Foolish Games

An April May Snow

Southern Paranormal Fiction Thriller

By

M. Scott Swanson

April May Snow Titles

Foolish Aspirations

Foolish Beliefs

Foolish Cravings

Foolish Desires

Foolish Expectations

Foolish Fantasies

Foolish Games

Foolish Haints

Prequel Series

Throw the Amulet

Throw the Bouquet

Throw the Cap

Throw the Dice

Throw the Elbow

Throw the Fastball

Throw the Gauntlet

Throw the Hissy

Never miss an April May Snow release.

Join the reader's club!

www.mscottswanson.com

Author's note- This is a work of fiction. Character names, businesses, locations, crime incidents and hauntings are purely imagination. Where the public names of locations are used, please know it is from a place of love and respect from this author. Any resemblance to actual people living or dead or to private events or establishments is entirely coincidental.

Whatever it takes
Cause I love the adrenaline in my veins
I do whatever it takes
Cause I love how it feels when I break the chains

**Imagine Dragons-
"Whatever it Takes"**

Chapter 1

Senioritis, spring fever, short-timer disease, and a bad case of "I don't care." I write the words neatly in the left margin of my yellow legal pad.

I struggle to focus on Kimberly Mason as she states why her client, Ivy Olson, should retain custody of Bailey. The terms I write down are listed under the heading of "what I have today," and I am attempting to come up with a fifth way of describing how I feel.

Under any other circumstances, I would be ashamed of my inattention to Roman Olson's—my client's—case. Given the context of the moment, I'll forgive myself.

Four hours ago, I was nude in silk sheets tangled up with a handsome professional ballplayer. Which is where I would prefer to be at the moment. Instead, I'm sitting through a dreadfully boring divorce arbitration.

Despite my ballplayer's request that I remain cocooned in the sheets with him, I left my hot man alone in bed. I showered, dressed, and made the drive to Huntsville, Alabama. The one-hour commute afforded me much time to sulk about having to work today.

Oh, but leaving my boyfriend alone in bed is only half the story. You see, he and I are moving to Baltimore, Maryland, in four weeks. This means, despite being a professional, I have extraordinarily little vested interest in this meeting. Shortly, I won't be an employee of the Snow and Associates law firm.

Technically I haven't exactly turned in my notice yet. However, Howard Snow, the firm's principal owner, who also happens to be my uncle, is well aware of when and where I will be moving. Since he is part of my family, he most likely knows that I skipped breakfast this morning, too. My family seems to have a GPS tracking system attached to my butt and a bodycam hidden on my forehead. No detail of my life is too insignificant for them to be made aware of, judge, and discuss.

It's another reason I am looking forward to leaving my hometown of Guntersville, Alabama. I would love a little bit of privacy.

I'm sure you can understand why I am highly distracted at the moment. Many things are changing in my life. Consequently, it has impacted my current attention to detail of my client's case just a wee bit.

Nah. Even if I had decided to take Howard's advice and remain in Guntersville as a partner in his law firm, I would find this case a bore. Bless it. I don't understand some couples. If both parties want to end the marriage, why can't there be more compromise to facilitate a quick end to the unpleasant part of the separation?

I mean, I have a dog, and we have a great relationship. When I'm lonely and no one else will talk to me, Puppy is there for me. When he can't find anyone else to feed him or scratch his ears, he comes and hangs out with me. It works out well for both of us.

If we were ever to separate, I would miss him, and he would miss me—occasionally. But for the life of me, I can't imagine delaying getting out of an unhappy marriage if my husband can't bear to part with Puppy. Puppy would come out a winner either way.

"April?"

Kimberly's voice is reminiscent of fingernails on a chalkboard. It brings me back to the task at hand. "Yes?"

She arches her eyebrows. "So, you agree?"

"Absolutely not." I have no idea what I'm not agreeing to.

Kimberly turns her attention to Roger Walsh, the Huntsville arbitrator we hired to settle the case of where the dog would live after the divorce. "Roger, this is why we had to bring you in. We are at a total impasse."

Roger has arbitrated several cases for me over the past few months. He is a thoughtful older man with a severely receding hairline and pooched tummy. Roger reminds me of a kindly professor. No matter how silly the case or how heated the conversation becomes, he manages to keep the room civil and on task without being overly autocratic.

"I understand, Counselor Mason. But I'm already aware that we were having some difficulties in the negotiation. Otherwise, you wouldn't have involved me." Roger looks at me and favors me with a smile. "Counselor Snow, do you care to enlighten me on why Mr. Olson should retain all custody rights to Bailey."

"Yes, sir. But first, I want to make it clear that my client is not averse to allowing visitation rights to Ms. Olson," I say as I shuffle to my presentation sheet.

"The last thing I want to have to do is coordinate visitation with that man to see my dog," Ivy spews.

In my peripheral vision, I notice Roman preparing to respond. I lay my hand on top of his forearm as I shake my head.

"Ms. Olson, I'll remind you to keep this meeting civil, or your counsel can handle it for you without your presence," Roger says.

I wait for a beat because Ivy is sputtering as if she might be dense enough to say something else and get thrown out. My wish does not come true as she wisely remains silent.

"Counselor Walsh, it's our assertion that Ms. Olson does not actually want custody of Bailey. She wants to get even with Mr. Olson."

"As you can see from the papers filed in the settlement ledgers to this date, Mr. Olson admits that the dissolution of the marriage was largely his fault. He has gone above and beyond the prescribed settlement for similar estates. The only point of contention at this juncture to bring this separation to fruition is the custody of Bailey." I pull out a communication I sent a week earlier to Kimberly. "Before arbitration, we sent this proposal, which by all accounts is little more than proposing a ransom settlement for Mr. Olson's dog."

Roger reviews the document, which I'm sure he has read earlier. "Counselor Mason, what was your response to this proposal?"

Kimberly crosses her arms across her chest. "Bailey is a living thing. You can't put a dollar amount on the love of a living thing."

Roger offers a faint smile. "We put a dollar amount to the value of living things all the time, Counselor. I take it you did not respond?"

"There was nothing to respond to."

Roger inclines his forehead. "All right." He turns his attention back to me. "Continue, please."

"To distill it all down, the important point is Bailey was two years old before Mr. and Ms. Olson met. Bailey is and always has been Mr. Olson's dog. It was Ms. Olson who moved into the household after the fact, not Bailey."

"At the time of marriage, all property is shared equally, Counselor," Kimberly says to Roger.

Roger raises his hand. "I assure you I know the marital laws for the state of Alabama, Counselor. But thank you for reminding me in the event I had forgotten that stipulation."

"Counselor, Mr. Olson has shown full contrition for not having kept his marital vows. He has apologized to Ms. Olson, her friends, and family that would listen. He has agreed to more than an equitable property division and other assets. Almost all these assets were solely created through his labor. The man just wants his dog. The one living thing that still loves him unconditionally and can keep him company as he works through his failings and strives to improve himself."

Roger twirls his gold pen back and forth as he appears to think through the situation. "This is quite the predicament."

I don't see much of a predicament. I'm beginning to view Ivy as not much more than a bitter extortionist. Yes, Roman should have kept his wee-wee in his pants as his marital vows commanded him. But what did Ivy expect? She didn't hold to those standards when Roman was married to Candace. Ivy and Roman's not-too-secret hotel excursions broke up that marriage, clearing the deck for this current train wreck.

Some people never comprehend the best indicator of the future is history. No, I know people can change. Still, if I have to make a bet, especially when I'm betting on something important like the happiness of my life, it makes sense to play the odds. If the man was sleeping with Ivy when he was married to Candace, Ivy shouldn't act surprised when he sleeps with somebody while he is married to her. It seems so rudimentarily simple. Yet, I see it too often in the divorce cases I have already worked on.

"Counselors, if you don't mind, I would like to ask your clients something directly."

I shoot a questioning look to Kimberly. She shrugs in response.

I guess we're in agreement on something as we both nod our heads.

Roger teepees his hands in front of him. Putting his two pointer fingers together, he gestures toward Ivy. "Ms. Olson, how do you feel this should be handled?"

She pouts as she answers. "I don't think Bailey should have to live with someone that he can't trust. I think full custody should be given to me."

Roger nods thoughtfully. He points to Roman. "Mr. Olson?"

Roman sighs. "I just want Bailey back. I raised him from a puppy. He's never been in any house besides the one I live in, and I'm not sure how he would adjust. I don't want him to *have* to adjust. I love my dog, and I want him to stay with me."

"You cheated on that dog when you cheated on me!" Ivy yells across the table.

"What are you talking about?"

"You broke up our family. When you cheated on me, you said you didn't care what happened to Bailey or me."

Roman's face contorts. "No, I didn't. You're crazy. You need to get that head of yours examined."

Ivy glowers at Roman. "I'll make you squeal like the pig you are—"

There is a blur of motion. Too late, I realize Ivy is coming after my client with a pencil held in her hand like a trench knife.

I fear she is coming after Roman's face. Her stab comes up well short.

Looking down, I realize I am wrong about her target. The girl's crazy is hundred-proof, and she is dead on her target.

Roman releases a scream that sounds like it belongs to a ten-year-old girl. There is way too much to see. I can't comprehend what has taken place.

I've been known to have a few issues with hiding my own crazy. For this reason, I'm in awe. I feel a momentary kinship with Ivy for the way she launched herself across the conference table.

Kimberly is trying to pull her client back across the table. She manages a handful of pantyhose. It stretches comically up toward her with no effect on Ivy.

Ivy is laid out across the table with her right hand extended toward Roman. Her teeth are bared, and her ice-blue eyes prove to me she is from a long line of crazy.

Roman's scream continues until his voice cracks. I finally look at him, and his expression of shock mixed with pain is so intense it is almost comical. I can't understand why having a hundred-and-ten-pound, crazy, bleached blonde throw herself across the table at him would scare Roman so bad.

"Remember that, you worthless piece of trash, the next time you go to grab some woman's butt!" Ivy screams.

Ivy moves her right hand back and pops up to return to her seat.

I see the pencil jammed into Roman's hand. My eyes blink rapidly as I try to comprehend what she has done.

"Are you crazy? What's the matter with you?" Roman hollers.

He has to ask? Yes, she is, and the fact her husband cheated on her is what's the matter with her.

Darn it. I was hoping for another typical, dull day. Instead, I get the crazy girl and philandering boy fireworks. Oh well, time to do what I can to keep the day on track.

"Let me see your hand," I tell Roman.

He is flailing his hand. The pencil looks like a lousy stage prop as spatters of blood fall onto the conference table. "She stabbed my hand!"

"Yeah, I see that." Captain Obvious is on a roll now. I catch his wrist as he flings his hand back in my direction and pull his hand toward my chest to get a better look at the damage.

"Is it bad?" he asks. "It hurts something fierce."

No kidding. I fight back a sudden lurch in my stomach as I examine where the number two pencil has gone cleanly between his middle and ring finger bones. I turn his hand over. The gray pencil lead pokes out of the palm of his hand. "Oh, quit being a baby."

"That ought to teach you to cheat on me, you jerk," Ivy snarls.

"Counselor Mason, please get control of your client," Roger commands.

This tiny hiccup is terrible news for me. I have a hectic schedule for the next few weeks. If we must reschedule this arbitration, it might involve me having to come back down from Baltimore. Plus, Ivy should be charged with assault. Since I was a witness, I would have to come down for that trial, too.

That can't happen.

"Will you hold still, you big baby?" I turn my body so my back shields everyone's view of Roman's hand.

"It hurts really bad."

"It's gonna hurt worse for a minute. I'm going to have to pull it out."

"No—no—no—no." Roman jerks his hand back, and I clamp it tighter against my side while holding firm to his wrist.

"Hold still," I warn him as I yank his elbow toward me and lock it under my arm. "One, two." I wrench the pencil clear of the wound. Roman's hand dribbles blood quickly onto the marble tile.

"Oh Lord, is that my blood?" Roman cries.

Geez, whose blood does he think it could be? I stretch both my hands to put his injured hand in mine. I have to hope none of the pencil lead broke off in his hand. Still, it is a risk I'm willing to take.

Besides, I sort of agree with Ivy. It would serve him right if he got a little gangrene in his hand.

Stop it, April. Concentrate.

Closing my eyes, I gather all my energy into the center of my chest. I draw a deep breath as I continue to wrestle to hold Roman's hand still while he jerks away from me. I push all the energy down my arms into my hands. I feel Roman's hand warm in between mine.

The heat rises until it is almost unbearable.

The heat dissipates, and our hands cool. I open my cupped hands.

"It itches," Roman complains.

I roll his hand over, examining the twin puckers of flesh on top and bottom. It is as if they have been healing for four weeks. "I don't know why you're raising so much commotion. It's not that bad." I release his arm.

Roman pulls his hand back and examines it. His brows come together. "But how? The blood?"

"I don't know. But you look good to go to me." I take my seat, folding my hands in front of me on the table. "Now, where were we?"

Roger looks at the blood on the floor and back to me. "Is your client alright to continue?"

"Yes, sir."

Roger looks past me toward Roman, who turns his hand over and traces the puckered scars with his fingers. "Mr. Olson, are you good to continue?"

"It's fixed." Roman shows his hand to Roger.

"We can reschedule if you are not feeling well," Roger offers.

"I think, given the stress level that this is putting on both parties, we would be best to soldier through this today," I suggest.

Roger ignores me as he asks Roman again, "Mr. Olson, are you ready to continue?"

Roman's eyes remain full of wonder, but he answers Roger anyway, "Yes. I'm actually feeling pretty good about things at the moment."

"Counselor Mason, I need you to make sure that your client does not have anything else in her hands that she can use as a weapon." Roger directs his glare onto Ivy. "Ms. Olson, I am holding that last outbreak in reserve. If you do any such action again, you will be charged with two counts of aggravated assault. Do I make myself clear?"

Ivy nods in agreement, but I wouldn't trust her with my worst enemy. That girl is unchained, and I'm not sure she will return to the land of the reasonable anytime soon.

"Now, I have to agree with Counselor Snow. It is a shame that everything has been taken care of in this case except for this one item. I find it difficult to believe that two adults can work through the challenges of dividing three properties, two successful businesses, and a large sum of securities. Still, we can't decide who gets the dog."

"That's just it, Counselor. My client's soon-to-be ex-husband has decided to be a complete pig-head about this. My client is highly attached to the dog and can offer it a far more stable home than Mr. Olson."

"You don't give a darn about that dog. The only thing you care about is yourself," Roman growls.

Roman pinky swore to me that he would not open his mouth during this arbitration unless Roger asked a specific question. I suppose Roman forgot that I specifically said if he felt compelled to speak at all, the one thing of utmost taboo was speaking to Ivy during the proceeding. So, what is my client doing? Talking directly to Ivy.

Some days I wonder why my clients even bother to hire a lawyer. I feel like the first question I should ask any prospective client is, "Do you plan on listening to my advice? If not, keep your money in your pocket and save me the headache."

I favor Roman my best "are you an idiot?" stare. His eyes open wider as he comprehends that he has made a grave tactical error.

"You don't know. I love that dog. If you weren't out gallivanting around and chasing every skirt in town, you might understand my close relationship with Bailey. You just proved my point that you're not a suitable parent for Bailey."

"I raised him from a pup, you ditz."

I hang my head in defeat. Obviously, my client is unable to follow the most basic instructions.

"Don't you call my client names." Kimberly jumps into the action.

I refuse to be pulled into the circus.

"All right, let's get this back on track. We need to figure out how we can negotiate this." Roger sounds uncharacteristically aggravated.

"There is nothing to negotiate. The dog needs to come with me, and then everything is a done deal. Then we can all go our own way," Ivy says.

"You are not getting my Bailey!"

Roger stands and claps his hands together aggressively. "Folks, this is not helping us reach a compromise."

"Forget your compromise, old man," Ivy spits.

My head is splitting. Thankfully it isn't one of my famous migraines, and it isn't a typical headache—which I never get. But I do have too much stupid being crammed into my head, and it is making me ornery. There is only so much stupid one person should have to endure.

"You don't love Bailey. You never loved him. How many times have you told me you didn't like him in the kitchen because you thought he stunk?" Roman asks.

"That dog is my companion," Ivy claims.

Roger clears his throat again. "We must come up with a solution for this last obstacle of separation."

"Cut Bailey in half and be done with it." I panic as everybody stops yelling and looks in my direction. "Did I just say something?"

Everybody nods.

I hate it when my mouth goes wildcat.

Roman still has a horrified look on his face as he says, "If that is the only option, she can have Bailey. It's not his fault I was stupid enough to marry Ivy. I'd rather him be alive, and the two of us have a chance of outliving Ivy."

Ivy's upper lip curls. "I say, split him down the middle. I want the front half. You can have the dog's back half. Since you're a butt man."

Roger is still looking at me with a curious smile. "Invoke the ruling of Solomon. Very clever, Counselor Snow."

Ivy might have shown her hand with her last comment. "Hand" makes me check that she hasn't picked up anything sharp again.

Roger remains standing, collects his paperwork, and sets it in his briefcase. "All right, folks. I have heard everything I need to make an educated decision. I will review my notes and let you know my finding by the end of the week. I wish each of you all the luck in the world."

Ivy turns to Kimberly. "That's it? When do we find out?"

I feel terrible for Roman. Some men are horrible at picking women. Not saying those men don't sometimes end up with the women they deserve. Still, it really makes for a rough life for all parties involved.

Roman remains seated, poking at the scars on his hand. The

confident man that accompanied me into the room no longer exists.

My Grandpa Hirsch, who died before Mama was born, set up a learning experience for me at Christmas time. Three ghosts came to visit me the three nights before Christmas. Each spirit took all night to show me in their own way that I'm a lousy friend, and I don't offer sufficient empathy to the people I know. I take well to most training, so if I plan to get better at showing compassion, now is as good of a time as any. Even if I have an impossibly tight schedule for the next four weeks.

I double-checked my calendar to confirm it is two o'clock before I'm due to meet with Dottie in Guntersville. That's plenty of time to take Mr. Loser "my wife stole my dog" to get ice cream. I mean, ice cream fixes everything. Right?

Chapter 2

"You really didn't have to do this. I appreciate it, but it wasn't necessary," Roman says as he looks down at his cup of ice cream.

"Let's just say this is about two people who are trying to do better, helping one another."

Roman looks up. His eyes narrow. "How do you mean?"

"Well, I know it's probably hard for you to believe, but it's come to my attention lately that I might be lacking in the empathy department. So, I thought it a good time to show some to a client who seems like they might need someone to talk to. Especially since their dog is presently a ward of the court until the arbitrator's decision." I can't help but smirk about the ludicrous arrangement.

Roman dabs his spoon on the top of his ice cream. "I might have exaggerated how good of a friend Bailey is to me. He is actually a pretty self-centered dog."

"Mine too. Bailey isn't a Keeshond, is he?"

"No. A black lab."

I shrug. "I was joking, Roman. I have pictures of Bailey in the folder."

"Oh, yeah. I forgot about that."

"Listen, on a serious note. Once we get this taken care of with Ivy and you two are separated, you really need to take a break from women for a few years."

Roman snorts. "Why do you say that?"

I raise my eyebrows. "I would think it to be self-evident, but if it would help you for me to lay it out, you are an awful judge of females. Plus, you are a cheat. Those are both serious strikes against your happiness. You should work on both before you hop back into the relationship scene."

Roman crosses his arms and leans back. "I'm not a cheat."

I stifle my laugh—poorly. "Did you have sex with Ivy while you were married to Candace?"

He looks away. "Well, yeah, but I thought I was in love with Ivy, and I knew I was going to marry her."

"And we already know that you are sleeping around on Ivy with—what was her name?"

"Star." He gestures with his hands in frustration. "You already know her name. The file—"

"I know. I just find it humorous to hear you say it out loud." I tap my head. "Does it not sound funny to you? Do you really believe you have a future with a woman named Star? Come on, Roman. You're smart and a successful businessman. You should know better than that."

"I never said I thought I had a future with Star. I've admitted to everyone that it is lust with Star." He points at me. "I bet you would be moved to lust too if you saw how she can wrap those long legs around the pole."

"Buddy, there are a lot of things that move me to lust, but a woman's long legs around a brass pole is not one of them."

"Well, you can say that now because you've never seen it."

"All right then. Who knows, maybe you're right." I shake my head.

"What do you think are the chances of me getting Bailey back?"

I scoop up the last of my pistachio ice cream. "I'd say a little bit better than fifty-fifty."

"Man, I didn't see this coming. I never thought she would stoop this low."

"Really? You really didn't see this coming?"

Roman scoffs. "I admitted it and apologized to her. And I feel like I have been more than generous with the division of assets."

"Sure, but Roman, you hurt her. She wants to hurt you. I can tell you are one of those guys who makes money, and it doesn't impress you. Giving Ivy a more-than-fair settlement didn't bother you because you're not wired that way. She's looking for a way to hurt you."

Roman scratches his chin as he thinks. "If that is true, it's just messed up."

"No, not really. I actually think she let you off easy."

Roman's jaw drops open as his mouth forms a perfect "O." His eyes open wider. "How can you say that?"

I wad up my napkins and put them in my empty ice cream bowl. "I'm just saying that if you had done that to me, you would have woken up and thought I was cooking you breakfast. Until you figured out the bed was on fire."

"What's the big deal? It's just sex."

My phone rings with perfect timing. Roman's obtuse nature regarding relationship fundamentals has begun to irritate me. This experiment in empathy has been a flaming failure.

I grin at the caller ID and answer. "Hey, baby. You out of bed now?"

"Oh, yeah. I've already gone for a five-mile run and taken a shower," Lee says.

Lee Darby is my delicious, tall, ball-playing boyfriend. We have history. We secretly dated briefly in high school. Our second act has already lasted longer. We are in love *and* lust for this go around.

Being with Lee feels second nature now. I hate being away from him. He is the first guy I have even fantasized about having a family with in the future. *Way* in the future. After I become a senior partner at a large law firm.

"Five-mile run? That's exhausting just thinking about it."

Lee laughs in his easy manner that warms me up on the inside. "So, are you in town? I thought maybe we would go get lunch together."

"Aww, that would've been really awesome. But, right now, I'm in Huntsville at the food court enjoying ice cream with a gentleman."

"Is he good-looking?" Lee asks.

I take note of Roman for the first time. He isn't an unattractive man. "No. Not even close."

"You'll let me know if I get any competition."

"There is no competition for you, baby."

He laughs again. "I'm gonna get me something to eat. I'll see you when you get home tonight. I love you."

"I love you, too."

"I do wish I had a girlfriend like you," Roman says.

"No, you don't. You know what I've noticed while I was on the phone?"

He leans forward. "What's that?"

"You leering at every female's butt who walked past us."

Roman suddenly has a goofy grin. "I did not."

"You did. Chunky, slim, blonde, brunette, college students, and even that woman in the walker, you eyed every one of them. You've got a serious women problem. You really ought to see if you can't just be without a woman for a year or two. Focus on something else for once, Roman."

"I do not leer at women. And I definitely did not ogle that nice elderly woman in the purple polyester pants," Roman insists.

"Denial is step one in the process. Hopefully, you won't stay stuck on step one. Otherwise, you're going to end up broke or, worse, dead. Seems like that pencil in your hand today should have taught you a lesson."

"It did. It taught me that pencils in the hands of a crazy woman are as dangerous as knives." Roman grins.

He can wipe that silly grin off his face. "You don't know the half of it."

Chapter 3

Driving back into Guntersville, I review the growing laundry list of issues confronting my clients. Given his marital incompetence, if I were to stay in Alabama, I'm sure to see a minimum of two more good divorce paydays compliments of Roman's future Mrs. Olsons.

If I trust my gut, Dottie Castle likely killed her husband thirty years ago. Going up against the FBI once they have a bee in their bonnet is never an easy task. Still, so far, the evidence says I'm wrong about her. Mr. Castle may have been offed by the Dixie Mafia for money laundering gone bad.

I must bring these cases to a successful end if at all possible before I leave for Baltimore. It's not that I can't turn them over to my uncle Howard. It's more a matter of pride. I need to finish them and not dump unfinished business in his lap on my way out the door.

As if the move and my crazy law clients aren't enough, I need to pay off my credit card bill for the Christmas gift purchases I made. Holy manger, what was I thinking? Plus, my student loans have matured and require huge payments each month. I have a teeny cash flow issue and am using the bonus check Howard paid me at Christmas to smooth out the added expenses. I'm afraid if I am not careful, the nest egg I had in my bank account the last few months that had helped me not feel so panicked all the time will dissipate into nothing soon.

If I were staying in Guntersville, I wouldn't worry about it too much. But I'm moving with no job lined up. I don't know how long it will be before I find employment, and Lee and I haven't exactly gone over who pays for what in Baltimore—since we're not married.

Visions of my disaster in Atlanta haunt me. Although I know it's unlikely, I may get to Baltimore and have the same difficulty gaining employment as in Atlanta.

I suddenly feel gassy, and my stomach roils, making me grimace.

At least I have options for now. I have a part-time job that pays significant cash money on the weekend. As long as I don't mind pawning off my sanity.

Today I am more fearful of financial failure than of my "gifts." I pick up my phone and call my brother Dusty.

"What's up?" he asks.

"I'm curious if you might have any work for me this weekend."

"You're calling me? Are you okay?"

"Yes. Can't I call to see if your team is working this weekend?"

"Sure. You can always call, and we can always use you if we're working. But you don't sound yourself. What's wrong?"

"Nothing's wrong," I insist.

"You're not, like, in trouble with a loan shark or something, are you?"

"No! Why would you say that?"

"I'm just saying if you were, I wouldn't have a problem with giving you an advance," Dusty explains.

"No. It's not like that. I just know I won't be able to pick up any side work with you once I go to Baltimore. That and I want to get in as much time as possible with the team."

"Uh-huh." He isn't buying it.

"No, I'm serious."

"All right. We are driving up to Bellefonte Friday afternoon."

"The nuclear plant?"

"No. The town and small foundry that was abandoned after the Civil War. I'll send you the folder that Miles put together tonight."

"And the team is going because—?"

Dusty guffaws. "Well, that's why I send you the report. Now isn't it?"

"And..." I press.

"The usuals. Strange voices, shadows. The activity level personally sounds pretty weak to me. Still, until we can get back into the Imperial Theater, we really don't have any outstanding leads."

"You still have the drowned girl over at the bridge on the way to Nana's," I remind him.

"True. I'm glad you reminded me. I need to have Miles check in on that and see if we can't do something next weekend."

"See, what are you going to do without me?" I tease.

"I'm not real sure, but I guess you're going to make me find out," Dusty says. "By the way, Chase mentioned this morning at breakfast that he plans to cook a pot of chili. It's hard to beat a bowl of chili on a cold night."

"That's a true statement. But I think I have the one thing that does trump a warm bowl of chili on a cold night."

Dusty chuckles. "Listen to little sis getting all cocky."

"I'm just speaking the truth."

"All right, well, if you two lovebirds get the munchies, you're welcome to crash our little patio party. Mom and Dad are gone right now."

That is the first I have heard of my parents not being home. I've spent every night for the last three weeks at Lee's lake house and lost touch with what is happening at my parents' house. I have only been by a few times to pick up more clothes.

"Where did they go?"

"Mom had some real estate training class up in Gatlinburg, and they decided to make a long weekend of it. I think they said they were going to be home Wednesday."

"Are you taking care of Puppy for me?"

"There's not really any need to. That dog eats every time Chase eats, which means six times a day. He also lets himself in and out, and if he's thirsty, he knows how to lift the commode lid," Dusty says.

"Don't let him do that. I just about had him broken of that."

"Well, he is a dude. Even if he is a dog. With you not home to train him, he's going to do what he wants. I'll warn you; I think he's starting to think he's Chase's dog." Dusty sighs. "Curious—why haven't you taken him over to Lee's yet?"

It is a good question. I wish I had a satisfactory answer for it. I've brought up bringing Puppy over several times to Lee. When I do, he abruptly changes the topic. I'm not sure if that's a no. Still, I haven't pressed the case yet since I know Puppy is comfortable being at my parents'. "I just haven't found the right time to talk to Lee about it."

The conversation comes to a sudden stop. I imagine I can feel Dusty's disappointment coming through the phone.

"Okay. Like I said, I'll send you the folder for the trip this weekend. If you two decide on home cooking instead of going out to one of those steakhouses, feel free to stop by tonight."

"Thank you, Dusty."

Man, it just gets under my skin how everybody is constantly judging me. I've been trying to think about what to do about Puppy. I love my dog, and he pulled me through some incredibly dark moments. Still, Puppy has a penchant for chewing on nice things. Lee is super particular about his home and has some expensive furniture. It's bad enough I've got my clothes strewn all over Lee's master suite. I don't want to be too much of a bother and bring my sixty-five-pound shedding machine over before Lee has been able to adjust.

Lee hasn't said as much, mainly because he changes the topic, but I feel like Puppy is a hard no with him. I get the feeling when he changes the subject that he is almost daring me to press the issue.

I feel awful. Puppy probably thinks I have abandoned him. I'm not fit to be a mother.

Highway 72 tees into Highway 79 as my phone rings. The screen reads *Doc Crowder*. "Hey, Doc. Do you have any results for me yet?"

"April?"

The unexpected voice startles me. I take another look at the caller ID. Yep, it reads *Doc Crowder*. "Shane? Is that you?"

His lazy laugh forces me to grin as I visualize his beautiful smile and handsome face. Shane is the one pleasant thing that happened to me during my brief stint in Atlanta.

I had romantic aspirations for our relationship. I mistook his generosity as evidence that we were becoming a thing. This was before I realized Shane is simply an all-around nice guy like my brother Chase, who would do anything they can for someone in need. That explains Shane and Chase's easy bromance centered around their mutual love for fishing and hunting.

"It hasn't been so long since we talked that you forgot my voice, has it? Remember I was at your parents' house last month when Chase and I went hunting."

"Yeah, it's not that. I didn't know that you were—are you working with Doc?"

Shane clicks his tongue. A familiar tick of his that makes me smile again. "Aw, you didn't know Doc was retiring?"

I knew Doc was retiring. I also knew he was marrying Jacob's grandmother and moving to Florida. What I *don't* know, and care about more than the details I *do* know, is what that has to do with Shane. "Yes."

There is a pause in our conversation.

"Well, I'm the new medical examiner, April," Shane says.

What? My eyelids blink in quick succession. "You are?"

"Sure. Doc cut me a deal on his building, and I'm buying him out."

I'm stunned. I know Shane works at the hospital in Atlanta. Still, I think he is an orderly or something. Even in rural Alabama, I'm not sure how that qualifies him to be a medical examiner.

"Wow. That's great, Shane. I had no idea you were interested in being a medical examiner."

"For real? You knew I was finishing up my internship at the hospital."

Ouch. The revelation hits me like a ton of bricks. Grandpa Hirsch really was looking out for me when he sent the three ghosts at Christmas to help me learn how to be a better person.

Shane has been one of my "lifeline" friends. The type of friend whom I can call when I hit the darkest space and I can't dig myself out of the hole of despair. Shane will talk to me even if it's two o'clock in the morning, and by the time we're done talking, I feel strong enough to face another day.

That's Shane. Yet, I never asked him about his life goals after all those phone calls and meals together as friends at my parents' home. I chose to pick up tidbits from our conversation and manufacture my own reality.

My version of Shane is superficial at best. Like my friendship *toward* him.

I am such a lazy friend. I will master this genuine empathy skill if it is the last thing I do.

"Well, now that I know you've taken over Doc's business, I'm going to have to get you a housewarming gift. Do you have any idea what you might like?"

"Nah, don't trouble yourself with that, April."

"No, I insist. Do you want a plant?"

"A plant?" He laughs. I blush.

"Sure. A plant, so that when people come in, it looks warm and cheery."

"Yeah, April. You know most of my clients are dead."

That's an excellent point I wish I had thought about before speaking. "Well, it will cheer you up."

He laughs again. "Okay. I suppose it will because it will remind me of you."

Now I feel terrible. I'm going to have to get Shane a huge plant. "Good, it's settled."

"You're crazy."

Somehow when Shane says, "you're crazy," it's an endearment. "What's crazy is you moving from Atlanta to Guntersville."

"I don't know about all that. I get to work for myself, my boat is at the marina five minutes away, and I can sit out on my front porch watching wild turkey in the evening and the stars at night. You don't get that in Atlanta."

That proves to me Shane was right to relegate me to friend status. He must have known all along that we weren't compatible. All the same, before Lee, if Shane had asked, I would have been more than willing to give it a try and deal with the breakup later.

"Back to business. I've got the report ready on that body y'all found in the drum."

"Gil Castle?" I ask.

"Hmm, did you have more than one body kept in a barrel of acid for thirty years?"

"All right, smarty. What do you have?"

"It's sort of complicated. I'm emailing you the folder. If you will give me a call back after you read it so we can go over it?"

"It might be late," I warn him.

"Wouldn't be the first time I got a call from you late, April."

I can visualize his infectious smile, and my mood continues to brighten. Shane always has that effect on me.

I have half a mind to cancel my visitation with Dottie until after I have had time to review the autopsy on Gil. Whatever Shane determined during the autopsy will have a considerable bearing on Dottie's trial. Shane's report has much more relevance to the case than anything Dottie can tell me. Probably more honest than anything I can learn from Dottie, too.

This is the worst-case scenario for me. Everyone who ever dreamed of being a defense attorney lives for the moment when they can secure the release of someone wrongly accused. It's the equivalent of a walk-off home run, buzzer-beating three-point shot, or a successful hail Mary touchdown pass.

Actually, it's better than all those sports analogies because it's not just the win. You are righting a wrong. I have experienced that feeling and am greedy for more of it.

Dottie Castle is the complete opposite of that dream case. First, I don't like Dottie. I'm big enough to admit the fact that if I were not Dottie's defense attorney, I would be rooting for them to lock her up for the rest of her life. She is mean, condescending, and is a sad, old, destitute woman who thinks she still has money and standing in the community. All those things make her an incredibly prickly person to be gracious toward.

There is a conundrum defense attorneys sometimes face. What do you do when your client is guilty of the crime?

Good question, right? If I had considered the point earlier, I would have angled to be a prosecutor instead of a defense attorney.

Still, not helpful.

Besides, with the notable exception of Dottie, being a defense attorney has been as fulfilling as I dreamed it would be. Not in the setting I had anticipated, but still, the job has held a wealth of opportunities for me to right wrongs and help someone in need.

It appears I have a true "suck it up, buttercup" moment. I have nothing that proves Dottie killed Gil, and I am her attorney. So, I'll do my job and proceed as if she is not guilty.

That does not require me to compromise my principles. I would never lie to win a case. Still, everything is based on the prosecution proving Dottie's guilt beyond a shadow of a doubt.

It's not precisely about if Dottie is guilty or not. It's about if the prosecution can prove their point sufficiently.

When I think about it that way and insert Dottie as the defendant—it seems like a pretty messed-up system of justice to me.

This is driving me nuts. As badly as I want to win every time I step into the courtroom, it sickens me to think that I might send a killer back onto the streets of Guntersville. Granted, she is an octogenarian killer, but a killer nonetheless.

When Agent King sent over his files during discovery, I was surprised to find how thin his case was against Dottie. All of his evidence is circumstantial and can be written off as coincidence. The difficulty of the case for the prosecution is compounded by the thirty-year memory of the few witnesses who don't presently reside *in* the grounds of Whispering Willows cemetery.

Dottie's contention is that Gil was money laundering for the Dixie Mafia. He got on the wrong side of a shotgun when the IRS came snooping, and his "partners" became nervous he might turn state's evidence. Dead men make lousy witnesses.

I admit. It is a compelling tale. Despite my dislike for Dottie, I'm inclined to believe it. That is until my grandmothers enlightened me that Dottie used to be a hot wife without Gil's consent, and when he found out, he threatened to divorce her.

Dottie came from nothing, and she had no intentions of going back to nothing. As good as the Dixie Mafia story is, the idea that Dottie killed Gil and buried him on the farm rings more authentic to me.

Then there was the first time Dottie and I met. I had forgotten about it before this weekend. With the constant random voices penetrating my mental partition and the accidental readings I purge from my memory, I had buried the unexpected transference I received from Dottie when we first met. It was dark, brutal energy, at odds with the diminutive elderly lady that sat before me.

Now that I know her, it's not a stretch to think of Dottie as a killer.

Chapter 4

Dottie's large, earlier-model luxury car is parked in front of Snow and Associates as I pull up. It still amazes me Judge Rossi released her until her trial. I'm equally surprised that Dottie has hung around *for* her stand trial. Then again, Dottie believes she is untouchable.

I gesture for Dottie to come inside as I unlock the office's mahogany door. I hold it open for her. "You don't want to be in this cold for long," I say as she gets out of her car.

I'm surprised to see her using a walking cane. That's a new thing.

"I warn you, young lady, old age isn't for sissies. That cold air is freezing up every joint I have."

Her civil, almost-human interaction catches me off guard. "Well, I'll put a pot of coffee on for us." I motion for her to sit by my desk as I move toward the coffee machine.

"I received a call from the medical examiner. He said they had completed Mr. Castle's examination. They plan to send the results over today." I want to let my statement hang in the air while preparing our coffee.

Dottie groans as she eases herself slowly into the chair. She cranes her neck as she looks at the documents I left on my desk last night.

"What do you think the report will say?" I ask nonchalantly.

Dottie adjusts in the seat so she can see me. "I suppose that he's been dead for three decades."

"True. The coroner tells me that he was in excellent condition considering how long he has been gone," I lie. According to the files, Gil's body had been converted to a pitted skeletal remain surrounded by liquefied slush.

"Oh, I'm sure Gil will find that a great consolation. He was always quite vain about his appearance."

There is the mean Dottie I know. Oddly, it makes me feel better. I can deal with nasty people, but I can't deal with unpredictability.

I pour two mugs of coffee and am right proud of myself for leaving out the rat poison. I offer Dottie a warm cup as I sit at my desk.

"Have you remembered any names from the Dixie Mafia Gil was working for since our last meeting?"

Dottie's lips narrow. "You're just not listening. I told you that I had no dealings with those people. Gil kept that all to himself. I only knew about it because they would come to the house occasionally, and I put two and two together."

I take in a deep breath and sigh. "That's just it, Ms. Castle. You say that you put two and two together, but if you didn't even know these people, how did you know they were criminals?"

"Oh, I knew."

Nice. Sometimes the most challenging part of my job is getting through to my clients without alienating them. "Understand, for us to defend against the prosecution's case, we need at least one of the jurors to think that somebody besides you killed Mr. Castle."

"I said I didn't kill him." She glowers at me.

"I understand. But again, we must make sure a juror believes us. With that in mind, you can see how important it is to establish that Mr. Castle dealt with criminal elements. Unfortunately for us, you are the only person who claims Mr. Castle was involved with the Dixie Mafia. That is why having the names of the individuals he dealt with would be so helpful."

"I can't just make the names up." Dottie's neck flushes red.

I feel as if I'm on a merry-go-round that I never asked to be on. Nana Hirsch all but chided me during our Christmas dinner for not using my talent on Dottie to get a reading.

Using my "gifts" on others is always a last resort because it is like voyeurism taken to the exponential power. I never feel right about it. It always leaves me feeling dirty. Still, Dottie is not helping, and I'm running out of options for effectively preparing her defense.

"I'm really not sure what sort of a defense we can mount. If we can't come up with some of the contacts from the Dixie Mafia days, it will be impossible to prove Gil's involvement." I continue to push on with conventional methods of persuasion.

Dottie shifts her weight, leaning onto her cane. "Dear, I sure don't want to spend the rest of my life in jail. If I thought I could come up with a name or two, I'd surely give it to you."

Maybe she doesn't know. It might be time for me to consider what a defense without mentioning another criminal element would look like. Pretty much it would be deny, deny, deny. And pray one juror looks at the mean old woman sitting next to me and sees their loving grandmother.

It could happen. There are plenty of people in the world who can't see evil sitting right in front of them. But if Dottie opens her mouth once, I think the "deny" defense would collapse.

Yeah, we're screwed.

Turning on my laptop, I see an e-mail from the medical examiner's office. I consider opening up the autopsy report from Shane in hopes there is some magical get-out-of-jail card buried in the report's details. At least it might have some hard facts that we can use to our advantage. Still, my heart just isn't in it. The day is almost up, and Dottie has sapped my momentum.

I lean back in my chair. "Tell me, where did y'all meet?"

Dottie raises her drawn-on eyebrows. "Me and Gil?"

"Yes. Was it like love at first sight?"

Dottie cackles. "Hardly. He was not the least interested in me in the beginning. It was all about Felicity Jefferson."

"Was that his girlfriend?"

Her eyes narrow as she shakes her head. "He wishes. Felicity was destined to be married to money. *Big* money. What is that saying? Money begets money?"

Dottie is asking me? I don't believe I have heard anyone under the age of fifty use the term before. "I think that's how it goes."

"Felicity was a beautiful girl. She had an hourglass figure with curves that men stopped and drooled over. Her hair landed below her shoulders, and it was an extra thick, silky auburn color. I remember her eyes being the most vibrant green." Dottie wiggles her wrinkled white fingers in front of her face. "Not really a jade color, almost a hunter green. They seemed to sparkle at times. I remember her lips being unusually wide and full. When Felicity spoke, I would be so mesmerized by her beautiful lips. I would concentrate so completely on their movement that I often found I didn't know what she had said to me."

"Did you go to school together?" I ask.

Dottie makes a derogatory sound. "Felicity went to the private school at the church. They don't have it anymore. But no, I definitely did not go to private school. I knew Felicity from when she would visit her daddy at the car dealership. During the summer, she would hang out to earn some spending money—as if she needed it—and she would answer the phones with me."

I cross my arms. "So, is this a dealership that you and Gil ended up owning?"

She appears perturbed by the question. "It was one of them, but the point I'm trying to make is that Felicity was, to this day, the most beautiful woman I have ever seen. She had more money than she could ever want. Yet, during the two summers we worked together, she acted like I was her equal." Dottie suddenly fixed her stare on me. "Why did she do that?"

Her question, so direct and unexpected, makes me hold my breath. "I guess she was a nice person."

"She was. She had no reason to be nice to *me*."

"Some people are naturally nice, Dottie."

Dottie exhales as she directs her attention to the wall. "I just never understood that. But what I did understand was that I wanted everything else she possessed. I wanted the house, the good looks, the popularity, and the money. I didn't know how to become Felicity, but whenever I saw her, she personified my goal."

I must admit that is sorta creepy. It may be the first time I've ever heard anybody acknowledge that they were crushing on someone they wished to emulate. I take a sip of my coffee as I wait patiently for Dottie to continue. Two girls sharing secrets.

She laughs, and I jump.

"Gil was nothing but a simple helper at Mr. Jefferson's dealership. He washed cars, changed the oil, and swept the floors.

"Gil wasn't that much to look at, but he was a big man. I prefer big men. And I could tell that he had an enormous amount of ambition. He didn't have a clue what to do with it. Still, it was there nonetheless."

Heck, this is more entertaining than watching *The Bachelor*. It sounds like Gil is about to get a rose, and he doesn't even know he is in the game.

"It was an interesting time, the sixties. Times were changing for women, or at least that's what everyone told us. But I knew it hadn't changed enough for what I needed. If I was going to run a successful business such as a car dealership, I would need a man. He might just be the figurehead, but in the sixties, it was a necessity.

"To be fair about it, Gil was never just a figurehead. He had a solid hold on the business aspect by the time he died."

Ding. There is my first red flag of the conversation. It's been so recent since he was dug up, I would think Dottie would say by the time he disappeared, not died.

"I approached Gil on several occasions. Each time he turned me down. It wasn't until Felicity went to college that he finally considered my offers."

"It didn't bother you that you had to be the one to ask him?"

Dottie frowns. "No, because I wasn't really looking for a husband. I was looking for a male to be the manager, in name only, of the business I planned to own. Gil was smart enough to help run the business. That's why I wanted him. With my know-how and his tenacity, we could end up with anything we wanted."

"How long before he started cheating on you?"

Dottie lolls her head to the side. "I'm sure you know by now it was a mutual thing."

I nod my head slowly.

"Gil was a good businessman. He was resourceful and persistent. He was a good provider and kind when with me as a husband. But the man had some serious issues. His entire worth or value was derived from how many beautiful women he could lay. It was an illness."

"You confronted him on it?"

"You're darn right I confronted him. I even threatened to shoot his pecker off if he kept it up." Dottie rubs a hand over her eyes. I notice how thin the crêpey skin is on her hand. "He would say he was sorry and promise never to do it again. And I think, each time, he really meant it." She shakes her head violently.

"What's the matter? Are you okay?"

"Yes. I remember how underfoot Gil would be after one of his bimbo flings. He would try too hard to make it right. There *is* no way to make it right. We had to move forward, that is all. There was no way to go back and correct it. He failed to ever comprehend that. It aggravates me to no end."

"Some people can forgive everyone in the world for their shortcomings, except themselves," I say.

"Yes, I think that may have been part of it. Or at least that sounds better than what I used to think. I believed Gil would be over-attentive during those periods because he feared he would do it again the moment I appeared convinced he wouldn't."

"You sound like you were unhappy. Why did you stay together so long?"

"We were a good team. Neither one of us had anything when we started, and we built a successful business together."

"Not to judge, but it seems like a poor reason to stay together," I say.

Dottie favors me with a humorless smile full of malice and contempt. "'Poor' is the operative word, dear. You have a highly supportive family, and you've always led a life of privilege. I don't hold it against you because I find you a smart and fair young woman. Still, until you have had nothing and no family to support you, it would be hard for you to understand my decisions."

"Fair enough. Do you want to talk about your affairs?"

"No. They were wrong. But I was just trying to wake Gil up to what he was risking every time he went after one of those floozies."

Dottie showed Gil by being a floozy herself. Her logic eludes me. "How long did that go on?"

"Two years, give or take a few months. I figure he played me for twenty years. Two years was just a minor infraction."

I don't believe Dottie is being overly cavalier. If anything, I think she probably had been lenient on Gil because of what the dissolution of their marriage would have meant for them.

Me? I would have been like, "Burn that house down." I don't see myself ever staying in a marriage strictly because of money. Don't get me wrong, I love luxuries. Still, I don't feel having a husband who only wants to sleep with me is a luxury. That's a requirement for a healthy marriage.

I believe Dottie and Gil had a business arrangement, not a marriage.

The marriage had gone totally awry somewhere along the way and became nothing but a farce. The bad thing is that they thought they were acting like a married couple, but to hear my grandmothers talk, everybody in our small town knew the marriage was over.

"So, how do you feel now that you know what happened to him?"

She exhales again. "I guess relieved. I think I had begun to think I would go to my grave not knowing what happened to him."

"Are you sad at all?"

"I don't think so. You have to remember, for all intents and purposes, for the last thirty years, Gil has been dead to me."

"You didn't know that. He might have shown up on a beach in Cozumel or something."

"Gil didn't care for the beach."

"It was a figure of—never mind." I extend my hands toward Dottie. "There is a chance that you're repressing your feelings. If it would ever help to talk about him, you can talk to me."

Dottie looks at my outstretched hands but does not take them. Instead, she struggles up on her cane. "Excuse me, the Number One China buffet in Scottsboro is half price for seniors from four to six. I better get a move on."

I have blown my opportunity to take a reading from Dottie. After discovering she still did not remember anybody from the Dixie Mafia, it had become my main goal of this little heart to heart.

I can't say I'm totally disappointed that it didn't happen. At least it would save me from feeling guilty for having intruded into the sovereignty of her mind.

I open the front door for Dottie. "Ms. Castle, whatever happened to Felicity?"

She frowns. "She married some extraordinarily wealthy banker's son in New York. They exchanged their vows in a hot air balloon when they got married. That became their ritual each anniversary. They would take a hot air balloon ride."

Dottie's eyes gleam as she smirks. "On their third anniversary, they had an accident during the ride. The basket became tangled on some power lines. Nobody in the balloon survived."

"My gosh, that's awful."

"It's one of the reasons why old man Jefferson sold to us at such a favorable deal. Felicity was his only child, and he was a widower. I think he figured there wasn't anything left to work toward." Dottie's drawn-on eyebrows come together.

"You know. I'm probably sadder about Felicity's death after all these years than what I am about Gil's."

After seeing her expression as she told of Felicity's demise, I'm left with a confused, uneasy feeling. I nod my head to cover my shock.

She turns and limps to her car.

I wait at the door to ensure she gets in her car all right. As she pulls out onto the street, I shut the front door.

Forcibly, I push the unsettling conversation from my mind and consider what to do with the rest of the workday. I won't accomplish much in the last forty-five minutes at the office that I can't achieve at home tonight. I opt to load my laptop, notebooks, and folders into my backpack, and close up shop.

It isn't dark, but I know we are only a few minutes away from dusk with the sun already dipping below the mountains. I swear, with daylight savings time gone and the shorter days, winter is darn near impossible to get through. It's, like, so depressing.

But what's not depressing is I am finally in love with a great guy. I know I shouldn't need a man to complete me. At least, that is what so many of my female professors told me at the University of Alabama.

I agree with them to a point. It's not like I wouldn't have value if I didn't have Lee. It's just I like being with Lee. I like being naked with Lee. And I like that Lee will be waiting on me when I get to his house. I don't know why that has to be a bad thing. It seems to me just to be a natural boy-girl thing.

Chapter 5

The last of my energy reserves drain away as I pull into Lee's driveway. I'm hungry, but the idea of going out for dinner does not appeal to me. Right now, I would be happy to get into my PJs, eat a bowl of soup, and go to sleep.

If I really desire sleep, I should have gone to my apartment.

I can't contain my grin as I slide my house key into the lock. "Honey, I'm home," I yell in jest as I enter Lee's house. I immediately notice that something smells delicious, and my stomach does a happy flip.

"Back here, baby."

I follow the sound of his voice, which thankfully is coming from the same direction as the delicious smell. I step into the oversized kitchen. Lee looks up and smiles at me as he uses some speedy wrist action on a large skillet. "You hungry?"

"I can eat." My curiosity has already kicked in hard. I crane my neck to see what is in the skillet. "What's that?"

"Mushroom and brown butter sauce for the linguine."

Looks fancy—and greasy. "Okay."

He gestures toward a dishtowel on the counter. "The steaks are resting under there."

"Resting? Now you sound like my brothers."

"Your brothers might know their way around a grill, then."

I perch myself on one of the barstools. "That would be correct. I suspect it's how they work off their sexual frustration."

Lee guffaws. "I assure you I'm not working off any sexual frustration by cooking. Now, if you'd care to work off some calories later." He wiggles his eyebrows.

"You're a goofball."

"That's the pot calling the kettle black." He fills a stockpot three-quarters full of water and turns the burner on.

My mind wanders back to my conversation with Dottie. "You don't know anybody that has ever married for money, do you?"

"Just half the players' wives I know," Lee says.

"Oh, yeah. I hadn't even thought about that crowd."

"Why do you ask? That's sort of a weird question." Lee smirks. "Even for you."

I ignore his jab. "I have a client who stayed married for thirty years in a bad relationship solely for financial reasons."

Lee drops the linguine in the boiling water. "Yeah, that's not optimal. It's sort of sad if you think about it."

"Does it work out for any of the ballplayers?"

Lee shrugs. "It seems to. To be fair about it, some of these guys are very athletic but not necessarily attractive in the face. They marry considerably more attractive women who pop out a brood of kids for them. In return, she gets the house she wants, any car she desires, and a black credit card that mysteriously pays itself off each month. Everybody gets something in that deal."

"Why does that sound cold to me?" I prop my chin on my hands.

"If I were to guess, because, in some ways, it's more of a business transaction. It starts with both parties being interested in marriage and having children. Still, it takes a weird twist with one exchanging money for better-looking genes."

I can't help but laugh. "Wow, the way you say it makes it sound so romantic. It's right up there with what I imagine taking out a mortgage would be like."

Lee dips his finger in the butter sauce, grimaces from the heat, then sucks his finger. "A mortgage isn't a bad simile. Nobody wants to pay the large bill each month, and nobody wants to pay twice the amount of money the house costs over the thirty years, *but* you do get a nice house today."

That totally goes over my head. "That doesn't make any sense."

"What part don't you understand?"

"Well, for starters, I understand that the players' wives get money they don't have to work for outside of the home. But before the kids are born, what do the ballplayers get out of it?"

Lee favors me with a wicked grin as he inflects his voice deeper. "Well, if you're confused about that, little girl, follow me over here to the bedroom."

I pick up a dishtowel and throw it at Lee. He catches it effortlessly.

"You're awful." I feign outrage.

"You're awfully naïve for your age."

I realize, as he stirs the linguine, I thoroughly enjoy just watching him. He is trim and muscular, but not puffed up like some of the gym rats I have dated. His muscles are from sprinting, throwing, and stretching. He is insanely sexy.

"What happened after thirty years?" Lee asks as he drains the linguine.

"What?"

He flashes a glance at me as the steam dances around his forearms. "The lady that stayed married for thirty years because of money."

"Oh, yeah. The funny thing is, she killed him."

"Nuh-uh." He stares at me. "Are you serious?"

"Well, it's up to the prosecution to prove it, but yes, I'm pretty sure of it."

"Wow. How much pent-up rage do you have to have for that?"

"I wouldn't think much, considering he was cheating on her."

Lee turns and pulls down two plates and two bowls. "Still, that's no reason to kill anybody. It might be a reason to leave the state and never call them again. Nobody has the right to kill their lover over something as stupid as that."

"What are you talking about? It's like the ultimate betrayal."

Lee fills both bowls with noodles. He frowns as he ladles the butter sauce over the top. "Yeah, yeah. Folks say that all the time. But last I checked, somebody breaking their marriage vows gives them zero time in jail, much less the death penalty."

I can't believe the nonsense I'm listening to. Lee is all but making excuses for adultery. Maybe this is the one percent that has kept me from fully committing. The one percent that is off with our relationship.

Lee lifts two beautiful sirloin steaks from the pan he had covered with aluminum foil and the dishtowel. The steaks steam, and their scent is heavenly.

"So, just to clarify. You think it's okay if someone breaks her marriage vows?" I ask.

Lee's expression sours. "Lord, no. It's never acceptable to break your vows. I'm only saying that it doesn't give your partner the right to go all vigilante and murder you."

"It's just forgive and forget?"

Lee retrieves silverware from the drawer. "It's always best to forgive if you can. But that doesn't mean to be stupid about it. At some point, if someone is a serial adulterer, the other partner will have to ask them to leave for their own health." Lee starts to hand me a fork and steak knife. He stops abruptly and pulls them back toward him. "Am I safe to give you sharp objects? You look like you have your fighting face on."

I hold my hand out. "Yes. I think we're a little bit apart on our feelings about this topic, and I must admit I'm disappointed."

"I'm sorry you are disappointed. Let's enjoy this wonderful meal your boyfriend cooked you, and not talk about those ugly things."

That makes all the sense in the world, but now that it is out there, I need to understand Lee's attitude. I mean, if we get married, and I decide I want to have an affair, does that mean he would just take me back? That would mean he expects me to do the same, too.

He cheerfully pours two goblets of red wine. The slight smile never leaves his face.

He probably would forgive me. Lee is so laid-back and easygoing, he probably wouldn't get worked up at all.

I sure know I'm not full of that much forgiveness. If he has been an excellent husband to that point, I *might* allow for one warning. A warning like burning his belongings, including his autographed jersey collection, in the yard as our neighbors watch. When he stops crying, I'll whisper in his ear that it will be him in the fire pit next time. That is April's style of forgiveness. And for the record, Snows don't *ever* forget.

All the anger I'm stoking evaporates as I taste the first bite of the linguine. Oh my gosh, this is good. I imagine I feel an extra pound of fat attach itself to my butt. "The sauce is delicious, Lee."

"I'm glad you like it."

My steak is so tender I press, more than I saw, with my steak knife. I nearly swoon as I take my first bite. It's a shame Dusty and Chase do not like Lee. The three of them need to enter some sort of grilling contest. "My steak is perfect."

Lee chuckles. "Good."

"What do I owe this beautiful home-cooked dinner to?"

"Honestly, sometimes I get tired of going out to eat. It's hard to beat a home-cooked meal."

When somebody else cooks it. "Well, it's definitely hard to beat this one."

"Tell me, how's the job search going?"

"Good. I've got a lot of different leads," I lie.

"I know it's tough interviewing long distance. I don't want you to sweat anything. If you need to move to Baltimore first and take a couple months to find the right job, I don't mind at all."

I feel something akin to panic tense my muscles,

accompanied by my shoulders creeping up toward my ears. "I know, and that's sweet of you. But I'm positive I'll find something before we move."

"I know. But I'm just saying in case."

I raise my eyebrows. "I said I've got it."

Lee laughs as he returns his attention to his meal. "I said I've got it," he mocks.

"Well, I do," I grumble.

"I hear you. I just don't want anything to make you nervous," Lee says.

Lee sets his fork down. "Darn. I forgot to mention, next Monday I need to fly up to Baltimore for a couple of days. If you can get off, maybe you should head up with me."

That makes perfect sense. If I were smart, I would line up several interviews. If I work it right, I will have my job before Baltimore. That would be a win.

"I'll check with Howard to make sure I can get the time off. It does make a lot of sense."

"I wish you could explain that to me. Why do you need your uncle's permission?" Lee asks.

"Because he is my boss," I scoff.

"Was…" Lee's lips narrow. "He won't be in a few weeks. If you need a few extra days, it shouldn't kill him. He might as well get used to it."

"Well, sure. But I don't want to leave Howard in a bind."

Lee favors me an "are you kidding me" expression. "April, are you leaving with me or not?"

I look down my nose at him. "What are you asking me?"

"I don't know." Lee looks away. "Some days, I feel like you're talking about leaving Guntersville, but somehow, when I get on that last plane to Baltimore, you're not going to be there with me."

"Don't be stupid. It's going to take wild horses to keep me off that plane. I am most definitely going to Baltimore with you, and I am extremely excited about starting a new life with you."

Lee's smile reappears. "Honest?"

"I absolutely am."

"I mean, I know it's asking a lot, leaving your family behind. But I'm serious about this relationship," he says.

I can't determine if he is alluding to me not being serious about our relationship. "I am, too. What's bringing this on?"

We lock eyes. "At times, I get this feeling that you are—I don't know—conflicted."

Conflicted is my natural state. "No. I don't know how many times I have to tell you. I'm excited to be going to Baltimore."

"All right then."

"All right then," I parrot.

"I suppose you can have dessert, then."

I would have left half the steak on my plate if I had known there was dessert. I can't eat another bite. "There's dessert?" I lament.

"Just follow me into the bedroom, little girl. Heh-heh."

Chapter 6

I'm able to beg off sexy time temporarily for an action movie and a cuddle on the couch. It's a good thing, too, because any sudden jostling would have had all that food coming back up on me. Incidents like that tend to put a damper on sexy time.

The sexuality of men will always be a mystery to me. How is it that Lee's hand is sliding under my bra during the most violent scene in the movie to cop a feel?

I don't know. Maybe I'm just weird, but watching random big dudes kill each other with machine guns and hand-to-hand combat doesn't exactly get my motor started.

When the movie ends, and Lee asks if I want to go to the bedroom, I tell him I need to review the autopsy on the Castle case. Lee, in response, kisses me so hard my right foot cramps.

Lee doesn't exactly play fair.

We undress each other on the way to the bedroom, and the violent movie doesn't even faze me anymore. By the time we crash onto the bed nude and his calloused hands run up my side, I have forgotten that we watched a movie after dinner.

As fast as everything started, Lee slows as he kisses my neck and shoulder. Yeah, I think my body is okay with skipping that whole foreplay section tonight. I'm ready for the main entrée, no appetizers for you.

As the second orgasm grips me thirty minutes later, the cramp that was threatening in my right foot finally strikes like someone shoving an ice pick into the arch of my foot.

As I yelp, Lee catches my foot in his hand and kneads the arch with his knuckles while he massages my calf.

"Your legs sure do have a lot of tension in them."

"It's because you keep making my toes curl." I laugh.

"I would think that would be a good thing."

"It is until my foot cramps."

"Hopefully, in a few weeks, your muscles will be used to it, and you won't cramp up. Sort of like spring training when we have to get our bodies used to playing ball again."

There is more truth to that than what Lee knows. Of course, I'm not going to share with him how long it has been since I had a reason to get a cramp in my foot while in bed. Some things your present boyfriend just doesn't need to know.

I roll to the edge of the bed. "I need to go pee."

Lee yawns as he grabs lazily at my thigh. "Leaving so soon?"

"I'll be back in a minute."

We have the heat turned up in the house, but leaving the bed after an excellent session of sex, the slight sheen of sweat chills on me immediately.

I stumble to the bathroom as my eyes adjust to the darkness. I'm shivering as I sit down on the cold commode seat.

The only thing I want presently is to hurry up and get back in bed. I make quick work of the task at hand and hurry back to the bedroom. I pull up short. Lee is lying on his back, his eyes closed and his mouth slightly open.

"Lee?" He doesn't answer me. I grab his big toe and move it side to side. "Lee, are you awake?" Still nothing.

Great. I am wide awake. I feel like I might not even sleep tonight, and Lee looks like somebody shot him with an elephant tranquilizer.

I might as well make good use of my time. I try to locate my panties in the dark and finally give up.

After searching in the dresser drawers I had dumped my overnight clothes into, I pull on my PJs and a pair of thick wool socks.

I retrieve my backpack from the kitchen and curl up on the sofa with my laptop.

How weird is it that Shane is now the medical examiner? In some ways, that's really cool, and in others, it's sort of disconcerting.

Oh, get over yourself, April. Shane is just a friend, and you have an awesome boyfriend. Nothing is disconcerting about Shane being the medical examiner. The only thing troublesome is that you assumed he was an orderly rather than an intern. That showed your natural lack of interest in him.

I hadn't been present when they found Gil Castle. From the detailed autopsy report Shane provided, I'm glad I wasn't on-site when they popped the lid on the fifty-five-gallon drum Gil's remains were swimming in. For the life of me, I can't figure out how the police ever located the body.

Cadaver dogs would have been useless given the amount of sulfuric acid and lime dumped on the body. All that as it was, a good deal could be learned from markings and striations on the skeletal system, which was mostly still intact.

When I told Dottie that Gil was in good condition, I had hoped to scare her if she was the murderer. Possibly make her decide to share the truth with me. But she didn't even flinch.

Shane's report concludes that Gil died of puncture wounds. There is a strong possibility from the angle of the striations on the neck vertebrae that he was asleep when he was killed.

Now, I'm not going to say that the Dixie Mafia never uses knives. Still, I know they have a real fetish for offing their opponents with either a fifty-caliber rifle or a twelve-gauge shotgun. They prefer you to have to identify bodies by birthmarks and tattoos. They want their victim's teeth to be missing, or at least a jumbled mess. You can't exactly do that sort of damage with a knife.

Still, burial in an oil drum full of caustic acid might trump a twelve-gauge to the face.

The truth is that as I review the autopsy, I believe Lee is rubbing off on me. Why didn't she pick up and leave if Dottie and Gil were having trouble? Why not start her life over?

Also, the theory about the criminal element isn't ringing true. It wouldn't make any sense if the killing was by the Dixie Mafia. They like to show off their violence as a threat and would have done something stupid like make sure Gil was found in the fountain in front of the City Hall. They wouldn't have wasted the opportunity by burying their victim on his farm.

Still, the ferocity of the murder is mind-boggling. Whoever killed Gil really disliked him. Surely the woman he was married to for thirty years couldn't do those horrible things to him.

I begin to feel like I'm on some invisible hamster wheel in my mind. I'm attempting to decipher what took place thirty years earlier with limited information, and it is making my head hurt.

A giant yawn comes over me. I decide I can't focus on the report any longer tonight. It's time for me to get back to bed.

Lee hasn't moved an inch. I snuggle up to him, laying my head on his chest as I pull the covers up. The rhythmic beating of his heart drives the anxiety from my mind.

Chapter 7

I'm surprised to see Howard's car as I park my car in front of Snow and Associates. I open the building's front door and holler toward his office. "Can I help you, sir?"

"You're funny, April."

I put my purse in my desk's bottom drawer and sit. "So, how is the pizza empire?"

"It's spicy." He appears in his doorway.

I roll my eyes. "Don't be coming at me with your lame wordplay. I'm not particularly happy about the way you have been disappearing lately."

He grins. "Point taken, mama."

"Don't start with me on that, either. What are you going to do in a few weeks when I leave for Baltimore?"

"Go fishing more?"

I flash a sardonic smile. "As if."

He rolls his shoulder. "Truthfully, I will probably close this down and go full-time into the pizza business."

I know Howard is having a good time working in the pizza business with his friend Colonel Mark Sullivan. However, his comment still catches me off guard. "No, you wouldn't. You can't close the law office."

"Why not?"

"Well, for one thing, this community needs your services."

"That's a laugh. There are still attorneys here in town, not to mention you can't swing a cat without hitting three of them in Huntsville and in Gadsden."

"But it's who you are." I can't understand how somebody could spend the time and effort to get a law degree and then decide to not practice anymore."

"No, April. If you don't hear me on anything else, hear me on this one fact. You are *not* your job. If you love your job and it makes you feel valued, that is the perfect situation. But the moment you no longer enjoy your job, or you don't feel valued, you owe it to yourself to make a change."

I make a derisive noise. "But you love your job. And everybody you work with respects you, so you know you're valued."

"I used to love my job, April. But I've been doing this for over thirty years now. That's a long time to do anything. Even something you love."

There has been no indication that Howard didn't enjoy his job. Well, there have been all the unexplained disappearances to Mobile. Plus, the fact that nearly all the cases in the last four months have been assigned to me.

"Oh my gosh, you don't like your job anymore, do you?" I blurt.

Howard laughs as he shakes his head. "No. I can't stand it. I am absolutely done defending people who should be put in jail to protect society and their own health. In the last five years, almost every new client has made me want to ask them, 'So, what did you think was going to happen?' Over time, what has worn on me is seeing the wheel turn and come back around. I don't want to be on it for the next round."

Howard will talk in code at times. He can be eccentric like that. I don't have a clue what he's talking about. "Wheel?"

He shifts his weight. "In my younger days, when I was your age, I thought of everything as moving in a straight line. Sort of like watching a line on a graph."

Howard studies my face for a second, grins, and must understand I still don't get it.

"Think of the stock market graphs." He moves his pointer finger up and down. "The line goes up; the line goes down. Things are getting better; things are getting worse."

"Sort of along the lines of—I graduated law school." I move my finger up. "I get fired the first day I'm in Atlanta," I swing my finger below my waist.

"Sure. On a personal level. But now, think about it from a community level. When I first started, I thought that by doing my job well and by defending people that needed help, I would be bettering the community." He runs his finger up in the air. "The goal being to continuously help people and, over time and in my own way, make things better for this town that I love."

I squint. "But you have. You've helped thousands of people in your community and made their lives better."

He favors me with a wistful smile. "What I wouldn't give to have that twenty-something attitude again. Not the body, nor the vigor, just that beautiful attitude where you honestly believe that somehow you are special, and your life is going to make a difference in this world."

I don't care for the direction this conversation is taking us. "Everybody can make a difference."

He inclines his head toward me. "That is exactly the beautiful attitude I'm talking about. You are me thirty-four years ago." He grins. "Well, you're an inch shorter with much better hair."

My eyes go to his thinning gray hair. "Much better hair."

He laughs. "Still, my attitude has been changed by reality."

Leaning back, I cross my arms. "You can change your attitude. It's the one thing you do control." I'm surprised that I regurgitated one of Granny's favorite mantras. Howard must have heard it thousands of times growing up in her home.

"Maybe 'attitude' is the wrong word," Howard says with a shrug. "It's that my understanding of reality has changed. I know this world does not operate in a straight line. It operates on a wheel. A circle, if you will."

"So, nothing ever changes? Is that what you're getting at?"

If so, it is a depressing thought. No wonder Howard is having difficulties engaging with his clients if that is his state of mind.

"The wheel can get bigger or smaller, but yes, it's uncanny how many things appear to be on autopilot or some sort of preordained fate." He raises his hand. "I'm not getting religious here. I believe in free will, you know that. But how many times have I cleared a man's record of a DUI just for him to commit another DUI two or three years down the road?"

"That's nothing to get a bad attitude about. You are doing your job. You can't expect successfully defending someone against a DUI charge will convince them to clean up their act. They are liable to be right back in court three months later with another DUI. You have no control over that."

"Good. It sounds like you have an excellent understanding of that reality already. I think I came into the profession believing if someone has a close call with the law and I help them, it will convince them to fly straight. I hoped their brush with imprisonment and my assistance would nudge them toward becoming a productive citizen of our community."

It is an odd thought, but I can understand that he may have believed that given his altruistic nature. "Well, you don't need to be concerned about me thinking I'll save anyone from themselves."

"Really? Then why did you have such an emotional crisis concerning Jethro Mullins's death?"

That is hitting below the belt. Jethro Mullins hanging himself is one of the worst moments of my life. I felt like I not only had failed in my job, but possibly, by not having done a better job, brought about his suicide.

I don't believe that anymore. Of course, my recovery was recently turbocharged by me getting to talk to Jethro at Christmas. He is my ghost of the present. He assured me I had done everything I could to help him. I hadn't realized until the following day when I woke how much I needed Jethro to absolve me for his death. One of the many gifts that came from Grandpa Hirsch arranging for the three spirits to visit me during Christmas.

"Perhaps that is what taught me I can't fix everybody. I'm good now. I've already walked through that fire."

"I see you grow with every obstacle you overcome. That's one of the reasons why you're an excellent attorney. Still, I don't want you to be surprised when the wheel turns. That day when it's no longer the man you cleared of DUI charges three or four times, now it's his son. Or the divorce papers are for one of the babies you hammered out custody rights for when her parents got divorced. It's when the wheel turns that you really come to realize how little your efforts affect our community."

Wow. I can't believe I'm hearing this from my uncle.

I feel my face squeezing into a tight frown. "Good to know. If you'll excuse me, I have a bridge I need to jump off of now. Or, if I don't want to cross the veil yet, I can forget this whole lawyer thing and ask Chase if I can work down at the marina with him."

Howard blows an exasperated breath of air between his teeth. "You're taking it wrong. When the job is no longer fun or interesting or intrinsically rewarding to you, I'm saying move on. If it's working at the marina, writing books like your brother Dusty, or teaching at the junior college, don't let your past investment in any career be a reason for staying in something that you no longer love."

What Howard is saying doesn't apply to me. Still, I can see where certain events he mentioned would weigh heavily on him. "So, baking pizzas is that much more enjoyable?"

He laughs heartily. "Yes. I have fun developing better pizzas and consistently showing our staff how to produce better pizza. It's quite challenging.

"And you know, for the first time in a long time, I feel like I'm helping the community. Everyone is nicer after they have had a couple slices of delicious pizza."

I can't argue with him on that point.

Chapter 8

At eleven, Howard announces he is going to lunch. Since he doesn't invite me, I figure he is going to Pizza King to check on his marinara dynasty. When he says it might be a long lunch, I know he is gone for the day.

It's "April in charge" again.

I don't believe I'm old enough for nostalgia. Still, as Howard walks out, I realize the business will close when I leave for Baltimore. I'm afflicted with a bout of melancholy. I guess I'm not as good with change as I pretend.

My daddy routinely visited my uncle's office when I was younger. He used to bring me along with him. Just me. He always said the boys were too rowdy for a respectable law office.

Howard's office has always smelled of leather and tobacco. I was drawn to the smells of his office as much as I admired his big, dark, oak desk and mahogany front doors. I think those things led me to want to be a lawyer before I even knew what a lawyer did for their clients.

My stomach rumbles shortly before noon as it threatens a total rebellion. As I pull my purse out of the bottom drawer, the front door opens, and Lane Jameson walks into our office.

He looks toward the back office. "I wouldn't suppose the boss would be in for a change."

Most days, I like Lane. For the most part, he is a pleasant

man. Lane also can be a jerk without realizing it. "He left a few minutes ago to take care of some business. What can I help you with?"

Lane runs his hand through his perfect salt-and-pepper hair. Every hair goes right back into place. "I need a public defender. Antoine Lattimore was brought in for impersonating a police officer, and he has requested counsel."

The familiar name brings back visions of a six-foot-nine giant, towering over all the other basketball players on my high school team. There is no way this is the same Antoine. Antoine finished two years at the University of South Carolina before going to the Euroleague to play professionally. He was a mini legend in the Sand Mountain community.

"The basketball player?"

Lane looks to the ceiling and sighs. "Today, the police officer, but yes, he was a good basketball player in his day."

This is like the twilight zone. I wasn't even aware Antoine was back in the area. "Why was he impersonating a police officer?"

"April, please don't make me try to explain crazy today. Can you get over there in the next hour?"

I point at my purse. "Well, I was about to get something to eat."

"As a favor, can you skip lunch and get over to the Annex as quickly as possible? I'm not sure how long Corby can keep Dorsett from restarting the interrogation. Dorsett seems to be worked up because Antoine was impersonating an officer. You know how Dorsett can make it personal in a flash."

Antoine graduated my sophomore year in high school. I didn't know him personally, but everybody talked highly of him, claiming he was very gentle and humble. That would be the opposite of Dorsett, who has a nasty tendency to believe that the ends justify the means. "All right, I'll get lunch after."

"Thank you. I owe you a dinner."

I follow Lane out of the office, and he waits while I lock the door. "When did Antoine come back to Guntersville?"

Lane opens his car door. "Truthfully, until I saw him sitting in the interrogation room, I thought he was still in Germany."

There is nothing like going into a case blind. But I'm used to it now.

This is where Howard is wrong. Neither the county nor the city had adequately funded the public defense department. They only have two, and one, Adam Shift, has been on medical leave for the last four years. He refuses to retire or take medical disability. Since he is over fifty, the department is afraid to fire him and end up with a discrimination suit. Without Howard, and lately, me, many defendants would have had their trial dates needlessly extended for lack of proper representation.

I enter the Annex and stride back toward the two interview rooms. I see Dorsett and Corby talking in front of room number one. Dorsett is highly agitated, and Corby is nursing a small styrofoam cup of coffee.

"Look at what the cat drug in. It's the wonder girl of the public defender," Dorsett says disparagingly.

"Shut your piehole," Corby directs to Dorsett. "Hi, Counselor Snow."

Corby is always a cool customer. I'm not sure if that is his natural state or because he is eligible for full retirement and can quit any day the mood settles on him. "Hi, Detectives. I take it Antoine is inside."

"Captain Crazy, you mean," Dorsett snarls.

Corby frowns. "You should know Antoine has changed. I'm not sure the man is playing with a full deck."

Beautiful. "Give me a few minutes alone with my client. Then I'll let you finish asking your questions."

Corby nods his head; Dorsett refuses to look at me.

The smell of urine and stale sweat greets me as I open the door to the meeting room. Antoine tries to stand, and his handcuffs catch on the table. He inclines his head toward me in greeting as he remains standing with his back hunched to allow for the shortness of the cuffs.

"Hi, Antoine. I'm April Snow. I have been assigned to be your defense attorney."

I'm shocked to see there are already numerous gray strands in Antoine's dreads. His face is heavily creased and weathered, not the shiny, full face I remember as always having a permanent smile.

"You can sit down, Antoine."

His expression changes, but I can't decipher it. He sits without comment.

I pull out my chair and sit across the desk from him. At six foot nine, Antoine has always seemed like a giant to me. But in high school, he was a long, lanky kid. These last ten years, Antoine has filled out considerably and probably put on at least fifty pounds. He is not just tall now; he's frickin' huge.

"You might not remember me, but we went to high school together. I was two years younger than you."

Antoine tilts his head to the right as his eyes narrow. His eyes open wider as his jaw slacks. "Chase's sister."

Of course. Antoine would have been a sophomore when Chase graduated. Because Chase played every sport except for golf, only because we didn't have a golf team, any male who went to our high school and played any sport knew my brother.

Hence, I'm Chase's sister. Never mind that, in the case of Antoine, I was a cheerleader at the end of the court, cheering him on for two years.

"That's right," I say.

Antoine goes quiet. His gaze appears to fluctuate between the one-way window and the ceiling. It is almost like I'm not in the room.

"Antoine, can I get you anything? A soda or maybe some crackers?" He continues to focus his eyes elsewhere. Concern tightens my gut as I consider what Corby said. "Do you know why you are here, Antoine?"

I think he may be staring at the one-way window, wondering what the detectives are looking at, saying, or thinking. That is not unusual for suspects.

"Antoine," I reach out to touch his hand. As I make contact, he jerks as if he has been shocked by an electrical current. The handcuff bracelets snap tight as they bite into his wrist. "Whoa, it's alright, buddy. I'm here to help you. I promise."

Antoine's eyes, yellow with red veins branching through them, open wider. "You know."

"I know what, Antoine?" Odd, but I believe I understand what he is speaking of, however I want to confirm it before I hit my panic button.

"You can see them, too." He juts his stubbled chin in my direction.

"See who, Antoine?"

He stands and leans forward until his long body reaches me across the table. I can smell fouled sinuses coming through his mouth. "Them," he whispers in a deeper voice.

I was *so* hoping to go to Granny's tonight, have a pleasant conversation and dinner, before driving over to Lee's and snuggling with him all night. Now I'm getting the impression Antoine will dramatically change my plans for the evening.

"Antoine, I don't know who you mean by *them*. Are you talking about the detectives?"

He squints his eyes. "No."

"The officer who brought you in?"

"No." He shook his head. "You know, the gray ones. The ones that you hear in your head, not your ears."

Oh boy. It is what I thought. Antoine isn't crazy, well he may be now, but he is a clairvoyant who doesn't know what is happening.

I sure wish Nana Hirsch was here to explain his condition to him. I consider denying it. Still, that isn't fair if I plan to ask Antoine to be honest with me.

"I don't see or hear anything right now. Just you, Antoine."

He nods vigorously. "But my hat. They took my hat from me."

"Sure, is that a problem?"

"The gray can read my mind. The hat keeps them from reading my mind."

I don't want to dispute his conviction in the power of his hat. Possibly retrieving the man's hat will put him at ease and make the interview run smoother. Still, I can't help myself. "Who told you that they could read your mind?"

He sits and leans forward in a conspiratorial manner. "If they can talk into my head, they have to be able to read my mind."

Not a flawed theory. I hadn't thought about it before. But that hasn't been my experience. "And what about the hat? Who told you that?"

Antoine laughs as if I have told a joke. "Everyone knows that. Besides, I put a piece of aluminum on the inside. They can't get through aluminum." He taps his temple with his long finger. "It's a thinkin' man's game, don't you know."

It's incredible what the mind will create when we have nobody to get answers from. "Would it be easier for you to talk to me if I get you your hat?"

"Safer. That way, the grays can't hear me."

Right. We wouldn't want the grays to hear us. "Okay. Give me a minute."

I open the door and lean out toward Corby. "Where is the police hat Antoine had on when he was picked up?"

Dorsett hops into the conversation. "In the evidence locker with the rest of the uniform."

I remain focused on Corby. "Can you get the cap for me? I think it will speed things along."

Corby screws up his face as he cocks his head to the right.

"Like you said, he's not playing with a full deck. I believe the hat acts like a security blanket. It may put him at ease and allow us to finish the interview without any interruptions," I explain.

Corby shrugs while a "what are you gonna do" expression is fixed on his face. "Sure. I'll send for it."

"We'll need it back. It's evidence," Dorsett says.

I favor Dorsett my sweetest smile. "Dorsett, I know you have your heart set on that hat. But with your abnormally large head, it just won't fit." I enjoy watching Dorsett's hand touch the back of his head as I close the door.

"Good news, Antoine. The nice detectives are going to fetch your hat."

Antoine lets out a breath as if he had been holding it for the last hour. "That's good. Them grays are sneaky."

"Now, in return, we're going to have to talk to the detectives and let them know what we were doing in the police officer's uniform. Is that okay?"

"I reckon."

"So, tell me. When did you get back from Germany?"

His expression tenses as he considers the question at length. "A week, maybe two weeks ago?"

"What brought you home?"

"My mama called and said she needed some help."

"Are you staying at your mama's?"

Antoine frowns. "Nah, Mama's house got rented out to some new folks."

"Where is she staying now?"

"She's staying up at Whispering Willows, G36. I'm camped out over by the north side of the Guntersville bridge."

Lord, help me. "Antoine, how long has your mama been dead?"

He stares down at the floor. I'm not sure he will respond. He clears his throat, but it still sounds like he has a frog in it. "The sugars got Mama about a year ago." He rubs his large thumb across his cheek to wipe away a single tear. "I wasn't able to make it back then."

"I'm so sorry, Antoine. I know that must be tough for you."

He stares at me, wheezes a breath in, and nods his head.

"You say she needs your help. Is she a gray, too?"

"No!" He draws away from me. "Mama could never be a gray. She's too bright for that."

"I'm sure you're right. I'm sorry, I just needed to ask." With the scarcity of background information, I'm doing little more than the equivalent of feeling my way through the dark. I have never had a conversation quite like this, and I don't need this huge man agitated with me, considering he could squash me like a June bug.

I can only imagine how disconcerting the voices in his head and the visions of his mama must be with no one around him to help navigate the clairvoyance.

The knock on the door is a welcomed distraction. Corby hands me the police officer's hat as I crack the door open.

What the devil? I turn the hat over in my hand. It looks like a prop from some 1960s cop show, complete with a few holes where the moths had a meal.

As I hand the worn cap to Antoine, he smiles, and for a brief moment, I see the big, beautiful, happy athlete I remember from high school. He pulls the cap smartly onto his head. His shoulders lower, and he slouches in his seat.

"Is that better?"

He nods his head as he grins.

"They can't hear you now, correct?"

He winks at me. "We can talk now. It's all safe."

It is apparent by this time that being charged with impersonating a police officer is the least of Antoine's concerns. I can help him with the legal matter quickly enough. Still, it seems more important to work with him on the extraordinary senses he struggles to understand.

"Tell me about the grays. How many of them are there?"

He rolls his yellowed, bloodshot eyes. "Hundreds—maybe more."

"When did you first see them?"

"When I came home and went to visit Mama. They were there, and they have followed me ever since."

"Antoine, you said your mama came to you and said she needed you to come help. I take it she was already a spirit by then?"

He nods his head and stares at the floor again.

"What did she tell you that made you come home?"

"It was like I told you. She said she needed my help."

"Yes. But, what sort of help, Antoine?"

He shrugs. "I don't know that I really understand it. All she told me was that an evil guy was coming to Guntersville searching for the lock. Because the key is not present, I must come home and help."

The hair on the back of my neck stands on end. "What kind of evil guy, Antoine?"

His eyebrows raise as he puckers his lips. "I got no clue. But I know bad guys don't like to see cops. That's why I got my uncle Vernon's old uniform when I flew into Atlanta. Then I took his Impala to Guntersville."

"You still have family in Atlanta?"

"My Aunt CeeCee is still there. She's not good in the head anymore." He taps his finger to the police cap.

Well, at least I have an explanation for the police outfit. Maybe it will help our cause that it was an Atlanta uniform from a few decades back rather than a Guntersville one.

"You said the grays did not start until you came back."

He narrows his eyes. "They're clearing the way for him."

I roll my hands palm up on the table. "Him who, Antoine?"

"The leader's left hand."

This time goosebumps break out on my forearm. I decide I do not want to go further down that rabbit hole with Antoine. It doesn't seem like he has much more information on the topic anyway, as he has gone quiet again.

Enough diversion. It is time I get down to our genuine business. "Antoine, I'm gonna let the detectives come in and ask you some questions. I don't want you to talk to them about your mama, the grays, or the bad man coming to town. They are not interested in that, and they don't need to know. But I want you to tell them that the uniform is from Atlanta, and you didn't mean any harm. You just liked it."

"They would get mad about the grays?" he asks.

"No, but they wouldn't understand. They have never seen them."

Antoine raises his eyebrows. "There are people who don't see the dead?"

"I believe most people don't," I answer him.

He clicks his tongue. "Some people have all the luck."

"Amen to that."

Corby keeps Dorsett on a short leash during the interview. Antoine follows my directions beautifully, so I know he isn't crazy. Although I'm unsure how long that will last if someone doesn't help him with some paranormal coping skills.

Corby allows Antoine to keep his uncle's hat as they lead him back to his cell as a goodwill gesture.

Leaving the Annex, I check the time and calculate that I have enough time to get to Granny's before sunset.

There is no doubt in my mind that Antoine has some level of clairvoyance. Ever since the moment he jerked back when I touched him, I was convinced. He probably experienced the same jolt I received from Nana and Granny occasionally when I was younger. Close contact between "gifted" individuals can result in a shock if caught unaware with no partitions up in their minds.

What I'm less convinced about is whether or not Antoine is sane. It does not escape me how fortunate I am to have multiple people to explain and help harness my talents. If Mama had tried to hide the truth from me when I was eight when the Man in the Lake grabbed my ankle, I might sound as bat crazy as Antoine does to everyone.

My ankle itches where the Man in the Lake had grabbed hold of me. It feels like a second-degree burn on top of a poison oak rash. I know it is a psychosomatic injury. Still, it haunts me twenty years later.

I could have written the interview off as the ramblings of a crazy man. But I have experienced numerous ghosts ranging from a molten gray to a sickly green or blue semitransparent. I also have experienced spirits so lifelike and vibrant that after the initial shock of seeing an acquaintance I know to be dead, I forget they are a ghost.

If Antoine's mama appeared in the manner of the ghosts

I encountered during Christmas, no wonder the man flew in from Europe post-haste.

Still, I haven't ever had a spirit warn me that someone was coming. No ghost has ever mentioned an army of grays preparing a city for someone's occupation.

By my thinking, that doesn't exactly put my mind at ease. As a matter of fact, if he is going to be proclaiming things like that, I really hope Antoine *is* crazy.

Chapter 9

As I pull up to Granny's gate, Maleficent sizes me up. "Don't you even think about it," I warn her.

The juvenile goat trains her calculating gold eyes on me, and I focus my attention on her as I drive through the open gate, get out of my car, and close the gate behind me.

I slink toward her to rub behind her ears as a peace offering. She turns her back to me, flips her tail, and dives into the woods.

Fine, I didn't want to pet her anyway.

Driving up the gravel drive toward the house, I'm surprised to see Dusty's restored GTO already in the driveway. I don't know why, but I have a small flash of jealousy. Tuesday nights are my night at Granny's. The two of them are sitting on the front porch.

"Hey, Sis. How was your day?" Dusty asks. It's apparent he has been drinking.

The whole situation just rubs my fur the wrong way, and I decide to hit him with both barrels. "Well, I was doing all right until our uncle informed me that he's closing his business when I leave. Then I was assigned a clairvoyant client. His "gift" is driving him crazy. He tells me that there's a legion of ghosts in Guntersville preparing the city for their master who's on the way."

"Dang. It sounds like someone had a full day." Dusty raises

the tumbler in his hand. "Kudos to you, Sis, for working a forty-hour week for a living just to pass it on down the line."

I favor my lunatic brother a droll expression for his Alabama reference. Granny spews her tea. Long Island iced tea, if I were to guess from the color in her cheeks and how she has doubled over in laughter.

"Really, you two?" I cock my hip.

"You should have been here with us. We're just sipping tea and watching the sunset."

I shake my head. "Did you hear me? Do you not find that odd, Dusty?"

He pokes his lips out. "No. I was kind of expecting Howard to close the law office once you left."

"Dusty—"

Granny cuts me off. "I think she's talking about the legion of ghosts preparing the city for their master, Dusty." Granny gestures to the rocker next to her. "Take a load off, Fanny."

Dusty snorts a laugh, covering his lips with his glass when I glower.

"I'll pour you some of the sun tea Dusty made me," Granny says.

"It's not sun tea, Granny," I grumble. "It's Long Island iced tea."

"It's refreshing, whatever it is," Granny says as I sit next to her.

Dusty lifts his tumbler toward the sun. "Look at that. It's not the least bit cloudy. It's tough to make tea without it getting cloudy."

Doofus. Tuesday nights are mine. I reach for the pitcher and pour myself a tumbler. "So, what's your take on it?"

"The ramblings of a crazy man? Who knows? Every once in a while, even a crazy prophet is correct." Dusty takes another sip of his drink.

"Did he happen to say if the master was dead or alive?" Granny asks.

"No, I didn't think to ask that. Why? Does it matter?"

Granny rocks vigorously in her chair. "Only because of the comment about a legion of ghosts. Ghosts don't typically like to follow directions. Think about it. They stayed behind when they were supposed to leave like everyone else. They're sort of rebels in their own way. The only thing strong enough to bind a few of them together, much less a hundred, would be a powerful necromancer or a demon."

I choke on my drink. "A demon?" I dealt with a low-level warlock once and nearly died. This is the first time anyone has mentioned that demons can actually be real. "You are kidding, right?"

Granny's eyebrows come together. "Oh no, dear. Demons are rare, but they definitely exist on this plane."

I take a long sip of that special sun tea. If there is even an outside chance some demon has aspirations of making Guntersville its home, I find that a little unsettling. "So, you're telling me that this could be true?"

"It most certainly *could* be true. But to Dusty's point, any day of the week, you can find some fool who will tell you that it's the end of the world today. But that doesn't rule out one of these days one of the fools being right."

I refill my tumbler. I hope Granny cooked tonight because I'm going to need to put some food on my stomach, or I'll be spending the night in her guestroom. I haven't eaten since breakfast. "I'm really not sure how helpful that is."

"Wow. Look how spectacular those colors are," Dusty slurs.

I look to the sky. The bruised-purple etching across the salmon-colored palette is indeed spectacular. I push my rocker back and enjoy the beautiful sunset.

I have been so busy today that I did not notice today was one of those "stolen days" from the dreary, wet, early days of spring. It is late March, and in Guntersville, it can often rain for a week, followed by days of tornado warnings and the required trips to our "safe" rooms or basements. But today is dry and crisp, with the lightest of breezes. I'm not even wearing a jacket.

"Is a demon something that we can exorcise?" I ask.

Granny exhales. "Only if a demon has taken over a nonbeliever. If it is strong enough to walk this plane without a host—" She shrugs. "Suffice to say that's a lot of juice."

Not exactly what I want to hear.

Chapter 10

I was pleasantly surprised this morning by an email from Roger Walsh. It's only Wednesday, and he has already come to a decision about Roman and Ivy's custody battle over Bailey. Roger has chosen to award Roman full custody of his dog and forbid Ivy from visiting Roman or Bailey. He cites his reason for imposing what is, in effect, a lifetime restraining order on Ivy, her propensity for random and unpredictable violence. Go figure.

I pick up my phone to give Roman the great news. Still, it's best to be thorough first. Instead, I should call Kimberly Mason and arrange to pick up Bailey today. I know Roman's first question will be where and when he can be reunited with his companion. It might be fun to deliver Bailey to him myself and see the surprise on his face.

I search my purse for Kimberly's number with good cheer as I swear I'll get better at adding people immediately into my contact list.

On the second search, I find her card in my wallet. Where I thought it was to start with.

I exhale and lean back in my chair as I cheerfully enter her number. When she doesn't pick up on the fourth or fifth ring, my spirits dim.

As I am preparing what to say to her voicemail, she picks up and, in a breathless voice, says, "I'm trying to find out, April. I'll let you know as soon as I can."

My nose wrinkles from my abrupt confusion. I lean forward as if that will help me understand Kimberly. It doesn't help, so I ask, "Find out what, Kimberly?"

The silence seems to last for eons. I hear Kimberly's rapid breathing. My gut rolls over, and I'm grateful I skipped breakfast.

"I assumed you had already heard, April."

I'm so nervous a random inappropriate laugh bubbles out of me. "Heard what, Kimberly?"

She sighs deeply. "This shouldn't be happening—it's not my fault," she blurts in a breathless, run-on sentence.

I put my head between my knees as I await the impact of the nuclear explosion I now believe imminent. The news will further complicate my already insanely complex life. I attempt to remain calm and in control. Instead, I sound as if I'm growling as I demand, "Kimberly, please bring me up to speed. *Now.*"

She pauses again, and I give thanks for not having this conversation in person, or I might be inclined to slap the hesitation right out of her. "Kimb—"

"When I called the kennel this morning to arrange for Mr. Olson to get Bailey, they told me Ivy had already picked him up."

Bless it.

The first electrical blast of the start of a migraine tags me on my C1 vertebrae. I rock side to side as I try to comprehend the implications of what Kimberly is telling me. Simultaneously, I run the scenarios that can unfold if this is the new reality.

"How? How does this happen?" I ask.

"I knew I never should've taken this case! That woman is crazy and dangerous, I tell you!"

I don't respond as I listen to Kimberly's meltdown. It's not that I don't care. I just don't have the bandwidth to deal with what is on my plate and to help her, too.

"She's the shallowest, most manipulative client I have ever

represented.

Yeah, well, Roman picked her, so what did you expect. "How did she get Bailey?"

Kimberly gets control of her emotions and straightens her lawyer façade. "The kennel informed me she came in with release papers. The only thing I can think is she cut and pasted the letterhead from Roger's communications and made some sort of release form."

"And the kennel didn't think that was odd? That she was picking up without counsel?" I ask.

"Come on, April. It's an animal kennel. I'm sure they are not used to standard operating procedures like the department of children's services. I saw the form. She did an excellent job of forging it. She ought to look into doing hundred-dollar bills in the future."

Despite the situation, I laugh at Kimberly's dry sense of humor. "Seriously?"

"I'm sorry, April. This is so embarrassing."

"It is what it is." I shudder as one of Chase's favorite sayings pops out of my mouth. "We'll figure this out."

"Lord, I hope so," she says.

"Where would Ivy go? Her parents'?"

"We've already checked with them. They haven't seen her."

I'm rubbing my forehead vigorously. "Friends, work associates?"

Kimberly barks a quick laugh. "She was married to Roman. She didn't need to work, and who in their right mind would want her for a friend?"

Valid on both accounts. Especially friends who have an attractive and wealthy husband. "Authorities?"

Kimberly groans. "It's a dog, April. Who can I call—the dog police?"

I'm now wondering if Kimberly was asleep during her law classes. "Kimberly, Bailey is still property. It's theft. Call your local authorities and report it, or I will. I assure you that *you* will make it sound less embarrassing to you than I will."

"There's no reason to take that tone with me, April. I didn't do anything wrong."

"Listen, I'm extending as much grace as I can under the circumstance, Kimberly. But, yes, you did do something wrong. *You* failed to secure the dog safely per the agreement of removing Bailey from Roman's home. *You* failed to press upon your client the importance of following the arbitrator's decision. *You* did a lot wrong, Kimberly. But that's okay. We all make mistakes. But please be helpful now and call the authorities so at least we can have that resource working in our favor." I disconnect the line before I have to listen to any more excuses.

Nothing aggravates me more than an immediate crisis and people worrying about assigning blame. It's just not helpful, and if you feel the need to place blame—wait until after the crisis is averted.

I know what *would* be helpful. If Vander were in town, I could call him. He would probably find Bailey and have Ivy in handcuffs before lunch. Unfortunately, I haven't heard from Vander for months now.

I call Howard. His phone rolls to voicemail. He must have worked late last night at Pizza King.

I can't wait for my mentor to wake up. Time is too precious with a mad dognapper on the loose. So, I call the only other person I can imagine could be helpful in this situation.

"What, Snow?" Jacob asks. He sounds aggravated.

I pause before asking, "Hey, I need a favor."

"Of course, you do," Jacob grumbles.

Somebody must have woken up on the wrong side of the bed. "Are you at work?"

"No. I just got in from a long night shift, and I was planning on going to sleep."

"I've got a situation in Huntsville, and I was hoping you could help me with it."

"Uh, April. I don't know if you realize this, but I work for the city of Guntersville. Huntsville is a little bit out of my jurisdiction."

"I know that, silly. I'm wondering if you know a private investigator in Huntsville. I would call Vander, but you know he has been MIA for a couple months now."

Jacob guffaws. "Vander's more than MIA."

Jacob doesn't have a very high opinion of Vander. Somewhere along the way, they seem to have gotten sideways with one another. Or Jacob is just a teeny-weeny bit envious. "So, do you know anyone or not?"

"Yes. Give me a minute," he huffs.

I notice the heel of my boot is tapping about 300 times a minute, and I force myself to stop. Man, I miss the days I could call up Vander and ask him to look into something. Hopefully, this new contact Jacob is looking for can be as effective. I could use an excellent personal investigator given the clientele I keep, if history is any indicator.

I slow my mind and find the irony humorous. I'm leaving in six weeks. Why does a reliable investigator contact matter when I won't be here, nor will Snow and Associates?

"Do you have a pen," Jacob asks.

"Yes, go ahead."

"The dude's name is Baker Diaz. I've only dealt with him a couple of times, and he has not worked for our department. But I've heard good things about him from the guys I know in Huntsville."

Jacob calls out Baker's phone number to me. "You're a lifesaver, Jacob. Thank you."

"Are you still heading up north in a few weeks?"

Oh, *now* he cares? Here I thought I would get the cold shoulder the entire conversation. "Yes, I still don't have a job up there. That may slow the process down."

"I'm sure Lee wouldn't care if you played housewife for a little while."

I don't care for the bitter edge in his tone. "Since we're not married, I can't play housewife. Besides, I think I may have a few leads on jobs. Lee has offered to take me to the Baltimore area next week. I hope to be able to land a deal then."

"That would be good." Jacob's tone is warmer. "Well, if that's what you want, I hope it all comes together for you."

"Thank you. I appreciate that. And thank you for Baker's phone number. Hopefully, he can get me out of this jam."

"Yeah, any time. Listen, I'm going to get some sleep. I'll talk to you later. Bye."

Jacob is gone before I can answer him. It doesn't feel good that my best friend is perpetually irritated with me now. I'm thankful for the vision my Grandpa arranged during Christmas. I didn't like it much at the time, but the insight was golden and has helped me better understand.

The majority of what is wrong with my relationship with Jacob is that he has always been willing to give. Any time I ask for help, he has always been there. But he has asked for little in return, and I'm not exactly the type of person that thinks to do stuff for you without you asking.

Shame on me.

I now understand that, in most people's opinion, it looks like I have taken advantage of Jacob's friendship. I suppose I did. He has always been the safety net ready to catch me without fail if I fall, and I took that for granted. Still, it was nothing I ever did intentionally.

I know his current foul mood toward me has more to do with him not having many people in his life. His mom recently followed his grandmother down to Florida. That was the last of his family left in Alabama.

My family dynamics are a complete one-eighty from Jacob's. Some days I believe I have too many people pulling me in way too many different directions.

I have been Jacob's primary focus since I moved home. We picked up where we left off at the end of high school.

High school was ages ago. We were very different people then, and without the pressures of long-term relationships. Heck, a long-term relationship in high school was thirty days. People are looking for a thirty-year commitment when you get to be our age.

The thought sends a shiver up my spine.

As much as it hurts and makes me feel bad, there really isn't much point in putting too much effort into correcting what probably can't even be fixed. It isn't like Jacob and I will continue to be best friends if I marry Lee. Plus, with me moving to Baltimore, it will become an occasional check-in phone call between us anyway.

The time to worry about fixing relationships in Guntersville has passed. I guess it was fun while it lasted.

Chapter 11

I'm typing Baker's phone number into my phone when it rings. I read *Doc Crowder* on the screen. "Hello?"

"I thought I would get a phone call the other night."

I smile. "I didn't want to make your girlfriend jealous."

Shane favors me a lazy, resonant laugh. "You know all the chicks in this place are dead, and I mean really dead, not figuratively."

"You're too classy to start with that mortuary humor, Shane."

"Aw, come on, it was funny."

"Maybe a little bit."

"Since you didn't call, I take it you understood the toxins listing?" Shane asks.

"On Gil Castle?"

"Did I send you somebody else's folder?"

"Hold on." I click my email icon reopening the folder Shane sent me.

"You didn't read that part, did you?"

"Hush," I say as I scan the report.

"And the defensive marks?" Shane asks.

"Defensive—what about them?"

Shane clicks his tongue. "Girl, do you need me to tutor you on remedial autopsy report reading."

Probably. "Hush your mouth."

"The point is there weren't any defensive wounds," he says.

I find the trace chemicals report. "What is methaqualone?"

"Do you know if your client and her husband were big partiers in the seventies and eighties?"

"I know that they were cheating on each other, but no, I don't believe they were into the party scene."

"Interesting."

"What?"

"I can't determine for sure the cause of death. I've listed it as a homicide because of the corpse's condition. But he had enough Quaaludes in him to kill an elephant, and there were no defensive wounds on his forearms or hands. He may have very well been dead before he was stabbed."

"So maybe he accidentally overdosed, and somebody hid his body?" I'm trying to talk the options out with Shane.

"Maybe, but why not just call the police and let them know what happened?"

"But why would the Dixie Mafia tranquilize him before they killed him?"

"Those crazies wouldn't have. The last thing they would have done was make Gil's death painless. Listen, it's just my job to tell you what I find. But off the record, intoxicating somebody with Quaaludes would be a terrific way to overpower somebody larger than you. And if someone is larger than you, a good way of transporting and disposing of the body is to cut it into smaller pieces. It's just easier to handle."

"That's so nasty, Shane."

He laughs. "Nasty? You should have seen the liquefied goo that was left in the barrel."

"Okay, stop before you make me lose my lunch."

"Speaking of lunch, I have to come into town for some supplies. Do you want to catch lunch with me?"

As heat flashes up my throat to my ears, my breath catches. "Oh, Shane. I'm not sure that's such a good idea since I'm with Lee now."

There is a long silence on the line. "Nah, baby. It ain't like that. I just meant to catch you up on the rest of the Castle folder and see what else you had coming up on your docket."

"Oh." Now I'm blushing from embarrassment. "I'm sort of covered up right now. I have a client in Huntsville with an emergency."

"Okay. I'll catch you some other time."

One of these days, I will understand that Shane is not interested in me. It's like the third or fourth time I thought he was hitting on me only to realize it is only Shane being friendly.

It's not my fault. Shane has such a high level of sexuality I feel like I've been in a heavy petting session every time we talk.

What he told me about Gil's murder does point the person-of-interest needle that much more toward Dottie. Shane is correct. The Dixie Mafia would have wanted Gil to be in pain. Dottie would have been more concerned with Gil overpowering her and foiling her plans. If he were tranquilized, Gil would not have been able to defend himself.

Although I try not to allow them to, the puzzle pieces fall neatly into place.

Dottie is a country girl. She would have known how to work their backhoe. It doesn't take much imagination to see her killing Gil, digging the trench, and placing a drum at the bottom of the grave. I can visualize her cutting Gil into manageable chunks and putting the drum lid on her crime.

My pun makes me frown rather than smile.

Dottie might be an extremely dangerous woman indeed.

Still, I've got plenty of time to consider what happened to Gil thirty years ago. I don't have time to dillydally on finding Bailey.

I make a second attempt to call the number Jacob gave me for Baker. My call goes to voicemail. I leave a message, hoping it sounds urgent but not panicked.

Well, that isn't nearly as fulfilling as talking personally to Mr. Baker Diaz. I would rather know he is already on the case. But I'm sort of out of options.

Part of me knows I should call Roman and inform him of what is happening with Bailey. I decide against it. If I call Roman, he will want answers I can't give him. What are Ivy's plans, where is his dog, and when will all this be fixed? There is no point in bringing him in until I have the answer to at least one of those questions, so the man has something to give him hope. Besides, Kimberly understands the urgency and doesn't want to be further embarrassed by her client. I'm sure she's calling in all the favors she has to bring this to a quick resolution. She may have Bailey ready for pickup before I can get Baker on the case.

I have a couple contracts I need to draft for other clients. Unfortunately, with the unwelcome news about Bailey and the information Shane provided all but proving Dottie butchered Gil, my heart isn't into doing a bunch of mundane paperwork.

I click over to the job board in Baltimore and scan through the different lawyer positions. It is pretty slim pickings. There is only one that is even close to being something I would consider. DC is even worse.

I can do this. While I was ultimately unsuccessful, Atlanta prepared me well for this situation. I'll simply go next Tuesday and pound the pavement of Maryland while Lee does his thing. I'm grateful I'll at least have that time to interview before I move up there.

I send a cover letter and my résumé to the one opportunity in Baltimore. Hopefully, they will respond soon to confirm at least one appointment before our trip.

Despite my bravado, the lack of opportunities in Baltimore and DC has me concerned. I know more than anything I want to be in the area of Lee's home base. But I don't want to play housewife, to borrow Jacob's term. If I'm going to live with Lee and not be married, I must carry my own weight.

When I began law school, I never believed I would have difficulty securing employment in my field. If I had thought for a moment I would have to move back home after school, I never would have spent the time, money, or effort to get the degree.

At the very least, I would have listened to Daddy and gone into mechanical or electrical engineering. As he always jokes, "People always be building stuff."

Too late to be changing careers now, April. You've got student loans to pay.

The silver lining? I don't need a bunch of opportunities on the job board. I only need one remarkable job tailor-made for me that I will locate when I'm in Baltimore. Yes. That's what I'm going to focus on. That's what I'm going to visualize and bring into manifestation.

My phone startles me with its ring. An unfamiliar number displays. "Hello?"

"April Snow?"

"Yes?"

"Baker Diaz, you called?"

"Yes. A friend of mine gave me your number and told me you do private investigation work?"

"Who's your friend?"

"Jacob Hurley from the Guntersville Police Department."

"Okay. What can I do for you?"

I explain the situation to Baker. He promptly tells me he has no interest in being a dog catcher.

Ten minutes later, he caves to my persistence, and I send him the file complete with pictures of Bailey, Ivy, and Roman. He informs me he will report back to me this evening.

Paradoxically, "this evening" sounds simultaneously like quick work by Baker and too long for Bailey.

Chapter 12

It is lunchtime, and still no Howard. I wonder if he is at the house or if he went straight into Pizza King today. This is not the behavior of the responsible lawyer uncle I grew up with.

Ugh. *Get it through your head, April. This is the end of Snow and Associates. Howard has moved on, and you should too.*

The truth is, I miss him. And I will miss working with him. Not enough to don one of those goofy, half-nylon-net, half-paper-boat-looking hats he is making his crew wear, but losing his mentorship weighs heavily on my heart.

I sigh as I pull out a fresh legal pad to write down a to-do list. While brainstorming, I remember I failed to pick up the case file on Antoine Lattimore from Lane. I also need to schedule an appointment to speak with Antoine's arresting officer. After that, it appears like I have a thinning agenda.

Perhaps I can work in an appointment at the beauty college to get my nails done. It has been *way* too long since my last manicure.

First on the list? A is for Antoine. To the District Attorney's office I go.

Normally I would walk to the DA's office, especially since we are having the second day of nice weather in a row. But I'm also hungry and want to get the task done as quickly as possible before driving to Petit Fours & Pimento.

I lock up the office. I point my car down Gunter Avenue and

make a series of left-hand turns to put me on Blount Street.

The day is looking up. I have a parking space in front of the DA's office and won't need to use the parking garage—which would have defeated the purpose of driving altogether.

Opening the door to Lane's office, I lean back as I'm greeted by an unfamiliar face. Lane has been changing office assistants lately like I change blouses. This one looks like she might be thirteen. I hope he had her parents sign an affidavit for underage employment.

"Can I help you?" she asks.

"Yes, I'm April Snow with Snow and Associates. I'm here to pick up the Antoine Lattimore folder. DA Jameson said he would have it ready for me."

The little girl favors me with a smirk with her lush lips before replying, "Yes, I have that for you. One moment please."

She disappears into the record room, leaving me to wonder what her coy smile was about. Maybe she likes doing a good job and is pleased that she knows why I am here.

Lane's office door is shut. Despite the blinds being closed on the interior wall windows of his office, I note that his office is dark. The boss is MIA at the District Attorney's office, too. There seems to be a pattern developing in this town.

The young assistant exits the records office. "You don't remember me, do you?"

That must be my least favorite question in the world. "I'm sorry, I don't."

"Stephanie Dunn. You were my cheerleading coach."

"No, I think you're mistaken. I haven't coached cheerleaders in almost nine years, and I only coached middle school. You're way too young for me to have coached you."

Stephanie smiled as she handed me the folder, and it reached her dark eyes. "I'm twenty-three, April. I graduated from Alabama A&M last year."

I do a double-take of the young woman's petite, lithe figure and round, girlish face. Bless it, I can't place her. "Oh, then you're probably right. Congratulations on the graduation. I bet your parents are proud."

"They are. I think it may have convinced my younger brother Kayden to seriously consider going to college, too."

Now I remember her. Stephanie was a talented tumbler and one of our best flyers. Her mama worked late, and she would have to bring her little brother to practice with her.

I remember how Kayden would throw the football up in the air and run under it, making crazy catches as he dove onto the padded floors. Effectively he was passing the ball to himself.

He was such a cutie with his flawless fade haircut and long, thick eyelashes. All the cheerleaders doted on him, making him uncomfortable.

"Okay, I have to ask, does your brother still play football by himself?"

Stephanie laughs as she shakes her head. "No. Once he got to the middle school, he found a few quarterbacks who could throw him the ball."

"Here I always thought *he* would be the quarterback."

"He played some of that, but he likes playing receiver and cornerback better."

"Too funny." I gesture with my hand. "I'm sorry I didn't recognize you at first."

"It's been a hot minute."

"It was good to see you. Tell Kayden hi for me."

"I will. Have a good day, April."

How cool is that? My memory of Stephanie is a little bitty stick with buggy eyeglasses and thick braids who was absolutely fearless with stunts that even made me shiver with apprehension.

Often, she was too shy to look at me in the eye when we spoke. Now, she is a polished young graduate working at the District Attorney's office. It is encouraging to see people attain their goals.

The next time we meet, I must ask if Kayden plays any sports besides football. If he plays basketball or baseball, maybe I'll get an opportunity to see him play before I head to Baltimore. I don't know why, but I really want to see what all those hours of self-practice might have done for him.

I get in my car and drive down Blount Avenue. The day is fifty-five degrees, sunny, and Guntersville Lake is visible on my right.

I think about Stephanie's update about her and Kayden's success while driving alongside a beautiful lake traveling to my favorite place for lunch. It is difficult to call today anything short of perfect.

I turn left off Blount in front of the Spanish House Antiques to travel back up Gunter, which is a one-way street. I make the turn and slide into the right-hand lane to claim a parking spot in front of Petit Fours & Pimento.

Did I mention today is perfect?

I slow as I approach the crosswalk since five women are crossing. One of the women catches my eye.

She is a big woman—six foot one and a Twinkie shy of three hundred pounds.

As she recognizes me, her bottom jaw drops, exposing large, chicklet-shaped teeth that would make a Clydesdale horse proud.

She spins. Which forces her fanny-length cotton skirt to swirl upward, exposing me to what resembles thirty pounds of mashed potatoes tied up in a clear plastic bag. Complete with a single red ribbon splitting it in half.

Bethany's thong scars my retina.

I stand on my brakes to give us space in hopes she will continue with her friends and not make one of her patented loud scenes.

Unexpectedly, my IROC's rear tires scream like banshees as a plume of gray smoke appears in my rearview mirror. My car fishtails to the left as I slide sideways into the crosswalk.

My right fender gets within a frog's hair of clipping my giant ex-sister-in-law as she freezes in between the white "safe zone" lines. In terror for her life, her lips pull back, forming a gaping "O" as her pig nose exposes both nostrils.

I clear the crosswalk in a slide, completing a full one-eighty before finding the brake pedal and doing what I originally meant to do. Coming to a stop, I lean against the steering wheel and offer thanks for somehow, miraculously, not having killed anyone.

Bethany slaps her hands on my passenger window before I can finish my prayer and gather my thoughts.

She's looked happier.

Against my better judgment, I roll the car window down.

"You think that's funny! What's wrong with you Snows?" Bethany screams at me. She looks over her shoulder and yells at her friends, "Call the police now!"

"It was an accident. My foot slipped," I explain.

"Accident my butt. You nearly killed me. Did your brother put you up to this? Tell me! Did he?"

"What?" I shake my head in disbelief. "Are you kidding me?"

"How much did he offer you? Whatever it was, it's not enough. You are going away for attempted murder."

"Oh girl, don't even." She is waking up my redneck crazy. She does not want to go there. "I guarantee you if I wanted to kill you, I would have run you down. For the record, I didn't even recognize you until you were almost past me. I was braking, and my foot slipped."

She screws her face up until her eyes disappear from view. "You just tell that to the police, April Snow."

A car behind us blows its horn. I'm blocking both lanes in my present position. I wave at the driver in my rearview mirror. "I gotta get out of the road."

"Oh, hit-and-run. That's great. That should get you another twenty years!"

"You know, Dusty said you were stupid, but I had no idea to what magnitude." I point toward the parking lot. "I'm pulling in over there. You might want to step back so I don't run over those barges that you call feet."

Her face turns red as she begins to tremble. "What did you just say?"

"I said move your feet, or they're going to be triple Es after I run over them."

She releases her grip on my passenger door. "Threatening me, too?" Bethany turns to her girlfriends, who are on the opposite curb. "You heard her, didn't you? She's threatening me now."

I take my time steering my car in reverse to stay clear of her. The last thing I need now is to actually hit her since the police are coming.

Man, what a drama queen. I would so like to slap her for being a miserable human being. Then I would punch Dusty in the face for being stupid enough to marry her and expose our family to Bethany's nonsense.

Thankfully, the parking spot I was eyeing is still available. I pull into the slot and double-check that I put the car in park. Checking that I'm in park is a story for another day that my brother Chase likes to tell about when Daddy taught me how to drive.

I lean against the driver's door of my car as I watch Bethany stomp her way to me.

If it were anyone other than Bethany, I might consider retrieving my forty-five from the glove compartment. She looks hostile, and Lord knows Bethany is a scary-looking woman when angry. Still, Bethany is all about drama and drumming up support for her victimhood.

A pair of noise-canceling headphones would be my first weapon of choice in this tussle.

A Guntersville police cruiser pulls up perpendicular to my car. A single *whoop* sounds from the vehicle's sirens.

"You are toast now, April," Bethany chides.

Crossing my arms across my chest, I take a deep breath and look to the clear sky. I wonder which officer we drew for this girl fight. I know it won't be Jacob, which is most likely a good thing for me, given his recent attitude toward me.

"I hope your brother enjoys having to visit you in jail," Bethany continues. "I've got four witnesses, April." She holds up four fingers and grins. "Four."

"Yeah? Well, I've got a secret for you, Bethany."

Her eyes narrow. "What?"

"Regardless of whether I go to jail or not, tomorrow you're going to wake up and still be the same mean-spirited, sorry excuse for a human being."

Bethany is stammering for a witty comeback as Justin Smith walks up with his reflective sunglasses. "What seems to be the problem, ladies?" I could understand him better if he would remove the golf ball-sized wad of chewing tobacco from inside his right cheek.

Bethany turns on Justin with the force of a hurricane. "Officer, you need to arrest this woman immediately for attempted murder, hit-and-run, threatening physical violence, and name-calling."

Justin grins as he looks from Bethany to me as if expecting one of us to announce that we are playing a joke. His eyebrows draw together. "You're serious?"

"Yes! I'm telling you she tried to kill me with her car. Her car is a lethal weapon." Bethany turns back toward the restaurant and waves for her friends to come toward her.

Justin is ten years older than me. He and his wife Lucy have three boys—I forget their ages—and they have had a boat down at my mama's marina for the last five years.

"April?" he asks as he points toward Bethany.

"Dusty's ex-wife," I confirm for Justin.

His eyebrows shoot up below the visor of his cap bill. "Oh, I never met her."

"Justin, Bethany. Bethany, Justin," I say in a droll tone as I wave my hand between them.

Bethany looks from me to Justin. "This better not be none of that small-town police-enforcement favoritism. We're talking about a serious crime here, mister. You need to do your job and arrest this woman." Bethany looks toward the diner and motions again for the four women to come to her,

"It's Officer Smith, ma'am," Justin corrects her.

"It's going to be administrative leave, mister. If you don't get your job done."

Justin ignores Bethany and directs his attention to me. "April, what's this fuss all about?"

I remain leaning against my car. Rolling my eyes, I say, "My foot slipped from the brake to the accelerator."

"It was attempted murder!" Bethany screams as her cheeks darken to beet red.

Justin pulls off his police cap and tucks it under his left arm. Justin keeps his head shaved. Combined with his thick, muscular build, he looks like a mixed martial arts fighter. "Do you have any wounds, ma'am?" he asks Bethany.

"Wounds?"

"Bruises, cuts, or abrasion marks from the car hitting you?"

Bethany turns to wave for her friends again. They have disappeared into Petit Fours & Pimento without her. She turns away from us as she realizes the posse is not coming to assist.

I swear I can see ropelike veins throbbing on her neck. They threaten that she may keel over with a stroke any moment.

While this would solve many of my brother's issues, I don't care to be in the area if Bethany has a life-ending event.

"Ma'am, any injuries?"

"No," she hisses.

"Ma'am, I don't know where you're from, but around here, we have a saying. 'No blood, no foul.'" Justin pulls his cap on smartly. "Ladies, I hope you have a good rest of the day."

"You're not gonna do anything?" Bethany asks as she follows Justin to his cruiser.

"There's nothing to be done, ma'am. I'd suggest you go enjoy your lunch or head back to Huntsville."

"This is ridiculous. This woman tried to kill me with her car. You're not even going to charge her with anything? That's a dereliction of duty."

Justin stops. He turns on Bethany, leaning toward her.

To her credit, she must have a little sense because she backs up a step.

"Ma'am, with all due respect. If April meant to kill you with her car, you're a big enough target she would not have missed."

Justin's comment leaves Bethany fuming on the curb while he gets into his police cruiser. She remains standing with her mouth open as he drives away.

Chapter 13

As much as I want chicken salad from Petit Fours and Pimento, I know I can't stomach being in the same restaurant as Bethany. Jerry's subs may not be what I want, but at least I don't have to feel uncomfortable there.

Pulling into Jerry's parking lot, I decide I might as well make it a working lunch and grab Antoine's folder.

Inside, I order a tuna melt, a sad substitute for chicken salad. Feeling oppressed for a simple mistake, I sit on the unbelievably hard seat and attempt to calm my nerves.

The tuna melt isn't doing it for me. No surprise there.

It is partially that I craved chicken salad and partially that my blood is still boiling from my encounter with Bethany. What a miserable person. I don't know what my brother ever saw in her.

Well, I do. Even with his money, Dusty is not exactly a babe magnet—but Bethany? He can do so much better.

Justin doesn't know it yet, but there is a free boat slip upgrade in his future as soon as I touch base with Mama and Chase about today's mishap. They're not Bethany fans either. Anybody who puts her in her place deserves a little extra consideration.

Take that for small-town justice, Bethany.

I open Antoine's folder and skim over it first. It appears that not only was Antoine arrested for impersonating a police officer, but there were some home burglaries in the area he was found. Nobody had seen him in any of the break-ins. Still, given his proximity to the crimes, he is a prime suspect.

I grin at my luck as I see Sheriff Becky Gray is the arresting officer. Now, if that isn't karma. Since receiving my Grandpa's Christmas gift, I have made a concerted effort with her. I think I'm wearing her down with kindness.

I dial Becky's number. She answers right away.

"Hi, April. What's up?"

"Hey, I just got assigned a client, and it appears that you were the arresting officer for him."

"Antoine?"

"Business must be slow if you know who I'm talking about," I tease.

"Not really. He has been on my mind a lot. So, I figured that's who you were calling about."

"I met with him yesterday. I would like to hear your take on the events leading up to his arrest."

Becky exhales. "It was sort of weird, April. I'm sitting at a red light. I look to my left, and I recognize him. You remember, he played basketball at our high school."

"Yeah, I remember."

"So, I was looking at him, and then I noticed his shirt has a badge on it. That doesn't trigger any alarms in my head. I thought maybe he moved back to town, and he was working as a security guard or something.

The light changes, and we pull forward. He was going a little faster than me, and I noticed he had Georgia tags. Then I noticed they were expired, and I pulled him over."

"Yes. He said the car was his aunt's from Georgia."

"Well, I don't know what the laws are in Georgia, but the tags were four years expired. I asked him to get out of the car while we ran all the information. That's when I noticed he was in an Atlanta police officer uniform. When I asked him if he was active in the force, he was honest and told me no. As a matter of fact, he told me that it was his uncle's uniform."

It sort of tweaks me that Antoine was honest with Becky, and she didn't extend him any consideration for that. "Why did you charge him with impersonating an officer when he told you right off that it wasn't his uniform? Maybe he was going to a costume party or something. You couldn't give him the benefit of the doubt?"

"I wanted to, April. But something wasn't right. He couldn't focus on anything I was asking him. His eyes were wandering all over the place. It was like he had a schizophrenic attack. I thought it best to at least get him in to have a doctor look at him and maybe get him some help."

"Well, they're giving him a lot of help right now, Becky. They have him chained to a desk in the interrogation room," I say before I consider how harsh my comment sounds.

"That's not at all what I intended to happen," she whispers.

"Look, it's okay. I'll see what I can do to help him. I didn't mean to snap at you. I'm sorry."

"No. I get it, April. Antoine was always nice to me in school. I truly did it out of concern more than anything. It makes me sick that I have caused him any pain."

"Like I said, it's cool. I'll figure something out."

"Will you promise to keep me in the loop? And let me know if there's anything I can do."

"Sure. And thank you for filling me in, Becky."

I feel like a heel as I hang up. Becky probably was looking out for Antoine's health. Still, like many things in life, you try to do the right thing, and sometimes it backfires in a big way. I will have to figure out how to help Antoine and make Becky feel she did the right thing. In short, I'll need to work some courtroom magic.

I'm wadding up my sandwich wrapper as Roman Olson storms into Jerry's sub shop. "There you are," he shouts. "I've been searching all over for you."

Man, if his comment doesn't have an underlying stalker tone to it. "It's just a lunch break, Roman. And my phone still works."

He props his hands on my table and leans toward me. I slide my butt an inch down the booth.

"I heard some scuttlebutt from Ivy's cousin that the arbitrator has already ruled."

Roman having phone conversations with Ivy's cousin piques my interest, but I don't feel overly nosy given his hostile stance. "It's true the arbitrator sided with you. But the coordination of transferring Bailey is going to take a while."

His brow furrows. "Why?"

I shrug. "There's a bunch of red tape that has to be taken care of before we can get Bailey released."

"But— You're going to do something about that, right? We need to speed things up."

"There's no speeding this up, Roman."

"I don't understand. It took them less than twenty-four hours to take the dog out of the only home he knew during his entire life. It shouldn't take them more than twenty-four hours to figure out how to release my dog back to me. Why does it take so long for them to release the dog to me, April?"

Fine. I shouldn't have tried to shield Roman from the situation in the first place. I must hold out hope that Baker Diaz will uncover something of consequence by the end of the day.

"Ivy took Bailey."

Roman smiles stupidly at me. His smile fades. "You're serious?"

"Dead serious."

"How does this happen?" he croaks.

"From what I have learned, I believe Ivy faked some release paperwork. The veterinarians didn't know any better and released Bailey to her earlier this morning."

"No! How is a dog held in protective custody, and one of the parties gets to just walk in and take the dog out?"

I shake my head. "I've got no satisfactory answers for you,

Roman. I do have a private detective working in the Huntsville area to locate Ivy and Bailey as quickly as possible. Once he does, we can retrieve Bailey."

Roman collapses into one of the chairs next to me, burying his head in his hands. "You're the one who said it first, but I didn't want to believe you."

I have no clue what Roman is talking about. "Said what?"

He lifts his face. Tear streaks stain his cheeks. "That she wants to hurt Bailey to get even with me." He breaks into a wet sob. "Oh, Lord, what is she going to do to him?"

Now there is an angle I failed to consider. I have been so focused on finding Ivy and Bailey that the whole revenge thing, so apparent during our hearing, escaped me this morning. "She's not going to hurt a dog." I try to calm his nerves.

Roman locks his watery eyes on me. "Yes, she will."

A cold chill climbs up my spine. Nobody is evil enough to hurt a dog. "She wouldn't hurt Bailey. He's her dog, too."

Roman draws a deeper breath as he wipes his nose with the back of his hand. "That woman is crazy and mean. You've seen her in action. She's like a rabid bobcat."

Roman makes an excellent point. The woman showed less than full restraint during the arbitration. Drawing blood during those meetings is usually frowned upon.

"Is there anywhere you can think of that Ivy might be hiding out with Bailey, Roman?"

He runs his fingers through his hair. "I don't know. Ivy was staying with her parents, but she sure wouldn't bring them into this."

"Friends? How about the cousin you were talking to?"

Roman barks out an abbreviated laugh. "No. She would definitely not be at her cousin's. They don't really talk anymore."

"I need you to think. I want this private investigator to be checking everywhere you believe she might have taken Bailey."

He squeezes his eyes shut in apparent frustration. "She's just such a loner. I can't see her taking a black lab to any of her acquaintances' houses. Her parents know Bailey, so that's not going to work for her." Roman hangs his head while making a groaning noise.

"What? What is it?" I ask.

"Uncle Neal's hunting shack up toward Tuscumbia. That's where she took him." Roman covers his mouth with his hand as he leans back.

"Why do you say that?"

"When we first started dating, Ivy told me she liked to go camping. It's not exactly camping, but I thought, what the heck, I'll take her up to the cabin. I hadn't been up there in years, and I needed to check on it anyway."

I make a circling motion with my finger, gesturing for Roman to get to the point.

"Right. We took Bailey on that fishing trip. I took him down to the river to let him swim since I had never taken him to the water before. Ivy kept telling me that the current might be too strong, but I insisted that all labs are naturally strong swimmers.

"Turns out Bailey swims like a boulder. He went under, and I froze. It was Ivy who pulled Bailey out of the river."

"And?"

"Ivy is like an open ledger. Her biggest fear is that she won't get compensated for something she's done. I know she's going to feel like she saved Bailey. Therefore, she can kill Bailey."

No, that's just too messed up, even for a psycho. "Roman, are you sure?"

"I'm going to kill her."

"Excuse me?" I say.

He leveled his bloodshot eyes in my direction. "I said I'm going to kill Ivy. I'm going to get a section of rubber hose and beat her to death."

No, that's not scary, and this is the same guy who hunted down my car all over town so he could speak with me. "I can't hear this. As a lawyer—your lawyer—I would have to report your intent to kill Ivy to the authorities."

"Consider it a professional courtesy. I didn't want you to be surprised when it happened, April."

I hold my hand out toward him. "Listen, let's let the private investigator do his job. I'm going to text Mr. Diaz and tell him he needs to check in the Tuscumbia area. Do you have an address?"

Roman gives me the address. I text it to Baker. Hopefully, that will narrow it down for Baker, and he can find something out on an even quicker basis.

I turn my attention back to Roman. "I need you to promise me you're not going to go looking for trouble with Ivy."

"Oh, there's nothing that woman can do to me now," Roman claims.

"Yes. She can get you stuck in jail for a long time. I would hate to see that happen to you."

"It seems like a small price to pay to make sure she doesn't do this to anybody else."

I haven't ever felt such raw brutality, but I can understand where Roman is coming from. "But the thing of it is, Roman, the courts will do their job, and this will be taken care of without you having to spend time in jail."

"I've lost my faith in the legal system, April. They can't even handle the protection of an innocent dog correctly."

"I understand your frustration, Roman. I really do. Still, give me a chance. If you can hold up for another day, this will all come to a satisfactory conclusion. You'll have Bailey back, and you and Ivy will be divorced."

"You don't know that."

"Sure, I do." I struggle to keep up my disingenuous, confident smile.

Roman studies me. He gives a nod of his head. "Alright. You win, April. I'll trust you to get it done."

Roman walks away, hitting the glass door too hard as he exits Jerry's.

My sandwich is sitting in my stomach like a rock now.

Chapter 14

I drive my car back to Snow and Associates and am pleased to see we don't have any customers waiting at the door. I retreat into our office and fall onto my chair.

In some ways, I'm beginning to understand Howard's point. Thirty or forty years of this circus would be absolutely exhausting.

I need a break, badly. I call Tiffany Bates to see if she has any appointments. She puts me down for a 3:30 manicure appointment.

I have a couple of hours to kill before I need to leave. The office is quiet for once, allowing me time to think about my upcoming cases.

I don't understand Dottie Castle's unsubstantiated claim about Gil's death being a Dixie Mafia hit. To my knowledge, Dottie is the only person to ever float this theory. The question on my mind is whether she made it up out of whole cloth or if there is any credibility to the root claim. I only need doubt. If I could prove their business dealings with Gil—well, it wouldn't be too difficult to imagine a juror going down that Mafia hit job rabbit hole.

I dial Ms. Castle's number.

"Hello?"

"Ms. Castle, this is April. Would it be okay to come over for a few minutes? I need to ask you a few more questions."

Dottie's home sits upon one of Guntersville Lake's many surrounding mountains. The conservative brick colonial commands a spectacular view of the north side of the lake.

As I walk up the sidewalk, I notice that only her glass door is closed. The front door is open. I ring her doorbell, and five teacup poodles charge the front door, yapping their warning.

Dottie is close behind. She corrals the miniature canine menagerie into the dining room to the right and puts up a doggy gate.

"Thank you for seeing me on such short notice, Ms. Castle," I say as she opens the glass door for me.

"Nice to have company, dear. It's just a shame it is not under better circumstances." She gestures to her right. "I set up tea in the living room if you would care to come sit and talk."

"Yes, ma'am. I promise I won't stay long. I've got an appointment at the beauty college to fix these disasters I used to call nails."

Dottie rotates her hand toward me. "I gave up on real ones forty years ago."

Yep. Those plastic talons really look good. "I might have to check into those. Maybe they have a stainless-steel version."

I sit, taking note of the china tea set on the coffee table. "You're probably the first person I've ever met who's offered me tea instead of coffee."

Dottie's drawn-on eyebrows jump. "I have coffee if you prefer."

"No, ma'am. I think the novelty would be nice."

"It's all a dying art. Customs that lasted three centuries in this country have dissolved in the last twenty years," Dottie laments.

Dottie lifts the tea kettle and holds the lid as she pours. I'm suddenly aware that she is no longer using her walking cane.

"I see you're getting along pretty well without your cane

today."

"That's the thing about arthritis. Some days it's bad. Some days it's nonexistent. I give thanks to the Lord either way."

Sitting down, she looks at me pointedly. "What do I really owe this visit to, dear?"

"I keep thinking about the Dixie Mafia. You told me Mr. Castle was working for them when he went missing. The fact we aren't able to identify any of the players is troubling me."

Dottie crosses her bony white arm as her lips tighten into a thin line.

"Of course, it won't be necessary to identify his specific Mafia contacts. Still, there's been no sign of organized crime in North Alabama since the sixties. We'll need some sort of tangible evidence that the Dixie Mafia was operating during that time and that Mr. Castle was the financial arm of their organization's activity. With that evidence, I know I can convince the jury to doubt the charges against you."

"I don't understand your point, dear," Dottie says.

I puff a breath from my nose in frustration. "Dottie, I need to know if the IRS returned the records they audited. Those records might hold the key to establishing Gil's participation with the Mafia as a money man." I gesture with my hand. "That then might provide a reasonable expectation that it was the Mafia who killed him—not you."

"Of course, they did. Why didn't you ask for them earlier?"

I grit my teeth and force a false smile. Taking a deep breath, I manage to hide my crazy. "Do you have access to them?"

Dottie laughs.

Her reaction startles me. Not because it seems inappropriate for the topics we are discussing, but because I believe it's the first time I have ever seen her smile.

She moves across the den and inserts a key into a Wedgwood vase. The chest-high bookshelf the vase sits on swivels forward two inches on the left-hand side.

I jump up and peer over her shoulder as Dottie slides her fingers into holes drilled in the side of the pine-framed door.

She gives a light tug, and the shelving swivels to a ninety-degree angle. I hear a whisper of creak from what must be a monstrous-sized hinge to hold such a heavily loaded shelf.

A stairwell, diving into pitch darkness after the first seven stairs, is before us. "What in tarnation?" I say.

Dottie looks at me over her shoulder. "Gil and I agreed that there are things that shouldn't be left out for snooping eyes. Especially if the law ever decided to make an unannounced visit. If you catch my meaning."

I nod. "I believe I do."

Dottie reaches into the darkness and a series of bare, yellow incandescent bulbs hanging by electrical cords from the basement's open-beam ceiling light up. I am not afraid of spiders. Still, the myriad of webs hanging low, speckled with long-limbed slender bodies, sends a shudder up my body from my toes.

"Yuck," I say.

Dottie reaches in and produces a broom from behind the door jamb. "Never mind them. I'll clear us a path, and they'll leave us alone well enough."

I hesitate despite her assurances.

Dottie takes a swing toward the ceiling and nearly goes butt over teakettle. I grab her bony shoulder before she falls.

An instantaneous flood of fragmented violent acts courses through my mind. My stomach tenses as if I have eaten something well past its expiration date.

"Whew. Aren't you the lifesaver," Dottie says.

I release her and offer her a wan smile. I try not to look her directly in the eye in case she might, by some odd intuition, surmise why my demeanor has changed so quickly.

Dottie turns and takes a less aggressive swipe at the cobwebs. "These itty-bitty spiders, they're only looking for a meal like everybody else. They won't hurt you." She continues down the stairwell, swinging the broom sporadically from side to side.

Given my feelings about Dottie and what I just pulled from

her thoughts, I'd be an idiot to follow her into the secret cavern below her home. Still, my ever-bothersome curiosity urges me to follow.

I expect to find a hidden lockbox or metal safe at the base of the stairs that sway with our steps. Instead, the entire basement is filled with decaying cardboard filing boxes. There is a narrow path separating the documents into four quadrants.

"What the devil is all this, Dottie? Are these shipping tickets for the vehicles?"

"It's everything. Shipping tickets, payroll, receiving reports, bill payments, and any dividend payments."

I feel my face tighten. "Dividend payments? I thought it was a privately owned company."

"Pay attention, dear. I told you there were investors," Dottie says.

My earlobes feel as if someone is holding a flame to them. All the time Dottie and I have spent discussing this case, and I'm only *now* finding out there were investors involved in their dealerships.

Some days I feel like my clients are actually working against me. Why won't they tell me everything initially so I have a fighting chance at helping them? "Do you know who the investors were, Ms. Castle?"

"Oh, no. They were all silent."

Of course. "Do you have any idea how many there were?"

She opens her mouth to say something, stops, and shakes her head. "I really can't remember exactly. I know it's more than two."

Okay. In April's cynical world, that means there were more than two people with a motive to kill Gil. But would they? What would be their motive to kill their business partner?

My spirits flag. All along, I thought the information surrounding me would be an effective deflection away from my client. Now I'm not sure partners, even if they had financial grievances, will be more compelling to a jury than a spurned wife.

My phone rings. I see *Lee* and gesture to Dottie that I need to take the call. "Hi, baby."

"Hey, love. Inquiring minds want to know what time you plan to be home tonight."

"Are you home now?"

"Yeah, I got done working out early and have already taken my shower. I was thinking about starting dinner."

"Oh, that sounds good," I blurt.

Lee lets out a low, rumbling laugh. "I didn't even tell you what I'm fixing."

"I'm sure it's going to be delicious," I say.

"I don't know. It's been a long time since I cooked worms and tadpoles," he teased.

"You're gonna spoil me, asking my brothers all my favorite dishes."

"So how about you wrap it up now, and you can come drink wine while I cook dinner."

"As inviting as that sounds, I have got to get a manicure. I'll be home just a few minutes past five."

"Ugh, you're killing me, babe."

"Stop that. You have me all night."

"I know," Lee says. "I just don't share well."

"Well, you won't have to share me with anyone when we travel to Baltimore next week," I remind him.

"I know. Look at what a mastermind I am."

"Right, let me finish up here with Ms. Castle so I can get on to my manicure."

"Okay, I'll see you at five."

I turn my attention back to Dottie. "Ms. Castle, are these in any particular order?"

She completes a slow pirouette as she points. Her agility catches me by surprise.

"Each section is one of the four dealerships. Outside of that, I really can't say what I'm looking at." She favors me with a smile that dares me to contradict her.

I have a conundrum. Something in my gut tells me Dottie is holding back some information from me. But why would she? Especially if it might help me in her defense.

I survey the boxes covering the cracked concrete floor. Many of the boxes are stacked waist-high, and several columns have collapsed, spilling the manilla folders and yellowing papers into the pathway.

What a record-keeping nightmare. The information I desperately need to connect the Dixie Mafia to Gil is somewhere in this mess.

Unfortunately, if I believe my client, she can't help me.

Bless it. How could Dottie not be kept in the loop with the inner workings of the enterprise she helped start?

There is no way I would be part of a family business and not have a solid foundation in all aspects of the company. Not to be the expert, but at least know whom we are working with and if those partners are legitimate.

For example, I have only worked at Mama's marina during the summer. Still, if heaven forbid I ever needed to, I know enough about it to step in and manage it. Not as well as Chase or Mama, but I know I could keep it running for at least a few months until we could find a buyer.

For being the original energy behind the enterprise, Dottie plays as if she has no business skills. From the looks of the records, she certainly doesn't have any organizational skills.

Was her only purpose in life to spend money—lots of cash—like a new-money socialite?

Somehow that doesn't ring true for me. Her home is impressive yet doesn't have the pretentious air I would expect if she was simply a country club trophy wife thirty years ago.

The incongruent fact is that if Dottie killed Gil, how did she know she would get anything out of the deal. Since she knew so little about the business, she would've been taking a massive gamble by killing Gil.

Again, another point, albeit weak, for our case. Only a crime of passion will fit neatly into the prosecution's case. With

Dottie's limited knowledge of the business, financial motives are off the table as a possibility.

"Ms. Castle, I'm going to have somebody come by later this week to pick up the records for the last three years that your dealerships were open."

"Which one, dear?"

"All of them. I don't want to leave any stone unturned. If we can find something that helps us point the prosecutor's finger toward another party, it will be well worth the trouble."

Her eyebrows jump. "They better come in a big truck and have a lot of energy."

She's right. I'll have to do some research to find a moving company willing to take the job.

Dottie gestures toward the stairs, and I follow her lead.

Bless it. When the crew moves the records out, I'll need to be here to determine which ones to take and which to leave. Maybe I can negotiate that with the movers, too. I'd prefer not to burn a day in Dottie's basement.

As we reach the top of the stairs, I start for the front door. "I'll call you when I have the movers scheduled, Ms. Castle."

I stop in my tracks as I notice my teacup and saucer. Cotillion training dies hard.

Lifting my saucer, I walk toward Dottie's kitchen. She holds out her hand for the set. As I hand it to her, my teacup shifts, sliding perilously close to the edge of the saucer. I catch the china cup against her hand.

My knees buckle. As if someone stiff-armed my forehead, my head jerks backward.

This vision is not fragmented like the kaleidoscope of violence and blood earlier. It is focused and steady through a vintage amber filter. Evil energy swirls in the atmosphere, laced with fear. The terror is so palpable my mouth goes dry as it is filled with the taste of bitters and salt.

The noose formed by the rope looped across the lowest branch of the gnarled oak tree sways ominously—absent a breeze.

"Sorry about that, dear. My hands aren't quite as stable as they used to be."

"No, ma'am," I say, regaining composure. "I'm terribly clumsy today."

"I suppose neither of us will be allowed to participate in the cotillion this year."

I freeze at Dottie parroting my recent thought.

Nonsense, April. She can't read your mind. Her comment is only a coincidence.

Trying to cover how disconcerting her quip is, I attempt to smile, but it feels all wrong. "It won't be a big loss on my part."

Dottie's eyes search my face. "Are you alright, dear? You look like you have seen a ghost."

Maybe because I believe I did. Or at least where one would have been created. "Yes, ma'am. The stress has been building on me lately. I have had a difficult time getting a good night's rest." I move toward the front door. "I need to leave if I plan on making my manicure."

She holds the door open for me. "Thank you for the visit, dear."

Yes, ma'am. Thank you for the tea."

I'm able to control my pace to my car and not run—barely. As I get in my car, I notice her staring from the porch, and I wave as pleasantly as possible.

My imagination is getting the best of me. I'm panicking that perhaps she could read my reaction—or more.

I can't get out of Dottie's driveway fast enough. If the vision captured isn't horrific enough. The desperate despair whipping in the air around the noose felt like the cold fingers of death caressing my cheeks.

Something else was in the image. Unseen, just out of my view. Not death, but an entity permeated with inky, oily wickedness typically reserved for evil warlocks and spirits that were unduly cruel humans during their lives.

Still, I wish I could have stood to maintain contact with Dottie longer. I still haven't confirmed anything.

I might have seen enough of the vision to prove Dottie is a cold-blooded killer with more contact. Instead, I managed to stoke up my fear about the woman and increase my intuition that I am defending a guilty woman.

As I drive down the mountain, the distance between Dottie and me calms my nerves. Regaining my composure, I replay the vision frame by frame in my mind.

It seems less impressive the longer I reflect upon it.

The vision only revealed a giant oak tree on the side of a mountain. A retaining wall kept the root ball of the oak covered on the severe slope. A storm was brewing in the air. The clouds flew by at a tremendous speed.

And, of course, there was a hangman's noose looped over the lowest branch.

There was no victim for me to see in the vision. Dottie wasn't there, either.

Still, I drew the vision from her. Doesn't that mean she was there? How else would she have the image in her memory?

Fudge! Why couldn't I have had another five seconds to look around while I was in her mind? Now I have more questions than I did before I went to talk to her.

Whether she was in the vision or not, and whether she killed Gil, I know Dottie has a profoundly evil natural core. Even if she is innocent and led a decent life, she would've been in constant conflict with her natural tendencies.

An involuntary shudder wracks through me. I can't imagine living with somebody like Dottie. You could have an argument before bed and wake up with a steak knife in your chest. Who wants to sleep for forty years with one eye open?

Chapter 15

After my disconcerting visit with Dottie, I'm torn between going home and asking Lee to hold me until the scary movie playing in my mind disappears or going on to the beauty college and relaxing while Tiffany does her magic on my nails. If I hadn't already scheduled the appointment, I would opt for going home to Lee. The sickly, evil feeling isn't rubbing off quick enough for me.

"What in the world have you done to these nails?" Tiffany rolls my hands side to side as she evaluates the damage.

"I think I've been chewing them in my sleep."

Tiffany's expression changes as she looks like she bit into something sour. "Nobody chews their nails while they sleep."

"Well, I don't notice myself chewing them during the day."

"My Aunt Judy used to get up and make red velvet cakes in her sleep when I was a kid," Glenda interjects.

"Nobody makes red velvet cakes in their sleep, either," Tiffany mumbles. "I've never noticed you chewing your nails before, April."

"I have a lot going on right now. Things are going really well."

Tiffany snorts a laugh. "That makes no sense. Folks

chew their nails when they are nervous because things are going *wrong*."

"That's not true. Some folks don't think they deserve success, and they get nervous that the other shoe's gonna fall when things are going too good," Glenda says.

Tiffany gestures between her workstation and Glenda's workstation. "See this right here, Glenda? That's the imaginary wall. You stay on your side; I'll stay on my side."

Glenda rolls her eyes. "Imaginary wall—I know somebody else has an imaginary wall," she grumbles.

"I heard you and Lee Darby are still dating. Is that not going well?"

"It's going great. We're going up to Baltimore next week. So, I'd say it's going fine. I'm going to be looking for a job up there."

Tiffany's mouth drops open. "Oh my gosh. You're going to live in Baltimore? That's so exciting!"

"I know, right?"

Tiffany gestures toward Glenda. "Glenda is right. You should be the last person chewing on your nails."

"I'm probably worried about other stuff, too. Mainly what my uncle is going to do when I leave town."

Tiffany starts on my other hand. "What do you mean? What he's going to do?"

"Well, he's got that pizza business now, and he's spending probably seventy or eighty hours a week over there. I hardly see him at the law office anymore."

Tiffany bobs her head as if she is waiting for me to say something else. "And then?"

I exhale in frustration. "Well, who's going to run the law office?"

"Why do you care?"

"Well, because..." Why do I care? I obviously do. I remain as particular as ever about staying an effective attorney for my clients. I remain dedicated to keeping the business financially viable, too.

Still, it is *his* business, dream, and choice.

Wow. Here I told him that the community needs him, but he's right. That's not enough to make you keep a business open if it's not what you want to do anymore.

I suddenly have an idea. "Glenda, do you remember Gil Castle?"

Glenda sticks out her lower lip. "Sugar, you gonna have to defund the wall for me to be able to talk to you. I can't see over it."

"You're insufferable." Tiffany sucks a breath of air through her teeth as she continues to work my nails.

Glenda giggles. "Yeah, baby, I remember Mr. Castle. I never bought a car off him. He was too expensive."

"Do you ever remember hearing him being in business with the Dixie Mafia?"

Glenda flares her nose. "Where'd you get that nonsense? Nobody's seen neither hide nor hair of those crazy white boys for decades. Good riddance, too."

I nod in response.

"Even if there were a few left trading guns and drugs, that doesn't sound right. Mr. Castle was a pretty boy. Not saying that he might not have gotten caught up in something, but he sure wouldn't have been properly prepared to run with those sorta boys."

"Thanks, that's kinda what I suspected."

Glenda narrows her eyes. "You didn't tell me where you heard that from."

"His widow, Dottie Castle."

Glenda jerks her head back as she makes a *pst* sound. "That woman ain't nothing but a liar. She'd tell you her mama was Diana Ross if she thought it would get her something she wanted."

That's kinda what I thought, too.

Tiffany has worked her magic again. I admire my civilized-looking nails as I walk to my car.

My phone interrupts my happy private moment.

I don't recognize the number. "Hello?"

"April, where are you?"

"Jade?"

"Who else is going to be calling you from the jail?"

"Uh—well—I." Note to self, save this number as "jail."

"How quick can you get down here?"

"To the jail?"

"Girl, did somebody knock the sense out of you? Yes, the jail."

"Maybe five minutes. Why, what's up?"

"The last shift put Antoine in solitary confinement. You need to get down here quick. The boy done lost his Jesus!"

Chapter 16

I call Lee during the short drive to the jail to explain that I'll be a little later than the five o'clock arrival I had planned. He said, "fine," but his tone made it sound more like "take a jump in the lake."

Apparently, I'll have a lot of boyfriend ego to pet when I get to the house. At least he didn't tell me not to bother coming over.

Jade meets me on the downstairs level as I come into the vestibule of the jailhouse.

"I'm so glad you came quickly."

Jade is usually a very jovial person. There is nothing even remotely humorous about her body language.

"You didn't say why he was put in solitary confinement."

Jade unlocks the gate, letting me in. "I don't think he's well." She taps her head with her finger. "The last shift said he was aggravating his cellmates to get them to leave him alone. He keeps talking about a demon waiting at the edge of the city. It was wigging out his cellmates, and the last shift said no matter what they did, he wouldn't hush."

As I follow Jade, all I can think is, *What am I supposed to do about it?* "They won't get him some psychiatric help?"

"You should know better than me, April."

We go up to the third floor, which I have never been on before today. Except for some unintelligible mumbling coming from the far end, the corridor is deathly quiet.

"Is that him?" I ask.

"I'm afraid so."

"Can you stay?" I'm not a small girl, but Antoine is huge. Jade would be a handy counterbalance in case things got out of control.

"I'm not going to let you in his cell. You'll have to talk to him through the tray transfer."

As we arrive in front of the last cell at the end of the hallway, Jade promptly pops open the six-inch by twelve-inch rectangle in the center of the solid steel door. I peer in and find Antoine sitting in the far corner, mumbling.

"Antoine." He continues to mumble. "Antoine!"

He turns his bloodshot eyes toward me. "Yes."

"Do you remember me?" I ask.

"Sure, you're Chase's sister."

"April."

He stands up from the bed and shuffles toward the opening. I take a step back.

"What do you need?" Antoine asks.

"I was about to ask you the same thing, buddy. The last shift said that you were pretty upset about the demon on the edge of the city?"

Antoine moves so quickly toward the opening it is creepy. He places a long finger across his lips. "They took my hat," he hisses. "The grays can hear me. If they know that we're talking about the demon, they will kill us."

"Who will kill us, Antoine?"

"The grays."

I begin to wonder if I misread our conversation earlier. From the onset, I assumed when Antoine was telling me about the grays, he was talking about ghosts. Still, spirits need tremendous amounts of energy. If they kill a human, it is typically vengeance regarding their death. While not entirely out of the realm of possibility, I now doubt that the grays are spirits, but something else.

"Are the grays ghosts?" I ask.

Antoine fixes his yellow, bloodshot eyes on me as he shakes his head side to side. "No. They are the condemned incarnated."

I have no idea what he is talking about. Sadly, he may be crazy. "I don't know what that means, Antoine." I turn back to Jade to ask her if Antoine has been talking like this the whole time. Jade's eyes are fixed open wide. "What is it, Jade?"

She shakes her head vigorously. "Nothing—nothing."

Antoine emits a loud moan. He begins to chant. "Ipsi resurgence, et non ambulabunt, quod imperare ejus."

"Antoine, what does that mean? They shall rise, they shall walk, they shall rule. That makes no sense to me." A cold trickle runs down my spine as I realize I translated the nonsense Antoine is spewing. The implication of what he is chanting chills my blood further.

I look to Jade. She is shivering as if she were standing naked in a snowstorm. "Jade?"

"Nah … nah … nah. That ain't right." She backpedals down the corridor as she forms a cross with her fingers. "It's one thing, Antoine talking a bunch of nonsense that nobody can understand. But you understanding it? Oh, heck no!"

"Jade, stay here with me."

She is halfway down the hallway now, still making a cross with her two pointer fingers. "Nope. This beautiful body has got room for only one spirit. I'm not letting some sort of demon hijack my body."

"Jade, it's not what you think. Stay here with me." She opens the door and slips into the elevator room.

I look back in on Antoine. He is silent now but laboring to breathe. I take a moment to try and understand what has transpired. Even though it sounded as if Antoine was the mouthpiece of some entity, he might have only repeated what he saw in a vision. I feel it necessary enough to know the truth.

"Antoine, are you with me?"

He looks up and nods. "You understood."

I smile and hope it gives his troubled mind some comfort.

"And you can see what I can see?" he asks.

"Probably more."

He covers most of his face with one of his hands. "Am I going crazy?"

I know where he is coming from. Even when I think I have a handle on my "gifts," some days it's too much, and I feel it will outstrip the capabilities of my mind.

Is Antoine going crazy? Possibly.

It's also possible that I'm going crazy today. We might all be crazy tomorrow, and we might all be eaten by an army of demons the next day. Who can tell?

"No. You're not going crazy, Antoine. You have a special gift that has turned on recently for you."

"I don't want it. How do I get rid of it?"

I burst into uncontrollable laughter. "I have no idea, but I'll make you a deal. If I ever figure it out, I'll let you know, too."

I sober enough to ask. "Antoine, the demon on the edge of the city, does he have a name?"

"I don't know."

"Have you seen his face?"

"Only in shadows. I don't know him and have never seen him before."

"I want to try something, if you will. Will you hold my hands?"

Antoine stares at me for the longest while. Then, appearing reluctant, he steps forward and extends his long arms toward me. I take his calloused hands in mine. Immediately I'm walking in a field. It's early morning, and a fog bank hugs the ground tight. I can see only a foot or two in front of me.

I can make out the silhouette of an attractive man's profile through the fog. I move closer and decipher the man's features in a blurred context. He is Caucasian with a well-constructed face. I want to get closer.

"You shouldn't come looking for things you don't understand, April."

I fall backward quickly as I attempt to retreat. I slip out of the vision and am left holding Antoine's hands.

Antoine frowns. "He pushed you out, didn't he?"

"Yes."

Antoine drops my hands and frames his face. "It's like I can feel him inside me. I want to scratch him out."

"No. He's not in you. He is only using your mind as a conduit."

"He doesn't like that you know he is here."

I'm not precisely pumped about knowing he's here, either. "I understand. He would prefer to keep his motives a secret. But your brave work has been spoiling that for him."

Antoine smiles. I had forgotten how beautiful his smile is. "Good. I like aggravating him."

"Are you going to be okay by yourself?" I ask.

Antoine shrugs and makes a clicking noise with his tongue. "I guess so. How long do you think they're going to hold me?"

"I'll do my best to get you released tomorrow."

"Okay, April."

He may tell me okay, but his body language says he has already spent more time incarcerated than he can bear.

Chapter 17

I'm halfway to Lee's as my phone rings again. It's the call I have been waiting on. "I was wondering if you were going to call," I say to Baker Diaz.

"It's been a little too interesting on this site," Baker says.

"Is something the matter?"

"I followed your lead out to Tuscumbia. By the way, nice area out here."

"I've never been."

"Your girl had been at the cabin. As a matter of fact, the cabin is stocked for a few days with canned goods, coffee, and the small fridge has milk and juice in it."

I'm tired and hope I didn't pay a hundred dollars an hour plus expenses to get a grocery list from a cabin in Tuscumbia. "You said 'had.'"

"Yeah, she's been gone ever since I got here. It's just a gut feel, but I think something might have spooked her, and she may have left for somewhere else."

"Do you think she saw you?"

"There's no chance of that. But I do think she is on the lam again."

"Well, that's a shame. I appreciate you checking the cabin out for me, Baker. If you send your invoice to me, I'll get you paid."

"Oh, wait a minute. No, that's not really why I called."

I can feel my mental eye roll. "Okay."

"Are you sitting down?"

I can't tell if Baker is messing with me or if he is one of those individuals who like to build up everything before telling you. "I'm driving my car."

"The dog we're looking for?"

"Bailey," I say.

"Yes. I'm pretty sure the dog is dead."

I should have pulled the car over before he gave me the news. A fierce sadness tears through my chest before I come to my senses. "What do you mean, pretty sure?"

"There are some good clues up here that she drowned that dog."

My mind goes to what Roman said about Ivy having saved the dog from drowning. My stomach turns as the probability plays out in my mind.

"What sort of a freak kills a dog?" Baker asks.

"A really ticked off soon-to-be ex-wife," I answer.

"Man, women are way more trouble than they're worth. Thank goodness for the Internet."

How convenient that Baker Diaz could sum up and confirm my initial impression of him in five succinct words. It doesn't matter. I have more significant issues on my hands.

For one, breaking the news to my client and then trying to keep him from going on a rampage that will have the sole intent of hunting down his ex-wife and gutting her. Nothing too difficult.

"Did you find Bailey? Or his grave?"

Baker exhales loudly. "I wish. Well, that's not true. I would prefer to find the dog alive, but I'm not gonna blow smoke up your butt and tell you that I'm not ready to be done with this case. I should have gone with my gut feel and stayed out of it. I have investigated kidnappings and contract killings, but I've never known somebody to kill a helpless dog. This is just not right."

Baker sounds thoroughly distraught, but I need better

information from him. "Mr. Diaz, if you don't mind, please focus. What is it that leads you to believe that Bailey has been killed?"

"The letter the dame left, of course."

"Letter?"

"Yeah, there was a letter on the table when I got into the cabin." Baker says it as if I should have already known.

"Ivy left a letter to be found?" I ask for clarification.

Baker chuckles. "I doubt highly that the dog wrote it."

I squeeze my eyes shut to hold back the snarky remark I want to cut loose on Baker. It is warranted but would not be helpful. "Will you read it to me?"

"Sure thing. You paid for it, boss." I hear him unfolding paper. He clears his throat.

"Roman, by now, you must know that I took Bailey. I never had an issue with the dog. It's important you know that because I want you to understand that you're the reason Bailey is dead. Bailey was the only way I could make you feel the way you have made me feel. No amount of money would ever hurt you like you hurt me. But now that your dog is dead, maybe you will feel like I do. Just remember, Bailey is dead because you're a jerk.

"Then there's a pretty good drawing of a female's hand shooting the bird followed by, 'Screw you forever! Sincerely, Ivy.'"

A letter is a good indicator that Bailey might be dead. But we still don't have a body.

Am I really holding out hope that Bailey is still alive? Or am I simply afraid of the blowup when I call Roman and inform him of what Ivy did?

"Baker, have you done a thorough search of the area?" I really don't know anything about Baker's background, so I don't know if he knows how to do a thorough search.

"Yeah. Since I found the letter, I walked the property in quadrants and triple-checked the river's edge. There are some dog tracks close to the cabin, but very few anywhere else on the property."

"It sounds like you've been busy. Why didn't you call sooner?"

"Honestly, I was hoping I would find the dog alive. If not alive, at least find it so that this Roman guy in the letter could at least bury his dog. It's just not right what this woman's done."

Baker just qualified for the understatement of the year. "Baker, are you in a hurry to get back to Huntsville?"

"I guess not. But I'm about to lose light here, and I don't know what good I can do in the dark. Are you wanting me to stay the night and start searching again in the morning?"

"Maybe. What I need you to do now is continue with your search on the property, widen it out if you see the opportunity to, and wait for me to call you back. I have some folks who might help us, and I need to touch base with them. Is that okay?"

"Yeah, go ahead and take your time on that. I'll just work the quadrants again, and once I've lost light, I'm going to go and get some dinner. But I'll have my phone with me the whole time."

"Good deal. Thank you, Baker."

"I just wish I had something better to report to you."

Yes, me too, I think as I disconnect the line.

Baker Diaz is no Michael VanDerveer. But then Michael VanDerveer is a one-of-a-kind individual. As far as private investigators go, Baker appears to be conscientious. The fact that he gained access to the inside of the cabin proves he is a man who will do what it takes to complete a job. Even if that means bending a few rules. He won't let a few pesky laws get in the way of achieving his mission.

A trait I admire.

I hesitate to make the next call. Not because I don't think they will do it for me, but because once I set this in motion, I will lose some autonomy on the job. I seriously consider any other way to get what I need done completed.

No. It is time to call in the cavalry. I dial Chase's phone

number.

"Hey, what are you doing?" I ask.

"I'm heading out to pick up Barbara. She won a bet the other night when we were playing Farkle, and now I've got to take her to the movie theater to see some chick flick. I always say I'm not a betting man, and I should've stuck to it."

Talk about terrible timing. The rest of the family and I have hoped Barbara and Chase would get back together for the better part of twelve years. The last thing I want to do is interfere with them spending quality time together. Even though Chase is not going to consider watching a chick flick as quality time.

This is a conundrum I could do without. I need his help now. Help that Chase excels at. Still, I really want Barbara as a sister-in-law and my brother happily married with a pack of kids to run with on the lake and in the fields in the longer term. Why does life always have to be so complicated?

"What's the matter, April? You sound weird."

"I was going to ask you to do me a favor, but I would rather you go to the movies with Barbara."

"What is it? I mean, if you really need my help and it's important, Barbara will understand."

"That's just it. I know she will understand, and you will take care of what I ask just because I ask you to."

"No. If I do what you ask, it will be because I decided I want to and can. There is a subtle yet important difference there. Now tell me what you were going to ask me."

I wasn't going to, but then I think about how bad it would be on Roman and how not having Bailey's body will make it even worse. "I'll tell you, but I need you to promise me that if you don't want to or if you think that it will make Barbara mad or hurt your relationship, you'll just say no."

"April, you sure do have a lot of ground rules considering you're the one asking the favor. If you don't mind, just spit it out."

"I've got a situation where one of my clients had a dog

disappear, we think in the river. Before we call him to let him know what happened to his dog, we would like to find the dog's body. We're running out of light on site, and we don't really have a way to effectively check the river. I just know with your equipment and your background for both fishing and hunting, you might be able to help."

There is a long pause. I become concerned Chase is formulating a pleasant way of telling me to bug off.

"That poor man. That is simply one of the saddest things I have ever heard."

Thinking about how tight Chase is with my dog, Puppy, his level of empathy does not surprise me even though I had not expected it. "The dog is pretty much the only relationship my client has left."

"Oh man, that's so tough. Where is this?"

"We're up in Tuscumbia."

"Now, if that's not like déjà vu."

I shift hands with my phone. "Why do you say that?"

"The boys and I camped up there last month for three days. We were hunting some whitetail, but we also dropped some lines in for bass."

"Are you serious?"

"Oh yeah. We had two doe tags, and Shane bagged a nice one. It's still over at David's being processed. It is excellent hunting up there."

"Do you think Barbara would mind you helping?"

Chase laughs. "She's not gonna mind me helping. She might mind missing the movie, though."

"I really don't want to put you out," I tell Chase.

"Let me just touch base with Barbara, and I'll call you right back."

"Okay. I'll wait for your call."

This is awful. I'm so bad about having a guilty conscience, even when trying to protect someone from the unknown. I seem incapable of keeping things under wraps until I can provide definitive information. I have this tremendous urge to call Roman and tell him we believe Bailey is dead.

There is no need to bring him in right now. It would be so unhelpful. Especially since he threatened—strike it from the record—to kill Ivy.

I have to hold on a bit longer. I may possibly have some excellent help who knows the area well. There is still a chance we will locate the dog alive. Even if the worst happens and we find Bailey's body, it will still be monumentally easier to move forward legally and emotionally for Roman.

With his companion missing and no clue what happened to Bailey, any conversations I have with my client right now would only serve as a point of aggravation.

Oh, I could skin Ivy alive. Right about now, I would love to wrap a handful of her blonde hair in my left hand while I throttle her with my right. I understand she is hurt by Roman turning to another woman. Believe me, I'm no fan of cheaters, and I believe Roman will get his comeuppance in due time.

But murdering an innocent dog? Who does that? What sort of monster is she?

I can't help but wonder if Ivy was born that way or if her cruelty was an acquired skill. Seriously how do you become so self-involved that no other living creature even matters?

My phone rings, and I see it is Chase calling me back. "What did she say?"

"You know Barbara, she's chill with it," Chase says. "Do you want to ride out there with me? Or are you taking your own car?"

"I'd love to ride with you if you don't mind."

"Pick you up at your office on the way out?"

"That would be great."

"Okay, I'll pick you up as soon as I get the boat on the hitch."

"You don't need any help with that?"

Chase laughs. "No offense, but the last time you tried to help me put the boat on the trailer hitch, I about had to buy a new boat."

That's the thing about older brothers. If you screw up once, they never let you forget it.

"Whatever."

"Sit tight. I'll be there soon."

How chill is Barbara? The woman just absolutely amazes me. I can't say I for sure wouldn't have a small drama episode if my man canceled an evening out on me.

My man—Peaches!

I hang my head in defeat.

Suck it up, buttercup. Better to pull the Band-Aid off now than let the soreness fester.

If I thought procrastinating would help, I would have. Still, there's no good reason to put this problematic call off any longer. I hit Lee's speed dial number on my phone.

"Where are you, April?"

"At the moment, driving back to my office."

Lee huffs. "Why?"

"Because I may have to go up to Tuscumbia tonight."

"Are you kidding me?" Lee's tone is full of venom.

"Yes. I've got to go up there and help my private investigator. We've got a court date coming up, and we need to get all this in order." I explain with a lot of words and few facts.

"I don't know how you find this acceptable, April. But I don't," Lee says.

"It's my job, Lee. This is what I do for a living. I help people."

"No, you're just sort of up in everybody's business, April."

His words punch the air out of me. I can't believe Lee said that to me. "That's not fair, Lee. You don't know what I have to do to do my job successfully."

"Obviously not. This road trip, where do you have to go?"

I don't care for the tone he is taking with me. "Tuscumbia, like I already said."

"Oh, wow!" Lee laughs. It sounds phony. "Are you even coming home tonight?"

"I don't know. It depends on how quickly we get what we need to get done completed."

"This is so rich," Lee grouses.

"I'm sorry you're upset, Lee. But what do you expect me to do?"

"Have a relationship with me."

I pull my car to the side of the road. I don't trust the shaking in my hands. "Why are you doing this? We do have a relationship."

"Whatever."

"Oh my gosh," I whine.

"Hey, since I might not see you tonight, riddle me this one question."

"What's that?" I whisper.

"Are you even planning on leaving for Baltimore with me?" Lee asks.

"What?" I can't believe what I'm hearing.

"You heard me. Are you actually planning on going to Baltimore with me this month, or are you getting cold feet? It's a simple question, April. Just answer it."

"You know how excited I have been about going to Baltimore."

"I hear you, but I don't know if I believe you. I mean, here you are just a few weeks away, and you're talking about having to go up to Podunk, Alabama, for some reason in the middle of the night."

"I'm trying to make sure my client doesn't kill his ex-wife," I explain.

"And I'm trying to figure out why you're still so concerned about it. Whether you do or don't, nobody's gonna care eight weeks from now."

"But I will," I say.

Lee releases a long, frustrated-sounding breath. "Whatever, April. Listen, I'm not gonna worry about it anymore. You know when we fly out. You have your ticket on your phone. If you can wrap up all the different law cases and ghost cases and whatever else when I'm leaving, and if you want to go, you're more than welcome to fly out with me. But I assure you I am not going to Lord over you and make you pack and force you to get on the plane with me. If you're going to go with me, I want to see you acting like you are excited to leave. Do you understand what I'm saying?"

"Yes."

"All right. I guess be safe, and I'll see you when I see you."

"Okay."

It doesn't seem fair for Lee to ask me to drop everything because of our plans. You can't simply stop in the middle of things. You have to bring them to fruition.

Where he gets the idea that I don't want to go to Baltimore is beyond me. We have been talking about where we might live, what kind of job I could find, and what his travel schedule will be for the last month. Heck, we've practically done everything except pull out a calendar and write down what we will do each day this year when he isn't on the road. I can't see how I can be any more plugged in to the idea of leaving with him. Does he need that much stroking, that much affirmation that I am in love with him and will follow him to the ends of the earth?

I want to scream. But my crazy has been bubbling up so quickly these days I push it all down and maintain control.

Once I feel like an in-control adult again, I put my car in drive and resume driving to the office.

This is what comes with relationships. We all have different needs and wants. It's expected that occasionally there is a rub between people no matter how in love they are and perfectly matched.

Poppycock. A relationship shouldn't be this difficult. Something is askew with Lee and me. I'll be darned if I can identify it, but it's there.

No. I'm probably projecting my male weariness onto the one man that I should be most concerned about.

The trouble is I have too many men needing things from me. I have Uncle Howard expecting me to cover the law practice he built from scratch. The District Attorney expects me to keep up with a full load of defendants because the county doesn't adequately fund the public defender's department. I've got poor Antoine sitting in solitary confinement thinking he is losing his mind. Roman is a privileged little twerp, but he doesn't deserve to be stabbed in his hand by his bat-crazy wife, and certainly, his dog doesn't deserve to be murdered. I really need a break from the men in my life. They are driving me nuts!

You know, that goes the same for Lee. Here I thought Lee was solid as a rock, and now he's starting to sound like a spoiled brat because I—what? I'm not making him feel special enough?

Do you know what would be really special right now? Some sleep. That's right, some rest and maybe a couple of days—no, make that weeks—of no men in April's life. That sounds like heaven on earth.

I've seriously got to work on getting some full-time girlfriends. I need girls that I can get together with and not have to be the one putting things back together.

I can't believe Lee. Like I don't spend every free moment with him? My gosh, I haven't even seen my own dog in three weeks. I'm concerned Lee will think having Puppy run around in his two-million-dollar house is too big a risk.

If he wants to be a titty baby, he can just go on up to Baltimore by himself. I wasn't looking for a boyfriend when I found him. It's not like I'm afraid of being alone.

Having someone who dumps on you is worse than being alone.

Does Lee honestly believe I'd rather wander the woods of Tuscumbia in the dark than have dinner with him and cuddle on our couch later to watch a movie? A movie I'm sure I won't remember in the morning? Seriously? How can he even think that?

I'll tell you how. Because he is a male. There must be something about testosterone that makes men turn into big crybabies if they don't get precisely what they want when they want it. Estrogen must be the "maybe next time I'll get what I want" hormone.

Chapter 18

As I park in front of Snow and Associates, I debate whether or not to go into the office. It's a short debate. I'm too frustrated about my discussion with Lee. If I go into the office and see all the folders on my desk and Howard's door closed, it will make me even crankier. I'm pretty close to not being able to stand myself.

Instead, I find an oldies rock 'n' roll station and let my seat back. It crosses my mind with a bit of humor as I listen to Joan Jett belt out her declaration of love to rock 'n' roll. The song probably topped the charts at the same time my IROC rolled off the production line. I wonder what it would've been like back in those times? No smartphones, no laptops, and games with the most basic graphics are all they had for entertainment besides their music and movies. No wonder everyone got married when they were eighteen. What else were you going to do for entertainment besides talking to your boyfriend and having sex?

I cup my hands in my lap and concentrate on the new trick I practice to pass the time. When I saw Grandpa do it at Jester's, I had a strong itch to master it.

Especially since Nana claimed only the strongest of magical beings could restrain the energy in such a manner.

Control is the key. The ability to direct with purpose is a sign of power. That's what I have learned from both Granny and

Nana.

The use of unbridled magic, or in Granny's case, the request for divine intervention, is a fool's game. My thoughts go back to the attic of an old home in Birmingham, where my ill-advised use of my newbie fire-casting abilities nearly spelled the doom of Liza and me.

Effortlessly, the glow intensifies inside my cupped hands. The tingle thrills me all the way to my toes, and I feel ten times more alive than any adrenaline hormone dump could make me feel.

Slowly, I rotate the glowing globe inside my hands. The flux from the magnetic field created by the movement sparks up the length of my forearm, forcing my biceps to tense.

Carefully, cautiously I roll my hands open—the movement where the magic fell apart most often last month.

Steady, the globe spins three inches above my right palm. Tiny bits of golden magic sling off the glowing sun as it rotates.

Yes, Nana and Granny have been right about everything except one significant detail. Magic, its use, does not drain me of my energies anymore. In fact, I believe my powers increase the more I practice.

I attempt to transfer the miniature sun that illuminates the cab of my car from my right hand to my left. I feel the tingle of the charge transfer hands, but as the globe slides across, it evaporates with a loud pop.

Dang it! I was so close this time.

I should have known better. I'm so stressed I can barely concentrate.

It's best I practice something less demanding. I practice creating a flame the size of a cigarette lighter by snapping my fingers—on my left hand. My off hand continues to be the weak link in my control progression.

Something moves in my left periphery and I shift in my seat to track it, but it is already gone. Just my imagination, I'm sure. Most likely, it was a random shadow cast by the streetlight.

It never occurred to me to ask Mama and Daddy how

Guntersville differs now compared to the 80s. I wonder what the population was in the 80s. I pull out my phone to search Guntersville's historical population.

As I look at the report, I see a shadow run the length of the passenger side of my car. My breath catches as I swivel to see what passed by me. Again, I don't see anything.

A wave of troubling energy washes over me as something unseen stirs evil into the air like a speeding car down a dusty road. The taste of copper and bitters merge in my mouth as the tiniest of electrical tingles creep their way up my shoulders. The hair on the back of my neck stands on end.

I clear my head the best I can of everything that has taken place today and focus on listening.

It is quiet. Too quiet.

Guntersville is old, and these streets are no stranger to death. Typically, if I lower my partition, I should feel many residual impressions and a few faint voices.

My partitions are fully down, and still nothing.

Don't work yourself up, April. You'll make this into something more than it is if you don't calm down.

Antoine and his half-baked demon story have gotten into my head. That's all it is. All his talk about a high-level overlord waiting on the outskirts of town for an army of "grays" to prepare Guntersville for his arrival has made an impression on me. Man, what was Antoine into?

I lie back in my seat again and am filled with sudden uneasiness. A human-shaped shadow reflects in my rearview mirror, and I swivel quickly to look.

Again, there is nothing.

"All right, I've had just about enough of this," I say as I open my glove compartment and fish out my forty-five-caliber Colt.

Everyone in my family would tell me the prudent thing is to stay in my car until Chase arrives. My middle name isn't Prudence, and I believe the most effective way to defend myself is to take an offensive stance.

I click off my pistol's safety and open the car door. As I lean to exit my car, a greasy thickness of evil envelops me. My senses shoot to high alert. I stand, and fingers run down my back.

Spinning, I bring my gun to eye level. I wrap my left hand around my right to stay the shaking of my pistol. I struggle to comprehend what I'm looking at on top of my car.

A nude, shriveled woman is crouched on all fours. Several strands of my blond hair clutched in her right fist float in the winter wind. Her lips pull back, exposing rows of sharp, triangular-shaped teeth.

I'm not sure how this supernatural entity will react to lead. Still, as much as I would like to experiment with this ghoulish woman, I don't want to end my time in my hometown by sending stray bullets down Gunter Avenue.

Sliding my right hand free of my pistol, I concentrate as I stare into her black fish eyes. With a twitch, I send a golf ball-sized pulse of blue energy at the woman's chest.

She leaps straight into the air, my magical projectile traveling harmlessly between her legs as she catches a branch of the oak tree in the green area. I watch in horror as she scrambles to the top of the tree with lightning-fast supernatural agility. She jumps from the tree top, arching her back while in flight, and lands on the roof of the Snow and Associates building.

She disappears momentarily.

I'd rather put a hole in our building than burn it down, so I switch back to a more conventional weapon for protection. I am not left waiting for long as she peers over the edge of the building.

I train my gun on her. It would be a difficult shot at an odd angle, even if the target wasn't a freakishly fast entity. I don't waste a bullet given her exhibition of the ability to avoid being shot.

Tauntingly, she smiles broadly, again showing the multiple rows of sharp teeth. She seems to understand that I am not going to shoot at her.

We size each other up for a few seconds. The ugly she-thing turns away. I hear her scrambling across the flat tar roof toward the back of the building.

What the heck was that? Whatever it was, it is not a ghost. Ghosts don't move like that, and they also don't seem to have that high focus level. She intended to touch me, and she meant to intimidate me.

And she succeeded on both counts.

I wish I had some of the team's special ammunition we use on supernatural excursions. The forty-five-caliber Colt I use on excursions fires a buckshot round with lead, silver, and iron. I might have had a chance of striking her with that round. Still, I believe I could shoot at her all day with a standard cartridge and never hit her.

My shoulders shudder involuntarily as I consider her sickening speed. She could've torn my throat out and been gone before I even knew she was on me.

But she didn't. She looked like she wanted to, but she held off. What was up with that?

I'm grateful that I have dinner with Nana tomorrow night. Maybe she can enlighten me. I'm at a total loss. I have never seen anything that looked human with mottled gray skin and shrunken flesh.

Headlights from a tall truck startle me. I breathe easier as I recognize Chase's black Ford 350 towing his ski boat.

Chase pulls up perpendicularly behind me. His heavily tinted passenger window comes down.

I choke as I'm greeted by Shane's familiar face. He leans back and knits his eyebrows as his eyes settle on the pistol in my hand.

"Is that how you greet friends now?" Shane asks.

My neck burns, and I suddenly feel on the verge of breaking a sweat despite the cool breeze caressing my cheeks. I click the safety on and shove the pistol in the back of my jeans. "I just had some witch—or vampire, demon, something—run their hand down my back."

"For real?" Shane smirks. "I never heard of them copping a

feel. Was Batman with them? Maybe Spidey, too?"

I roll my eyes. "Real funny."

My brother leans forward and adds, "You called the wrong twin if you need help with that. I thought we were going to try and find a pooch."

I look back toward the roof of Snow and Associates to make sure that we aren't going to have another surprise attack. "We're going to get the heck outta here and save this for another day." I open my car and retrieve my purse and backpack. I keep the pistol.

Shane hops out of the front of the cab and holds the door open for me. To my surprise, Barbara is sitting next to Chase.

"Do you want to ride shotgun?" Shane asks.

I pull the handle on the back door. "No. I'm tired. I may want to lie down." As I open the door, I get my third surprise. Patrick McCabe sits on the back bench seat, complete with a goofy smile.

"Hi, April."

"Hi, Patrick." I attempt to act natural as I pull myself into the truck. So much for taking a nap. I'm not going to be especially comfortable laying my head in Patrick's lap.

"Chase said we're trying to find a puppy, and I wanted to help," Barbara explains.

"The more eyes, the better," I tell Barbara. "It's good to see you."

"It's good to be seen," Barbara says.

I don't know why I'm the least bit surprised. After getting over the initial jolt, I realize what Chase has done for me. He has assembled a small collection of some of the best hunters he knows. Shane and Patrick both have gone hunting with Chase before. Barbara and Chase used to hunt squirrels together when they were in high school as a pastime.

I said they were close. I never said they had a normal boyfriend-girlfriend relationship.

Still, what an odd combination. My brother is driving his truck with his ex-girlfriend, twelve years removed, sitting next to him.

Next to her in the front seat is a mutual friend of ours. At one time, I was in total lust over Shane. He never has thought of me as anything but a friend.

The guy in the back seat with me? Patrick and I dated for a few weeks, and I had myself convinced he was the man I was going to marry—until he introduced me to his eight-year-old son. I ran out on them like an immature fool without explaining. I did call a few weeks later and apologize. We haven't talked much since, and that's all on me.

How delectably embarrassing. The entire cab of the truck is one dysfunctional group of awkwardness.

"So, how long has the dog been missing?" Chase asks.

"Well, there's a little more to it than that. The dog was actually kidnapped by the soon-to-be ex-wife of the owner. An arbitrator had awarded full custody of the dog to the husband this morning. Since it's more than just you, Chase, I wish I had told you that we may have to move the search to recovery at some point. There is a real chance we may find Bailey, the dog, is dead."

"Why would you say that?" Barbara asks.

"I've got a private investigator in Tuscumbia. There was a letter from the wife explaining why she had killed the dog."

Everyone in the truck is silent for a minute. Shane interrupts the somber moment of reflection. "That's just messed up."

That's what I was thinking. "I might believe it was only a threat, except I've met the wife, and she is totally unhinged. In truth, I think she would kill her husband if she thought she could and serve a reduced sentence."

"I think that's the majority of ex-wives from what I've seen," Chase says. "Justin Smith told me you had a close encounter of the Bethany kind."

"Yeah, well, I'm not exactly proud of it. I let her get me riled up, and I'm trying to do better. Granny keeps telling me I need to love my enemies or I'm gonna bring myself down."

"I just want to know one thing," Chase says.

"What?"

"How in the world did you miss her?" Chase laughs and shakes his head.

"I wasn't trying to hit her in the first place, you bonehead. My foot slipped!"

"For the record, Justin's not buying it, and neither am I. He played along because he can't stand Bethany."

"I don't really care what you think. I know I didn't do it intentionally."

We ride in silence for a while. I rest my hot forehead against the clean, cold window.

"In case any of you need something to do Thursday, the memorial for Gil Castle will be held then," Shane says.

I guess that signals the end of any further investigation into Gil's murder. It's hard to find much out from an urn of ashes.

"Not to be morbid, Shane, but a body that has been put through that, how do you handle that?"

Shane looks over his shoulder at me and grins. "One bucket at a time to the crematorium."

"That's so gross. I guess that was the only option, considering."

Shane snorts. "Considering Ms. Castle insisted on it. She even prepaid me. She also paid the funeral home for the service to be held as soon as I completed my investigation. I am going to cremate him in the morning."

Knowing Dottie's financial situation, I find all this to be odd. "She paid for the cremation?"

"Cash money. She didn't even bother with a check or ask for a receipt," he answers.

This doesn't add up. I will have to remember to check on this once the current dog crisis is over.

We are thirty minutes away from the cabin, and I call

Baker to inform him we will arrive soon. He advises me he commandeered the place since it looks like Ivy has left the area.

Baker will never be Vander, but I have to credit him for his resourcefulness. I like him more the longer he works with me.

As we turn off the main state highway and drive toward the river, it begins to sleet.

"This might add an extra layer of challenge to the search," I grumble.

"We all have rubber boots and ponchos. We'll be okay." Patrick says.

I have a colt forty-five, a flashlight I'm not positive has batteries, and a phone. Everybody else is a little bit better prepared for this search than I am.

Chase points ahead. "Is that it?"

A restored metallic blue Nova Super Sport is parked next to the cabin. If that is Baker's, he is my new permanent detective.

I catch the address on the mailbox, confirming it is Roman's abandoned cabin. Smoke tendrils spiral out of the chimney. "Can you park the boat to the side, or do you need to go ahead and drop it in the water?"

Chase stops his truck as we come up the driveway. "I'll let you two girls go on in and talk to your private investigator. The three of us will get the boat in the water."

I'm not arguing with that plan. Dropping the boat in the water is not my favorite activity.

Barbara and I stomp the mud off our boots on the front porch. We open the front door to find Baker sound asleep on one of the four beds in the large living area.

"Is that your private investigator?" Barbara asks.

"Don't judge. He has been on the job all day, and the last few hours, he's been rechecking an area he had already examined."

I walk over to Baker's bed, and I tap his boot. "Baker," I whisper.

Baker pops up like a jack-in-the-box swinging a gun in his left hand that I had not seen. I back up two steps and almost fall on my butt. "Easy! It's April."

He lowers his gun. "Sorry. I dozed off."

I'm so pleased not to have a hole in my head that I don't even tell him how close he came to shooting me. "Did you find anything new since I called?" I know he didn't because he was asleep. I'm trying to calm down from my near-death experience.

"No, this one so far is a real stopper."

"Do you still have the letter?"

Baker reaches into his shirt pocket and pulls out the yellow legal pad sheet. He hands it to me.

Ivy definitely wrote it. I can visualize her shaking her platinum-blonde hair as she explains to Roman how he killed his dog. Not her.

"And nothing else?" I ask Baker.

He exhales loudly. "No, ma'am. Like I said, I saw some dog tracks outside the cabin. But there's none in the fields or down by the river."

"Could she have carried him?"

Baker shrugs. "I suppose she could have, but why put yourself through lugging around a heavy dog?"

"What's your gut feeling, Baker?"

"Honestly?" he asks.

"We're not paying you to lie to us."

He grins. "I think the letter's a fake. I don't have anything to base it on other than gut feeling. But it just feels off. It also feels off that Ivy bought supplies and left. Almost like she never intended on staying here but wanted us to think that."

"To what end?" I ask.

"It's more believable that she would've left the area if she actually did kill the dog. If for no other reason than her own personal safety, she should leave town."

"Do you run into stuff like this very often?"

Baker raises his eyebrows as he shakes his head. "No, and I hope I never do again."

The three boaters come in the door and stomp on the wood

floor. Snow sprinkles from their boots and quickly melts.

"Game on now," Shane says.

"What's the matter?" I ask.

"It's snowing some huge flakes right now," Patrick says as all three move toward the fire.

"This is some real grilled cheese and chili-type weather," Chase remarks.

"Can we get started with the search?" I ask Chase.

He shrugs. "We can, but you're not going to find anything in this storm. The best thing to do is to hunker down for the night and get an early start."

That isn't what I want to hear, but I know it is probably the right call. I check my phone, and it is after nine PM. I point to the four beds. "How do you want to work the bed assignments?" I can't work out a good sleeping order with four beds.

"Barbara and I will take one, your PI takes the other, and then you take your choice of Shane or Pat sleeping with you. And some lucky guy gets a bed to himself."

I'm horrified. I'm sure my mouth gapes open as I think about the different implications. Sleeping with Patrick would be way too awkward, considering I'm only still his friend because he is a forgiving soul. Shane, I am sure, would have no issue sleeping with me, but I wouldn't get half an hour's sleep because my lust button would be stuck all night while he never even stirs.

"Oh, that's ridiculous," Baker says as he starts toward the door. "I've got my camping equipment in the car. I always come prepared."

"I can't let you camp outside in that weather," I say.

Baker looks at me like I've grown a second head. "I'm not going to. But I am going to bring my sleeping bag and pillow inside. I'll camp out in front of the fireplace."

Well, that sounds a lot better. "You really don't mind?"

"If I minded, I wouldn't have offered."

As Baker walks out into the snow, I turn to Shane and Patrick. "Lucky us, we each get our own bed."

"Cool," Shane says as he falls backward onto the bed Baker had been sleeping on.

"You good with four AM, Shane?" Chase asks.

Shane fishes his phone out of his pocket. "Yeah, I'll go ahead and set my alarm, too."

"Sounds like a plan," Patrick says as he, too, pulls out his phone.

Four o'clock in the morning? My gosh, who does that? If it had been up to me, I would have been thinking five-thirty or six at the earliest, hit the water by seven. Oh well, on the positive side, the earlier we get started in the morning, possibly the earlier we find Bailey, and I can put the Olsons behind me. It won't bother me to be done with my philandering client and his crazy ex-wife.

Baker comes in with his bedroll. "I think if we wake up at four and get started after breakfast, it would probably be best. This little squall is supposed to blow out in the next couple of hours, but there's a larger storm behind it that is supposed to be hitting tomorrow night."

I suppose I should have been listening to the weather station instead of Joan Jett when that weird-looking, naked old lady appeared on top of my car.

As everyone settles in bed, I consider calling Lee and explaining the situation better since I obviously had not done an excellent job earlier. That seems like a lot of work.

Instead, I text him that I'm with Chase in Tuscumbia and that we had to spend the night. I don't bother to fill him in on the fact that Patrick and Shane are with us, too. There's no point in adding additional gas to that fire.

While I was trying to go to sleep, it started to tickle me that this was like an adult version of a sleepover. I want to tell myself that this is good for my maturity growth. If I'm to marry Lee and remain friends with Patrick and Shane, at some point, the weirdness of us having dated had to be lanced and cleaned. What better way than to sleep with both of them at the same time in the same room. I don't know why, but I find it all insanely funny. Perhaps I'm overly tired and stressed. I'm feeling quite slaphappy.

The wind continues to whip outside. The snow changes to sleet and hail every few minutes, making a tapping sound on the windows before it reverts back to snow. The warm yellow flame of the fire dies down to red embers glowing from the hearth.

I prop up on my arm and scan the room. No one is stirring; everyone is asleep.

I can't sleep. I'm tired enough to sleep for two days, but something is brewing in the air. Something evil and sticky clings to all the energy forces. We're out in the secluded woods. There should be few voices, if any, but I can feel them press against the partition in my mind. If I were to let it down, I would have a flood of incoherent sounds crashing into my mind. It makes no sense to me.

I drop back down on my pillow and punch it under my neck in frustration as a sloppy attempt to fluff it. Could that crazy thing on my car have been one of the grays Antoine was talking about? Just being honest here, if that's what is following the demon that is waiting on the outside of Guntersville, I sure don't want to ever meet that demon.

It occurs to me that it is the first time I have run into an entity that is not connected to a specific place in ages. Well, let's just say I was unaware that my parking spot was haunted before six o'clock this evening.

Are there things now roaming the streets of Guntersville hunting for certain people? Man, that sends chills up my spine. Especially since I would be one of the names on their assassination list.

What does the demon have to wait outside the city for the grays to do? It seems that if something is powerful enough to control a group of what I ran into this evening, there's not anything in Guntersville that could prevent them from coming into town. Why wait? Better yet, why come at all? What is this all about?

Now I'm glad we're getting an early start tomorrow. I want to get out to Nana's and get some answers. If not some solutions, she can point me in the right direction, plus I can pick up my paranormal shotgun, and forty-five ghost-shot cartridges. Right now, I'm more worried about needing to evaporate a spirit than putting a hole in a human attacker.

Curious, as usual, I tilt my head to look in the direction of Chase and Barbara. They have their backs turned to each other and have placed a pillow strategically between their shoulders. I can't help but grin at the fact that both have put a hand behind them and on each other's hip. Their minds might be telling them they're friends, but their hands are calling them a liar.

Tightwad Dottie somehow came up with the cash to cremate Gil. I don't know why that is sticking in my head.

For all I know, she might have had a life insurance policy payout now that Gil's body has been found. I wish I could let it go, but I don't seem ready to just yet. I keep having the gut feeling that I'm going to get halfway in on Dottie's trial, and it will be like, "Surprise, your client is as guilty as they come."

Man, there are just way too many things to be thinking about right now. I believe I'm making my head hurt. Some days life is just too tough.

Chapter 19

Puppy lies against my legs. I'm cocooned in luxuriously soft cotton sheets as the morning sunlight kisses the room with a warm yellow-and-pink glow. The rhythmic rumble of waves crashing rolls to me through the open French doors. The tang of saltwater mingles with my two favorite scents in the world: frying bacon and dark coffee.

Puppy stirs and plops off the side of the bed, I assume to investigate the source of the mouthwatering sizzle. I watch him exit the interior door to the left with one eye still closed.

I stand to follow him but notice I'm naked. When did that happen?

An extra sheet is folded at the end of the bed. How convenient. I wrap it around me like an oversized shawl and follow Puppy.

Nothing looks familiar. Everything *feels* familiar.

An athletic man in sweats and a long-sleeved T-shirt is barefoot frying bacon in a cast-iron skillet. His back is to me, and I approach him. I want to reach out and touch him.

Something wet slides into my ear. My brain short-circuits. My eyes open, and Chase is leaning over me.

"Rise and shine, Valentine," he says way too loudly for four o'clock in the morning. He looks over his shoulder and, with an air of pride, says, "Wet willies works every time."

"Dang it, Chase," I complain as I wipe my ear with one hand

and backhand my brother's rock-hard belly with my other. "You know how much I hate that."

"Which is exactly why I continue to do it," Chase says as he walks away, satisfied that I am sufficiently awake.

So, there is no beach and no sexy guy in the kitchen. Still, Baker is frying bacon in the kitchenette, and I see coffee in the Brew Master. I'm aware that doesn't balance out that Chase gave me a wet willy, but with Puppy in the bed in my dream, it was a fifty-fifty possibility he would have given me one, or worse, a whole cheek lick.

"The bacon is almost done. Somebody find some plates," Baker says without turning around.

I consider hunting for them, but Barbara beats me to the punch. The first cupboard she opens is full of multicolored plastic plates reminiscent of the set I took to Alabama.

It's uncanny how Barbara knew precisely where to go as if she had stayed here a hundred times. She will make some lucky guy a great housewife. I can only hope my brother gets his act together.

While I consider everyone else's love life, I float toward the coffee. The sour taste in my mouth reminds me that I forgot my toothbrush. That is strike three. No rubber boots, appropriate coat, or toothbrush. Today will be most unpleasant.

I open the refrigerator and smile as I spy an orange juice container. I pour myself a glass by the sink, thinking the citrus might cut my stale breath.

Baker is transferring the last of the bacon, and our eyes meet. "Where'd you get that?" he asks.

I gesture toward the refrigerator. "The fridge."

He shakes his head, "Don't drink that. I didn't buy it."

"Why?"

He pours the bacon grease into an old can. "If that woman is mean enough to kill a dog, what makes you think she wouldn't poison one of us accidentally while attempting to poison her husband. It's his cabin. She knows he'll be up here at some time."

I pour the orange juice down the drain and decide to own my fuzzy teeth and bad breath. Sometimes sound logic can be inconvenient.

After a quick breakfast, everyone begins to put on their snow clothes for the search. I'm feeling particularly sorry for myself as I psyche myself up in preparation for freezing my tail off all day when Chase comes back in from his truck.

He drops a small duffel bag on my bed. "Barbara reminded me you weren't living at home right now. She had me bring your hunting gear."

My eyes well with tears of gratitude. "Thank you."

He gestures toward Barbara. "Thank Barbara. I was prepared to let you freeze your fanny off."

"Thank you for being more civil than he is," I say to Barbara.

"Don't pay him any mind. He's just sore because you're not around the house anymore," Barbara says with a laugh.

"I am not," Chase retorts.

Being mean doesn't exactly entice people to be close to you. But I suppose in Chase's world, being mean is showing affection?

"I think we should walk the quadrants first. After we complete that, there should be better light for a water search," Baker recommends.

I'd been so tired when I came in last night and then caught off guard with the number of beds versus people that I had not taken serious note of Baker. He is of average height with dark black hair, rich brown eyes, and a ruddy, heavily pocked face. He is muscular and sturdily built. There is a seriousness about him that gives me confidence that he knows what he is doing. This isn't just about a paycheck for him.

"I agree, but in pairs, so we have an extra set of eyes on each quadrant," Chase says. Everyone nods in agreement.

Baker gestures toward Patrick, and he steps toward Baker, pairing off.

"Looks like you're with me, Bama." Shane zips up his parka.

"Just don't talk me to death. It's distracting, and I'll need to concentrate."

Shane favors me with a slow, low-pitched laugh. "You're a hot mess, girl."

Shane doesn't know the half of it.

Baker's level of organization is incredible. Last night when we arrived in the dark, I hadn't noticed it, but he had marked out each quadrant with stakes. The quadrants travel out from the cabin to the east, north, west, and south. Each is divided into four arcing sections every hundred yards out. There are four arcing sections on each side, totaling sixteen sections to search.

Shane and I take the east quadrant grouping. The ground is frozen and crunches under our feet. A few snow patches cling in the spots without vegetation. Still, most of the precipitation last night must have been freezing rain that refroze once it soaked into the mud.

As we begin our second section, I can't stay quiet any longer. "Why did you never tell me that you were a medical student?"

Shane's lips draw back, exposing his perfect white teeth. "What did you think I did at the hospital?"

"I don't know. An orderly, a maintenance technician, or maybe even somebody who signs folks in at the emergency room?"

"And why would you think that, Bama?"

His question makes me uncomfortable for some reason. "I don't know, probably because I don't know anybody who's gone through the trouble of becoming a doctor?"

Shane continues to study the ground, looking for any hints of Bailey. "That's not true. Both your father and your brother Dusty are doctors."

"That's not the same," I protest. "They aren't like *doctor* doctors."

"I think you're looking for MD."

"Right."

Shane exhales loudly. "Does it really matter? I mean, would you not have been my friend if you had known I was studying to be a doctor?"

"No, that's silly."

"Then it's all good. Right?"

But it isn't all good in my mind. It is yet another illustration of my failure in fundamental relationships.

I never cared enough to ask Shane what he was doing at the hospital. In hindsight, it was incredibly shallow that I never asked and yet had such strong feelings for the man.

"Just for the record, I'm not going to be happy if I find this dog dead," Shane grumbles.

"Me either."

"Do you think she is mean enough to have done it?" Shane stops and trains his golden-hazel eyes on me.

I nod my head slowly. "I'm afraid so. She's like a riled-up bobcat."

"That's so messed up."

"Yeah. It is," I whisper.

Our search party had inspected all sixteen sections Baker had lain when the sun melted the last of the frost and snow. I can only speak for the sections Shane and I worked, but every rock and every fallen branch was scrutinized to ensure it was not part of a dog. If the rest of the team treated their sections the same, I'm confident that Bailey is nowhere on the cabin's five-acre plot.

"Do you want to check along the riverbank or try the boat first?" Chase questions Baker.

"I don't know about you, but I think I would prefer a pleasant boat ride and give my feet a break," Baker says.

I find it interesting how even though Baker is the new

person in our group, everyone is already deferring to him. There is something about the man that lets you know he is all business and is capable of developing a sound plan.

Let's face it. If I were in charge, I would have us searching willy-nilly. The idea of the areas ringing out from the house being marked in separate quadrants first seems like a genius idea. It looks like the only logical decision that could have been utilized for an effective search—now.

I usually love boat rides. But with the occasional stray bit of hail falling from the sky and the biting northern wind, I know it will be less than fun. That's before I consider that our mission is to find a murdered dog.

Chase hands everyone a life jacket as we board his boat.

Patrick unties us from the dock and pushes off.

"What area do you want to check first?" Chase asks.

"I spent a lot of time yesterday on the bank looking out." Baker points to the riverbank on the cabin side. "I don't know why but I have a gut feeling that if she killed Bailey, she might have dumped him in the channel. Let's run it first."

"Works for me." Chase accelerates until we create a small wake. He turns us toward the channel.

Baker steps toward me. "If you want to do something different, let me know. It's your investigation."

"No. You seem to have a good handle on it."

He smiles. "I appreciate that."

"Just wondering, Baker. What's your background? Where'd you learn these skills?"

Baker looks out toward the water. "Compliments of Uncle Sam."

"Military, huh?"

"Hundred and first airborne, did my twenty and got out."

I can't help but laugh as I look him over. "There's no way you're that old, Baker."

"Well, that's because the Army will let you enlist on your twelfth birthday."

I shake my head. "And here I thought you didn't have a sense of humor."

"I do with the regularity of a lunar eclipse."

Baker is a good guy. I'm thankful Jacob put me onto him. "Is your gut still that she faked all this."

"I think so." He shrugs. "But then again, I'm just human, and it may be wishful thinking on my part."

The motor of the boat reverses, and I stumble forward. Baker catches me with an arm and steadies me.

"More to the left, Chase," Patrick yells.

I move toward the front of the boat and stop in between Barbara and Chase. "What is it?"

"Patrick thinks he sees something," Barbara says.

"That's it, a little further," Patrick hollers back to Chase.

I watch as Patrick leans out over the nose of the boat. Shane hops into action, too, and leans out next to Patrick with a fishing net.

All I know is if they pull a drowned black Labrador out of the water, I'm going to have a fit. No, I'm serious.

I was never really a dog person growing up. Still, ever since Granny gave me Puppy, I now understand people's attraction to their dogs.

If Ivy murdered Roman's dog, I'm going to be so angry I will want to hunt her down and pull every strand of her hair out one by one. Forget about trying to protect her from what Roman might do.

Baker pushes past me as he goes to help at the front of the boat. I'm not sure I want to see what the boys have found.

"What is it?" Chase asks.

The three men do not answer. They are intent on their task. Patrick raises his left hand and gestures for Chase to back the boat up.

I brace myself, and Chase puts the motor in reverse briefly.

Shane lurches forward as he reaches out with the net.

"Got it!" Patrick yells as he pushes up onto his knees.

Whatever they caught is in the net Shane is holding. I'm filled with dread as Shane starts to stand. The last thing I want to see is the dead dog. I turn away from them.

"What is it?" Barbara asks.

"A dog harness," Baker replies.

I spin around, now knowing there is no dead dog in sight. Baker examined the harness closely.

Our eyes meet. "It's your dog. Bailey," Baker says as he flicks the octagon-shaped brass tag.

I turn my hands palm up. "Where is he?"

Baker walks toward me. He holds the blue harness out for me as he points at a frayed cut on the top torso portion of the harness. "It looks like something cut the fabric," he says.

I don't comprehend his meaning. "So, he got away?"

Baker's eyes narrow as he frowns. "Doubtful. At least not while he was alive."

I take the harness from Baker and examine it myself. Shane and Patrick sit at the boat's bow with their feet resting on the cushions as I look up. Their wrists are draped over their knees, and they have frowns fixed on their faces. "She cut the harness. Why?"

Baker shakes his head. "I don't think that's how the events went." He takes the harness from me and runs his hand down to the end of the leash. It, too, is slashed. "It's all theory, but if I had to guess, she drowned the dog with his leash and harness on. She probably put a weight of some sort on the leash side."

My chest constricts, and it is suddenly harder to breathe. "But why did she cut the harness?"

"She didn't, Bama. That's a prop cut," Shane interjects.

I feel Chase's arm come around my shoulder. I don't want it there. I'm too aggravated to be touched, but I don't shake him off because I know he means to comfort me.

"The doggy's body probably floated up and then got ran over by a boat, April," Chase tries to explain.

I turn toward him. "Then where is the blood?"

He shrugs. "The dog was in the water. There's a chance the blood would've dispersed before it stained the harness."

I close my eyes and shake my head as I imagine having to call

149

Roman. "Oh, this is not good."

"I'm so sorry, April. We were all hoping for better."

I open my eyes and look at everybody who has pitched in. We *all* feel awful about what Ivy has done to Bailey. We *all* had a vested interest in finding the dog alive. This is the worst of all possible outcomes.

Get over yourself, April. These people helped you when they didn't have to, and they feel as lousy about it as you do.

"Thank you all for taking the time to help with the search. I really appreciate it and know that you didn't have to."

As Chase drives the boat back to the dock, we are a somber group. We pack up our vehicles in near silence.

I walk over to Baker's car as he is closing the trunk. "I want to thank you for such a thorough job."

He frowns. "Thanks. I just wish it had a better ending."

"Well, we didn't write the ending. Ivy did. We were here to find out the truth and bring closure."

Baker nods his head. "Sometimes, that's all you can do."

"Do you have all the information to email me your invoice?"

"Yes, I have all that from earlier." He extends his hand to me. "I enjoyed working with you."

I shake his hand. "Same here. Do you mind if I call you in the future?"

"Sure, anytime I can be of service."

"Good. Have a safe trip," I say.

"You, too. Say hi to Jacob for me." Baker Diaz gets in his car. I watch him drive away as I walk to Chase's truck.

As I am about to hoist myself into the back of the cab, the most amazing thing happens. The thick snow clouds we dealt with all morning open up a gaping hole, and the sunlight shines through like a gigantic flashlight. It is as if cables of gold extend to the earth's surface.

"That's almost worth enduring a snowstorm to see," Patrick says, his voice full of wonder.

"Sometimes beauty appears when you least expect it," I say.

Chapter 20

It is a long, quiet ride home. I still have not heard from Lee, and I wonder if I should go to his house tonight or stay at my apartment. It hurts, and my eyes tear up when I think about it, but I sort of feel like maybe I should spend the night at my place. Give us some time to think things over.

Face it, our situation has moved at a lightning-fast pace since Lee came back on the scene. Until he bought his vacation home in Guntersville, I had decided a long-term relationship with a man was not in my near future plans. If you told me I would be moving to follow a man, I would have asked if you were into hallucinogenic drugs. It simply wasn't part of my plan, but I didn't know Lee Darby was an option when I formulated my life strategy.

Still, what Lee said to me yesterday hurt me terribly. It stings because I made a conscious decision to do better with our relationship than what I have in the past. I am actively attempting to be more of a giver than a taker—and it still isn't good enough.

That's right, Grandpa Hirsch's lessons during Christmas did not fall on deaf ears. Until then, I never realized how shallow I was with some of my past relationships. That's why I have begun to make a concerted effort with everyone I deal with, to know more about them and let them know I care. For some people, this is easy and comes naturally. It's hard work for me.

But I really thought I was doing a great job when it came to Lee. Obviously, he doesn't see it the same way.

It's enough to make me wonder if I'll ever be able to have a "normal" relationship. Given that so much of my life is abnormal due to my "gifts," it only seems fair that I have a comfortable, zero-drama marriage to a great guy.

There I go again, believing life should be fair.

My phone dings, and my heart flutters. Maybe Lee has forgiven me.

I sigh. It's a text from Nana. *Are we still on for tonight?*

Bless it. How did I forget about our dinner? I really need to visit with her and discuss Antoine's situation, too.

I'm also exhausted, and the idea of getting home and crashing on my bed seems awfully tempting. Oh, who am I kidding? I won't sleep until I know what was on top of my car and I am confident they can't just appear inside my apartment. I text Nana that I will be at her trailer at six.

Chase and I are the only two awake in the truck when the snowstorm starts. He looks in the rearview mirror at me. "If you think this is bad, imagine still being on the water with this coming down."

"That would not have been fun," I agree. "The weather has been so whacked this year. It's been years since it has snowed this late in winter."

"True." He sighs. "So, are you all set to go to the big town of Baltimore?"

I roll my eyes. "I don't know now."

"Uh-oh. Sounds like trouble in paradise."

I stare out the side window at the clumpy snow falling down. "He's upset that last night I didn't make it home for dinner."

"Well, I'm never going to defend him, but as a point of observation, you didn't just miss dinner. You missed making it home," Chase says.

"I was in the middle of the case. Lee can't expect me to drop everything on a whim and run home because he wants to have dinner with me."

"Whoa, Nellie. Like I said, I'm never going to defend him, but there are worse things in the world than your boyfriend being upset you didn't make it home for dinner. You could have a boyfriend who doesn't care whether you did or didn't."

I blow a frustrated breath between my teeth. "Why can't I just have a boyfriend who understands that sometimes I'm not going to be able to make it, even though I want to."

Chase shrugs. "Nobody says you can't. But Lee Darby is telling you he's not that man, and you should respect that. Lee Darby wants his woman at the house for dinner and in his bed at night. That doesn't make him wrong. That just makes him maybe not the best choice for April."

"That's not true. I want those things, too," I argue.

Chase wags a finger in the air. "Yet you didn't make it home last night. Understand that in some people's books, as odd as it may seem to you, actions speak louder than words. You may *say* you want to be home every night, but if you're willing to sacrifice family time for your job, your words are just a bunch of hot air."

"That's harsh."

Chase shakes his head side to side. "You know that's not my intent. But I do want to make sure you don't move across the country with somebody that you're not compatible with."

Chase giving relationship advice. If that isn't rich. He is sitting next to the woman who would love to marry him, but he's too much of a bonehead to understand it.

Lee and I aren't incompatible. I just have more on my plate than I can say grace over. Things will be quite different once we are living in Baltimore. I'm sure of it.

I know where all this is coming from, anyway. Chase has some sort of beef against Lee. Lee has never said an unkind word about Chase, so I know it is my brother's issue.

I turn my attention back out toward the snow that continues to get heavier, and I ignore my brother. If he tries to continue the conversation, I'll pretend I've fallen asleep.

The phone call I need to make to Roman weighs heavily on my mind. When we were at the river, I told myself I would make it when we were in the truck. Now that I've been riding for a couple of hours, I've decided that it's best to wait until I am alone in my apartment. I hope that I'm not procrastinating.

As morbid as it may sound, I do wish that we had found Bailey's body. The harness is substantial proof of his drowning once it's explained in detail. But I would be lying if I said it feels like it is one hundred percent proof positive. There is still a slight opportunity that Bailey could have somehow survived. But it's most likely wishful thinking.

On the positive side, once I call Roman, I'm mostly done with the Olsons and their dysfunctional marriage. The property and money have already been divvied up. The dog was the last item standing between their separation and official divorce.

That will leave Dottie Castle's and Antoine Lattimore's cases on my immediate docket. What extraordinary luck to be left with a possible sociopath and spouse killer, and a clairvoyant one step from insanity? Man, I've got to get into a better market.

"You want me to follow you over to Lee's?"

I realize Chase has stopped in front of Snow and Associates. We have two inches of snow, which in Guntersville is considered a blizzard.

"I think I'm gonna stay at the lake house tonight. Just let me follow you over there."

Chase's eyebrows rise as he puckers his lips. "Okay."

To his credit, he doesn't press.

I hop out of the truck and walk to my car. I freeze when I see the barefoot and hand imprints in the snow circling my car and streaked in a line over the hood and roof of my car. Instinctively, I look to the top of the oak tree and then to the roof of Snow and Associates. Nothing. For now, at least.

The thought of the grays circling my car as recently as the snowfall is making me so scared, I can barely unlock my car from my hands shaking.

I want desperately to see Nana this evening to discuss these creatures with her. Still, I'm too petrified to travel to her house by myself.

Chapter 21

Back at my parents' lake house, I help the rest of the search team unpack their gear and load up their cars. Patrick and Shane head out, but Barbara follows Chase inside.

As I watch the two of them go up the stairs toward Chase's bedroom, I decide to take a moment to call Roman about Bailey and Ivy. I walk into the den to have privacy and find Puppy on the leather sofa.

I bribe him for forgiveness with a quick back and neck massage. Lucky for me, he's as forgiving as the rest of the men in my family, unlike my boyfriend.

"Are you going to stay here and help me tell this man about his dog?" I ask Puppy. "He's going to be really, really sad that his doggie won't ever be coming home."

Puppy stretches a paw out, placing it on my thigh. He can be supportive at times. When he wants to be.

The time for procrastination is over. I pull out my phone and dial Roman Olson. I flinch with each ring of his phone.

"April, did you find Bailey?"

I push through my hesitation and break the news to Roman. "I'm so sorry, Roman. We did not—"

"Blast it. I've been searching my mind trying to think of anywhere Ivy might be hiding out with him."

"Uh—listen, Roman. That's helpful. Keep thinking of possibilities where Ivy might be, but I've got some terrible news to share with you."

Roman lets a choked, nervous laugh escape. "Honestly, short of a bomb threat at my house, I don't see how things can get any worse."

"Roman, please. Let me finish."

He sucks in a breath, and the line is quiet. "Okay," he says.

"Bailey isn't with Ivy, Roman." I bear down to free the words from my mouth. "I'm sorry, Roman. Bailey is dead."

"Wh—"

"We found his dog harness in the river, and it had been cut by a prop blade. I believe she drowned him as you suspected."

"It could have been any dog's leash…"

I exhale. "I'm so sorry. It has Bailey's tags on it."

"It—" Roman chokes. "—you're sure—it's blue and—oh, no!"

"I'm so sorry, Roman."

I'm not prepared for the screech. Long-winded and high-pitched, Roman's scream seems to last forever as I pull my phone from my ear.

As he sucks in a breath, his cry transforms into a pitiful mewing noise. My heart aches for him.

I clutch the soft fur at the base of Puppy's neck. It helps me stay steady with resolve.

A year ago, I would consider Roman's reaction overboard for a pet. Puppy has forever changed my point of view. If something were to happen to my furry buddy, I, too, would be reduced to a wailing blob of misery.

"Roman, are you there?"

He sniffs loudly and clears his throat. "Yeah."

"Are you going to be alright? Do I need to call anyone for you?"

"Yes." He wheezes. "A hitman. I've got money, and I don't care how much it costs. I want—"

"Roman, no!" Bless it. He has shot my blood pressure out the roof. "I am not having this conversation with you."

"You don't understand."

"Yes. Yes, I do. But you are not going to say or even think that again. Are we clear?"

"But she needs to—"

"Ah-ah-ah, stop. Listen to your counsel. You will do whatever you need to do to deal with your grief *except* for hurt, talk to, or even think about Ivy. You focus on the good times you and Bailey had together. Let me and the courts take care of Ivy. Are we clear?"

His hesitation makes me fear I won't be able to reel him in this time. "I suppose."

My shoulders, which had crept up to my earlobes, drop back to their normal position as I draw a deep breath. "I'm truly sorry for your loss, Roman."

"Uh. I got to go, April."

"I understand. Take care."

I hang up and think evil thoughts about Ivy. I don't like to, but I'm still horrified at what she has done.

I scratch Puppy behind his ears again. "I appreciate you staying here for moral support. Is Uncle Dusty here? I need to see if he will go with me to Nana's."

Puppy grunts as he stands. He drops off the sofa and lumbers toward the basement. I follow Puppy. I hear Dusty on the phone as we reach the stairwell landing.

Reaching the bottom, I see Dusty is alone, on the phone, and monitoring several different screens. It appears like he might be editing some film from one of our excursions.

He turns, and our eyes meet. "Hey, let me call you back." He puts his phone down. "Hi, stranger, what's up?"

"Are you covered up tonight?"

Dusty steals a quick glance at the screens. "Well, I'm putting together some footage for the television series. This episode is due next Friday. But I can free up some time if it's important to you."

"I need to go out to Nana Hirsch's tonight. Thursday night's our dinner night." He doesn't seem to be following me, so I add helpfully, "It's when I talk to her about stuff. You know—paranormal stuff."

Dusty squints his eyes as if he is waiting for me to finish the thought. "Right."

"Would you ride out there with me tonight?"

He grins. "Sure. Any particular reason?"

"I don't want to be out in this wacky weather by myself." The lie slips out so quickly and easily I don't even know where it came from. I don't even feel my face heat.

He nods his head. "No problem. Let me finish this one section, and we can head out."

That went easier than I imagined. Besides, this could kill two birds with one stone. I've intended to get Dusty out to the Willoughby covered bridge so he could meet the little drowned girl. If she makes an appearance tonight, it will undoubtedly make the journey worth it for Dusty.

Since I'm getting what I want, my anxiety level comes down. That allows me to pay attention to the film Dusty is editing. "Is that from the Imperial?"

"Quick eye," he says as he looks over his shoulder. "I thought I would review the old footage to see what could be salvaged for a show since we're running light on material."

Dusty's voice creeps up an octave, and he touches his nose. Telltale signs that he just floated a tiny lie of his own. I push in closer. "It amazes me that we got so little considering all the lousy juju in that place.

"Yeah. I keep feeling like there is something to be found in this footage. But I've been over it several times and don't see anything."

The Imperial is a movie theater in Shelbyville, Tennessee, that we researched during the Christmas season. We believed we had cleared the building of a malicious spirit, which was the condition of our access to the site. Still, scaffolding on the site collapsed under mysterious conditions two days later, breaking one of the worker's ankles.

I had warned Dusty we were leaving business undone. I'm not sure if it was our desire to start the Christmas holiday or if Dusty's minor "gifts" warned him to leave the theater.

Whatever the reason, he called the investigation and had the team head home.

I can tell by his body language that he sorely regrets the decision.

"Would you like another set of eyes?"

Dusty nods as he strokes his unruly red beard. "Yes, please."

I roll a chair over to the monitors, and he runs the footage from the beginning. Settling in, I note that the take is twenty minutes long.

As we approach the end of the footage, a few seconds of unexplainable shadows stretch across the ceiling in the extended back hallway. Still, they are not nearly defined enough for our purposes.

The footage cuts at the eighteen-minute mark. It's of Liza and me working on releasing the spirits of people tragically killed in a fire at the theater. It warms my center that we could give so many tormented souls the peace they deserved after so many decades in purgatory.

The footage cuts again with thirty seconds remaining. It's Dusty holding the back door open for me in preparation for locking the theater and leaving for home. The same chill that ran up my spine that day makes an encore appearance.

Something on the screen catches my eye. "Hey, back the film up."

Dusty moves his mouse. "What did you see?"

"I'm not sure just yet."

He reruns the last minute of footage. It is like one of those crazy black-and-white puzzles where I know I'm seeing something, but I can't identify it. After staring at the puzzle for an extended period, a friend would point out that the word "fly" is in the drawing. After that, all I can see is "fly."

The trouble with this puzzle is that whatever is raising my hackles isn't popping out at me.

"Again?" Dusty asks as we reach the end of the footage.

I circle my finger in the air. "Play it again, Sam."

It's the footage in the last thirty seconds of the tape.

Something flashes on the wall behind Liza as we make our way to the exit. "Stop the tape."

"You see it?" Dusty asks.

I frown. "I see something. But I can't make it out for some reason. Can you slow the tape down?"

Dusty rewinds the tape and plays it at one-tenth speed. It is slightly easier to make out the shadowy movement, but I still can't identify precisely what I'm looking at. I point to the spot right behind Liza. "Do you see that?"

"Liza's shadow."

Sorta, kinda, maybe. It just doesn't look right.

Perhaps I'm making too much of it. I may be trying too hard to see something that isn't there since I *felt* something. It is understandable, given that the night we left Shelbyville, I sensed something was hiding from us as we locked the door.

"Have they had any other disturbances since the scaffolding accident?" I ask Dusty.

He scratches the back of his neck. "They tell me it's getting worse than ever. The spirit, or whatever it is, gets bolder and bolder by the day. They've even been spotting disturbances on the square now."

"Outside the theater?"

Dusty guffaws as he rewinds the footage again. "Yes. The last I checked, the town square was outside of that theater. Unless you're counting the mural on the ceiling."

Yeah, that was kind of stupid. "I'm just surprised. They never reported anything on the square prior, correct?"

Dusty adjusts the audio. He backs down our voices and increases the background. "It wasn't like a never occurrence. But no, they did not have anything happening regularly."

My ears perk up, and my back straightens. "Did you hear that?"

Dusty looks at me and shakes his head. He rewinds the tape and plays it again, making the background even louder.

It is unmistakable to me. Something giggles in the background as if it has a great secret. The laugh is cut short, followed by a low-pitched, guttural, coaxing voice. "Go on, go on" is what I make out.

It is the voice I heard the night we left Shelbyville. But that night, I thought it was in my mind.

I rub my temples as I consider the implication of the voice being picked up by our equipment and not energy resonating in my mind. How tired was I to mistake it that night?

Cut yourself some slack, April. It was the third incident on that trip.

I force myself to let it go. Ultimately, it didn't impact the research. It just chills me to the bone to realize that so many things are merging together. It's as if my two realities, both sides of the veil, are so merged I can't always tell which side of the veil I am on.

Nana warned me my veil was thinning. With that comes the possibility of accidentally time traveling or teleporting— which means the chance of being lost in the void forever.

I shudder to shake the negative thoughts from my mind. If I don't take care, I'll manifest what I fear.

Purposefully, I lean in closer to the display. There is certainly something off with Liza's shadow. It can't have been the lighting because my shadow is not moving in the same manner.

Dusty rewinds the footage again, and I grab his hand. "Can you play this backward?"

Dusty shrugs. "Sure."

He resets the meter and plays the film in reverse. Liza's shadow on the wall is whole. It splits in two at the waist as the film continues in reverse.

"Well, I'll be darned." Dusty clicks his tongue.

I watch in horror as the second shadow splits from Liza's. I can make out a hunched-over humanoid figure with extended claws and a long tail like a rat. "What the heck is that?"

"Huh." Dusty pokes his lower lip out. "I'll have to get verification, but we may have recorded our first demon."

It is as if somebody has jammed an enormous metal straw

into my chest. All the air escapes my lungs, and my muscles involuntarily flex. I want to ask Dusty to clarify, but I know I heard him correctly. Even if I don't want to believe him.

"That would explain its movement outside of the theater. Demons aren't held to specific locations."

"What do we do with that?" I ask.

Dusty chuckles, somehow finding humor in my question. "Liza is an excellent expeller. It didn't work that night because, from what I know of it, demons are a precise and different process than expelling spirits. Now that we know what we're up against, we can get back down there and take care of business."

I pull away from Dusty as I shake my head. "No. This thing is different, Dusty." I point to the frozen frame that shows the shadowy demon. "This thing here is smart. It made sure we didn't notice it before we left Shelbyville. I don't think we should underestimate it."

Dusty considers what I'm saying. "Okay. Let me think about it. You might be right, and we may need some extra backup. The main thing I need to know right now is if when we get done with our trip to Bellefonte on Saturday if you could ride with us to Shelbyville."

"I'm not an expeller."

"No, but your animism protection spells have come in handy in the past."

I study what I see on the screen, and my blood chills. There is no way I want to go back to the Imperial theater in Shelbyville, Tennessee. I especially don't want to if a short-tailed demon is running around. According to Antoine, I've got demons of my own to deal with right here in Guntersville. I sure don't need to bring one down from Shelbyville.

"April? Are you in?"

I chew my lower lip and look away. I want to say, "Heck no, I'm not going to go with you!" But how can I ask him to ride with me tonight because I'm afraid of the grays and not be willing to put my health at risk in a reciprocal manner?

I blow out a breath. "Alright, I'll go. I'm not sure what good I'll do you. But I'll be there."

"Awesome. I'll let the rest of the team know." Dusty flips the switch, thankfully turning off the screen that displayed the long-tailed demon.

He grabs his backpack, shoves his laptop and two notebooks into it, and slings it over his shoulder. "Are you driving or am I?"

"Do you want to see the little drowned girl ghost?"

"Does a fat baby poot?"

I roll my eyes. "Fine, then I better drive."

Chapter 22

Ghosts, warlocks, and demons are all scary. But my anxiety is focused on an icy county road while I fight the steering of my rear-wheel-drive vehicle.

Dusty's cream-white skin appears even whiter than usual. "Man, I wish we had brought one of the four-wheel-drives."

"At least you're not driving." I open my right hand, which is cramping from me gripping the steering wheel too tightly.

"I didn't think the roads would be this bad out here."

"That makes two of us. But they're not going to salt the roads this far out of town," I say.

As we make the right-hand turn toward the Willoughby bridge, I notice a green luminescent light glowing from the bridge. I decelerate my IROC down to a slow roll. "Something's not right up ahead."

"If I didn't know better, I'd say that's the northern lights," Dusty says in awe.

"If so, this is going to be the first reported case south of the Mason Dixon."

Dusty chuckles. "There has to be a first time for everything."

I'm still waiting for the first time I go through a day without something stupid, weird, or scary happening. To date, it has never happened. "The only other way to get to Nana's is to go up to Grant and come back around the mountain."

Dusty narrows his eyes. "Why would we do that? It would

add at least thirty minutes to our trip."

That is true, but at the moment, thirty minutes of extra driving looks like a minor inconvenience compared to whatever is making the bridge glow green. "Nana won't mind if we're late. You can call her while I turn around. "

Dusty waves his hand dismissively. "Forget that. Let's go up there and see what this is all about."

I don't need to drive to the bridge to know what it is all about. If I had a twenty-dollar bill to bet, I would say that drowned girl has gotten some extra juice, and she's showing it off. "You sure?"

He looks at me as if I've lost my mind. "Sure, I'm sure. Do you need me to drive?"

"No, I've got it." I put the car into gear and cruise at walking speed toward the bridge. We get within fifty yards of the bridge entrance, and I stop and put my car in park. I can't believe my eyes. Nothing could have prepared me for this spectacle.

"What in the world…"

"Dusty, let's go back. We can circle back through Grant. We don't have to use the bridge," I beg him.

"I can see them," he says.

That is even more reason he should listen to me and forget about using the bridge. "Good, then you know we should just circle back around."

He points with his finger. "The shorty in the center, is that the little drowned girl you're always talking about?"

"Yes." But she's just an annoyance. The two shriveled, naked women flanking on either side of her look like they can do some severe damage if they are so inclined. I have never seen such an ostentatious display of power as the creation of the two grays. The undulating green light surrounds the covered bridge and towers fifty feet into the air.

It's meant to intimidate. For me, it does its job.

"Drive up closer," Dusty says.

I turn and gawk at my brother. "For real? You must be out of your mind."

"No. I want to see what these are all about."

Against my better judgment, I put the car in drive. "Bloodshed, chaos, and evil, that's three things they are about, I can guarantee you."

"I swear, April. You are so melodramatic," Dusty says as we approach the three female apparitions.

The first hint of putrid gas fans through the car's heater when we are five car lengths from the bridge entrance.

"What is that?" Dusty coughs into his fist.

The smell resembles a run-over skunk combined with a rotten egg on a hot August afternoon. "Dusty, I'm going to gun it."

"No, April. I want to get a closer look."

I stomp on the accelerator, and my IROC tires spin for an eternity before the car fishtails forward. The two wrinkled, naked women move closer to the little drowned girl in the center as I gain speed. All of them are lined up in the center of the path. If they think I'm stopping, they are sadly mistaken.

"April, stop!" Dusty hollers.

I know what Dusty wants to do, but he has no idea what he's messing with. The little drowned girl is scary in her own right, but the grays are just a step below that demon I saw in the video. Things like the grays want folks to take their time and prey on people being mesmerized by their grotesqueness.

I'm not falling for that game.

I refuse to close my eyes as I approach the moment of impact. I expect to see all three bounce off the nose of my car.

Over the roar of my engine, I hear a loud hiss. Both shriveled women jump straight into the air, and I drive under them.

As my car hits the bridge's icy planks, I notice several planks have been removed from the bridge's floor, leaving a four-foot gap in the middle of the bridge. I need some sort of ramp.

With every ounce of energy I can muster, I visualize a small ramp at the lip of the missing planks.

I close my eyes and press the accelerator all the way to the floorboard. Dusty screams like a panicked little girl next to me.

There is a jolt that pile drives me back into my seat, forcing my teeth to clash together. My stomach drops out the bottom as we go airborne inside the bridge.

As we land, my chest crashes into the steering wheel, and the vehicle turns sideways, sliding out the far end of the bridge and coming to a stop on the roadway.

I lay over the steering wheel, struggling to catch my breath.

I'm driving up to Grant next time.

"Are you kidding me?" Dusty rants. "You could have killed both of us back there."

"Just for the record, I'm pretty sure they would've killed us back there." I notice movement in my rearview mirror. I do a double-take in the mirror, and the little drowned girl favors me one of her evil smirks from the back seat. I push off from the back of my chair. "Fudge! She got in the car."

"Who?" Dusty swivels in his chair. "Hey, little girl."

The little drowned girl holds her doll in one hand and the doll's head in the other. She holds both out toward Dusty.

"Do you want me to fix your doll? Put her back together?"

The little girl's mouth drops open to her belly button, and razor-sharp spikes grow from her jawline. "Fix her, or I'll eat you!" she says to Dusty.

Apart from fear and wanting to protect my brother, I remember this drill from earlier encounters. I slam my car into gear and accelerate. I'm not sure what the rules are with the grays, but I know little drowned girl can't follow me to Nana's.

The abomination dissolves in the back seat. As I Tokyo drift onto Nana's gravel drive, I check the mirror, and she is gone altogether.

I steal a look at Dusty despite me wrestling for control of my vehicle at a high rate of speed. He looks like toast to me.

"Are you okay?" I ask.

He stares at me, eyes open abnormally wide, and takes his time in answering. He stutters slightly, "I think I might've peed myself."

Chapter 23

I pull up Nana's driveway and park on the side of her trailer. "Are you okay to go in with me?"

"I'm sure not staying out here alone." Dusty quickly opens the car door and walks toward the trailer's porch.

He beats me to Nana's front door and calls out to Nana as he goes inside. I hold up and look back from where we came. I have an uneasy feeling that we are being watched.

Of course, they are angry. We made it to Nana's, which has more spirit catchers on the trees than leaves.

I don't care how much Dusty wants to complain about it. We are definitely going the long way home.

As I step inside the trailer, Nana coaxes Dusty to drink something. "It'll calm your nerves," Nana tells Dusty.

I watch with much interest and mirth. Sue me. I'm curious if he is foolish enough to take one of Nana's potions.

"Thank you, but I can't drink that, Nana. It smells like rotten bananas and motor oil," Dusty complains.

"All Nana's potions smell like that. Don't be a wimp. Go ahead and drink it. It'll calm your nerves," I cajole.

"How about we split it?" Dusty says.

I continue toward the kitchen. "I'm used to that circus at the bridge now. I don't need anything to calm me down. I *am* hungry. What's for dinner, Nana?"

She follows me into the kitchen, leaving Dusty in the living room holding the tonic he is reluctant to take. "Fried pork chops, mashed potatoes, biscuits and gravy, and a smattering of green beans to give it some color."

"Man, I should've stopped and picked us up cupcakes to round out the caloric explosion," I say.

Nana lifts a Tupperware cover. "No need, I have a fresh carrot cake."

"Well, that's not even fair, Nana."

"Hey, it's just once a week. Let your Nana take care of you."

I move in and give her a hug. "Thank you, I appreciate you."

And I do. This strikes me as incredibly odd considering how I felt about my grandmothers before moving home.

Nana used to scare the bejesus out of me. I knew she claimed to be a witch, and that was enough for me to write her off as the crazy lady living in the trailer out in the woods. Or possibly worse, an actual witch. While other kids hid that their grandfather was a drunk and their brothers did meth, I was petrified that someone would remind my friends that my Nana is a witch.

Granny, though I had fond memories of staying with her in the summers on the farm, I couldn't relate to in the least. An uber-conservative holy roller isn't the sort of person an enlightened, college-educated young woman wants to burn a couple of hours visiting. I had better things to do than sit on the porch and watch the ryegrass grow.

Never have I been so wrong.

It's as if I am half of each of the two extraordinary women —their scared and unsure half, for sure. I didn't inherit their mental strength and commitment to their beliefs. My brothers seemed to have taken all of that gene by the time Mama got around to making me.

Still, I got their curiosity and ability to adapt to what the world throws at us—even though I complain about it.

And, of course, I got their paranormal "gifts." Skills they have spent untold patient hours explaining to me the past few months. Advising me on how to bring them forward and, just as importantly, bring them to bear in a controlled manner.

Thinking about what they have meant to me as I have struggled with this surge of abnormal skills and power makes my eyes water with gratitude.

Nana cocks her head as she studies me. She smiles and asks, "Did you have anything interesting happen this week?"

I roll my eyes as I shake my head. "Oh, please. I have so many things to ask you about it's not even funny."

Nana stirs the gravy. "Perfect. That should make for some enjoyable conversation over good food."

"It's obvious you two are going to act like this is a normal occurrence," Dusty says as he comes into the kitchen, still holding his tonic. "But I would really like to know what I witnessed out there at the bridge."

"That was the drowned little girl, the ghost I keep telling you about, Dusty."

He shakes his head. "Okay. Little girls don't open up their mouth like an anaconda and show rows of great-white teeth."

I try to contain it, but I laugh at his current state of fear. "That just means she likes you."

Dusty shakes his head. "No. I'm not going to let you make light of this. She most certainly did not like me."

"Yes, she does. She is sweet on you, dude."

"And those two shriveled-up old broads with the—?" He forms a hand-bra at his navel.

"Watch yourself there, boy. I resemble those remarks," Nana says as she fixes our plates.

"What were they?"

"They were the reason I needed to come out and talk to Nana tonight," I say.

"Ah, you ran into a new entity?" Nana asks.

"More like they're stalking me," I say.

Dusty interjects, "But what about the missing section in the bridge?"

"What's the matter with the bridge?" Nana asks.

"It's missing about a four-foot section of its boards."

"Oh my gosh, I need to call the Sheriff and tell him to close it off." Nana picks up her phone to call.

"It might've been a hallucination," I offer.

"Hallucination or not, it's best the Sheriff checks it out, April."

I can't argue with her logic. I would hate for someone to have an accident and get seriously hurt.

Dusty crosses his arms. "But what about the ramp?"

"What about it?"

"Where did it come from?"

To not be rude, I decide to answer Dusty. But I'll be darned if I'm going to spend a bunch of time explaining it. I tap a finger to my head.

My answer leaves Dusty with a dumb look on his face. It is priceless. I only wish I had a photo.

I hand Dusty a plate of pork chops and mashed potatoes. "Have some food. It'll make you feel better."

If I hoped Nana would put my mind at ease, she does precisely the opposite. She urges me to discuss both the grays and the demon at the theater with Granny tomorrow.

She makes Dusty and me a charm pouch for protection but advises that it will have a limited effect against demons or spirits working in conjunction with demons. Again, not what I desire to hear, considering how the grays seem to be tracking me.

Nana agrees that they may be stalking me, especially after telling her about Antoine. She says that it would only make sense that they would be attracted to my powers. My "gifts" would act the same as GPS for them, and being as strong as they are, be considered a threat. Something to be eliminated or captured.

"And you agree with Dusty, Nana? You believe we are dealing with a demon in Shelbyville?" I ask as we stand at her front door.

"There's always the possibility it could be something else. But the probability runs toward the demonic."

"Something else like a different type of ghost?" I feel my spirits rise as I hope I saw something other than a demon on the film footage from the Imperial.

Nana's face tightens as her brow furrows. "Oh no, honey. I'm talking about demigods. Demons can be nasty, foul creatures and extremely dangerous, but they are nothing compared to the alternative."

That is not what I want to hear right now. Here I had come to Nana's in hopes of getting answers, and instead, I will walk away with more questions than what I had when I arrived.

She waves her hand dismissively. "But again, that's your Granny's skill set." She gives a shoulder shake. "All that stuff makes me feel like someone stepped on my grave."

Nana moves closer and gives me a hug. "You be good now, and don't forget to go by and talk to Loretta tomorrow. If it is a demon, she'll know what to do to help you."

"I hear you, but I don't know that she's run in that circle for a while. I doubt if she would know anybody that could help now."

Dusty stands opposite me. His face screws up dramatically. "April, Granny's the best expeller east of the Mississippi."

I burst into a bout of laughter. Dusty is such a card. I don't know how he can joke about such things, given we're both going to be in danger in Shelbyville. And I know he's mentioned it before that Granny dabbled as an expeller, but come on—a demon?

Neither Dusty nor Nana is laughing.

"What?" I ask as I sober.

"It's true. Loretta and I have our differences, but she is the most talented exorcist I have ever known."

I look uneasily between the two of them. "*Riiight.* Because every demon fears a five-foot-tall granny with a white powder-puff hair helmet."

"Think what you want," Nana says as she turns her attention to Dusty and gives him a hug. "Keep your eyes open, big'un. Don't let your sister get you into any trouble you can't get out of."

"I'll take care of her."

I shouldn't have let them get my goat, but some folks don't know when to stop their nonsense. Most talented exorcist—I'm so sure.

Yes, Granny has confirmed that she has some abilities to cast out demons. Honestly, though, she hardly speaks of it and only when I directly question her.

These two want me to believe that Granny's a peer of Lorraine Warren. I expect as much from Dusty, or even Chase. My brothers' sole purpose in life has always been to punk me. But, Nana?

I can't believe she would assist him.

Stomping down the porch, the freezing air slaps the warmth from my skin. As I yank on my car door, locked, I can sense them watching. I can't see them, but I feel their keen interest, and it sends a shiver up my spine.

"What are you so sore about? We got the information you needed and a free meal." Dusty opens the passenger door.

I raise my hand to shush him. "Do you feel it?"

Dusty studies my face. "Yeah, I'm feeling a little gassy myself."

Why are my brothers perpetually goofy? "No," I hiss. "Do you not feel them watching us?"

Dusty spins around. "Who?"

"Well, don't look."

"Well, then how am I supposed to see?" Dusty complains.

"Never mind." I get into the car and slam the door.

"Man, if I knew you were going to be like this, I would've just stayed at the house."

"Don't give me that. You now have a potential new case at the Willoughby bridge." I raise my finger in the air as I raise my eyebrows. "Oh, and as an extra bonus, you and Nana got to play a joke on April. Ha, ha, ha."

"What joke?"

I start the car and do a three-point turn in the gravel. "Oh, I don't know, maybe that Granny is the best exorcist this side of the Mississippi?"

"She is. Everybody knows that."

"Everybody knows that..." I mock him.

"Fine. If you don't believe me, you don't believe me." When I turn right coming out of the driveway, he asks, "Where are you going?"

"Home," I say curtly.

"You turned the wrong way."

"Not when I'm going around the mountain and through Grant to get home."

Dusty shakes his head. "For Pete's sake, it's going to take forever to get home."

"At least we'll get home," I grumble.

Dusty lets his seat back as he turns his head toward the passenger window. He begins a light snore almost immediately.

I suppose I should take it as a compliment that he feels comfortable enough to sleep given the poor driving conditions. Then again, he may be sufficiently perturbed with me that he would rather fake sleep to avoid any further conversation with me.

Fine. I wouldn't care to talk to me either in my current cantankerous state.

Something besides the grays tracking me has me on an emotional pendulum lately. I wish I could identify what it is since it is making it quite challenging to be the "new and improved" April I want so desperately to become.

I steal a look at my brother. His head has lolled to the side, and his mouth is open wide enough to drop a ping pong ball through without touching his lips.

That's a good thing since the road conditions are treacherous, and I need to check if Lee ever called. Whenever I look at a text while driving, Dusty acts like I'll wipe out three Greyhound buses and kill two hundred and thirteen people because I'm distracted.

That's so silly. I'm perfectly capable of giving my full attention to two things simultaneously.

There is no text from Lee. I wish I could say it doesn't matter, but it crushes my heart. I realize I might not be going to Baltimore after all.

I could call and try to make up with Lee. I could tell Lee that I'm sorry—but sorry for what? I was doing my job. If he can't understand that, what am I supposed to do?

Does he expect me to sit around the house and wait on every one of his needs? Sure, some days that sounds like a fairly good gig, but I still have aspirations of my own. I might not be planning on being the most-sought-after defense attorney in the South anymore. I will be the best in the mid-Atlantic area if I go with Lee.

Yes, the location may change, but the goal is still there in my DNA.

If Lee can't let me be my own person and give me the latitude to do my job correctly, maybe my boneheaded brother Chase is right after all. Perhaps Lee and I are incompatible.

Put that in your pipe and smoke it, April.

Man, my life sucks. Why can't I get traction with any of my long-term goals? How do I go from being so excited that things are going my way to being right back where I was when I borrowed Shane's truck to come home to Guntersville?

Again, the pendulum effect in my life.

It's the paranormal events I'm forced to deal with constantly. That's what is bringing—has been bringing—these swings into my life.

You know I don't even want to do the paranormal. It scares me. It has always given me a severe case of the heebie-jeebies.

Still, I needed the cash, which is my issue, and I'll own it. That's why I chose to help Dusty. But that paycheck does not give him the right to make fun of me.

If our working relationship was not so close to the end, we would need to realign the rules on how we interact with one another. I might not be Mr. Big Shot Paranormal Writer. Still,

I've earned my stripes as a valuable associate, and he shouldn't spread false information as a joke.

True, it isn't the first time someone in the family has alluded to Granny having significant powers. She's also helped me hone my manifestation abilities. Which is a powerful skill.

But the best exorcist this side of the Mississippi? Why do Nana and Dusty believe I'm so incredibly gullible?

Then Nana puts the cherry on top by saying, "Be happy if it's a demon, better than the alternative, it could be a demigod or even a god." Yeah right.

Sure, everybody teases April. Hardy, harr, harr. Never mind, we nearly lost our lives on Willoughby bridge minutes earlier or that I had some crazy old chick naked on all fours waiting on top of my car the other night. No, we can still make fun that demons can be afraid of little white-haired ladies.

I draw in a deep breath and release it slowly. I roll my head side to side to release the tension in my neck.

Memories from my past flash slowly through my mind. The first time I heard a voice in my head—the old man in the river grabbing my ankle—Nana's knowledge of how to build mind partitions. The flashes increase their pace until each is a blur, which I hold intimately dear as part of my history.

The deck flips its last card. It shows Nana's expression as she tells me about things worse than demons. There is no humor in her eyes. All I see is concern and profound sadness.

Peaches! What if I've been wrong?

A wave of vertigo overcomes me as an epiphany—that I desperately want to discount—rolls into my mind. There's something larger at play in Guntersville—that involves me—and I have missed the clues all along.

Chapter 24

The lights are on at the lake house as I turn my car up my parents' driveway. I see both of my parents' cars. I'm surprised they are back from Gatlinburg, then remember tomorrow is Friday.

Dusty wakes when I stop the car. Stretching his arms, he says, "That didn't take near as long as I thought it would."

I get out of the car and walk toward my apartment. I do not want to sleep alone tonight. It's odd how quickly I became acclimated to sleeping with Lee.

I consider sleeping in my parents' home so I don't feel isolated, but they may still be unpacking and settling in from their trip. If I crash on the sofa in the den, they might feel they have to be quiet, so I can sleep. I don't want to inconvenience them.

"Hey, do you have time to go visit with Granny in the morning?"

"Are you serious? I've got a law office to run." After my epiphany, I need time to regroup before layering on any additional information.

Dusty narrows his gaze as he runs his hand through his hair. "We're leaving for Bellefonte at three. You're going to be able to make the trip. Right?"

"As long as everything goes fine at the office. Fridays are always a wildcard."

"Are you ditching me?"

"No." Maybe. I don't know.

He moves toward me. "I know you're leaving in a few weeks, but I really want you to go with us this weekend."

"I'm not saying no, but if I don't, you've got to figure out what you're going to do in a few weeks anyway."

His eyebrows shoot up as he releases a short laugh. "Oh. Okay." He rubs his hand across his mouth. "Well, we're leaving at three. I would love for you to come with us if you can."

"Yeah," I say on an exhale.

"All right, have a good night." Dusty walks toward the glass door of the lake house.

"Thank you again for going tonight," I yell to him.

He lifts a thumbs-up gesture into the air without turning toward me. I watch as he opens the glass door and turns out the light on the porch.

I feel lousy and am not motivated to do anything productive tonight. I scan a couple of my favorite retail sites, but nothing catches my eye. I check social media for thirty minutes. Inexplicably, somehow, that makes me feel even worse about my situation.

Lee Darby or no Lee Darby, I have to get out of this town. Especially if I am right that I am at the center of the supernaturalism in Guntersville.

I slip the crucifix Liza gave me around my neck and pad over to my refrigerator. I dig in the freezer, moving around several nearly empty containers of ice cream.

Pulling the two Tupperware containers of ice forward, I swallow so hard I hear it in my ears. I stroke the crucifix I'm clutching in my left hand with my thumb.

Inside their separate blocks of ice, both items come to life as they sense my proximity. The amulet changes from its "at rest" bruised-purple color and turns red as it emanates dazzling pink rays lighting the freezer's interior.

The surface of my vision stone roils as the cloudy white crystal turns transparent, opening sight into future and current events. It senses my attention and shows me Lee's face.

I promised myself I would stay here a couple of months when I ran back from Atlanta with my tail between my legs. I was no longer the same confident woman who left Alabama with my Juris Doctorate.

The events in Atlanta damaged me. They made me question everyone and doubt my own abilities.

Moving home had only exacerbated my condition. Wounded as I was, it was all too easy to fall back into the role of the pampered Southern princess I was when I left for college. It was too easy for me to be Ralph and Vivian's daughter or Chase and Dusty's kid sister again—not April Snow, professional attorney.

Atlanta marked another "first" that has proved tragic. Shane was the first man I wanted who put me in the friend zone. It's okay now. I'm getting used to him as strictly a platonic relationship, but only because he *is* such a thoughtful individual.

Still, that first-time event had me questioning myself, too. Suddenly it was as if I *had* to have a man in my life.

That fueled a reaction where I allowed things to speed up too quickly. I allowed myself to think long-term before I knew the men and had a tight grip on their goals and expectations for our potential relationship. Essential questions like what do you do at the hospital, or are you married, and of course, do you have a cute son that looks just like you?

I groan as I put my forehead against the top of the cold rim of the freezer. I am such an idiot.

The vision stone swirls, whipping Lee's face away and replacing it with a jack-o-lantern. The vision makes me smile, forcing a crease in my gloomy disposition.

Yes. Summer on the lake was a blast, and the next thing I knew, it was Halloween, one of my favorite seasons at home.

Thanksgiving, my favorite meal, was a few weeks after that. And let's be serious, who can leave at Christmas time? Not to mention I had thirteen weeks' worth of Alabama football overlaying those incredible holidays.

And here I am in Guntersville a year later. It wasn't an accident. I made choices all along.

However, I had not planned on Lee Darby and a move to Baltimore.

Does Lee Darby and Baltimore fit neatly into my life plan? Before yesterday it seemed to like a glove.

Now, I'm not so sure.

I knew better than to fall in love with Lee Darby. Not because he's Lee Darby. Just a man in general. I have so many things I want to accomplish, I don't have time to work in a personal relationship.

This Christmas fling was doomed to fail regardless of what man had come into my life. It's nobody's fault. It's strictly a case of great idea, terrible timing.

If not Lee Darby, why Baltimore? Sure, my friend Marty works in DC, but there wouldn't be a need to be in Baltimore. Why limit myself?

It's time to broaden the job search again. That should help speed up my exodus from Guntersville. Hopefully, that will let things return to normal for my home town and me.

It was fun while it lasted.

I pick up the three ice cream tubs separately. The butter pecan is the heaviest, so I select it. I begin to shut the door and stop.

Why not?

I know that each has its own addictive qualities.

That's why I encased them in ice. In the event I got the itch to use them, I'd be forced to wait and hopefully return to my senses before they thaw.

Still, I'm leaving as soon as I find a job. I will be leaving all this paranormal funny business behind and be normal like I always wanted. I can leave the artifacts with Granny to stow when I leave.

Also, I have some right dangerous adversaries tracking me down for reasons I don't know. Extra juice and a heads up could be the difference between surviving the next few days or getting a permanent residence at Whispering Willows cemetery.

I set the tub of ice cream down and fish each of the Tupperware containers out, putting them on my dinette, too. I retrieve a large spoon and commence to improve my attitude with butter pecan.

I scrape the older, darker skin off the butter pecan, and it tastes better. Propping my elbows on the table, I eat directly from the container as I keep a close watch on the two artifacts.

The dog door flips up, and Puppy comes into my apartment. "Hey, buddy. How have you been?"

He wags his butt as he approaches me. He focuses on the ice cream container and spoon. He turns and trots toward his doggy door.

"Hey, stay in here and keep me company."

The doggie door slams behind him. I think Puppy realizes that ice cream equals drama. Puppy doesn't do drama.

It's alright. Daddy always told me I couldn't count on other people to make me happy. Likewise, he impressed the importance of understanding you can't make other people happy, either. He would coach that we are each responsible for ensuring our own happiness, and if we are successful at it, we might cast some sunshine to encourage others to be happy.

When Daddy would tell me this, it always convinced me I was adopted.

Now I think I get his point. I am all that I can control—and too often, I am out of control. It's time April focuses on April and doing better. Everything else will happen as it will.

I'm startled to see that the block of ice the amulet was in has completely melted. I dip my hand in the surprisingly warm water to retrieve it.

Tingling tendrils of energy work their way up my arm and

settle at the base of my skull. A sudden dopamine release triggers a warm sensation throughout my core.

I laugh as I watch the last drops of water drip from the scrolled gold casing that holds the glowing stone. Why did I ever put this up? It feels so good.

Separating the chain, I duck my head through. As the warm stone settles on top of my crucifix, I stand. Becoming used to the increased dopamine surge, the urge to giggle has left me.

I've worn the piece before, but it did not have this effect on me last year. Then, I knew it was of great power, a dangerous magical tool. Despite my dead aunt's urging that I was the heir to the amulet, it always felt borrowed and too potent.

Now I feel like what can only be explained as an apex predator. I feel taller, faster, and stronger.

Curious, I walk to my full-length mirror to see what has changed. Nope, same height with the same start of a muffin top I went to work with this morning.

I step closer to the mirror. Squinting, I lean in for an even closer look. The lighting in my apartment is casting an odd glare from my skin.

I move in several directions, and the result is the same. My skin has a faint glow to it.

I'm not sure how I feel about this new side effect. Could this be harmful? Could it cause cancer? I reach for the amulet to remove it and notice it is purple, its resting color. As I pull the chain over my head, the stone turns red again as the weird glow leaves my skin.

Thank goodness. At least the condition is not permanent.

I consider what to do with the artifact. It would be impossible to wear, even though the urge to do so is compelling. It's not like I can go around glowing. It would be particularly awkward at night.

There's only one answer. So, I slide the stone back into the water. I'll refreeze it tonight.

Some things are best left alone.

It's a shame since I felt like a superhero as soon as I slid it around my neck. That was cool, but the only superhero power I need is the ability to get innocent people out of jail—legally.

My fingers continue to tingle as if there is too much blood in them. The sensation is similar to after I light a fire with my magic. Still, I haven't used any since I was waiting on Chase yesterday.

Something small to practice. I should practice control.

I know plenty of energy is accessible before I begin. I can smell the ionization of a surplus of energy floating in my apartment.

It whips about me as I center myself and draw the surplus into my chest—I remind myself to keep it small—and clamp down tight on the request as I visualize it.

The *tic-tic-tic* of the watermelon seeds falling onto the table makes me proud of myself. I was trying for five, and there are less than two hundred on the table.

"Stage two," I mumble.

Without touching them, I separate a seed from the pile. As it approaches the edge of the table, I make a flicking motion with my finger, sending the seed across the room and bouncing off the far wall.

I repeat the process over and over. I'm able to build the velocity and accuracy of the seeds as I aim at the wastebasket next to my closet. Seed after seed makes a satisfying ping as it strikes the outside of the stainless-steel container.

That's some extraordinary control.

A noise startles me, and I send a seed through the drywall across the room. "Fudge."

I fret about the hole I'll have to fix as I wait to catch the noise again. Footsteps coming up the driveway.

Moving to the counter, I retrieve a knife and wait. Someone knocks on the door.

Bless it, Dusty. I guess I will have to pinky swear I am going with him tomorrow, or he will not let it be.

I set the knife on the table and pull open the door. "I said I'll go with you if—" I take a step back in shock.

"We need to talk," Lee says. "Can I come in?"

Talk about what? I gesture for him to enter without saying anything. I put the lid on what's left of my ice cream and put it and the Tupperware back in the freezer.

Lee moves forward, bracing himself against my counter. "About last night."

Here we go. "If you expect me to apologize for doing my job last night, we really don't have anything to talk about," I say.

"What?" Lee shakes his head. "Lord, no. No, April. That's just it. I realized I was really being selfish last night. It has nothing to do with the fact you were working. I know how you are about your career, and it's one of the things I like about you. You want to be productive. You want to do things of value."

I raise my hands palm up. "Then what was that all about?"

Lee stares at the floor. "I don't know. I just really like spending time with you. When I think I'm going to get to hang out with you and something goes wrong, it *really* frustrates me.

"Then I get all these insecurities floating around in my head about maybe she doesn't love me, or maybe she doesn't want to spend time with me, or maybe this is a temporary thing for her. But for me, it's not. When I'm with you, I feel at peace for the first time in my life. I feel like I know who I am. And then, when I'm not with you, I feel lost and disinterested in everything."

I'm so confused. It's like Lee read my mind and repeated it right back to me. "Are you serious?" I croak.

He looks up from the floor. "Yeah. I'm afraid I am, and it scares the living daylights out of me."

I fight back a sniffle. "I'm scared, too."

"Can you forgive me?"

"Only if you promise to be fairer next time. I felt awful all last night and today, and I was only doing my job."

He nods. "I know. I'm sorry. I never want to make you feel bad."

I wipe at my nose. "Okay."

He steps toward me with open arms. "Can I have a hug?"
I move in and give him the hug we both need.

Chapter 25

I wake and shower in the morning while Lee sleeps in my bed. As I dry my hair, Puppy comes into the apartment, starts to jump on the bed, notices Lee, and huffs.

Puppy stares at me with accusing eyes. He head butts the doggie door on his way out.

A familiar uneasy feeling bubbles up from my gut, washing away all the warmth from last night's makeup sex. I wish it were only that my dog disapproves of Lee, and I still need to convince Lee that Puppy and I are a package deal.

It's the one percent hesitation factor I have with Lee. The "yes, he's perfect, except…" feeling I have inside. But except for what?

I huff as I shake my head. Picking up my brush, I do my best to push it from my mind. There will be plenty of time to ponder the question once I get the last details of my Guntersville life in order.

If I plan to leave with Dusty today at three, which I should to keep our relationship intact, I must get a handle on all the paperwork that piled up while I was searching yesterday for Bailey. Besides, I want to check with the Huntsville police and see if they uncovered any leads on Ivy.

If she is smart, she will have already ducked out of the country because I'm not sure Roman will hold his anger in check. Heck, I'm not so sure I wouldn't beat her to within an inch of her life if I saw her myself.

I kiss Lee on the forehead and whisper that I will see him tonight. I suppose we'll go back to his lake house now that we have cleared the air about our feelings.

I close my door and see Barbara slowly sliding the glass door to my parents' home closed, her shoes dangling from her other hand.

"Busted," I tease as I walk toward my car.

Startled, she turns and rolls her eyes. "It's not like that."

"That's what I always tell myself, too."

"Whatever." She laughs and leans against the porch railing to pull her shoes on.

For someone who claims it isn't like that, she sure does have the shine as if it *is* like that. "Don't be a stranger now that you remember where we live."

She waves at me. "Have a blessed day, April."

Barbara code for "mind your own business." I would tease her some more, but I have some lawyering to do.

Driving into town, what Shane told me begins to itch at the shadowy corners of my brain. The fact Dottie has already paid for the cremation of Gil. How? Dottie has zero savings.

Something isn't right with that. One more odd thing making me believe my client is not telling me the truth.

Luckily, I know exactly who can help me with several mysteries that continue to pinball in my mind. I have come to understand that experience isn't only about getting more proficient at your job. It's also about learning whom you can get information from when you need it.

I unlock the front door of Snow and Associates, collect the

mail accumulating on the floor from the door mail slot, and make my way to my desk. I get situated and call Elsa Long.

Elsa was recommended to me by Mama when I needed help determining the valuation of a client's business—which turned up an off offshore and off the books bank account. Mama has the talents of every resident of Marshall County indexed in her mind. It's sort of scary, and very useful.

Elsa is the flesh-and-blood brunette version of a Barbie doll. Except if Barbie was a feminist.

She's also one of the most brilliant people I have known. That's saying a lot, as I have been exposed to many intelligent people in my life.

Nowadays, Elsa is a work-from-home CPA. I believe I bought that line the first time I met her. The longer I work in my profession and see that often things are not as they seem on the surface, I don't really think Elsa is a CPA. Her profession might be really close to that acronym. It would probably be spot on if I replace the P with an I.

How else can I explain her being able to track down a supposedly anonymous bank account on an undisclosed Caribbean Island in a matter of hours?

Adding additional credibility to my thoughts that she is CIA, the woman looks like she could kick Conor McGregor's butt, run a marathon, and then kick McGregor's butt a second time without breaking a sweat. She is the last woman in the world I would pick a fight with.

"Long, CPA."

"Elsa, it's April Snow. How are you?"

"Doing well. You?"

I grin. It is funny to hear Elsa do small talk. It is probably like shoving needles in her eyeballs. "Great, thank you for asking."

"So..."

"I was wondering if you might be able to do some research for me again."

"Research," she says like she has no idea what I'm asking.

"Find out if one of my clients has an account they're not

disclosing?"

"Oh. *Research.* Okay. I was sitting here binge-watching *Hart of Dixie* because it's an incredibly slow day at the office. I was hoping someone would call and ask me to do some research for them."

"Really? What great timing. But *Hart of Dixie* really is a great show. What season are you in?"

"April, that was sarcasm, dear."

There isn't a spot of skin on me that doesn't heat with embarrassment. "Well, of course. I was just joking."

Elsa lets out an aggravated breath. "I'm sorry to be such a witch. I've been submerged in this special project for the last forty-eight hours straight. Now that you call, I don't know when was the last time I ate, and I don't think I've had a shower this week."

That forces an involuntary shudder from me as I consider that Elsa wouldn't have any stubble on her legs like I would after a week of not showering. She is always all-natural. The woman has leg hair that would make a golf course rough envious.

"I'm sorry I bothered you. I'll figure out some other way to handle it."

"Oh, bollocks." She huffs. "I've obviously hit a brain bubble here. Working on some quick and easy project would do me some good and let me look at my employer's spreadsheet with a fresh eye afterward."

"Are you serious?"

"April, when have you known me not to be serious?"

Like never. "Thank you. This means a lot to me."

"Oh, you owe me. I'll have to think about how you can pay me back."

That causes an uneasy tickle across my chest. "We'll figure something out."

"Yes, I'm sure we will. Now, who's your subject?"

"She's a local, Dottie Castle."

Elsa grunts. "Is she that blue-haired widow who used to own

car lots?"

"Yes."

Elsa lets out a delighted cackle that sounds remarkably close to how I imagine a witch would sound. "Oh, this is going to be fun. I do not like that woman."

"Do you know her personally?"

"She tried to hire me three years ago for a job, and I turned her down. Then the egotistical woman reported me to the Better Business Bureau."

"Did it damage your business?"

"Nah, I went in and deleted her report and posted several rave reviews instead. Then I shut down all of her credit cards for kicks and giggles."

Elsa has an odd way of entertaining herself. I feel like a laggard for binge-watching shows at my parents' lake house. "Are you sure you can work it in?"

"Oh yeah. I need to take a break and get something to eat anyway."

Maybe take a shower, too. "Thank you, Elsa."

"No problem, love. I'll call you as soon as I'm done."

I hang up with Elsa and question what in the heck I'm doing. My job is to defend Dottie, not to convict her. Maybe Dottie does have some hidden savings accounts in offshore banks she squirreled away. Perhaps she doesn't. Either way, it does not answer the question driving my behavior.

Did she kill her husband?

The trouble is, I'm her defense attorney. It has nothing to do with the truth. My job, and what should be my only question, is can the DA prove that Dottie killed Gil. That is all, as a professional, I should be concerned about.

Still, I've got to know.

I'm going to defend Dottie either way since I have been assigned her case. But I *need* to know if she's guilty or not for my own peace of mind.

Chapter 26

I set about the task of going through the mail. I want to make sure there aren't any bills needing to be paid or any old-fashioned payments by check among all the advertisements. This has been one of my duties at Howard's law office from the beginning.

At first, it aggravated me that I had to do basic bookkeeping as part of my job. Now I find it relaxing in a mind-numbing sort of way.

I pull out the three checks from the pile, as well as the power bill and the Internet bill. I make out the deposit slip and set up the two invoices for payment. I'll drop off the deposit on the way out to meet Dusty this afternoon.

That is assuming I remain motivated to go to Bellefonte tonight. I still haven't fully committed in my mind, although I am leaning toward going with the team.

Paranormal excursions have become like a drug to me. I hate the supernatural, and it really messes with my mind. Still, I have a difficult time not going when I know the rest of the team is headed out for a research trip. There is something about the camaraderie and the adrenaline rush that has me loading up into the van every time. Even when I have been swearing all week, I'm not going.

I understand it sounds conflicted. But that's the story of my life.

Before closing the online bank account, I review the company's cash flow and current savings. We are flush. We have made a handsome profit in the last few months. Business is excellent.

It wasn't always this way. When I first started, we were running a small deficit. Our cash flow was weak due to Howard's aversion to collections. I was constantly worried if Howard could afford to have me working for him.

Now I look at the books and wonder how Howard can consider closing the business. I mean, I'm sure he makes a nice profit selling pizzas, but it seems like you must sell a lot of pizzas to cover what we've been clearing at the end of each month. I know I wouldn't mind putting it in my bank account if it were my business.

To each his own, though, and it's Howard's decision. I just hope that he never regrets his decision.

My emails are a mess. I attempted to keep up with most of them yesterday, but there is still a slew of them I didn't read. I clamp my teeth as I come across an unopened email from Judge Phillips's office. Antoine Lattimore's hearing is scheduled for ten o'clock this morning. I look at the clock in the bottom right hand of my PC screen—9:35.

Peaches! I've got to double-time it to Judge Phillips's chamber. I slide my laptop into my backpack and yank my purse out of the bottom drawer.

Normally I would walk to the courthouse, but I hop into my car and drive the two blocks. As I approach the courthouse, I pray for a parking space.

There is one available. Unfortunately, it has a blue handicap sign mounted in front of it.

I can't let Antoine Lattimore spend the weekend in jail because I couldn't get to his trial on time. Surely, I won't be more than an hour. Nobody should mind. What is the probability someone will need the spot?

Guilt and shame suffocate me like a wet blanket over my head as I put my car in park.

Fudge! How can I possibly be "good" when there are so many things to consider, and I have more on my plate than I can say grace over.

I back my car out, nearly side-swiping a minivan, and rev the engine as I race to the parking deck. My IROC bottoms out as I turn off the street into the garage since I forgot about the gully for stormwater.

At a full sprint, I take off toward the courthouse in heels, focusing on staying on the balls of my feet. I focus my vision straight ahead, ignoring the folks I pass who gawk at me as if I am running from an assassin.

A sizable bead of sweat races down my spine as I slam into Judge Phillips's courtroom door. It flies open, hits the backstop, and vibrates back toward me, making the most annoying sound that echoes throughout the room. I always forget the door to Judge Phillips's chamber is looser than the others.

Antoine is seated at the defense table, and Katie Tipton, Lane's newest prosecuting attorney, stands at the opposite table. I take my seat next to Antoine and nod to Katie.

"I was worried you weren't going to show up," Antoine whispers.

I give Antoine my best "as if" expression. "I wouldn't leave you hanging, Antoine. I'm here for you."

"I need to tell you something," Antoine says.

"That you're thrilled you have the best defense attorney in Guntersville?" I tease.

"Sure, that. But probably more important is that the demon is not waiting outside the city any longer."

The hairs on my arms stand up. "He's in the city?"

"No. He's waiting in a different city. That's why the grays have left."

I guess it's a good thing the demon has set his sights on another town? Or maybe Antoine really is crazy, and I'm on the verge of following him down the same rabbit hole. Sometimes it's difficult to tell when people are crazy or truly gifted with supernatural sight. Bless it, I know my visions usually make me feel like I'm going crazy, and they're often as clear as mud.

Judge Phillips enters the courtroom, and Hal, the bailiff, calls us to order.

I turn to Antoine. "That will have to wait. We've got to get you out of jail first."

Antoine nods in agreement.

Judge Phillips addresses Katie first. I don't know her that well. She recently came on board when Lane secured a temporary position exception. Katie is a nondescript thirty-something who moved to Alabama when her dad retired from his job in Connecticut and the family moved south.

Katie does a commendable job explaining the state's contention that Antoine committed a felony. Still, she isn't going to win any litigation awards. Her delivery is monotone. I can tell even Judge Phillips, a stickler for courtroom decorum is about to nod off if she doesn't inflect her voice more.

It startles me when Judge Phillips calls my name. I must have fallen asleep with my eyes open. "Yes, Your Honor?"

"How does your client plead to the charges of impersonating a police officer and reckless endangerment?"

I have a spontaneous moment of clarity. "Your Honor, my client pleads not guilty to reckless endangerment. I would like that charge dismissed because there is insufficient evidence that Antoine Lattimore caused or was in the position to cause anybody harm.

"To the charge of impersonating a police officer, we plan on pleading no contest with the stipulation that my client is charged with a misdemeanor rather than the normal class C felony. Mr. Lattimore, while dressed in a vintage *Atlanta* police officer uniform, did not attempt any act as a police officer while in uniform. Again, if the prosecution cannot prove that he was attempting an act, the charges would need to be thrown out."

Judge Phillips angles his nearly bald head. "Counselor Snow, is your client pleading no contest to the impersonation of an officer, or are you making a case for the charge to be thrown out."

Good question. It would be a question I would be better prepared for if I had known the trial was at ten this morning. I wish I had the time to review his file again. "Your Honor, I'm going to move to throw out the impersonating an officer charge as well. Criminal code 13A-10-11 states explicitly that the suspect must commit an act while in the uniform. My discussion with the arresting officer revealed Mr. Lattimore was simply driving his vehicle. He was pulled over for an expired tag."

Judge Phillips raises his eyebrows. "Is that your final answer, Counselor Snow?"

"Yes, sir."

"Now that we have that settled." He shuffles papers around on his desk and raises a gray sheet of paper. "This is the written affidavit from Sheriff Becky Gray. Counselor Snow, her account backs up your claims."

He addresses Katie, "Counselor Tipton, before I rule, is there anything else the state wishes to enter into the record?"

She shakes her head slowly. "No, Your Honor."

"Very well, I'm going to move to dismiss the charges at this time." Judge Phillips looks pointedly at Antoine. "Sir, I hope you put that uniform away for good. If you ever come back in here and I know you wore that uniform, I will make sure you spend some significant time in jail. Our citizens must know who their police officers are. It is a dangerous game you're playing. Do you understand?"

Antoine nods. "Yes, Your Honor."

Judge Phillips slams his gavel. "I move to dismiss all charges against Mr. Lattimore. This court is adjourned."

I stand until Judge Phillips disappears into his antechamber.

"What does that mean?" Antoine asks.

"It means you're a free man. However, if they ever catch you with that uniform on again, they'll pour you into a concrete slab under the jail."

He clicks his tongue. "Harsh."

"So, what are you going to do now?" I ask him.

He shrugs. "I'm not sure. I don't like being here without protection, but Mama seems to think I'm supposed to be here for some reason. Maybe supposed to be here with you."

"I doubt that." I look around and notice we are the last in the courtroom. "Are you sure you'll be okay?"

"Sure. I'll manage."

I'm racking my brain trying to think of options for Antoine. The best one I can think of is going back to Atlanta and living with his aunt. There isn't anything left for him here in Guntersville. My phone rings, interrupting my thoughts.

I answer, "April Snow."

"Did I get you at an inconvenient time?"

I grin in anticipation. "What did you find out?"

Antoine taps me on the shoulder and waves goodbye. I return the gesture.

"Well," Elsa extends the word uncharacteristically for her. "As we all suspect, Dottie Castle is not who we think she is."

"What's her real name?"

Elsa actually chuckles. "No, love. I mean, she's not the goodie two shoes widow that we all believe her to be, and she's definitely not broke."

That penny-pinching, complaining, overbearing woman. I consider all the times I changed her will for free.

"Are you serious?"

"Love, I have already asked you once today. When have you known me not to be serious?"

I've got to stop asking that. "How rich is rich?"

"What I've been able to track down so far looks to be somewhere in the neighborhood of between sixteen and seventeen million."

I choke on my saliva. I was expecting to hear Dottie had sixteen or seventeen *thousand*. Perhaps, on the outside chance, something like fifty thousand. To hear Dottie has as much as seventeen million in the bank makes me want to throttle her. She could live an extravagant life, and I'm doing lawyer services for her for free.

Where is the justice in that?

"Are you okay?"

"Yeah. I'm just madder than I've been in ages. I've been doing free legal work for that woman."

"Oh, don't feel special. Ten percent of this town has done something free for *that* woman. I probably would've ended up doing something, too, if I hadn't already known she was impossible to work for."

A funny suspicion comes into my mind. "Who told you about her?"

Elsa is silent for the longest moment, and I think she won't answer me.

"Vander. Vander told me about her."

Makes sense since she knows him. If he knew, why didn't he warn me? Did I ever mention her to him?

Hearing his name from someone besides the echo in my head makes me melancholy. "Have you heard from him lately?"

"Lord, please. Are you looking for him?" Elsa sucks in a breath of air. "Oh, my gosh! You're sweet on him. How cute."

"No, I'm not. I'm engaged."

"Being engaged doesn't make you not have the hots for somebody."

"It does when you're in love with your fiancé," I correct her.

"Sorry. That's a misnomer. Vows really don't control the lust meter. People say they do. But people lie all the time."

"Why would I lie about being in love with my fiancé?" I notice my voice getting shriller.

"I didn't say you lied. I said people lie. Is there something you need to come clean about? I'm all ears."

"What? I don't know..." I sputter.

"Hey, don't get me wrong. I get it. If I were straight, I'd ride Vander like a rodeo champion. He's kinda handsome in a dark, bad boy sort of way. I know a lot of girls are all into that whole Mr. Mysterious thing."

"I am not into Vander!"

"Because you have a fiancé. But if you *didn't*, you would be into Vander—wait"—Elsa guffaws—"would that be *he* is *into* you?"

Oh, she's driving me crazy. "I didn't say that."

"You didn't need to, love. I can tell by the way you asked if I heard from him. And I bet if I could see you, I would see a pretty blush across your chest."

I cover my neck with my hand. "I asked like a friend who wants to know what is happening with him."

"Have you heard from Vander?" Elsa mocks with a breathy, sexual undertone. "I can only dream that you ask people about me with that same tone."

"Whatever. You're just mean."

Elsa lets loose another one of those weird witch cackles. "Are you just figuring that out?"

No, but I had forgotten. Bless anybody unfortunate enough to be Elsa's sibling. It would've been impossible to grow up with her. "I'm glad I could be such great entertainment for you."

Her tone changes dramatically. "Oh, don't be that way. I was only playing with you. I'll send the information I found about the bank accounts over to you. If you want to give her a major tweak, we can always contact the IRS. I don't see where any of this money has had taxes paid on it."

Oh, that's a crafty bit of leverage I can use with Dottie. "Thank you, Elsa. I do appreciate you taking time out of your schedule for this."

"It came at a good time. I needed the distraction." She lets out a soft sigh. "Well, I've got to get back into the torture chamber. My boss is a jealous god."

The vision of Elsa in a full-body latex suit, high-heeled boots, and a whip in her hand pops into my mind at her mention of a torture chamber. Great. It will take me a thousand years to un-see that.

Chapter 27

So, Dottie is a multimillionaire, after all. More importantly, she is a conniving, secretive fraud. As if I hadn't thought that from the moment I met her.

The question is, what are you going to do about it now, April Snow?

I know what I'm going to do. I'm going to defend her. That's what you do when you're a defense attorney. You get your clients cleared of the charges leveled against them.

This does change the game plan, though. Since I no longer believe in Dottie's innocence, my play is to throw enough shade on other people in Gil's life to take the spotlight off of Dottie.

There will be twelve jurors hearing the case. I only need one of them to believe the DA has insufficiently proven the case against Dottie and be dogged in their conviction.

I have to sit. The dirtiness of defending a woman I believe to be guilty makes me ill.

Maybe it's Pollyannaish, but I always held an image of being a good lawyer. The one who brings truth and clarity to a situation so my innocent defendant can go home to their family.

Now, to do my job, I must introduce confusion and doubt into the process. All to allow a mean, old, probably murderous octogenarian to live out her life in relative luxury. The new job description sucks. There isn't any way to sugarcoat it.

Maybe I *can* sugarcoat it. Petit Fours and Pimento is around the corner. If Tonya Bryant is in today, there will be some awesome cupcakes in the bakery. My experience is, there is little in the world a cupcake can't fix.

There is something special about holding a miniature cake in your hand especially made for you. Not a slice of some community cake, your *own* private, fist-sized cake complete with an inch of pure sugar and butter icing and special seasonal sugar candies on the top.

Yeah, forget lunch. It is time for a cupcake fix.

As I walk across the crosswalk, I double-check to ensure no car is coming. Since my close call with Dusty's ex-wife, Bethany, I have this uneasiness that she is lying in wait, ready to run me over with her Mercedes crossover. I know it's irrational, but so is some people's fear of spiders. To each their own.

Walking into Petit Fours and Pimento, I swear I can taste the sugar on my tongue. I don't have to ask if Tonya is in. Whipped butter and sugar hang in the air like some sort of magical air freshener.

I scan the menu for the lunch side, so it's not overly apparent that I'm a sugar junky in need of a fix. Chicken and dumplings is today's special. That is one of my favorites, and I consider opting for lunch and a small sugar cookie. That would be the responsible decision.

I opt for full-force sugar therapy and turn toward the bakery section.

Tonya is a sturdily built brunette about my height with a perpetual smile. What isn't to smile about when you are surrounded by pastries all day? She swaps out an empty tray in the case for a fresh tray of cream horns.

She stands, and our eyes meet. "April Snow, I haven't seen you since before Christmas."

"Did your girls enjoy Christmas?" I ask.

Tonya rolls her eyes. "Their mee-mom spoils them so much."

"I hear that's what grandparents are supposed to do."

She raises her eyebrows as she purses her lips. "All I know is that's not the same woman who raised me, and surely not the same woman who kicked me out of the house when I got pregnant."

"She has to make amends some time, Tonya."

Tonya giggles. "Lord, don't you know that's the truth."

I'm biting my thumbnail while reviewing all the possible choices. Truthfully, I have moved past choices and am considering combinations.

"The petit fours were put out this morning, and you saw I just brought out the cream horns. Of course, if you're feeling adventurous, I have a really healthy banana nut, and a very popular bran muffin. Judge Phillips gets one every day."

As constipated as Judge Phillips acts in court somedays, he should start eating two. I'm not interested in the muffin. They won't help my sugar therapy quest.

"Cupcake?" I'm shocked to hear my own voice. I thought I was thinking it.

"I was just decorating them." Tonya gestures toward a dozen softball-sized cupcakes on the counter behind her. "I have chocolate, strawberry, white cake, and German chocolate."

"Yes, please," I say with a laugh.

Tonya's smile dims. "Are you having a tough day?"

I blow out a frustrated breath. "I've actually had a few things go my way today, so I should be grateful. Still, everything is going by so fast, and I can't figure out how to get off this train."

Tonya's smile reappears as she laughs. "Very carefully is all I have to say about that. It seems like the train's always been going too fast for me to hop off."

"I know. Right?"

"I suppose the key is to make sure you get on the right train to start with."

I raise my hands above my shoulders. "Yeah, but it's not like they are conveniently labeled."

Tonya juts her chin out as she smirks. "Oh, I think we know what train we're getting on. We just choose to ignore the signs."

Dang it if there isn't a lot of truth in that. It's not like anybody has forced me on any of the trains I've been riding. I've always been a willing passenger at the start.

"Well, if nothing else, I am a responsible sugar pusher. No, you can't have all the cupcakes. Which *one* would you like?"

Man, a health-conscious pastry chef is as rare as a defense attorney who requires an innocent client. We are both doomed in our chosen profession.

My eyes dart from one delicious cupcake to the next, and I feel close to having a panic attack. I have to have the German chocolate—that is a must. Still, the strawberry looks especially unique and tasty. I could use some uniqueness right now. "I want the German chocolate for me, but I'm going to take the strawberry to Dusty. I'm going on a road trip with him later this afternoon."

Tonya favors me a droll stare. "Alright, your call, April Snow. I just hope you don't do anything you'll regret." She boxes the two cupcakes for me and rings me up.

As I lift the pink box, I smile at the significant weight. That German chocolate isn't going to last very long. "I'll see you later, Tonya."

Friday is always busy at Petit Fours and Pimento, and I struggle to find even an open countertop stool when I hear my name. When I turn, Randy gestures for me to come toward him. I do an internal eye roll. I just want to eat my German chocolate cupcake in peace.

Reluctantly, I step toward him and see that Jackie is sitting with him. Our eyes lock, and where I half expect her to narrow her eyes in a glare, she gestures me over, too. Darn it, now I don't have a choice.

I remember what the ghost of Christmas present showed me during Christmas. And I appreciate the fact that Jackie and

Randy still consider me a friend even though I know I'm less than perfect. But I don't need friends at this moment. I need a quiet place where I can devour my cupcake.

Oh, get over yourself, April. How difficult is it to just be friendly and neighborly for a few minutes?

What's the point of learning that you're a loser in the friendship department if you won't start to make small baby steps toward improving? I wave as I approach them. "How are my favorite two newlyweds?"

"Awesome," Randy gushes.

"We're figuring it all out," Jackie says.

Randy pushes a chair out for me and motions toward it. "Sit down. It's hard to find a seat in here this time on a Friday."

I check Jackie quickly. She gestures emphatically for me to sit down.

"You really don't mind?" I ask more to her than Randy.

"Oh, no. Randy and I eat here every Friday just like clockwork."

Jackie's tone is a little peeved-sounding. I know it has nothing to do with my appearance at their table and everything to do with a ritual that has already lost its shine.

Bless his heart, Randy is a super sweet guy, but he can also be OCD about his schedule. While we dated, I don't think we ever saw a movie at any time other than the seven o'clock showing on Saturday. If it's what works for Randy, there's no point in changing it.

"Ever since I started working at the hardware store, it's a lot easier to have lunch with Jackie on our Friday afternoon date."

Randy working at the hardware store is news to me. "You're not doing bodywork at Lou's anymore?"

"I still help him on the weekend if he's running behind, but you can't do that work forever. Besides, there's a lot of toxins in the paint."

Randy has some issues, but I doubt they were caused by paint. If I were to guess, it is more to do with genetics. "And you like working at the hardware store?"

"It's okay. I've got a lot to learn, but Mr. and Mrs. Rains are great teachers. Besides, someone has to take it over when they retire."

I look at Jackie. "Your parents are getting ready to retire?"

Jackie shakes her head and purses her lips. "No."

"We're looking to buy a house," Randy announces.

"Really? Where at?"

Randy glances sideways at Jackie before he continues, "I want to buy a house over by my mama. That way, when we have babies, she can take care of them for us."

"Your mom is not watching our kids, Randy," Jackie insists with a mouthful of BLT.

"Why not? It's a perfect setup."

"No, it's not. And we've been over this already about a thousand times."

Randy grins as he cuts his hamburger in quarters. "Maybe a thousand more times, and you'll see what a perfect plan it is."

I take the opportunity to unpack my German chocolate cupcake. It is gorgeous, but so is the strawberry one, and I linger before closing the top of the box. I look up and find Jackie is eyeing me. I know the look.

"Is everything okay, April?"

"Yeah, things are going great." I'm hoping if I keep telling myself that I will believe it eventually.

"I heard through the grapevine that you and Lee Darby might be moving up north. Is that true?" she asks.

"Well, it's not really up north," I scoff. "It's only Maryland. But yes, we're supposed to be moving in the next few weeks."

"That's good. I'm happy for you," Jackie says. "I hope everything works out for you two."

"Thanks." Perhaps the friend thing isn't as difficult as I thought.

I'm beginning to see a common thread in my life. Complicated relationships can become pleasurable if you don't avoid them.

Chapter 28

After my cupcake break with Jackie Rains, now Jackie Rains Leath, I realize what is bringing me down is my client Dottie Castle. I can't stomach the idea of having to act as if I believe her innocent while defending her. I'm not a saint, and I'm surely not above a white lie, but I need to have an honest conversation with her. I need her to be aware I know she killed Gil.

I know it won't fix anything. But for some odd reason, I have a burning desire to see her expression when I call her out. She needs to know that I am doing my job as a professional, but I'm no rube.

I'm so lathered up I don't even bother with the courtesy of calling her in advance. Besides, I *want* her surprised.

Her old luxury sedan is tucked away in her carport, so I know she is home as I ring the front doorbell.

My aggravation with Dottie rises another notch as a tiny middle-aged woman with a heavy accent opens the door. I pass judgment on Dottie again, Lord help me, as I suspect she is not paying this woman a fair wage for her services.

That's a fair assessment, given she is paying me nothing for being her defense attorney while she holds millions in reserve. It's safe to say Dottie is also abusing her house cleaning service, knowing Dottie's dollar-clutching habits.

"Hi, is Ms. Castle available?"

"She said that if it's her lawyer to tell you that she is asleep. Are you her lawyer?"

"Oh, no. I'm her new banker, and I need to talk to her about some investments I don't want her to miss out on," I say.

The woman narrows her left eye as she appears to appraise my response carefully before nodding. "She is in the kitchen." She pulls the door open and gestures me into the home.

Now that I have been invited in, I will go exact my pound of flesh. I stride toward the kitchen, and the maid, unconcerned, walks in the opposite direction.

As I near the kitchen, I hear Dottie call, "Felicia, was that her?"

"You're darn tootin' it is." I step into the kitchen and savor the shocked look on Dottie's face. "Hiding from your attorney is not the best way to build trust. Just an FYI."

Dottie glares at me. "I wasn't hiding from you. I have a horrendous headache. I can't bear to sit through one of those hideous interview processes again and relive you dragging out the details of my poor departed husband's untimely demise."

"I know. I wish I didn't enjoy torturing you so much, Dottie."

Dottie shifts her head back as she thrusts her bony chest out. "Are you sassing me?"

"It's called sarcasm, dear." Oh, I like the way that one rolls off my tongue. I'm going to have to thank Elsa for that.

"I declare. I suppose I'll need to call Howard and inform him of his niece's behavior."

"Please. See if you can get him away from the pizza dough long enough to care. You'd be a better woman than me."

"I see." Her eyes fill with contempt as her lips form a thin, frosted-pink line.

"Oh, I doubt you do. But I promise you will be enlightened after this conversation."

"What are you talking about?" Dottie asks.

I brace against the kitchen center island. "It's time you and I have a come-to-Jesus moment."

Dottie shudders as her eyes open wider. "Have you been

drinking?"

"No, just eating cupcakes."

Her drawn-on eyebrows draw together as she mouths the word cupcake in apparent confusion.

"I'm going to defend you regardless, Dottie. But you need to be truthful with me and admit that you killed Gil."

"I killed Gil?"

"We both know you did."

Her eyebrows jump toward her hairline. "We do?"

"Come on, Dottie. Enough of the lying. Just come clean and tell me."

"Sure, as soon as you tell me why in the world I would kill my loving husband."

A brief laugh escapes me. "I can think of about sixteen million little reasons down in Nevis. And I'm not talking about drinks or palm trees."

What little bit of coloring Dottie has drains out of her. "I don't have the faintest idea what you're talking about. Quite frankly, I have had quite enough of this conversation with your conjecturing and accusations."

Un-freaking-believable. The level of some people's privilege obviously runs so deep they believe they can continually tell the same lies, and eventually, people will believe them. Well, I'm about to pop this woman's privilege bubble in a big way.

"You're going to sit there and continue to lie to me?" I ask.

Dottie points in the direction of the front door. Her finger is shaking. "No. You will remove yourself from my home this instant, or I'll call the authorities. Oh, and I'm getting a different defense attorney."

"I don't think so. At least not a free public defender. Once I tell the district attorney about your offshore funds, I believe he will request you hire your own attorney."

"You will do no such thing!" Dottie challenges me.

I feel my face stretch into a wide, demented smile I'm sure is worthy of the villain in any horror flick. "I cannot think of anything I will enjoy more." I raise my finger. "Wait, I thought of something I will enjoy even more."

We stare at each other for a moment before she asks, "What is that?"

"I cannot wait to call the IRS and tell them that there are sixteen million dollars of untaxed earnings in a Caribbean bank account owned by Dottie Castle."

Where Dottie previously turned the color of flour, her face now takes on a green hue. "You would do that to a poor old woman? Where is your compassion?"

"I guess I lost it when my client decided to lie to me."

"You don't understand. I know your family. I know your background. You've always had everything you need. You can't possibly understand where I came from."

My face contorts. "What? That gives you the right to kill somebody?"

"I'm not saying that—"

My phone rings. I glance at the screen.

Mother of pearl! Can this day get any more whacked?

I motion for Dottie to hold up. I draw a deep breath as I reread the screen and note the time, 3:05.

I can't believe I'm holding up Dusty's team.

I answer. "I'm on my way. Where do you want to meet?"

"Are you closer to the house or the Marina?" Dusty asks.

"The marina."

"Good. Meet us there. I'll ask Chase to get your car back to the house."

"Thank you. I'm sorry I'm running late."

"No worries. I'm only glad you are making the trip with us."

I hang up and fix Dottie with an "all business" stare. "I have to leave right now, but we're not done. I suggest you think about your answer long and hard before we talk again."

Chapter 29

Dusty calling was fortuitous for Dottie. I was about to grab a handful of her white, cotton-ball topknot and have a serious "tell me the truth, or you'll be wishing you did" conversation with her. I will defend her, but I'll be darned if she will continue lying to me.

I pull into the marina parking lot and realize it has been three months since I visited. The new drydock storage building Chase began constructing during the Fourth of July holiday is up and operational. I see the paranormal team's van at the back of the parking lot. My brother Chase is leaning against the driver's door, talking to Dusty.

I pull up close to the van. *Dagnabbit.* I didn't pack anything for the overnight. I can't go.

I get out and walk around to the driver's side of the van. "I can't go."

Chase and Dusty break off their conversation. "What's the matter?" Dusty asks.

"I didn't pack anything to change into."

Dusty looks me up and down. I can tell he thinks I can wear the same clothes for three days.

"No. I'm going home and packing, or I'm not going at all."

Dusty frowns. "We're going to lose light here in an hour. I'd hate to set up the site in the dark."

Chase taps his hand on the open van window. "Did you say it

was up at Bellefonte?"

"Yeah."

"Shoot. I can run her to the lake house and then run her up to the turnoff for the nuclear site. That way, it won't hold you guys up."

Dusty winces. "Are you sure? I hate to put you out."

"No, it's fine. It won't take me that long to drive round trip. Besides, April is right. She won't be comfortable with what she's wearing now. You can't expect her to go camping in a business suit."

Dusty looks from me to Chase and nods. "Alright, we'll go on to the site and get our campsite set up."

"I expect a hot dog once I get up there. I like mine crispy black," Chase says as he pats Dusty's arm.

Chase turns and holds his hand palm up toward me. "The keys to the pumpkin, please, Cinderella."

"It's okay. I'll drive." Chase is a very conscientious driver when anyone other than family is in the car. All bets are off if it's Dusty or me in the vehicle with him.

He shakes his finger from side to side. "That's not the way it works. I called first dibs."

I hesitate but relinquish my keys. I don't have a choice. Everyone knows that you can never break first dibs. It's a law.

"Have you heard anything else on your dead puppy case?" Chase asks as we leave the parking lot.

"No, not yet. But I'm going to assume it signals the end of the divorce negotiations. There's nothing left to be divided."

"Yeah, but they're gonna put that crazy lady in jail, aren't they?"

I shrug. "I don't know, Chase. It's really not any of my business what the prosecutor wants to do."

"Geez. How do you let all that go so easy?"

Good question. I'm starting to believe I don't, and that's part of what's tearing me apart on the inside. "It's part of the job description, I guess."

Chase turns his attention back to driving as he grumbles.

"Well, that part of your job kind of bites."

Tell me about it. There's been a lot of things in my life lately that don't make a lot of sense.

Thankfully, Chase does not follow me into my apartment when we arrive at the lake house. I pull out my small carry-on and pack the essentials. Underwear, yoga pants, sweatshirts, hoodie, and sports bras. I shove an older pair of tennis shoes in the bag while I lace up my hiking boots with the jeans I changed into.

I step outside with my backpack. Chase is throwing a tennis ball for Puppy.

That's one more thing I need to decide. Puppy technically is mine. But Puppy sees himself as his own being and has become more a family dog than an April-only dog.

At least that's what I'm telling myself. But I might be trying to justify leaving him at his home rather than cooping him up in a small apartment in Baltimore.

He loves my family, and he loves the lake. It's a painful decision. The idea of living without him makes me hurt as I watch Chase wrestle the tennis ball from Puppy's mouth and toss it again.

"Hey, I'm ready when you are," I announce.

Chase tilts his chin up in acknowledgment. "See you in a couple of hours, Fang. Stay out of trouble."

I get into my car. I have long given up on trying to get Chase to call Puppy by his correct name. When you're a Snow, you learn to pick your battles at an early age.

"That's pretty lucky that y'all's event is so close to home this time."

"Oh yeah. Otherwise, I wouldn't be able to go," I agree.

"What are you hunting for out there? Aliens that glow in the dark from the nuclear plant?"

Oh, Chase. "We're not going to the nuclear reactor. We're

going to the town."

Chase scoffs. "There's no town out there. Just the reactors."

I look out the passenger window. "I'm just going on what Dusty says. He believes there are ruins of an abandoned town to research. He says it was burned down by the Union troops."

"For real? That's actually sort of interesting."

"I didn't realize you were a history buff."

"I'm not. But I like to know about the towns around me."

"Then you should go with us," I tell him.

"I don't know. We'll see."

"Did Barbara go home?"

Chase nods his head. "She had to go into work today."

"Are you officially an item now?"

Chase shoots me an "as if" expression. "Why would you even ask that?"

I can't conceal my grin. "I don't know. Maybe that she was sneaking out of the house this morning?"

"It's called being respectful and not wanting to wake up Mom and Dad."

"You sure? Because I kinda thought like..." I make a vulgar gesture with my hands.

"Lord, April, grow up. It's not like that," Chase says with an eye roll.

"Sure does seem like an awful lot of people are telling me it's not like that when it looks just like that."

The speed of my vehicle is increasing. "I think you just need to pay attention to your relationship, and everything will be fine for you."

"I am paying attention to my relationship."

"Lee seemed pretty bent the other night."

I smiled. "Yeah, until he showed up at my door begging for forgiveness, and then we had crazy makeup sex."

Chase's face twists. "Oh, for Pete's sake, TMI."

"What? Does it embarrass you that your little sister is having sex with her fiancé?" I tease.

We are hurtling down State Highway 72 in excess of one

hundred miles an hour. The car dances to the left briefly as we fly around a cluster of four cars doing the speed limit. The pine trees on either side fly by so fast on the shoulder of the two-lane road they are only dark brown, gray, and green blurs.

I want to punch Chase on the arm and tell him to stop it. But at this speed, the slightest flinch could put us into the shoulder and then flip us into the trees. It would be a spectacular, albeit quick, death. I'm not ready to leave just yet.

As the towers of the never-activated nuclear reactors come into view, Chase backs down the speed. "I did an excellent job on her. I didn't hear a single screw loose," Chase comments on his bodywork of my IROC.

"Oh, there's plenty of screws loose in this car, but they all belong to you."

Chase laughs. "Don't be a spoilsport."

"I wasn't the one trying to kill us."

"Sometimes a man needs some peace and quiet."

"You could've just asked," I grumble.

A three-story brick structure comes into view. It has a chain-link fence built around it. "That's awfully big and tall for an abandoned house fireplace," Chase says.

I see the van with two of the pup tents already up. "There they are." I point.

As we come around the corner toward the van, I identify everyone. There is Luis, Miles and Liza, Chet and the Early brothers. There is also a short, white-haired woman. I gesture toward her. "Is that Granny?"

"Yeah. Dusty said something about you were supposed to meet him at her house this morning to discuss something. She decided to ride up with the team."

I cover my face with my hands. "Bless."

"What's the matter?"

"My life is moving too fast, Chase. I can't seem to catch up with it." I grimace at Granny in her powder-blue polyester pants and hiking boots. "Is it safe for her to be out here?"

"Are you for real? She's your granny, not an invalid."

"I'm just saying. It seems like she is at that stage of life where she should be slowing down."

Chase gestures in the direction of Granny as he parks the car. "We are talking about Granny Snow. Right? Because I don't think she is one to slow down."

As much as I hate to admit it, Chase is right. Granny isn't exactly one to sit back take things slow, at least until it is sunset time on her porch.

Before I can get out of the car, my phone rings. Chase motions for me to go ahead and take my call. He opens his door and moves to the trunk of my car.

"Hey, baby."

"Hi, what do you want for dinner?" Lee asks.

"Uh, I think Dusty is planning on us cooking on the campfire," I answer.

There is a long, tense pause. "What are you talking about?"

"The paranormal team. I told you I was going with them this weekend. We're up at Bellefonte."

"Why?"

"Because we check on paranormal disturbances."

"So, you won't be home tonight?"

He's a little slow at times, folks, but he does finally get it. "No. We're camping here at Bellefonte, and then Saturday night, we will be in Shelbyville. I'll be home Sunday night."

"When did this happen?"

"I texted you the schedule earlier this week."

Lee's voice goes up an octave. "I don't remember getting this text that you're talking about. But I do remember being at your apartment last night, and the least you could've done was mentioned it to me."

My voice becomes louder. "Why would I mention it to you when you've already got my calendar? There's no reason for me to beat you over the head with information."

"Obviously, there is. I don't remember ever hearing about this. What am I supposed to do this weekend?"

"I don't know—go pitch?"

"Don't even."

"What? I was just trying to be helpful."

"You know what, forget it. You don't want to be here, I get it. I'm not going to be the stupid fiancé pining for his girlfriend to come home."

"Lee, I sent you the information."

"April, I didn't get it. But I don't care. Have a great weekend. Obviously, you're with people that mean more than me."

"How can you even—" He is gone. I stare at my phone in disbelief. What just happened?

Tell me how we go from him showing up at my apartment begging for forgiveness last night, foot-cramping sex, and me thinking wonderful thoughts all day only to have it blown up because he didn't remember I would be gone all weekend. This is teetering on the edge of ridiculous. As much as I love Lee, I can't deal with making sure he knows where I am twenty-four seven.

"Trouble in paradise?" Chase asks as he leans his head into the car.

I open my mouth wide to say something, but I'm speechless.

"I hate to be the one to tell you I told you so, April."

"Then don't."

"I can tell he's one of those guys who likes for his partner to be home. He's not going to do well with you leaving him by himself in the evenings."

"I'm supposed to change what I do for a living and the time schedule for those things simply because he wants me conveniently around in case he wants company?"

Chase frowns. "Lord, no. But what you're supposed to do is find a guy who understands and doesn't make you feel guilty every time you need to do something on your own."

I open my car door and yank my backpack out. "Chase, how about you do everyone a favor and save your advice for people who ask for it."

"All right," he says, shutting the car door. "I think you're upset because I'm spot on."

"I think I'm upset because my boyfriend is becoming impossible to keep happy."

Chapter 30

Looking out to my left, I see the Bellefonte Towers. A multibillion-dollar project that has never created the first kilowatt of power. What should have been a boon for this town ended up being the biggest of teases.

Granny and Liza are talking next to a fire that makes more smoke than flame. As I approach, I say, "I wasn't expecting to see you here. Were you looking for a side job, Granny?"

Granny gives me a quick hug and a kiss on the forehead. "Dusty described to me what you have going on in Shelbyville. I thought it best if I travel with you."

"Your grandmother thinks that it might be a mid-level demon," Liza remarks.

"Or it could've just been a really odd shadow on the back of the wall," I say.

"That's always a possibility," Liza says. "Still, the whole time we were closing up, I felt like something was watching us. Like it was waiting for us to leave."

A cold tingle runs up my spine. What I wouldn't do to go back to that night and insist more strenuously that we continue the site's blessing. Liza felt it, too. Unfortunately, that bodes well for Granny's theory of a demon being present at the Imperial. "We did our best with the information we had, Liza."

"*Ahí está mi loca belleza rubia,*" Luis says as he embraces me. He smells like coffee and pepper.

"You're not so bad yourself, Luis. And I'm not crazy. I'm stressed," I answer him.

"You're way too beautiful to be stressed. The world should be your oyster."

"Flattery will get you anything you want. I'm a girl presently with a low self-esteem." I can't believe that popped out of my mouth.

He favors me with a smile that crinkles the laugh lines framing his big dark eyes. "This too shall pass. You're a strong woman, April Snow." He points toward Liza. "You're almost as strong as Liza and a lot nicer than her."

"Who brought the food to this picnic?" Chase hollers as he strides toward the van.

Chase is always thinking of his stomach. As much as he eats, he should weigh 500 pounds. To be fair, my cupcakes are starting to wear off, and I could use a hot dog, too. "Are you hungry?"

Liza exhales loudly. "Might as well eat. This place is dead as a doornail."

Between the angry phone call from Lee, the advice I didn't ask for from Chase, and seeing all my friends, I neglect to mentally scan the energy in the area. Realizing my error, I calm myself and pull my powers inward.

I lower the partition of my mind, preparing to push out with my collected energy. Residual emotions tumble into me, crashing roughly and sparking raw, sympathetic emotions.

I do not know if there will be any ghosts or dancing lights on this excursion. Still, there are plenty of residual energy fields to investigate.

I don't see any point in mentioning it to the others. Describing residual energy fields to readers won't exactly sell books for Dusty. Presently it is like a montage of voices saying the same thing repeatedly but overlaid on one another. I can decipher some of the statements. But for the most part, they are rather mundane.

There is, however, a strong pull toward the north side of the fields. The energy is pulling me in the direction past the three-story chimney up on a knoll spotted with gnarled old oak trees. I point toward the trees. "Cemetery?"

Liza and Granny nod.

"You don't feel it?"

"Feel what?" Liza asks.

"Nothing, I guess. I thought I felt something pulling me in that direction."

"Do you want to go check it out?" Liza's eyebrows raise.

"No, I want to get some food in my stomach first."

As if I summoned him, Chase walks from behind the van with four fire pit forks in either hand with a hot dog on the end of each.

"Who wants to eat a weenie?" Chase chants.

If I wasn't so hungry, I would be disgusted at him. Instead, I walk over and grab one of the forks from him. "Thanks."

After dinner, the team walks the grounds of the old town. The city has disintegrated into mounds of bricks.

The only structure still standing is the three-story fireplace that was supposed to be for a large boardinghouse. A hundred years is a long time for something to be abandoned.

Miles sat with me during dinner and explained that the town had been a thriving enterprise until the 1860s when Union troops quartered here and stripped the county of all resources. If that wasn't enough, they went ahead and burned the town down on their way out.

The town never fully recovered from the Union occupation. To add insult to injury, the rail line that was run later was put five miles to the north, and Scottsboro was created. What little bit of commerce was left in Bellefonte moved at that time, and by 1920, there wasn't a single soul still living in Bellefonte.

The only residents now are in the city's cemetery. I'm being drawn toward the knoll where the cemetery is located. The sensation is more than a nudge. It's a pull.

I consider going to bed and leaving it be, but instead ask Liza, "Do you want to check out the cemetery?"

She rolls her shoulder. "I don't know. I'm kinda sleepy."

"I want to go," Granny, who is sitting next to her, says.

"Are you sure, Granny?"

She stands and brushes off the back of her pants. "I'm positive."

"Oh fine, you overachievers," Liza grumbles as she stands. "The fire is too warm anyway."

I consider letting the boys know, but they are so involved in their conversation around the van I don't see the point in interrupting them. Besides, I sense only the standard cemetery sort of vibes. I'm not receiving anything that would indicate we might experience something worth recording.

"It's a good thing we are headed to Shelbyville tomorrow," Liza comments.

"Why would you say that?" I ask.

Liza snorts. "Because we *know* something is there. This place is quiet."

"Speaking of overachiever, I seem to recall someone was considering turning in her ghostbuster badge the last time we were in Shelbyville."

"Hmm ... things change. It's amazing how your perspective can change when you have the right help," Liza says.

Dusty did everything he could to encourage Liza to stay with the team when she quit New Year's Eve. It was a devastating loss for the team.

They struggled through the next few months as the contract for the television show went into effect. While the cases were satisfactory and the show received good ratings, the team wasn't the same. It was as if the team's spirit had been sucked out of it, leaving us all hollow.

Then after having no contact with the team for two months, Liza showed up at my parents' house asking Dusty when the next project was and what we should expect to encounter. She acted as if she had only been away for the weekend.

That's one positive about hanging around Liza. She may be odder than even me.

Since coming back, while she has always been a competent practitioner of her craft, she has been more confident. It's hard for me to judge, but I get the feeling her powers are also more significant than when she left. But again, I'm but a newbie in the skill set she utilizes. It may be a simple case of control envy on my part.

Granny holds up her hand. "Do you hear that?" We freeze in our tracks and listen.

I believe I hear something, but I can't distinguish it because it is too faint.

Liza is the first to speak up. "Weeping?"

Granny nods and gestures for us to follow her. The area is saturated with moisture, the ground so soft it clumps to the soles of my boots.

The weeping intensifies as we reach the base of the knoll. Starting up the slight incline, the voices begin.

The last thoughts of the living or the greatest regret are spoken repeatedly. It makes me feel as if I am stuck in a sound booth with a fifteen-second tape on a continual loop. The multitude of voices overlay one another in a cacophony of sounds and emotions flooding over me.

Slowly I raise the partition in my mind to squelch most of the noise. It will improve my chance of hearing the voices on this side of the veil and help maintain my sanity.

As I block out the voices originating from the cemetery grounds, the weeping becomes louder to me. "It's on this side of the veil."

"Yes, but faint," Granny says.

Granny pulls up abruptly. Liza and I nearly run into her backside. She grabs onto both of us to steady herself and gestures in front of her.

I can make out the ancient slab tombstone in the faint dusk light that we almost walked across. As I look out further, the area under the large oak trees is littered with hundreds of similar flat gray-and-bone-white stones.

"Abigail Jones, 1792 to 1832. Our beloved mother," Liza reads out loud. She looks over her shoulder. "That's only forty."

"And with more than one child." If things don't work out with Lee and me, I will be doing well to have a child *before* I'm forty, much less have multiple.

Granny steps around the stone, weaving her way through the cemetery, careful not to step on graves. I realize she still has extraordinary dexterity for a woman her age as I follow her.

"It's a little to the left," Liza tells her.

I still hear the faint weeping, but I'm also picking up another louder sound. "Do y'all hear water?"

Granny climbs up another small hill and is at the peak of the cemetery. "Sure enough." She points down the other side of the knoll. "There's a small stream running behind the cemetery."

"What manner of idiots bury their dead next to a stream?" I ask.

Liza giggles uncontrollably. "Well, now we know the rest of the story."

Her using the famous line from one of my daddy's favorite radio shows brings a smile to my face. "I give. What's the rest the story?"

Liza flashes a full smile, a rarity before her mysterious absence. I forgot how beautiful she is.

"The Yankees didn't kill off the town, but the backwash from the cemetery into their drinking water did."

My face contorts into a grimace. "Oh, that is so gross. I think I'm gonna be sick."

"Shhh. Y'all hush your mouths," Granny hisses as she crouches.

Instinctively, I hunch over and share a look with Liza. She shrugs and duck walks up the knoll toward Granny. I follow.

Granny has dropped down onto her knees and hands, intent on something down by the river. I go to all fours next to Liza.

A soft-blue hue illuminates the base of the trees by the

swollen stream. Another bout of weeping comes from the direction of the faint glow. I tap Liza on the arm and point toward the light. She nods her head.

I'm expecting to see a shadow or, if the team is fortunate, perhaps a floating orb in the luminescent blue mist by the trees. I am unprepared for the thin apparition carrying a tattered bundle of rags in her arms. I draw back at the clarity of the spirit walking barefoot along the river's edge.

Liza turns to me. "Nearly a full apparition."

I nod in agreement as I continue to watch the pale-blue apparition walk along the stony stream bed. The young woman looks to be only fifteen or sixteen years old. Her hips are not yet flared, and her overall physique is emaciated.

As she walks toward the east, she draws closer to the cemetery and where the three of us are hiding. My eyes are continually drawn down to the intricate details of her bare feet —cut, dirty, and bleeding. I shudder to think how it had to hurt walking on the stones when she was alive.

The weeping woman draws even with us and is positioned between us and the river. She unbundles the rags in her arm.

My breath catches in my lungs as she reveals an impossibly small infant. She clutches the premature child to her chest and releases the most sorrowful weep I have ever heard.

She gazes out over the swollen stream. I realize how this story ended, and I am overwhelmed at the sense of helplessness. I want to stop the inevitable—but this scene took place a hundred and fifty years earlier. There is no stopping the past.

The malnourished woman with the dead baby walks barefoot into the stream. Her body is buffeted by the fast-moving water, and as she nears the center, she falls and disappears under the flowing current.

I remain in a dumbfounded shock as I attempt to square what I just witnessed. A profound sadness washes over me, and I feel like lying down and crying for a few minutes. I believe I have come to the realization there may be too much meanness and pain to bear in the world.

"We'll need to find her burial to help her. We'll need to locate any younger female graves that have babies buried with them," Granny says in a rush of words.

"They wouldn't be buried together," Liza says.

"Why not?" Granny asks.

"The baby will be in the cemetery as long as the body was recovered. Mama committed suicide. She won't be in hallowed ground."

Granny shakes her white helmet hair. "I forget about that at times."

I am working my way back from my trance. "I can't believe we didn't bring the camera crew with us. Do you think we should have them set up?"

"It may be done for the night, but it wouldn't hurt for them to set up and try," Granny says as she rises and slaps the dirt from her knees.

"She looked like a baby," Liza says.

"There was a lot of death and destruction left in the wake of the fighting. Starvation and disease were common in counties where the troops foraged," Granny says matter-of-factly.

I've had enough. I don't want to think about it and be sad any longer. "We can look for her gravestone tomorrow. It could be by the river if I were to guess. Maybe we can help her. I will inform the boys where they need to set the equipment by the river and the cemetery."

I step away, not concerned if they will follow as I make my way down the knoll back into the marshiness of the lower field. I'm in desperate need to be alone with my thoughts as the images of the young mother's feet are etched into my mind.

Chapter 31

Darkness has fully engulfed the small valley we were in, and the moisture hanging in the air makes it feel even colder. I look up at the stars in an attempt to put something happy in my mind.

The human condition tears at my heart some nights. At times it seems like there is an unfathomable amount of meanness in the world. It is as if the world has a fixed amount of evil always present and always striving to be in control no matter how many good people try to love it out of existence.

The fire has all but died down, but the boys' conversation is livelier than ever. They don't see me approaching them. "Y'all might want to get some equipment up there on the hill."

Everyone drops their conversation and turns toward me. "What's going on?" Dusty asks.

"A full female apparition," I inform him.

"No kidding," Miles says as he pushes his glasses up the bridge of his nose. "And here we thought this place was going to be a bust."

Chet and the Early brothers move toward the equipment when Luis says, "We've got this, Dusty."

"You're probably going to want two cameras and two external microphones," I tell them.

"Was it detailed or just a blur?" Dusty asks.

"Very detailed." I pull a water bottle out of the cooler and sit on the cooler's lid.

Dusty and Miles collect their electronic notepads and follow Luis and the rest of the team to the cemetery. They talk excitedly as they go.

"Are you alright?" Chase asks as he sits next to me on the cooler.

I roll the cap of the water bottle in my hand. "I don't know. Some days this stuff just puts me in a funk."

"I get it. It's tough seeing dead people."

I cut my eyes to Chase. "How in the world could you get it, Chase?"

"Well, I've been to enough funerals to know that being around dead people makes me sad. I would think it would be the same if they were dead and in ghost form."

Somehow *that* Chase logic makes perfect sense to me. I always worry about myself when Chase's statements make sense. It's probably an indication I'm on the verge of a nervous breakdown.

"Some days, this stuff just scares me," I admit.

"Well, if it makes you feel any better, it scares me every day."

I glance at him sideways. We both burst into a fit of laughter.

He's such a goof. I love my brother.

Chase points at the blue tent on the opposite side of the fire. "While you were packing your bag, I put my tent and bags in your trunk. If you want, you can bunk with me tonight. We can be scared together."

I laugh again and nod my head. "Yeah, I would like that."

The smell of burning lumber and the acrid smell of fired gunpowder envelop me. The light cavalry rides through town with torches, tossing them indiscriminately on our buildings.

I hug tightly to the brick wall of the old courthouse. I don't understand how I know what the building is, but I do.

The general store owner, Mr. Ferrell, comes warily out of his store and attempts to talk the Union soldiers out of torching his store. One of them draws his service revolver and shoots Mr. Ferrell in the chest without warning. The shop owner drops to his knees as his shirt grows a large, circular red pattern.

Mr. Ferrell's hands frame the growing red stain as he looks at it with an expression of disbelief. The soldiers throw their torches onto his business, but he never notices it.

I'm shaking uncontrollably as if I were caught in a snowstorm. The fear has gripped me to my core and stripped away all my higher functions of thought. I am in an all-out panic when I see one of the Union cavalrymen lift my friend Marissa and throw her across his saddle before he gallops out of town.

I flatten myself further against the brick side of the courthouse, hoping, praying to be invisible. If the good Lord can see fit to get me through this raid, I will never ask for another thing.

The sound of a twig breaking wakes me up. I open my eyes but do not move as I hold my breath, listening for a repeat of the sound.

There is a rustling of leaves on the opposite side of the tent. I look across to Chase. He is sleeping, unaware.

I can feel the power brewing outside the tent. I find it disconcerting that something that powerful and obviously so highly skilled could be stupid. If I'm correct, there are three of them, and they are creeping their way slowly toward the tent, attempting to remain undetected.

Their power is dark and filthy. The texture repulses me when I reach out and touch it, not unlike accidentally putting my hand in someone else's bodily fluids.

With each step closer toward Chase's tent, they become more and more emboldened. They are sure they hold the element of surprise.

If I am going to do anything to stop them, it will need to be now. I can't allow them to fall on my team unaware. If possible,

I must make them turn and run.

My hands shake fiercely as I gather the nerve to attack. Still, I'm so afraid I feel as if I may vomit at any moment.

Cowgirl up, April. You can't afford the luxury of being scared.

Pulling all the swirling chaos into my chest, I attempt to steady myself and develop a game plan. I position myself at the front of the tent with the zipper in hand.

I must move quickly. They outnumber me and are more skilled with their art than I am. I'll only get one attempt to make this work. If I don't, there's no telling what will happen next.

Unzipping the tent, I stride out as if I am a warrior queen in full command of the battlefield. The red eyes of one of the ancient witches are directly in front of me.

I take a step to the left and throw out an energy blast toward the fire pit. The entirety of the camp is lit with bonfire-quality flames, and I watch two of the witches retreat further into the darkness.

I drop the partition in my mind entirely. It is a dangerous move, but I need to communicate to them that I am madder than a wet hen, and they need to leave me alone, or I'll jerk a knot in their tails.

"Leave us in peace or die in pieces!"

Their laughter pierces the clear, cold night air. The sound of their cackling makes the hair on my arms stand on end.

"Thee talks as if thee are in charge," the witch who did not retreat says as she swipes at the fire, sending the camp back into darkness.

"I am in charge when it comes to dispelling you."

The shriveled, naked witch who did not retreat circles to the side of me further from the fire. Her lips draw back, and I see a multitude of sharp teeth in her purple mouth.

She does not move her lips, but I hear her perfectly. "You will serve our master, or you will die."

"Yeah, I hate to disappoint your master, but I already have too many jobs. I'm already busier than a one-legged cat in a sandbox."

"I warn you. Do not toy with me." She takes a step toward me in a threatening manner.

"I don't know what you think you're doing, but me and you are gonna mix," I warn her with false bravado.

She raises her ugly face to the night sky and releases a gosh-awful cackle. "You will find that to your detriment, lock witch. I have studied the dark art for over five hundred years."

"Well, I'll be, and here I wouldn't have put you a day over four hundred." I can feel the other two grays circling behind us even though they have not shown themselves yet. The nastiness of their power weighs on me, and I find myself subconsciously rubbing the crucifix hanging around my neck. The crucifix that Liza gave me on our second excursion. Whenever I touch it, it fills me with love and appreciation.

"There's no point in fighting. My master will own you, lock witch. If you come on your own accord, he will lavish luxurious gifts on you and offer you eternal life."

"I don't want eternal life if I have to look like you. Have you seen yourself?" I ask. "Because it's like you fell out of the ugly tree and hit every branch on the way down."

"You try my patience. I will ask you to come quietly one last time."

I sense the other two close enough to pounce. I have seen their jumping capability previously and know they can strike me at will.

As I stroke my crucifix, an idea pops into my head that makes me smile. The probability of it working is pathetic, given my lack of experience with casting spells. Still, I'm beyond worrying about an errant stream of magic.

I pull all the energy I can hold into my chest and visualize the crucifix. I throw out my powers in three specific cones, striking all three witches simultaneously.

I'm as shocked that I hit them as they are.

The witch communicating with me stumbles backward three steps as she clutches at her chest. She moves her hand out of the way with a scream as if she were touching a hot stovetop.

I watch with morbid glee as the crucifix I hung around the lead gray's neck burns a crucifix brand into her chest.

I scan my flanks and watch the similar reaction by the other two witches. They leap up from the ground they were crawling on and swipe wildly at the crucifixes dangling from their turkey-like necks.

It is a risk because I still have memories of the fire I caused in Birmingham, but I throw a fireball toward the campfire. To my surprise, it works perfectly, and a full blaze appears, illuminating the entire campsite once again.

Between the witches screaming and bright fire, the rest of our team spills out of their tents.

Liza and Granny take a position on my flank, drawing crucifixes while chanting blessings for the team.

The lead witch charges at me on all fours in a creepy-fast bear crawl, and I prepare for a collision with her. She leaps high in the air going over me at the last moment. She continues running as she screams in pain. Her two lieutenants spin and follow her toward the knoll.

"Y'all come back now, you hear. Not!" I yell after them.

I watch as they scamper up the hill and across the cemetery into the oak trees at the river's edge.

Hopefully, they'll run all the way to Chattanooga.

Granny touches my shoulder, and I flinch. "Are you alright, dear?"

I'm shaking so hard my knees threaten to come unbuckled. "Yes, ma'am," I lie.

"That was some seriously nasty magic those witches were dealing with," Granny remarks as she puts her arm around me.

"Why didn't you wake us?" Liza complains.

"I sort of didn't have time."

She has a bout of shoulder shivers. "That's just messed up. Did you see how that one was running?"

"Don't remind me," I say.

Dusty parts Liza and Granny, handing me one of the team's bullpup shotguns. He shakes his head. "I guess we are going to have to always carry these nowadays. I'm sorry. I didn't think this site was active enough to warrant the need for us to have to deal with the guns."

"It's not," I say as I take the proffered weapon. "Those witches have nothing to do with Bellefonte and everything to do with some demon that one of my clients keeps warning me about."

Dusty's brow furrows in confusion.

A sudden wave of exhaustion courses through me. "I'll explain in full tomorrow." I motion over my shoulder to the tent. "But I'm going to get some sleep for now."

I enter the tent before he can ask another question.

Chase is sound asleep inside our tent. I believe he will sleep through Armageddon.

I crawl into my sleeping bag. I know there is no way I can fall asleep after all the excitement, but at the very least, I can lie still and let my body rest as I stare at the shadows outside our tent.

There is no proof of what I told Dusty. It's just my assumption that these scraggly witches following me have something to do with the demon Antoine keeps referring to. I'm not sure if they are the grays, but I certainly could understand Antoine referring to them as grays if he does not know that witches do exist.

What was with the promise of eternal life if I served their master? Eternal life might sound like a pretty good deal if you could appear under thirty for all eternity. Still, if you have to look like some old, dried-up living mummy, the appeal drops precipitously.

One thing is for sure, if they were trying to get my attention, they've got it now. Every twig snap, odd shadow, and moment Chase's breathing is irregular, I tense as if one of those crazy, weird-moving witches is about to jump on me and suck out my life force. It makes it a little challenging to calm down and go to sleep.

Chapter 32

"April."

Someone pokes me in the rib. I flip around quickly, ready to fight the witch off me. Chase recoils, gathers himself, and grins. "You act like the Devil's after you."

Close enough to the real thing as far as I'm concerned. "Why are you poking me?"

He waves toward the tent's zipper door, which is open. "I think your team is about to search for some young mom's gravesite?" He wrinkles his nose. "Or something like that. I'm going to pack up my gear and drive back to town."

I sit up. "Oh, yeah. Sorry about that. Do you want me to help you pack?"

He furrows his brow. "No, I got this. But you might want to run along and help your team."

I zip out of my sleeping bag, pull on my boots, and grab my coat. Stepping out of the tent into the bright morning air, the temperature is at least fifteen degrees cooler, and the wind is howling.

From my vantage point, I see my team at the crest of the knoll in the distance. I hear Chase come out of the tent, and I turn toward him. "Thank you for the help yesterday, Chase. I can't tell you how important it was for the team and me."

He winks. "That's what big brothers are for." He makes a shooing gesture. "Now, run along and play with the rest of your supernatural friends."

I roll my eyes. "Whatever—be safe."

"Play nice."

He's such a goof.

As I walk toward my team, it occurs to me the probability of us finding a grave outside the cemetery is next to zero. In all likelihood, if the young mother were banned from a proper burial in the graveyard, she may not have been afforded a proper tombstone. Her grave may have been marked by a simple wooden placard that has long since deteriorated.

I push my hands further into my coat as I cup my shoulders against the wicked wind blowing in from the north. This winter has been the longest. This may be the year that the once-in-a-lifetime event happens again.

Mama told me that she and Daddy had picked out Savannah for my name. But when a freak snowstorm dropped eight inches of snow in northern Alabama on April 1st—and it took Daddy an hour and a half to drive Mama to the hospital so I could be delivered, they changed my name to April May.

Ever since, I have wanted it to snow on my birthday. I don't know why, but I would prefer for one less thing about the circumstances of my existence to be unusual.

I pass by a small pile of red brick and wonder if it had been a house or some sort of shop.

It is depressing to think of all the structures built by the city's inhabitants. Buildings expected to stand for hundreds of years are now being reclaimed slowly with each rainfall back into the soil.

Nothing stands the test of time. Some days it makes me question why we try so hard to make our mark in the world when it is as fleeting as our name written in the sand on the beach at low tide.

The odd tracks in the mud make me stop. They are where the hardpacked chert gives way to the saturated red clay. They appear to be long-toed human tracks, possibly size seventeen, with some sort of sharp claw at the end of each toe. At least that's what the print looks like. I'm sure they were made by the nasty, gerbil-footed witches during their getaway last night.

I can't focus on them right now. I have work to do. But I would be lying if I said it doesn't give me pause that I have never seen tracks like these before.

It is a struggle to ignore the danger signals tingling up my spine. But the grays are gone. I sent them packing, and they have matching crucifix brands on their chests this morning.

I climb up the knoll and walk to Luis and Miles working on one of the cameras. "Good morning. Did y'all get anything last night?"

"We got the south end of something ugly heading north," Miles says.

That amuses me, and I snort a laugh. "What are you talking about?"

Luis shudders. "Those things you cast out of our campsite last night, they weren't human."

I laugh again. "No kidding, Sherlock. What was your first clue? The fact that they look like they were four hundred years old, or the fact their skin was gray as if they were petrified?"

Luis and Miles share a look. Miles extends his electronic notepad toward me. "No, what was in the campsite may have looked like ancient witches. But that's just how they wanted to appear to you."

I mean to laugh, but it comes out as a strangled croak. What Miles is saying creeps me out.

"Here, you need to look," Miles insists as he pushes the notepad toward me.

"That's okay. I'm good." I wave my hand as I stare past them.

"*Perras demoníacas,*" Luis declares.

The blood chills in my veins. It is the last thing I care to hear. But even in Luis's native tongue, I understand and know he is correct. There is no other explanation for what has been following me.

"I am sorry, April. I didn't want to be the one to tell you. But you need to know."

I favor Luis a droll stare and accept the notepad from Miles. He taps play, and my mind briefly short-circuits as I watch three unidentified beings cross in front of the camera. One stops a few feet from the lens and glares back down the knoll toward the valley where we camped last night.

The bodies of the beings look like a cross between a kangaroo and a T-Rex with grayscale skin. They have long, serpent-like tails and stunted arms with spindly hands. Their faces are humanoid with no eyebrows, extremely swollen lips, and ear holes rather than ears.

"What am I looking at?" I ask Miles.

He huffs. "I have no clue. But your Granny and Liza say they are some sort of low-level demons. Your Granny referred to them as some sort of hunter demons."

"*Perras demoníacas*," Luis says. "My grandmother used to tell tales about them descending on children who did not say their prayers at night and devouring their intestines while the children were alive."

"That's like so twisted I can't comprehend it, Luis. Please stop."

He shrugs. "Eh, it got me to say my prayers every night, and I was not the best of boys."

"But you saw them at the campsite. They didn't look anything like this," I continue.

Luis scratches the back of his head. "Yes, that is probably the difference between their normal state and what they think you will respond to. They are hunters, April. Don't hunters use camouflage?"

"That's rich. They think I will respond to a five-hundred-year-old witch?"

Luis points at the notepad. "Would those things make you feel more comfortable?"

Yeah, no. Whatever Miles captured an image of, it looks like something out of a nightmare. If I had seen it in person, I would never sleep again.

"The point is, whatever they are, they're not what they're

trying to look like. The first rule of trust is, don't trust anything that doesn't appear in its natural state."

Luis is beginning to sound like a commercial for organic vegetables. I salute him. "Yes, sir. If we're good, I'm going to try and find the weeping mother's grave." I turn and put my hands on my hip. "Did y'all get any film footage of her?"

They both frown. "The audio picked up something, but it's too garbled to make out. The video has the slightest blur in the field of scope, but no, we have no full apparition, or partial for that matter."

"Figures. We have a full apparition that most people would have empathy for, but all we get is the weird butt image of three lower-level demons."

Miles shrugs. "I don't make the demons. I just film them."

Granny, Liza, and Dusty are on the opposite side of the knoll, searching by the stream bed. I make my way down the steep slope, grabbing hold of an oak tree root to steady myself.

I fall into line, matching pace with Dusty as he searches the edge of the stream. "What did you think of the film footage?"

He shakes his head without looking at me. "Interesting. I'm not sure if we have enough background information on them, though, to run with that as the story."

"I think you're sort of missing the point that they're not tied to this land."

Dusty turns toward me and cocks his head. "I'm not missing anything, April. I just don't know what we do with it at this point."

We walk a little further down along the water's edge, and I get a tingle. I'm too far away from the cemetery for it to be emanating from there. "Hold up. Do you see anything?"

Dusty makes a slow turn. "Just more of the same."

I frown. "I'm starting to feel something."

Dusty looks about quickly. "Are you expecting those demon

ladies back?"

"No, it's something different." Liza and Granny are fifty feet ahead of me, and I call out, "Granny, Liza, are you two feeling anything?"

They both turn toward us. Granny answers, "Something faint. But I can't identify it."

Yeah, me too. I move forward with Dusty for a few more yards, and the feeling lessens. I tap him on the arm. "Let's backtrack for a moment."

"Are you sure?"

This time, as we backtrack, the sound increases further. It is the sobbing of the lady from last night. It is coming from the far bank of the stream. "Is there a way to get across this?"

Dusty gestures toward the west side of the stream. "We found a ford upstream about two hundred yards."

"I need to get to the other side."

He looks nonplussed and shrugs. "I guess you do what you gotta do. Follow me."

I follow Dusty's lead.

"Bethany's lawyer called and told me you tried to run her over," Dusty says nonchalantly.

First, I'm shocked that Bethany's lawyer would be peddling such poppycock. Second, I'm surprised Dusty would wait this long to bring it up if her lawyer made those charges. "It wasn't like that."

"Well, you're a lawyer, so you play the odds all day long. What do you think the odds are that the sister of your soon-to-be ex-husband accidentally gets the accelerator stuck right as you're walking across a crosswalk?"

"Probably a million to one, but that doesn't mean it's not the one time it isn't an accident?"

Dusty shakes his head. "Don't try to peddle that BS to me. I know you don't like her."

"And you do?"

Dusty waves at the ford in the stream. "At least I have enough sense not to try and run her over with a car."

I follow him onto the ford. "My foot slipped."

"Well, you need to be more careful. You might want to practice more with your car so you don't end up hurting somebody."

"That's rich coming from you. Given what she is putting you through."

"Yes, but it *had* quieted down considerably until you tried to mow her down."

"Fine, I see I have been proven guilty without the opportunity to plead my innocence." We come off the ford and head back east along the stream's bank.

"Tell me, what made you bring Granny along for this trip?"

Dusty looks over his shoulder at me and raises his eyebrows. "You really have to ask?"

"Well, yeah. I think it's a fair question to ask why you brought a seventy-year-old woman on an excursion."

"Honestly, what's going on down at the Imperial theater has me extremely concerned. Even loaded for bear with all the extra weaponry you worked to secure for us, I don't feel safe for my team or me."

"And your seventy-year-old Granny makes you feel safer than a bullpup shotgun loaded with paranormal buckshot?"

"No. But having a highly skilled paranormal expeller when I'm dealing with a probable demon does have a tendency to calm my nerves."

"Everyone sure is throwing that D-word around a lot."

"Does any of this feel like a normal ghost hunt to you?" He lifts his hands into the air. "Do those three things from last night seem like normal apparitions to you?"

"Well, no—but..." I stammer.

"Everybody has their unique skills. Some people try to hide them. But if they love you and you need their help bad enough, they'll use their skills."

I hold up my hand and stop. The feeling has intensified. I step slowly a few more feet up the path, and the energy weakens considerably. I backtrack and note that we are directly across the river from where we saw the ghost walk into the stream last night.

"Have you found something?" Dusty asks.

I roll my hands over. "It feels like it should be right here, but I don't see anything." I scan the rocky stream bed. There is no sign of a headstone or mound of rocks marking a possible gravesite. Walking up from the stream, I fight through the heavy vegetation.

I don't feel Dusty behind me. Swiveling, I find him still standing near the stream. "What are you doing?"

"I'm not sure I want to get into a bunch of weeds when I don't know where those three from last night ended up."

I don't worry about that. I have already felt them, and they are far to the west of us. Watching, but not willing to get new crucifix burns on their chests just yet. "Suit yourself, but I think you're safe."

Finding what we are looking for is a lot like playing Marco Polo. I track fifty yards further into the vegetation, fighting the briars and sawgrass. Soon the feeling becomes weaker, and I return toward Dusty. I do the same east to west until I home in on where the most potent energy emanates. It's a large briar bush surrounded by dried sawgrass.

"Are you planning on another excursion out here, Dusty?"

He scowls. "No. There's something about this place I don't like. Plus, the footage we got is barely usable."

I nod in agreement as I kneel to investigate the enormous briar bush. I wonder if it would work since it is not directly her body, but I feel that most of what remains of her will indirectly reside in the briar bush. I say a silent prayer for her safe passage and for the peace of her soul. I say another prayer for my abilities to be sufficient.

"What do you see?" Dusty asks as he comes alongside me.

"The devastation of a young woman's dreams. The uncounted casualties of war and the desperation of a world gone mad," I whisper as I admire the ferocity of the two-inch studded spikes set in the center of the myriad of gnarled, thick briar canes.

"Huh, I don't much care for briar bushes, either," Dusty says.

I shake my head to bring myself back to the present and push lightly on his chest. "Step back if you don't mind. I don't know how big this is going to get."

A concerned expression crosses his face, but he abides by my request. Once he is sufficiently out of the way, I turn back to the briar bush and spread my arms wide.

I sense their excitement to the left. They hid in a small grove of hickory trees a bit further west of the ford we crossed. If they are hoping to see a display of my powers, I will give them another small taste of them.

I pull everything good, clean, and forgiving in the world into me and push it out violently toward the briar bush. It shakes as if a strong wind passes through it and bursts into flames.

The heat warms my cheeks, and I back up until I am beside Dusty. "Fair journey." I bless the young mother as I watch the briar bush be consumed by the odd blue flame.

"Did you do that?" Dusty asks in awe.

"Yes, Granny's not the only one with some sick powers."

"Remind me not to tick you off."

Chapter 33

Chase has already left in my car when we arrive back at camp. We pack our gear into the van and head out for Shelbyville, Tennessee.

We reach Huntsville and Dusty pulls the van into the Pancake Pantry for brunch.

The team's tension is palpable. Last night was supposed to have been an easy warm-up before the sweep of the Imperial. Instead, the grays have sapped the confidence of our group.

We order and are waiting on our meal. Granny asks, "During the last trip to the Imperial did the team use any crucifixes or holy water?"

Liza nods her head. "I used some, but I thought what we were dealing with was just some lost souls. I would have treated the situation differently if I had known it was possibly a demon. I feel terrible that I didn't take care of this the first time."

Granny shakes her head. "You work your way up from the most likely to the least likely, Liza. There would have been no reason for you to think you were dealing with anything other than a run-of-the-mill ghost to start." Granny exhales. "Besides, if this happened to you, you're not the first to miss something at that theater."

My ears perk up. "What do you mean, Granny?"

She sighs, hesitates, and then whispers, "Your Great-grandmother Polk, that's my maiden name, dear, took an assignment at that very theater."

"Wha—your mom—why don't I know this?"

Granny raises her eyebrows. "There's a lot you need to know, April. You've chosen not to ask the right questions."

What the devil does that mean?

"My mother was a talented woman. Her skills were slightly different than mine, but powerful. She believed she had cleansed the theater. But I remember her remarking one night over supper that she felt the real abomination at the theater was Austin Tate. She said the man made her blood chill, and she felt the darkest of cores in the man." Granny squints her eyes. "You need to understand, Mama Polk never spoke ill of anyone. That's why it has stuck with me all these years."

"The spirits from the fire were hiding in fear. I understand how she would have thought she cleared them."

Granny bites her lower lip. "It would have to be something strong and evil to hold that many spirits in line."

"But what about Mr. Barker's ghost."

Granny waves dismissively. "That was much later, dear. Ted Barker and Ross McQueen were hung in the town square several years later."

"Hung?" I blurt.

"Miles said the newspaper reported they committed suicide together," Liza says.

Granny raises her eyebrows. "The town paper? Please. I highly doubt they would report how a mob of locals pulled the two men out of the theater and strung them up at the oak tree on the west side of the town center. I suppose the reporter considered it suicide that the men, Ted and Ross, "jumped" to their death when the bench they were standing on was kicked out from under them. Never mind the noose around their neck or that their wrists and ankles were bound."

"I can't even..." I mutter.

"Tell me about it. I've watched the world change many times over in the short seventy years I've been here. But one thing remains constant. There is always evil. The only hope is that there will be enough good people to risk all to impede evil's progress."

Dusty taps his water glass with his spoon. "I want to make sure we are in larger teams than usual for this excursion since we know we are dealing with a violent entity. We need to remain in groupings of three, and each group needs to have one of the specialists," Dusty says.

By "specialist," I assume he means spiritual expeller and not audio or video specialist. "I think we need to set our operation parameters, Dusty. I am a little confused. Are we attempting to get a video of this, or are we trying to cleanse the building of it?"

"We're always trying to get footage or audio if possible, April," Dusty says.

"Yes, but is it our first objective?" Travis asks. "I'm a little confused, too. In some ways, this sounds more like a straightforward exorcism. I'm just not sure why the video and audio team are here."

Dusty's face reddens as his temper uncharacteristically flares. "You're here because I'm paying you to be here, Travis."

Travis rocks back in his seat as he looks away from Dusty. "Yeah, well. A paycheck is not worth anything if you're too dead to spend it."

"If you have a problem, you need to tell me now, Travis," Dusty says louder.

I'm shocked by my brother's behavior. I've not seen him this worked up in ages. Something is definitely agitating him, and I don't believe it is Travis.

"Dusty, Travis isn't complaining about the job. He's simply expressing a safety concern." Luis's voice has a calming effect on all of us. "That's why we have these meetings, so we can work out our concerns. Your idea of teams of three is a good start. What else can we do to ensure everybody's safety, and what is going to be the line of demarcation between trying to get something on film and remaining safe?"

There is an awkward moment when I'm not sure if Dusty will renew his attack, this time on Luis, or if he will calm down. Luis favors him with one of his patented charming smiles, and I know Dusty can't remain angry for long.

Dusty nods his head. "You're right. Both of you. And thank you for bringing it to my attention. First and foremost, everyone that is comfortable being armed, I want you to carry weapons with you at all times and make sure they are fully loaded. Second, we will attempt to capture footage of this entity." He directs this at Travis. "I need to remind you that this could be a hallmark case. This may be a different sort of supernatural being that we've never dealt with before.

"If we can capture footage safely, it could mean a significant boon to the business. That being said, we are going to do a general sweep first. If we find that it is quiet, we will set up our audiovisual equipment and settle in for the night."

"And if we find this thing is spoiling for a fight?" Liza asks.

"Then the heck with it. We'll rely on you and Granny to send this evil back to where it came from while the rest of the team protects you. There's no video or book sales worth one of the team members getting hurt."

"I have to agree with Travis," Chet kicks in. "I think this should be one of those rare occasions where anybody should be able to call broken arrow."

This is all rather interesting to me. Other than Liza, probably because we room together, I have never really heard any of the guys voice their fears. Sure, you would listen to an occasional "I thought you were going to get killed," but it was always someone showing concern for your well-being. This is the first time I can remember people on the team being actively concerned for their own safety.

It makes me wonder if I'm underestimating what waits for us at the Imperial. I'll admit it gave me the heebie-jeebies that I initially missed it hiding in Liza's shadow in the video Dusty and I reviewed. Seeing it so well defined on the videotape gave me pause. Still, almost every excursion gives me pause. This one doesn't seem like anything particularly special other than the spirits or demons having the ability to avoid detection.

I'm surprised that Chet requests preapproved permission for any team member to call broken arrow. The ability for any of the nine of us to say, "That's it, we're all leaving now." Considering that Dusty funds the entire operation, that is a significant request.

Dusty pulls at the red facial hair under his chin as he looks around the table. "Fine. I trust all of you and know you understand what's at stake when we lay down finances for one of these excursions. But yes, anybody can call game over, and we pack and leave as quickly as possible."

I scan the table. Team members are exhaling and shifting in their seats. If they are relieved, I can't tell it.

"Codeword is Lakeside. Say it three times fast, and everybody exits as quickly as possible with anything they can carry." Dusty looks at each team member individually. "Do we all agree?"

I nod my agreement with everyone else. Until ten minutes ago, especially after being attacked by the weird witches last night, I had become comfortable with the thought of the Imperial excursion. I figured we would go in, do some blessing, burn some sage, and throw some holy water around—easy-peasy. This request from the team members puts everything in a new light. I now wonder if this might be my last paranormal excursion.

Chapter 34

We pile back into the van, and Granny hops onto the backbench seat with me. She waits until we are back on the highway, then leans close and asks, "Do you want to tell me about last night?"

"What about last night?"

She flashes a crooked grin. "We could start with the ten-foot-tall blue fire and maybe end with three lesser demons screaming in pain as they tucked their tail and ran."

"What about it?"

Granny huffs impatiently. "Child, if you want to make me sit here and pump you all day for information, I want to remind you that I'm a lot more patient than you are."

That is the truth. "I meant what do you want to know?"

"How did you make it happen? Was that an animism spell or manifestation?"

That's the value of having two excellent mentors. I could have gone several years and not ever questioned *how* I created what I did last night. It was enough for me to bring it to bear when needed. I didn't particularly need to know the how.

But I do need to know. There is something dangerous about not knowing what bag of tricks you're pulling your magic from.

The problem is, as I search my memory from last night, I can't be sure. I chew on my thumbnail as I try to re-create the seconds after hearing the stick break outside our tent. It is one long blurred flash of colors and decisions. I can't determine how I created what I did.

I decide to be honest. "I'm not sure, Granny. What do you think?"

Her blue eyes cut into me as she confirms I wasn't fibbing to her. The concern comes over her expression as she speaks. "I'm not sure, either. You will be the only one who can say. The signature was unlike any I had seen before. It should not be possible, as they are like oil and water, but if I were to guess, I believe you somehow mixed the two last night."

I lean back and grin from ear to ear. "Nah, that's not possible."

"I would say *can't*, but in your case, I say you *shouldn't* do that. It could end up with dire consequences if you were to lose control."

I blow a breath through my teeth. "I don't think that's what happened."

Granny sighs. "Okay. I said only you could know for sure. But I do want to ask you to make sure which skill you're using next time. With you having both, it could be dangerous for you. Or for the people around you."

"Yes, ma'am."

I take her advice to heart. It does concern me that I don't know which skill set I pulled from last night. Why don't I know? Surely, I should be able to feel the difference.

Granny's head ends up on my shoulder. I peer down at her and find her to be sound asleep. I suppose a demon sneak attack is a bit more excitement than she's used to these days.

I draw a deep breath and attempt to reconstruct the event in my mind again. I remember stroking the crucifix Liza gave me, so I obviously used the law of love for manifestation. Right?

But then, I've never used manifestation for fire. I have always used animism to create fire.

I suppose it could have been either—bless, it came so easily. It was right there for the taking. It wasn't like I had to reach down and figure out which one I was using. It was simply *my* power. Not some sort of religiously divided doctrine. I had command over all my abilities.

That infuses another level of confidence into my spirits. Still, I'll need to spend more time clarifying my skills if I continue to dabble in both of them.

Chapter 35

We reach Shelbyville at two in the afternoon. The weather has warmed, and there is no gusting wind here.

Dusty parks the van in front of the Imperial. The team, except Liza, Miles, and Luis, who are uncomfortable with weapons, load our guns and stashes them on our bodies. If the Shelbyville police come by at this moment, we are all going to jail.

We look more like a posse than paranormal hunters as we enter the Imperial. Heather White, the owner of the Imperial, waits for us as we enter.

Her chocolate hair is pulled back severely into a French braid, her ocean-blue eyes narrow, and her lips thin into a line as we approach. "You're almost an hour late," she directs toward Dusty.

"We had a situation this morning we had to take care of," he explains.

"More pressing than what I have going on here?" Before Dusty can comment, she continues, "You realize I'm now three weeks behind on construction. It's doubtful we will be open in time for the Spring Gala. Do you understand what the construction loan is costing me right now?"

"I'm sure it's very stressful, Ms. White," Dusty says.

"It's Miss, and I doubt you really understand how stressful it can be." She points her finger at Dusty. "You promised me that you had cleared the theater of ghosts. I paid you for that."

Dusty rubs the back of his neck. "We did clear it of ghosts. Unfortunately, we believe you may have a demon in the theater."

Heather offers a sardonic smile that displays her exceptionally full lips as she nods her head. "Of course. Demons this week, vampires next week, and werewolves in April? I'm sure they will all require change orders and additional cost."

Dusty chuckles, and Heather's neck flushes red. "What may I ask is so funny?"

Dusty struggles to regain his composure. "I was just thinking there must be a school on ball-busting, and you earned a Ph.D."

Her eyes open wider. "Excuse me?"

I can't believe Dusty said that to Heather. I stare at him in shock and then have another disconcerting thought.

I've seen that awkward body language with him before. His tucked chin, crooked grin, and stance with more weight on his right leg than his left is a dead giveaway that he is interested in *Miss* Heather White.

Oh, bother. Dusty must like a challenge.

"No, Heather. There's no additional charge. We're here to get you back on schedule if possible."

She relaxes her stance. "Oh. Okay." She lifts a ring of keys. "Here are the keys for tonight. Umm—do you need me to stay or anything?"

Oh, Lord, no. I can tell Dusty will ask Heather to stay while we investigate.

"It's best you don't," Liza interjects. "Your presence could affect the accessibility of the demon. We wouldn't want anything to interfere with that."

"Oh," Heather's coral-colored lips remain in a perpetual "O."

Dusty shoots Liza a look that reminds me of an incident as children when he licked a double scoop of pistachio almond ice cream too eagerly. It rolled off the cone onto the blistering hot sidewalk.

"Yes, contaminating energy forces are always an issue with paranormal expulsions. We want this to be a success," I pile on.

"Okay. I understand." Heather turns her attention back to Dusty. "Well, give me a call in the morning when you're done." She mimics a phone with her thumb and pinky.

I want to break her pinky.

As I think violent thoughts, my vision shifts and for a millisecond Heather's facial coloring is muted. I rub the back of my neck, which is still tight from the stressors last night. I need a good night's sleep.

Dusty's disappointment is apparent as we watch Heather sashay out the lobby doors. I must give Dusty credit. He might still be picking troublemakers, but at least Heather is an attractive woman, unlike Bethany.

I'm partnered with the Early brothers. Liza is with Chet and Luis, while Granny is partnered with Miles and Dusty. I don't mind so much since the Early brothers are big guys that follow instructions well. Plus, like me, they have no problems carrying weapons. If anything goes south, we will be the ones with the best chance of shooting our way out of trouble.

That's where the positives end. On the last excursion, I had been assigned the upstairs. That's where I found the ghost of Ted Barker and his lover Ross McQueen.

We also found no paranormal activity on the main level, but a tremendous amount of activity behind the stage and in the hallway that looped behind the stage. The Early brothers and I are assigned the backstage area. This is where Dusty and I saw the demon shadow separate from Liza's in the video.

When we were in the lobby, I had not sensed anything. Which I consider being a positive compared to our first trip. On the initial investigation, there was a continuous thrumming noise. A noise we later determined to be the ghosts of the movie patrons trapped by the locked steel back door during the fire of 1936.

The thrumming noise is gone. That issue is solved.

The brothers and I walk down the far-right aisle past the seating, and still, I sense nothing. But as we open the backstage door, I feel a fleeting emotion. Surprise? Yes, something was surprised to see us, and not in a good way. As quickly as I felt the emotion, it slides away into the shadows, and I lose its presence.

It is such second nature to have Liza next to me, I almost turn to the brothers and ask them if they felt anything. Other than bringing overwhelming firepower to bear, my team isn't going to be any assistance to me.

"Y'all want to walk the hallway first or check the offices as we go?" I ask them.

They share a look, and then Jason speaks for them. "If you don't care, we'll follow your lead."

Alrighty then. Fair enough, I suppose.

I choose to walk the hallway first. I take my Colt forty-five out from my waistband and click the safety off. I hear both brothers chamber rounds into their bullpup shotguns.

Making our way to the first left-hand turn in the hallway, I ruminate on the fact that in a few weeks, this will all be behind me. Demons and witches, casting spells and shooting paranormal ammo, and road trips with my brother's team.

I wonder how I will shove everything back into Pandora's box. Will I still want to?

When I was younger and first found out about my "gift," I hobbled it from day one and kept it shut up as much as possible. That doesn't mean I didn't lean on it every once in a blue moon. Still, I never let it grow in its strength.

It is intense, and I am learning how to use it effectively. It seems like it may be difficult to shut it down for the rest of my life, even though I know it will be in my best interest long-term.

There is one undeniable fact, though. No matter how much it scares me, there is no adrenaline rush quite like a paranormal excursion.

The brothers and I complete our first circuit of the hallway and search each office and dressing room. For some reason, this is a bit more disconcerting than walking the hallway.

"Liza, what do you have?" I hear Dusty's voice across the radio that Jason carries for us.

I open up another dressing room. For a moment, I believe I feel a temperature change and then disregard it as my imagination.

"There's nothing up here, Dusty. All signs of the Barker and McQueen ghosts are gone," Liza reports.

Liza's team has been assigned the upstairs that I scouted during the previous excursion. It is good to know that burning the chairs from the Barker box has released the trapped spirits. That confirms to me we had done our job. The two famous apparitions from upstairs were freed, as had been the auditory-only souls that were trapped in the hallway fire."

I'm so deep in thought about our last excursion to the Imperial that as I open the door to the dressing room, I do a double-take at the man standing inside the doorway. He gives an amused laugh. By the time I react, leveling my forty-five at eye level, he disappears.

I remain frozen in place, staring straight ahead.

"Holy crap! What the heck was that?" Travis asks.

"That's messed up, man!" Jason says.

I turn and watch both of them fanning their shotguns in 180-degree arcs. "Hey, guys, watch the weapons. I don't need one of you going off half-cocked and putting one of us in the hospital, or worse, in the ground."

They become aware of their guns and lower the barrels to their sides. "Sorry." They say in unison.

"What was that?" Travis asks.

That is a good question. The experience with the three gnarly witches the night before helps me today. "Whatever it was, I don't think it is what we saw," I say as I pull the door shut.

Jason wrinkles his nose. "I don't understand."

"It means that he was in costume," Travis says.

"It wasn't much of a costume," Jason comments.

"No. What I'm telling you is that when a demon appears in front of you, it shows you something that it thinks won't shock you. It probably is not some man from the eighteen hundreds; it might very well be another gray kangaroo humanoid with sharp teeth.

Jason curls his lip. "I'd like to pop one of those if I could."

"Stick with me, and you'll probably get the opportunity before the night's out." I mean it as a joke, but it falls flat.

Both brothers look at me as if they are waiting for me to laugh. I guess it really isn't a joking matter.

As I open the next few rooms, I automatically see shadows that cause me to jump. I can't get the vision of the man out of my mind.

He was not attractive, but he was unique looking. Of average height with a slight build, he has wavy, dark black hair slicked back with hair product. The goatee and partial mustache on his face are salted with a few strands of gray, and his skin is a ruddy brown. His nose is a pointed beak, but not too large. The most startling feature was his cobalt eyes that appeared to glow in the dark. But that couldn't be. I must have imagined that.

"April, does your team have anything to report?"

I consider delaying the report of the man until he makes another appearance. Still, looking at the Early brothers, it is apparent that it will not fly. "We found something in one of the dressing rooms."

"Do you need backup?"

I need my head examined. "I'm not going to turn it down, but you can wait until you finish your sweep."

I hand the radio back to Jason. "Let's go check out the dressing area," I tell the brothers.

I have seen that man with cobalt eyes before today, though I can't remember from where. Now I wish we had allowed Heather to stay behind. She would be a good source for history on anything we couldn't explain.

For heaven's sake, Dusty looks at Heather like he is entirely gobsmacked. What's particularly odd to me is, it's not the first time they have met. I don't recall him being all google-eyed about her during our last visit to Shelbyville. Of course, she had her hair down last time and wore jeans. With some men, it's a particular look that flips their switches.

With Dusty, troublemakers seem to be what power him up.

Look at me hating on my brother and his choice of women. April Snow, who can't even keep the fiancé who loves her happy. I'm the worst person in the world to be judging who someone else hooks up with.

The dressing room has already been remodeled. I turn the light on. There is lots of bluish LED lighting and a brand-new tile floor. The room is so sterile it makes me feel like I am in Doc Crowder's autopsy room. Well, now I guess it is Shane's autopsy room.

Jason points at the tall lockers. "We don't have to check those, do we?"

I understand his point without him explaining further. The lockers look like the perfect place for something to hide, and if I had my druthers, we would skip over them. This means there is probably something vital to our investigation inside them. "We're going to have to check all of them."

Travis pushes past Jason and opens the first locker. "I can't believe you're afraid. Are you squeamish you might find somebody's skid marked tighty-whities?"

"It's not like that," Jason grouses.

Travis points to the lockers across the room. "I'll give you the ones under the dressing mirrors."

"Thanks," Jason says as he moves over to open the smaller cabinets under the makeup counter. "I don't know what we expect to see in here other than some leftover hairspray and possibly an old stick of deodorant."

The point is we shouldn't find anything. The cabinets are new from the renovation, and the event center has not opened for business yet. There shouldn't be anything in the lockers other than dust from mounting the units to the wall.

I notice four more lockers behind the shampoo station. I walk over to search them, too. Each has a small tumbler lock. I jiggle the handle of each locker in case they are unlocked. None of the units open.

This strikes me as odd to find locked lockers. Then again, maybe the construction teams are using them to store their tools.

The lights flicker, and a whirlwind of negative energy whips across me. Rather than a light or two flickering, all the units turn on and off and in a sequence. Long-long-short, pause, short-long.

"Is that morse code?" Jason whispers.

I have never been so proud of being a Girl Scout dropout in my life. If that is morse code, I don't want to know what is being communicated to us.

I glance at my teammates. Catching both brothers' eyes, I know I'm seconds away from a mutiny. "No," I say. "It's new construction. I'm sure somebody left a wire loose, and it is short-circuiting. You know how difficult skilled labor is to find these days."

I'm uncertain if either of them believes me. Lord knows I didn't convince myself, but I set about rattling the handles on the locked lockers again as if I will get a different result.

Travis whistles and says, "Mother trucker. Will you look at this?"

Turning toward the commotion, I'm forced to grab the counter to steady myself as my legs buckle. Travis holds up a crucifix by the chain in his right hand.

The crucifix in ornate sterling silver has four rubies, one set at each end of the cross, and one at the center. It appears to be an exact duplicate of the one Liza gave me.

My hand goes to my chest. I relax as my hand lays over the familiar shape of the cross.

"Let me see that, Travis."

Travis steps toward me, and the chain slips from his fingers.

He crouches to pick up the chain, and it slides two feet out of his reach. We share a look of disbelief.

I step forward and attempt to pick up the chain, and again it slides out of my reach.

This can't be good. It is as if some unseen force is playing keep-away with the crucifix Travis found. At the same time, the lights continue to strobe in a rhythmic repeating pattern leaving no doubt that it is some sort of code.

I run toward the chain in a less-than-graceful movement and dive on the floor to catch it. It is as if the necklace is a negatively charged magnet, and my hand is also negatively charged. It shoots across the room at a high velocity, sliding under one of the cabinets.

Standing up from all fours, I try to reclaim my pride by acting like I meant to do that. "Must have been some sort of illusion," I offer.

Travis shakes his head. "That ain't no illusion; I was holding it."

"And I heard it strike the ground." Jason backs up his brother's claim that the crucifix exited.

They can claim it was real all day long, but I just can't go there. It all but disappeared in front of me. Natural objects don't do that. "Do you want to undo the cabinetry and retrieve it from under the cabinet, then?"

Travis gives an awkward laughing noise that tells me he is on his last strand of sanity, and it's being pulled too tight. "Check the baseboard. There's no way anything could've gotten under there."

I don't want to because I know he is correct, but I squat and inspect under the cabinet as he suggests. The cabinetry sits on a minor setback, but it is a solid base with no place for something to slide under. My gut clenches. It is as if the crucifix and chain have disappeared into thin air.

The knocking noise makes all three of us suck in our breath. The lights stop flickering.

The three of us are staring at the ceiling as Dusty and Miles stroll into the room. They both look up at the drop tile ceiling, too.

"So, what did y'all find?" Dusty asks as he squints at the ceiling.

Travis and Jason stare at me. Great, the mutiny is over, and I'm in charge again.

The trouble is, I don't know how to explain what we just experienced. "We did see an apparition in one of the dressing rooms. Miles, do you have any photos from the research you did? I sure would like to look at them to make sure we're not missing any clues."

Miles pulls out his electronic notebook. "No trouble at all. Let me pull up the folder for us."

"Travis and Jason, if you don't mind, please start bringing in the equipment cases and travel bags. Dusty looks around the room. "This would make a good room to set up in."

Miles stands next to me and sorts through the photos of the Imperial theater file. We're so close I smell the citrus of his cologne.

There are several black-and-white photos of Ted Barker and Ross McQueen. Several pictures were taken at different angles of the old gnarled oak tree on the west side of the town square. There is a sprinkling of images from events at the theater and one from the reopening in 1943.

My heart skips a beat when I see the intense stare of the man in the reopening photo. The photo is a black-and-white, so I can't be sure if the eyes are the same astonishing bright blue, but his delicate features and medium skin color are the same. He is dressed in a suit, but it is him. I stick my finger on Miles's screen. "Who's that?"

"Austin Tate," Miles says it as if I should already know.

"The man who bought the theater after the fire?"

Miles grins. "Were you even here last time?"

Yes, but I was inundated with supernatural happenings that day. Excuse me if I didn't read all the historical memos. "You know I was."

"Yes. Austin Tate bought the theater after the fire. He got it for a fire sale bargain." Miles laughs as he raises his eyebrows. "Get it?"

"Yeah, but it's not funny. Is Austin related to Heather?"

Miles nods his head. "He was her maternal grandfather. That's how she owns the property."

I chew my thumbnail. "It was extremely brief, but I believe whatever it was we saw in the first dressing room, it was Austin Tate or an Austin Tate look-alike."

Miles closes the protective cover on his notepad as he stares at me. "Are you positive?"

"It was way too quick to be absolutely positive, Miles. But yes, I believe so. Except he wasn't a ghost. He was right in front of me, and then he disappeared."

"Okay, I believe you," he says.

"But what does it mean?" I ask.

Miles pushes up his glasses as he sucks in his lips and shakes his head. "I haven't a clue, April. But we'll figure it out."

Chapter 36

I don't like the idea of setting up in the dressing room one bit. I would have argued the location, except it is the largest room behind the stage. With Dusty setting his mind on the room and given his cantankerous mood earlier today, I decide it's not a battle I wish to fight.

The men busied themselves setting up the video and audio. Even though they didn't find anything where the Barker box once was, we set a camera up there, too.

The other four cameras are placed strategically behind the stage. One in our dressing room, one in the dressing room where I saw Tate, and one in each long hallway. It isn't a perfect setup, but I'm relatively pretty confident it will work, given this spiritual entity is not shy in the least bit.

Austin is more than "not shy." He is so confident he is taunting us with his display of power.

It is impossible to explain, but I felt him craving me. Not sexually, but as if I am something to be consumed.

It has made me fearful of using my "gifts." I sense that he wants me to use them, and he is excited about the prospect of me using them.

Logically, Austin would only taunt us because he has grown so powerful, he believes he can overwhelm me. Interesting. Last month he hid in the shadows from me; now he is taunting me. I must wonder what has changed so markedly in such a short time.

I signal to Dusty that I'm leaving the room to make a phone call. I step into the hallway and dial Lee's number as I pace.

My call goes to his voicemail, and I hang up.

I know guys will despise it when it is created, but mark my word, one day, a woman will develop a fantastic app that takes the temperature of the owner's phone case and reports it back to the caller. That'll give you an indication that the owner is holding their phone when you go to voicemail. But because the app has not been designed yet, I have no way of knowing if he is swamped and can't get to his phone or if he is done with me and just not answering.

I redial his number. This time when the voicemail message ends, I say, "Hey, baby, I hope everything is going fine. We're all safe here, and as long as everything goes all right, I'll see you tomorrow. I love you."

That's all I can do. Throw messages blindly in hopes it softens Lee for another round of making up. Even though this time, it is strictly on him.

Trust me, I won't beg, but I also won't let my pride get in the way. There is too much at stake for that.

Why has our relationship suddenly become so difficult? It started out so well, too. I never would have guessed it would become so complicated.

Shake it off, April. We're getting too old and have too many responsibilities to have private pity parties.

Fudge. Speaking of difficult relationships, I was supposed to find a mover to get the company records out of Dottie's basement so I could review them.

I rack my brain and am amazed that I don't know any movers. Smiling, I remember that the day I met Shane, he was helping his uncle's moving company. I'm sure he is out of that line of work now.

Wait, I know someone better than a mover. I have a direct hotline to a reviewer of moving companies.

I go to favorites and hit the top phone number.

"April, is everything alright."

"Yes, ma'am. I'm hoping you can recommend a mover for me."

She sighs. "Don't you think you should at least let your Daddy know you're moving to Baltimore before the moving van shows up? I know it won't be a pleasant conversation about you moving in with Lee, but you're an adult. He will respect your decision."

I quit pacing and struggle to lift my jaw, which has dropped open. How does Mama know that? I haven't had the nerve to tell her yet. "Uh—it's not for me, Mama."

She sucks in a breath. "You're not leaving!"

"You want me to go?"

"I'm confused, April. Back up a minute. What do you need a mover for?"

"I need to move business records out of Dottie Castle's basement over to the law office, so I can review them."

"Oh."

"Did Uncle Howard tell you?"

"About Dottie?"

"No. About Baltimore."

"Lord, April. Howard wouldn't have told me unless you asked him to tell me. Before you get any bright ideas, that is not how you will inform your father. Do you understand?"

Hmm … sounded like a promising option until she slathered the wrath of Mama all over the idea. "Yes, ma'am. So do you know any good movers?"

"Yes, I'm texting Ben Talbot's information to you now."

"Thank you, Mama."

"Wait, April. I need to know. Are you leaving for Baltimore or not?"

"Dang, Mama. I feel like a little bird being kicked out of the nest right about now."

"Please drop the dramatics, April. This is important."

"I mean, I'm going. Or at least I think I am if Lee hasn't decided we're a bad match. We've had sort of a rough week.

He keeps misunderstanding my work schedule and getting his feelings hurt. I don't feel it's my—"

"Baby, you're killing me here. I've got meetings double booked this afternoon. If you want to come over tomorrow night and split a bottle of wine while sharing your man troubles, that would be lovely. But I need to know if you are moving out of Guntersville soon."

Harsh. "I am moving, but it may still be a while, Mama. Why?"

She pauses so long I wonder if she plans to answer me. "Promise me you'll come by tomorrow night."

"Uh—okay. Why?"

"April, please. Just promise me. If you stay here any longer, there are things you need to know. Things that maybe I should have told you sooner, but there's nothing to be done about that now."

"Mama, you're scaring me. Are you alright? Is Daddy?"

She makes a choked laughing sound. "Oh yes, baby. This is about you."

Her tone triggers the suspicions piling up in my mind the last year. Like an avalanche, the pile moves, and the parts of the puzzle click together in my mind, the most recent piece being from the previous night.

"Mama, what is a lock witch?"

She sounds as if someone punched her in the gut. "Where did you hear that?"

"Last night during our investigation."

"Listen to me. You tell your brother to get you home straight away. Do you hear me?"

"Mama, stop. You're spooking me. Besides, Granny and Liza are here with me."

I hear her breath faltering. "Ask Dusty to bring you home. In the meantime, please be careful."

I'm frowning so hard my eyes are almost closed. I choose to at least tell her what she wants to hear. "Okay, Mama."

"Thank you, baby. I have always loved my April Fools girl."

"Foolish girl," I correct her to the nickname that has always stung."

Mama laughs. "No, when I was nursing you, I always referred to you as my April Fools Snowgirl. Your brothers thought it was funny to shorten it to foolish girl, and it stuck. Please be careful. I'll see you tomorrow."

"Thank you, Mama."

I hear a laugh from the end of the hallway. I slide my phone into my back pocket and begin down the hallway to investigate

As I make my way down the hallway, I am forced to stop as the uneasiness in my gut rolls over. I have a nagging feeling that I am no longer looking for something. Something is toying with me. I seriously consider taking Mama's overprotective advice by asking Dusty to take me home.

Something falls at the end of the hallway. Fine, there's no way my curiosity will let me ignore that.

As I march down the length of the hallway full of purpose, I pull the bullpup shotgun out of the sling on my back and chamber a shell. If Austin Tate wants to try and spook me again, he's in for a rude reception. I'm gonna blow him into the middle of next week, looking both ways for Sunday.

As I near the end of the hallway, I hear that giggle in my head again. Now he is starting to anger me, and I pick up my pace.

The ceiling grid lights strobe, seeming to keep rhythm with the step of my boots. The sickly-sweet smell of rotting flesh and sulfur hangs heavy in the air, forcing my face to contort in disgust.

As I turn right around the corner, Austin is six feet in front of me. I swing my riot gun up toward him, and he opens his left hand, raising it toward the barrel of my shotgun. I pull the trigger, and nothing happens. I pump the shotgun for a fresh shell. Nothing happens as I pull the trigger.

Austin chuckles, but the humor in no way reaches his cruel eyes. The cobalt color illuminates and appears to swirl around his tiny silver pupil.

"Don't be a foolish girl. Accept the honor of being the lock witch at my side," Austin mocks.

I think to turn and run back to the rest of the team. There's safety in numbers, right?

Austin raises his right fist. Then opens it, allowing the crucifix I saw earlier to dangle from his hand.

He continues to laugh as he rocks the crucifix side to side. I've seen the likes of the expression on his face before; it's the one that says, "You're an idiot."

I could pull my forty-five, but Austin is so close into my personal space I decide to back up and wait for the right moment to break into a run for the dressing room.

Austin points his finger at his sternum. My hand goes instinctively to my chest in a sympathetic motion.

My heart stops. I double-clutch at my shirt, pulling it forward. I'm horrified as I confirm my crucifix is missing. Where the sterling serpentine chain and blessed crucifix should be, I have a first-degree burn in the shape of a handprint.

Antoine's words come back to haunt me. Then the attack by the witch at Snow and Associates and later the attack by the three witches at Bellefonte. The demon was never waiting outside of Guntersville, at least not like I thought. No, the demon the grays were preparing Guntersville for was lying in wait for me in Shelbyville.

It is as if Austin realizes I understand what he is attempting to show me. He is giddy with his accomplishment.

I point my useless shotgun at him and incline my forehead toward him. "Put the necklace on the barrel."

Austin shakes his head as another broad smile consumes his face.

"Give it back," I growl.

Austin lifts the crucifix above his head and opens his mouth exceptionally wide.

"Don't you dare!"

It is too late. Austin drops my cross into his gaping mouth and swallows it whole.

Chapter 37

I can't believe my eyes. Before considering the ramifications, I swing my shotgun like a club, slamming it butt first against Austin's right temple.

The gun's stock bounces off Austin's head as a secondary crack echoes in the hallway. His head lays grotesquely sideways, the left side of his face lying on his left shoulder.

Austin lifts his head off his shoulder with both hands, setting it dead center on his neck and pushing as if reconnecting some morbid Lego set.

He favors me a shoulder shimmy. "I like my witches with some fight in them!" His wild eyes and maniacal smile almost make me give up the ghost, and in a panic, I swing at his head a second time.

He disappears before contact. My momentum spins me around, and I fall rudely on my butt.

Great. Austin ate my crucifix. How do you get something back after a demon eats it? For Pete's sake, I have difficulty getting something back from Puppy once he eats it.

I stand and rub my offended posterior. I'm shaking, but at the moment, I can't discern if it is because I'm scared or angry. I know if Austin is demon enough to show his face again, I'm aimin' to skin his hide and nail it to the barn door.

"What! Are you scared of me, Austin?" I spin on my heels. "Aww ... don't be like that. Come on back for round two. Or do you only play when you can pop in and out and surprise folks, you low-life, egg-suckin' dawg?"

Rubbing my bum, I make sure that I didn't crack my tailbone with my fall. Then I check and make sure I didn't pee myself, which is what has me particularly infuriated.

Satisfied that I didn't, and I can return to my team without having to change my pants, I walk back toward the changing room we have commandeered as our control center. I'm minus my crucifix, and my ultra-cool, ghost-busting shotgun has been transformed into a Cro-Magnon-era weapon. I look down at my new club.

"Aww ... for the love of—" The butt of my bullpup shotgun is fractured.

I'm embarrassed, too. I wasn't paying attention, and that's what gave Austin the advantage. If I'd had the Early brothers with me, I doubt Austin would hazard such a prolonged encounter with me.

He thought with me being alone, he had the advantage. Yet, look who ended up having to use his disappearing trick.

It's Lee's fault I almost got eaten. If he hadn't been such a little crybaby the last few days, I wouldn't have felt the need to call him. I'm seriously reconsidering the risk-to-reward factors of a relationship with Lee Darby.

Stepping into the command center, I recognize the unmistakable scent of pepperoni pizza. My eyes scan the counter space, zeroing in on the six large pizzas and four, two-liter Cokes. My stomach growls so loudly I look nervously about the room to see if anyone heard.

"Is that your stomach, or do you have a medical condition you need to tell us about?" Chet asks.

"I have a condition, Chet. I have hypoglycemia," I say with a classic "bite me" expression.

Chet's eyes open wider. "Oh man, I'm sorry. I think I have a cousin who has that. It's bad news."

"Well, you shouldn't go around making fun of people. You never know what they're dealing with." Like a severe case of the lies today. Good thing I'm indoors. I'd hate to risk a lightning strike right now.

Chet steps to the side and gestures toward the pizza boxes. "Don't let me get in your way. Hurry up and get you something to eat."

I'm famished. Any other time I could've easily wiped out half a pizza or better on my own as hungry as I feel. Still, my interaction with Austin has left me feeling queasy. After just one piece, I feel a case of indigestion coming on.

You should never go into the water right after you've eaten. And you should never eat right after you've had the bejesus scared out of you.

Liza, Granny, and Dusty are to the side discussing something. I wrap my arms around myself and interrupt their conversation.

"So, what's, like, the plan here, boss? We're actually just gonna camp out here?" My voice has a little more venom than I intend.

Dusty's eyes narrow. "What is it with everybody questioning this mission?"

"I don't know, maybe most sane people don't like poking demons?"

Liza snorts a laugh. "She has a point, Dusty. We've got film on those three from last night, and film's not even necessary because it's burned into everyone's mind."

Dusty waves his hand dismissively at Liza. "But that's what you do. You expel supernatural beings. Plus, we've got Granny for backup."

Granny shakes her head lightly and speaks barely above a whisper. "Because something can be done, Dusty, doesn't make it easy. Have you ever considered that I quit for a reason?"

"Sure. Everybody's got to retire sometime, right?"

"Retire from what, Dusty? Five or six trips a year to help a family in desperate need put their life back together? Do you really think I'm selfish enough not to help because I want all my time to myself?"

Dusty shifts his weight from his left to right leg. "Well, no, ma'am. I didn't mean it like that."

"That's the issue, Dusty. You don't mean it, but it comes across that way. These 'gifts' have their price. We see things we can't ever unsee. We use energy that we can never get back, and in the end, it warps our reality.

"You and your brother enjoy doing bodywork on cars. Let me ask you if I take a baseball bat to a car fender, how would you fix it?"

He crosses his arms as if he were about to take a test that he is sure to ace. "Nowadays, I would go to the junkyard and get an undamaged fender, or worst-case scenario, order an aftermarket fender online."

"And if you couldn't?"

His brow furrows. "Like a different fender isn't available?"

"Precisely. You must use the car's original fender. How would you repair it?"

He shoves his hands in his pockets. "I suppose we could pull the dent out and then fiberglass patch the hole from the bolt. It would be okay if you were just looking at it in passing, but there's no way to get it back to a pristine state."

Granny nods her white helmet hairdo. "Exactly. That's what happens to my mind if it gets warped too many times. In passing, it looks fine, but it's not. *It's not fine at all.*"

"So, you quit because you couldn't take any more of it?"

"That, and I was starting to wonder if one day I might make a mistake and make matters worse. The more my reality becomes warped, the easier it is to make judgment errors. Errors that may put other people in danger."

Dusty looks around the room at the setup and makes a circling motion with his finger. "You think setting up in this room and spending the night is a mistake? I was planning on us sleeping in shifts so that someone would always be watching the equipment."

Granny holds up her hands. "I'm not trying to change your program here."

"I am," I interject. "I believe we need to get rooms and come back in the morning."

"But why? We're already here, and we're set up. If we're lucky, we'll get something in the next few hours, and we can all go home," Dusty reiterates.

"Yeah, well, this place ain't right, and we're pretty stupid if we spend the night here. I'd rather us not all die because you've gone hardheaded." I can't help it. Once I start talking, the truth flows out my mouth.

Dusty rocks back on his heels. "Wow. I didn't know you felt that way. Tell me again why you bothered to come?"

"Because you guilt-tripped me into it," I retort.

Dusty rubs his forehead. "Alright, you know what. I'm going over here to talk with the guys. I'd like you to think about what you need to do, and if you want to go to a hotel, I'll be glad to call you a taxi."

After everything Dusty has done for me, I probably should be ashamed of myself. Still, I have all the emotions swirling around me from my encounter with Austin. Truthfully, all I can focus on, the only thing that seems to be a reasonable course of action, is to get the entire team out of the Imperial and never return to Shelbyville.

What if I am correct that the demon Antoine has been raving about, the demon that controls the grays, is actually Austin? What then? The grays are already hot on my trail. Didn't Antoine say the grays are supposed to destroy anyone that might stand up against the demon?

Wouldn't that also mean Austin is coming to Guntersville? Which would negate anything we can accomplish in Shelbyville.

I want to laugh. It is all so preposterous. Of all the cities in the world, why Guntersville, Alabama? I mean, it's the antithesis of "go big or go home." Doesn't this demon and his horde of gray hunters understand that they set the bar way too low?

Set your sights on New York, LA, or Tokyo for goodness'

sake. If you're scared to go that big, shoot for Vegas or Atlantic City. Who knows, you might even be able to find some sympathetic allies there.

Wishful thinking never got anything accomplished. I can wish all day that this demon had some common sense and set its sights on controlling a city that would bring it some credibility in the world.

The facts are, the grays are hunting me, and a demon has made it personal. Like it or not, the fight has come to me. I will have to either stand and fight or flee.

I wonder if Dusty would spot me cab fare to the lake house rather than a motel in Shelbyville?

"What's gotten into you?" Granny says as she puts her hand on my shoulder.

"You were kinda rough on your brother there," Liza says with a smile.

I purse my lips and attempt to stare Liza down. She raises one eyebrow as she otherwise ignores my mean mug.

"What did you see?" Liza asks. "Was it him?"

I point my finger at her. "We promised each other we weren't going to do that. That we wouldn't use our 'gifts' on one another."

"Psst. Please, I don't need any special talent to read you like a book. Whenever you see something, and you don't want to share with the rest of the team, you turn flour white and get this pursed-lip constipated face." Liza mocks me.

"I do not."

"Yeah, you do," Granny agrees.

I look from one to the other and exhale. "I don't want to talk about it."

Granny giggles. "Lordy, you've never changed. You still think not talking about it makes it go away."

"You said during manifestation training talking about it makes it come about."

"There's a little bit more to it than that."

"Well, yeah. The 'little more' part being that I believe this whole 'haunting' is a hoax to get me back here. To Austin's homefield, per se."

Granny's coloring changes to a shade whiter. "Why do you say that child?"

My hands become over animated as I speak in a harsh whisper. "Because he all but told me so. The fool keeps talking about me being the lock witch by his side. I'm telling you this isn't normal. It's like this demon, ghost—whatever it is—has a stalker issue and I'm the center of his attention."

"Oh, my." Granny braces against the wall.

I catch her arm to steady her. Tears leak out the corners of her eyes.

"Granny?"

"It's nothing. Just a little short on breath." She pats my arm.

"Okay." I know she's not telling me something. Still, I have too much information to process as it is.

Granny takes a deep breath and exhales slowly as she locks eyes with me. "Possibly with the three of us, we stand a chance. I felt it. I didn't want to alarm you, girls, until I had a better feel of it. But mark my word, it's a bad booger. It's mean, old, wise, and canny."

"Well, make me feel better, why don't you." I roll my eyes at Granny.

She smiles with good humor. "Let's put it in perspective. Most demons inhabit an unsaved human. Basically, animate a meat suit with their own spirituality."

"I hate that term." Liza grimaces.

"Which is probably why they use the term. They know it bugs us." Granny motions toward me. "But what's this demon animating?"

I had not contemplated it until Granny brought it to my attention. The demon animates nobody, and it isn't for lack of opportunity. There have been plenty of workers present over the last few months, not to mention Heather and our team. Yet the demon was animating a ghost? How can that even be? "A ghost?"

"It can't be," Liza says.

"And yet that's exactly what we're experiencing. Understand, I believe that this demon occupied Austin while he was alive. Yet even though living hosts have been available to it, to date, it has preferred to inhabit a spirit." Granny seems to peer blankly at the ceiling. "Yep, there's no textbook on that one, girls."

"What now?" Liza asks, her eyes intent on Granny. "What do we do if there's no plan of attack for this situation?"

"Because there's nothing in our books of instruction doesn't mean that there's no successful plan of attack available. It only means that we have to devise it ourselves and hope that we've chosen wisely," Granny says.

"I'm not real high on that choosing thing. Something tells me if it goes wrong with this entity, the three of us might be his next three humanoid-faced gray kangaroos."

Granny laughs at me. "Oh, I assure you that's what he's after. Otherwise, I believe he would've locked the doors and burned us all alive in here."

Liza's eyes narrow. "Why did you say that?"

"That he would burn us alive?"

"Yes."

Granny raises her eyebrows. "Because he's done it before when he didn't get what he wanted."

My blood chills as I think of the movie patrons who died in the hallway. It is gone, but I swear the *thump, thump, thrumming* I heard on our first visit still plays in my head. The idea of anyone or anything being so innately evil is beyond my comprehension.

I know there's evil in the world. I'm not naïve. But in my experience, most evil is in search of something, typically power. Whether political, financial, or sexual energy, it is what all evil seems to crave. But evil for the sake of being evil? That's a unique and quite sick condition.

Anger floods my emotions again. This cannot stand that anything so evil can exist unchecked. My fear has dissipated as

I resolve to rid the world of this dangerous demon.

"What can we do?" I ask Granny.

"It does pose a specific problem, doesn't it," Liza says. "How can we expel when there's no physical body?"

Granny nods in agreement. "It does. But something tells me since he is bending the rules, we can too."

"How do you know that?" I ask.

Granny shakes her head vigorously. "Oh, honey, I don't know for sure. Understand, everything we're doing from here on out is just spitballing. But we either come up with a plan that makes sense to us, or we walk away." She inclines her head toward me. "But something tells me this thing and its witches have your scent. I don't think I'm prepared to let my granddaughter live her life looking over her shoulder for the rest of her days."

That is the perfect description. With all the tracking and taunting, it is as if the demon and his horde have my scent. There is no way to shake them from my trail.

Great. A few days ago, the most significant decision on my mind was whether to go to Baltimore with the fiancé who makes my toes curl in bed before or after I land a job in Baltimore. Now I'm having to create demon-dispersing spells out of whole cloth. Lovely.

"Will a demon trap even work without a physical body?" Liza asks.

Granny nods her head. "I'm not sure how it's affected given that Austin is not a solid being."

"Says you," I say with a sarcastic tone.

Liza and Granny break off their discussion to stare at me. I add, "I'm just saying that he's been able to grab solid items, I can smell the stench of him, and he's appeared several times now looking as solid as you or me."

Granny shakes her finger. "Now, if there was some way to get him in the trap in the solid form..."

"And if we add the incantations that eliminate his ability to change form," Liza adds.

They smile at each other like a couple of loons as their heads bob up and down. I have no experience in demon traps or incantations and am totally lost. "What? Is this like something you're gonna draw on the floor?"

Granny looks at the tile floor at her feet. "I don't trust the grout lines."

"Me either," Liza agrees.

Granny passes by me for the door. I follow her and Liza out of the dressing room.

Granny points at the smooth concrete floor as the dressing room door clicks behind us. "This is what we need."

"We'll need to get some paint," Liza says.

I hold up my hand as it comes to me what they are saying. "Wait a minute. Let me get this straight. Heather White has spent a fortune remodeling this dump, and now you want to paint a demon trap on her brand-new concrete floor."

They look at me with a "yeah, so what" expression.

"Don't you think we should run it by her before we start painting graffiti all over her floor? I mean, it might not come up."

"Oh yeah," Liza rolls her eyes. "I'm sure she'd much rather have a murderous demon occupying her facility. That'll be great for business."

"Okay fine. Maybe you're right. But just being the devil's advocate..." I wave my hand to clear the unintended pun. "Making sure we're thinking this all the way through. After we deface Heather's costly concrete floor with fresh graffiti, how do we get Austin into the trap? I mean, I don't like the guy at all, but one thing's for sure ... he's not stupid."

"Well, I have been thinking about that, too," Granny says. "Now, remember this is all just theory, but I think we might be able to use his ghost state against him. What's the one thing that spirits on the wrong side of the veil can't resist?"

Once again, I feel like the failing student in a class full of geniuses. I'm not aware there is something that ghosts can't resist.

"A séance in their honor," Liza whispers with an awestruck tone.

"Exactly!" Granny praises her.

My mouth is hanging open. "That'll really work?"

"It's all..."

"Theory," I finish Granny's words for her. "But ghosts really do answer séances?"

"Don't you occasionally call out to spirits when you're on an excursion?" Granny asks.

Only when Dusty makes me. "Yes, ma'am."

"No difference. You're just not sitting in a circle holding a bunch of people's hands," Granny explains.

Now I understand séances to be like making tiny punctures in the veil. Granny explaining it to me sends a chill up me as I realize I'd been running around poking holes in the veil all along. Something is quite disconcerting about that revelation.

Whatever. I'm beyond arguing about any of this. Besides, if it does work, it seems like I'm the one who stands the most to gain. I see an opportunity to get out of the building for a few minutes if nothing else.

"How much paint do you need, and do you need specific colors?"

Granny tells me that she wants a gallon of black, a gallon of red, and a pint of gold-colored paint. She also instructs me to make sure that it is exterior grade because it will better hold to the concrete.

I step back into the dressing room while the two of them discuss what they will draw and to what scale.

Walking over to Dusty, I extend my hand. "I need the company credit card. I need to go get us some paint."

He squints as he pulls out his wallet. As he removes the card, he pauses and looks like he is about to ask a question.

"Probably best you don't know," I tell him.

Half a smile pops onto his face as he gives a nod of his red hair.

"I'll take Chet with me if you don't care."

"Be my guest."

Chet is watching the monitors on one of the laptops hooked up to the remote cameras. I tap him on the shoulder. "My hypoglycemia is acting up again. Will you help me find a hardware store?"

Chet frowns. "Sure."

That's what I like about Chet. Where some folks work best under pressure, he works best under confusion.

Chapter 38

It feels terrific to slip outside, even if it is only a temporary reprieve. The gentle breeze caressing my face lowers my anxiety. I realize how discombobulated and stressed I am from my interaction with Austin. My body and mind are perpetually stuck in a state of high alert.

"Care if I drive?" Chet asks.

"Please, be my guest."

Hopping up onto the passenger seat of the van, I shiver. The inside of the truck must be ten degrees cooler inside than outside. As Chet starts the vehicle, I turn the heater up to full blast.

"You ought to let the motor warm up before you turn on the heat," Chet complains.

"I heard somewhere that even when it feels cold, the air is a degree or two warmer than the inside of the car, and it helps heat the vehicle."

"My feet beg to differ," Chet grouses as he drives the van out of the parking lot.

As we drive around the town square, I admire the enormous oak tree that stands prominently in the courtyard. "That oak tree during the day is gorgeous. At night it looks like something out of a Hans Christian Anderson fairytale. Way heavy on the scary," I say.

"Did you see the pictures Miles had?"

"Of the tree? Yes."

Chet cut his eyes to me and then back to the road. "No, the ones from the lynching of Barker and McQueen."

"No." Thankfully.

"Crazy. The whole town must have been there. It sent a shiver up my spine." Chet looks my way again and furrows his brow. "I can't believe he didn't show you."

"I didn't even know they had been murdered until today."

"Huh. That's odd. I thought Miles told all of us."

I try to recollect if I had missed the team's premeeting for the last trip to Shelbyville. Still, I specifically remember eating pizza as Dusty and Miles went over the details of the haunting. This means somehow Miles kept the information out of the general meeting and only shared the history of the so-called double suicide—murder—for the guys.

He may have been trying to protect my sensibilities by not showing me a graphic photo, but leaving out the detail altogether was a mistake. The information changes the complexion of our last case. It explains why Ted's and Ross's ghosts did not pass to the other side of the veil before we burned the chairs that contained their residual energy.

"I thought the city of Shelbyville celebrated Ted because of his success in the movies."

"They did. Still do," Chet says.

I raise my hand in a "what gives" gesture. "Then how did they end up hung?"

"I should let Miles tell the story because he remembers the details better."

"Yeah, well. Seeing as he forgot to tell me last time..."

Chet snorts. "Right. So, the Shelbyville newspapers glossed over the two men's deaths. You know, unexpected, tragic deaths. That's how they reported it."

"Since when is it unexpected that you die if somebody hangs you?"

"I heard that." Chet laughs. "Still, the real reason the city whitewashed the event is that it was all a huge mistake. Barker and McQueen hadn't done anything wrong."

"Mistake? How do you accidentally hang two men?"

"No. It was a mistake that they were accused of kidnapping that boy for a sex slave. See, a son of a prominent businessman went missing. After a couple of days of searching for the boy, the crowd got worked up. Someone floated the idea that Barker and McQueen kidnapped the boy, the theory grew legs, and they marched them into town by rifle point."

Sex slave? As stupid as what Chet is telling me sounds, I can visualize that happening. I once was involved in a protest on campus that suddenly morphed into a fistfight. It put an early halt to my social activism career.

There's a specific line of demarcation where a gathering of concerned people steps over the line and becomes a mob. In my experience, for every twenty people you add to a group, there is a subsequent ten-point drop in the group's average IQ. Soon the IQ dips so low that the most absurd idea becomes believable. That's when folks get hurt.

"Did they find some sort of evidence? Blood? A basement with chains?" I ask.

Chet's eyebrows shoot up. "Heck no. A couple days later, he came on home. The boy had been hiding in the shed at a friend's house because he took his Mama's car for a joyride and backed it into a pole. He was afraid his dad would tan his hide."

I'm beyond mortified. "Did the law bring charges against anyone in the mob?"

"Nah, you know how towns were back then. It's like, aw man, we hung them, and they were innocent. Well, there's nothing we can do to bring them back. You want to go get a beer?"

I'm frustrated for two reasons. First, Miles had no right to withhold the information about Ted and Ross. If he didn't share in the planning session, it should have been the first item mentioned by him—bless it, or any of the menfolk—as soon as we identified them in the theater.

Second is the human condition that *somebody* must be

blamed, and a trial is unnecessary. Over the last year, I have defended several wrongfully accused people. Their emotions were always highly charged, and often they were fearful. And they knew they were going to be afforded defense *and* a fair trial.

I can't begin to imagine the disbelief of Ted and Ross as they were dragged from their home, the realization they were being tried by the mob with no opportunity to defend themselves, and the final horrible moment when they surrendered to their fate as a noose was pulled tight around their necks.

When I believe I cannot experience any more meanness in the world, here comes another story that shocks me.

"I bet the boy and his family acted like nothing ever happened. If he had only stayed home and taken his medicine for having gone on the joyride, two men—innocent men— would have been allowed to live."

"True that, but the Tate family fell on tough times not long after that. They lost most everything over the next six years. I'd say that's a case of karma righting things."

"Tate?"

"Yeah, it was Austin Tate's only child."

Like dominoes, the facts fall one after the other, and I'm horrified at what we have caused. When we removed the apparitions we could see, we inadvertently set loose an evil entity on the world.

Since Dusty told us the worker was injured at the theater, I wondered why the hauntings increased. More importantly, why they were increasingly violent.

Now I have no choice but to recognize that Ted Barker and Ross McQueen were acting as guardians of the Imperial theater. Guardians that kept the demon that had possessed Austin Tate marginalized.

Oh, how Austin must have hated them even more in death, being imprisoned by them in the property he murdered innocents to facilitate the purchase.

There is no way we could have known. Plus, Ross had even

acted aggressively toward one off our team. What were we to do? We couldn't leave a violent apparition in a special events venue.

Plus, Heather specifically mentioned the ghosts in the box seats and the crowd beating on the fire exit door. She never made a mention of a possible third supernatural in her building.

Now I really am making excuses for us.

I can't help but fixate on the fact that if Miles had given me the information about Ted's and Ross's deaths, I would have pieced it all together sooner. But I'm not sure that's true, either.

One thing I know. The demon possessed Austin Tate early and controlled his life. Now he owns him in death, too.

It makes me sick. This is one of those cases where we've done more harm by attempting to help. If we had never gone to the Imperial, Austin would still be under the control of the guardians.

I share in the pain. I would be safer, too, since the demon would be unable to summon the grays to hunt me.

This is majorly messed up. I lean forward and struggle for a solution.

Chet and I must move quickly in the hardware store. They close in twenty minutes, and the older gentleman at the paint station is less than pleased that we have three cans of paint that need to be tinted.

I feel better once we have the paint in the van. I don't know what to do, but Granny and Liza do, and I trust them fully. We'll be able to set this right. I know we will.

Of course, I have no clue how a demon trap works or how often they are successful. Still, there's no need to get bogged down in probabilities and such. I just know it will all work out. I hope.

"You're awfully quiet," Chet says. "A penny for your

thoughts."

"Dark and foreboding."

Chet flashes me a grin. "That good, huh?"

"No. There's so much of this on the relationship side that I can't wrap my head around. Barker had specially reserved seats at the theater. Why would anybody think that he would hurt the child of the man who owns the theater?"

"Come on, you know how ignorant people can be when they're upset. Especially if they feel a child has been hurt."

"But Austin and the town turned a blind eye to his relationship with Ross. That's no small thing for that period. Why on earth would folks believe Ted would risk destroying that by hurting Austin's son?"

"People are crazy, April."

No. People are not, as a rule, crazy. They certainly do crazy things. But those things are done from a position of motive. They do what seems inexplicable until you know their goals.

There are too many moving parts in this story. I know I'm missing something.

We pull back into the theater lot. In silence, we gather up our supplies.

As we enter the front lobby, my senses heighten as I smell the sickly-sweet rot in the air. It seems we have been visited by the toilet demon.

"Crap, what is that nasty scent?" Chet complains as his face contorts comically.

"Yep. I think *the* Austin Tate was up here crop dusting the front door so we would walk through it."

"That's so wrong."

I swallow my gorge and duck for fresher air as I move through the lobby. "Dude may be dead, but he has an oddly familiar sense of humor."

I'm looking at Chet as I'm talking. The can in his right hand strikes my thigh as his eyes enlarge. "Stop!"

"What the..." I follow his line of sight to a giant blob in the middle of the threshold we are passing through. I first think someone has gutted a deer. No, it is a pile of excrement the circumference of a manhole.

"Somebody took a dump up here?" Chet asks with astonishment.

"I think that's our demon sharing with us."

Chet's lips draw back, exposing his teeth as his nose wrinkles. "That ain't right."

"You can say that again."

Chet stoops as if to get a closer look.

"What are you doing?"

"I see something shiny in it."

"Come on, that's just nasty. Let's get back to the rest of the team."

Chet sets his paint cans down. "No. One second." He disappears behind the front desk.

I listen intently for Austin's laugh that I figure I should be able to hear at any moment. I'm positive he must be watching and getting a laugh from his prank.

Chet is gone only a minute. Still, I'm relieved when he comes from behind the counter. He is carrying a broom and walking toward the demon excrement.

"What in the world are you going to do with that broom?"

"Go fishing in this nasty pile o' poop," Chet jokes.

My gag reflex kicks in as he jams the broom handle into the massive pile of waste, swishing it side to side. An even more unfortunate stench rises into the air, overpowering the original sweet rot.

"Stop that, Chet!"

He is intent on his task. "Give me just another second."

"I'm serious. You're gonna make me hurl."

Chet lifts the broom handle. Clumps of coagulated black matter make splatting sounds as they fall back into the pile of waste.

"Ta-da." Chet grins broadly. "I got it!"

It is nearly impossible to identify with all the muck attached to it. As more waste falls from its surface, I recognize my crucifix.

Even though I am grateful for Chet's chivalry and tenacity, I'll never wear that crucifix again. "I don't think I want it anymore."

Chet squints. "You gotta be kidding me. There's nothing on here that can't be washed off. Spray a little Windex to boot, and it'll be good as new."

I'm not going to have this argument right now. "You're right, thank you."

Chet combines one of the bags of painting supplies into the other and drops the nasty necklace into a plastic bag. "While y'all are painting, I can clean this up for you."

He retrieves his paint cans, and we walk gingerly around the mess on the floor.

It does not escape me how Chet took everything in stride. I mean, we were greeted by the smell of death followed by the most enormous human cow patty I've ever seen, and then Chet fished out a piece of jewelry for me.

I watch him carry the paint as if nothing out of the ordinary has happened. Are we that numb to it?

Chapter 39

When we arrive at the control station, we find the Early brothers and Miles already tucked into their sleeping bags, sound asleep. Miles better be glad that he is asleep. His temporary reprieve will allow me to cool off over him not disclosing everything he should have about Ted and Ross. I have to exert great self-discipline not to walk over to him and snatch him baldheaded to wake him up.

Liza takes one of the cans from Chet. "C'mon, April. Help me with the border while Loretta does the script."

Reluctantly, I drop in behind her.

"I want to help," Chet says.

"Do you have a steady hand?" Granny asks.

"Yes, ma'am."

"Then you can help me with the script."

Painting is not my forte. I stunk at fingerpainting, and my artistic growth was stunted after that.

Liza pulls out one of the three-inch sponge brushes and makes to hand it to me. "If you start on the left side with the circle, I'll start on the right, and we can meet at the halfway point."

"Can't I just watch?"

"You're not going to help?"

From my point of view, I am helping. I'll probably only mess it up if I work on the trap. I don't want to be the one to make it fail. "I'll be moral support for you."

Liza frowns but thankfully doesn't argue the point.

I feel bad for Granny and Chet. Granny because a woman her age shouldn't be on her knees on a concrete floor. Chet because it should be my task, not his.

I cross my legs and lean my back against the wall.

Chet has some sick skills. He uses a fine-point paintbrush to fill the boundary with the additional script once the outer border has dried. As the symbol nears completion, the intricate detail the team has put to it in such a short time frame is mind-boggling.

My phone rings, and I jump. Pulling it out of my back pocket, I see it is Lee.

I would be lying if I said I'm not surprised. After him not calling me back or taking my calls, I thought we were done.

Okay, April. No smart-mouth, scorned-woman talk. Use your pleasant voice.

"Hi, Lee," I say as I walk away from the rest of my team.

"Hey." His voice sounds odd and halting. "Where are you right now?"

That's an odd question. "I'm in Shelbyville with the team."

He is quiet for a moment. "Okay."

His uneasiness concerns me. "Why, what's up?"

"Uh, it's nothing. My mind must be playing tricks on me."

"No. Seriously, tell me," I insist.

He clicks his tongue. "You're going to think I'm crazy. But I met Marty for dinner. And well… Never mind."

Oh, he can be infuriating. "Tell me."

"When I left, I swear all the TVs were off. But when I returned, the TVs in the den, kitchen and main bedroom were all turned to the shopping channel."

It feels like a platoon of daddy long leg spiders works their way up my spine. I don't want to give in to my anxiety. "Maybe you forgot to turn them off?"

"Well, I mean maybe, but I never watch the shopping channel, and the other thing that's got me a little wigged out is, you know that special flavor of chips you got that neither one of us likes?"

"Yeah."

"They were open on the kitchen counter, and you're not gonna believe this, but when I went to throw them away, I swear I smelled your perfume in the air."

My breath catches in my chest. I can't be sure of it, but my thoughts go immediately to the grays. Even if Lee and I do not stay together, I would never forgive myself if something happened to him because he was involved with me.

"Where's Marty now?"

"In the john. He's about to drive back down to Birmingham to spend the night with his mom."

"Lee, if I ask you to do me a favor, would you just do it?"

He lets out a nervous laugh. "That's a pretty big ask. Could you narrow it down a bit for me?"

"I would really appreciate it if you went with Marty and stayed at his mom's until I get back."

There is another long pause. "Why?"

Why indeed. "What you told me wigged me out. You staying there by yourself makes me worry about you."

"I'm perfectly capable of taking care of myself."

"I know you are. This isn't about you. This is about my idiosyncrasies. I'm out here on the road, already stressed and all worried about you. Besides, you like Marty's mom. When was the last time you saw her?"

"Yeah, I guess it has been a while."

"All those meals you told me the woman has cooked for you. You two go down there and buy her breakfast in the morning."

"Hey, that's a fantastic idea. I could take her to the Waffle Shop."

How a boy can be so wealthy and his tastes run so cheap remains an eternal mystery. "Or Pancake Pantry."

"Yeah, that's not bad, either. Sort of a chick place."

"Which Linda is..."

Lee laughs. "I get your point now. That's a better idea."

"So, are you going? For me?"

"Yeah. But when you get back, we got to talk. This ducking out on the weekend thing, I'm not real fond of it."

"I know, but remember, once I'm up in Baltimore, I won't have any of these weekend excursions."

"That will be better. Oh hey, Marty's coming out of the bathroom. I'll catch up with you later."

"Okay." I wait for the three magic words that will let me know that all is right with us again.

"Bye now, Babe."

Those were not the words I was looking for. I stare at my phone after Lee hangs up. I speculate where our relationship is now. I also wonder who the heck is wearing my cologne in his house.

I should not be on a paranormal excursion right now. I have way too many distractions in my life, and I know I am not giving any of my present situations enough focus.

Chet comes down the hallway from the men's room. I see my crucifix dangling from his right fist.

"Who's the best?" Chet says as he holds the crucifix out toward me.

"Thank you." I take it even though I am skeptical. I can always drop it in my backpack.

"Loretta and Liza are about to begin the séance. I figured you could use the extra mojo just in case things went sideways."

He wiggles his eyebrows, and I laugh. That releases a large portion of the stress I'm holding inside, and I am thankful for Chet. I inspect my crucifix and find that it is cleaner than it has been in months. "This was sweet of you," I say as I put it around my neck.

Coming around the corner, it looks like a movie set. Dusty has brought all equipment to bear in the narrow passage, setting up directly behind Granny and Liza, with the demon trap directly in front of them on the otherwise polished concrete floor.

Chet, step to the side of Liza.

"Where do you want me?" I ask Granny.

She holds out her hand. "Between us so we can keep you safe."

Liza takes my other hand. I can't catch my breath. Liza winks at me, and I croak. Which is not helpful.

"Ladies, this usually does not work, but it is safer if we do not call the spirit by name out loud. For now, focus your energy inside you and visualize the man who has been possessed."

Liza leans forward and looks past me to Granny. Her forehead wrinkles as she frowns.

"Patience, Liza. It's safer. And if it works..." Granny says.

Liza and Granny close their eyes as they set their mouths. I'm so intent on watching them I'm late to begin my meditation.

The thought of dealing with Austin again today is not appealing. Still, if Granny believes it can put an end to this nonsense, it's worth the pain.

I cannot bring Austin into my mind. His face begins to materialize, and then it dissipates. Again, in the background, I am surrounded by crumbling, burning buildings rather than being in the theater.

Bearing down, I try to refocus my energies. I see Austin's cobalt-blue eyes, struggle to hold them steady, and then I fall through them and am in a burning town again.

For the love of all things holy, what in the dickens is going on? If there were ever a time for my "gifts" to actually work, now would be it.

The extended screech of nails on metal runs chills up my spine, and my eyes pop open. I can't see him, but I feel the grimy, evil, chaotic wave roll forward, buffeting the three of us as if we stood in the ocean.

Four large slashes appear in the plaster fifty feet away, and the slashes grow slowly down the wall.

Liza grasps my wrist. I had not realized we had become separated.

Run, April, run.

I can't tell if that's my survivor intelligence speaking to me, or if Austin has tapped into my mind and he wants me to run—to separate again from the group. No, I'm not going to leave my team if I can help it.

"Hmm … smells so tasty."

I think I peed myself.

A massive black creature appears ten feet in front of me.

Yep, I peed.

As if through a trash can, I hear the commotion of the boys talking excitedly behind me. Good, at least my painful, impending death won't be for naught. They'll get some excellent footage for their television show.

"I thought I'd let you see the real me, April. Relationships are better when they are based on transparency. And we're going to have a long, long relationship. I'm so glad we had this time together this weekend. I have learned so many valuable things about you."

I take in the enormous creature standing before me. Crouched so as not to bump his black, rat-like head on the ceiling, he is easily ten feet tall and a lean two hundred and fifty pounds. He barely opens his leathery wings, blocking the hallway completely. His tail, shiny black like the rest of him, is a long, muscular whip shape. As it swishes side to side, it leaks a trail of liquid across the floor from the stinger at its tip the size of my forearm.

His eyes remain cobalt blue.

I glare at him and take a step toward him. My arms pull behind me by Liza's and Granny's firm grips.

I'm shaking so hard I swear my teeth will rattle out at any moment. Still, I muster all the false bravado I can because I know what I must do to save my team.

"Kiss my grits, you impotent bully!"

With a blur of speed, Austin reaches for me, and I fall back with the help of Granny and Liza, landing on my butt.

A roar splits my eardrums.

I look up and find Austin with his muscular arms to the

ceiling, talons tearing through drop-tile ceiling, and I fear he may jump up and out of the trap. Scrambling to my feet, I work on conjuring a chain to hold him in place.

Before I can cast anything, a ball of black smoke appears inside the trap. Austin is gone.

I recoil as the black fog disperses.

"Dagnabbit, that boy's got some wretched gas," Chet complains.

Chapter 40

I prop my butt against the wall and brace my arms on my knees as I work on getting my heart to slow down. I'm too young for a heart attack—but I still might die of one today if I can't get my blood pressure down.

"Is it over?" Luis asks.

Nobody answers him.

Granny sits down on the concrete; Liza does likewise. We stare at one another. Our mutual expressions say it all. That was way too dangerous to be winging it in that manner.

Granny swallows then says, "That was a Hell Kite."

I don't know what the demonic handbook classifies what I just saw as, but I think death animated would suffice. I slide down the wall and sit on the floor, too.

"I've seen two before today. I never thought I would see a third in this lifetime."

"What's the significance?" Liza asks.

Granny sighs. "Hell Kites are the lieutenants of Archangels. They carry out high-level tasks and also have the ability to bind other supernatural entities to them. Ghosts, lesser demons, necromancers—witches—" She looks in my direction.

"But it's over." Dusty squats next to Granny.

"Only one way to be sure." Granny holds out her hand, and Dusty helps her up. "Girls, time to do a full sweep. The slightest blip, call everyone to your area.

We take our time with the sweep. Nobody wants to have a threepeat at the Imperial.

While I work my section with the Early brothers, my mind keeps straying back to how the demon was hiding in the corners on our first visit. It was a testimony to the amount of goodness that must have been in Ted Barker and Ross McQueen.

Granny has said before that some people are Light Keepers. They are the opposite of the pathologically evil. Austin picked the wrong couple to tangle with. He would have sensed their goodness like he senses my power, and he would have thought his plan to have them murdered, genius.

Instead, he imprisoned himself for decades. And we were the ones to set Austin free.

At least we were able to set it right in the end. All's well that ends well.

We're the last to finish our assigned sweep, and the rest of the team has our equipment packed and sitting in the lobby. As we approach, Liza gives a thumbs up and raises her eyebrows.

"All clear," I say.

I look past her, and Dusty is talking with Heather. Her expression does not look like what I would expect from someone whose building has just been swept of supernatural issues.

Curious, I approach them in case I can add some helpful details. And eavesdrop.

Heather notices me. Her head twitches, and I have that weird sensation of looking at two pictures overlaying one another.

I blink hard, and it clears the anomaly.

"I'm so glad everyone is safe," Heather says as she looks over my head. I turn and look behind me.

Nope. Nothing is there. She's such a weird chick.

If I had room to lie down in the van, I would sleep all the way home. Still, it's a good thing I can't. Once we put an end to Austin, all the other demons in my life popped back up.

My life is one long game of whack-a-mole.

First, I need to secure the documents from Dottie's basement. Yes, I hope to find evidence of the Dixie Mafia in Gil's paperwork.

Sue me. After dealing with Austin and the demon, Dottie is looking more like a little old lady accused because of lazy police work.

Plus, I really want to see where all her honey holes are that Elsa found. Seventeen million! That just makes my head spin.

I call Ben Talbot, forgetting that it is the weekend and early in the morning. He agrees to meet me at Dottie's on Tuesday with a crew to move the records out and over to Snow and Associates.

Against my better judgment, I give Dottie a call to tell her we'll be there Tuesday, and I'll need her to let us in the basement. She doesn't answer, so I leave her a voicemail.

It's okay. I didn't really want to *talk* to her, anyway.

Next, I call Petals and More's owner, and I'm glad Rhonda Applewhite sounds like she just woke up. I helped her avoid serious jail time for unethical behavior at her florist shop.

"Hello?"

"Rhonda, this is April Snow."

"April? Why are you calling at this hour?"

"I need to ask a favor, and I don't want to forget."

"Okay..."

"What's the most expensive bouquet you have?"

She hesitates. "I have some triple-layer sorbet peonies."

My stomach rumbles as I think of ice cream. "Are they pretty?"

"Yes."

"I need you to make me an arrangement—with a vase— ready for a pickup tomorrow."

Rhonda clears her throat, "That's a big ask for on the house, April."

As if. If Rhonda were to give them to me, she'd probably be stealing flowers out of the cemetery again. "No. I'm paying for these."

"Oh." Her voice inflection changes. "Great. I'll have them ready for you by noon. You can pick them up any time before five."

Her excitement gives me pause. "By the way, how much will it be?"

"Two hundred and fifty."

Bless it! I draw a deep breath and relax. Two hundred and fifty is cheap compared to what this person has done for me. "Great. I'll see you tomorrow, Rhonda."

Dusty and Miles are carrying on a conversation about an antebellum home in Franklin, Tennessee. The rest of the team is asleep.

Comfortable that I am caught up on my to-do list and grateful to still be on the living side of the veil, I turn sideways and rest my head on the back of the bench seat. I could sleep for a week...

Chapter 41

I stumble out of the van when we arrive at our parents' home. The early-morning air carries a chill on it from the lake. Instinctively, I look across the water's surface at the heavy mist as the sun filtering through the boughs of the tall pines thins the pewter-gray blanket. Few things can lift my spirit like dawn at the lake.

I draw a deep breath, pulling in the cold, humid air. It's a familiar and cleansing breath that helps wipe away the strangeness of the past two days.

The battle is won. The grays, the demon that inhabited Austin Tate, they have perished. Figuratively and literally, it's a new day.

I stand in the driveway with Dusty and Granny to my side. We wave to each team member as they drive their cars out of the gravel lot down by our mechanic's shed.

It's a bittersweet moment, and its poignancy does not escape me. Our collection of eclectic, skillful people became my "geek" family, people who risked their lives with me in search of things the average person would avoid. This is our last goodbye after one of our research trips. It is truly a turn-the-page moment for April May Snow.

Sure, my skill set will be difficult for my brother to replace, but the team was doing well long before I showed up, and they will continue to be successful. I'm not going to kid myself in regards to that. No one is ever indispensable. That includes me.

However, no matter how much I despised these trips at first, they have come to be a "high" that I know I will miss gravely. Especially since I'm finally gaining control and understanding of the "gifts" I was born with. And yes, I do now consider them all *gifts*.

It has been fun learning to control my skills and interesting to find out their different applications. Sadly, I must put them back in the box and seal it forever so I can move forward.

Once I get my career on track in Maryland, there will be no time for flying down to Alabama to traipse around an old house looking for things that go "boo" in the night. Just like I put away my Barbie dolls and tricycle when I was younger, so will I have to put away my extraordinary "gifts."

As the three of us watch the taillights of Miles's car, the last to leave, I look at Granny, and tears pop up in the corner of my eyes as a lump forms in my throat.

How badly am I going to miss the two women who helped me learn to cope, and then master—on most days—my skills? I'm regretful that it took me this long to realize what special people they are and what they could mean to me. Now I'm sorrowful I will be leaving just as I have come to love and appreciate our relationships.

It's as if I was in a special, secret club with each of them. The club was made for only the two of us. It was a club my brothers and parents weren't entirely privy to. I am blessed I got that experience with *both* women because of their differing powers.

I am now so grateful for this time back in Guntersville.

But it is fleeting. I understand when I leave, like when I went to college, the further I am from Guntersville, the weaker my powers will become and eventually atrophy completely. Likewise, I know that every day away is one day closer to when I will not be able to speak to my grandmothers on this side of the veil.

"Oh, honey, what's the matter?" Granny says as she grasps both of my hands.

"I am—just—I don't know," I croak.

"Aw, honey—" Granny pulls me to her. Her head rests against my shoulder while I lean into her hair as the scent of Aqua Net engulfs me. "You're okay. You did a spectacular job. I don't know if I told you or not."

"I'm so glad you were there," I whisper.

"Me too."

I feel it coming on, but I can't stop it. I cry and tremble. Embarrassed, I try to push away, but Granny embraces me tighter.

"You're okay, April. You're safe, your team is safe, and you did your job. But I understand. I do know what this takes out of us."

"I really thought, there for a moment, we were all dead."

Granny offers a rueful laugh. "If I were betting money in Vegas, dead would've been the safe bet." She grabs my shoulders and holds me at arm's length. "Look at me."

I tilt my head up and swipe at a snot bubble with the back of my right hand.

She shakes my shoulders lightly. "April May, I am so proud of you. Do you hear me?"

"Yes, ma'am," I say, the words catching in my throat.

She pulls me in for another hug. This time she tries to squeeze in a bear-hug manner. I'll gladly take all she can give.

"Now, you go get you some rest," Granny says.

That sounds like the best idea ever. "Yes, ma'am. Goodnight."

She grins and raises her eyebrows. "I think you mean good morning."

I favor her a smile and raise my hand to Dusty. "See you tomorrow, Dusty."

"Not if I see you first, Tink," he says with the wink of an eye.

Tears pop into my eyes again as I favor him with a wan smile that frees a tear to streak down my cheek. Bless it. What's with the blasted water works?

I heave my backpack onto my shoulder and shuffle toward my apartment. Motion catches my peripheral vision. I watch four ducks transform from a silhouette against the rising sun into gray-tone versions as they land smoothly to the side of the boathouse.

I lay my backpack on the kitchen table and quickly get into my pajamas inside my apartment. To make myself feel civilized again, I run a brush roughly through my tangled hair and scour my teeth for several minutes with my toothbrush.

As I pad toward my bed, the thought of how close we came to the end of our lives today rolls over me. I redirect my path to the freezer.

I take both the amulet's and the vision stone's ice blocks from the freezer and set them in the sink to thaw.

Sure, Austin has been sent back to wherever he came, presumably taking his witch entourage with him. And I'll be leaving Guntersville soon, too. Still, until then, I will be traveling with all the firepower I can muster.

What's on my mind is the Old Man in the lake. My lifelong nemesis was on my mind during the trip home.

It seems all too apropos for him to quit voicing his idle threats and act on them before I am gone forever. He's been quiet for the past month. I ease my mental partitions halfway down to see if I can hear him.

Lowering my protective barriers down, I redouble my focus, listening for any hint of the old ghost.

I jerk quickly to the slapping sound at my door as I have a mini heart attack.

Puppy freezes and studies me intently.

"Peaches, Puppy. You scared the devil out of me."

He accepts that for hello and struts over to the side of the bed. Puppy leaps onto the foot of the bed, shaking the footboard against the wall.

"You might want to slow down there, big guy. You're getting sorta heavy," I say as I punch my pillow and turn on my side.

Puppy snorts and twirls around five times as he punches the bed quickly with his four paws. He plops down across my legs, effectively pinning me.

I pull my legs out from under him. "Space, dude. We're sharing," I complain as I position my body diagonally on the bed to account for the boulder in the center now.

The ring of my phone wakes me.

"You need to get dressed."

"Jacob?"

"Yes."

"Get dressed. Why?"

"Isn't Dottie Castle still your client?"

He knows she is. "Yes."

"Her house is on fire."

"What—"

"I said your client's house is on fire," Jacob says exceedingly slow, enunciating each syllable with an exaggerated tone.

I struggle to get Puppy off my legs as I look at the time on my phone. I have been asleep for 30 minutes.

"Is everyone all right?"

"Can't say. We've got the entire Guntersville Fire Department out here, and Boaz is on the way to help."

My stomach tightens at the news. "Have you seen Dottie?"

"Not yet. To be honest, I was hoping you might tell me that the old battle-ax had gone somewhere to visit family."

I hop up and down to pull my jeans on. I must still have stress bloat from my interaction with Austin. "No, I haven't spoken with her this weekend."

I recall her not taking my phone call from the theater. Different contingencies, all bad, play through my thoughts. The first my mind latches on to is the paperwork in her basement.

Could she have been telling the truth all along? Could the Dixie Mafia have come back to cover their tracks?

"What did you do last night that you're still asleep?" Jacob asks.

"I was—"

Jacob sighs. "Never mind. It's none of my business. Listen, I've got to get back to playing policeman. I'll see you in a bit."

I frown at my phone as if Jacob can see my displeasure. I know why he is perpetually curt with me now, and I understand his feelings thanks to my grandpa's thoughtful, albeit supernatural, gift. Still, I can't help that Jacob feels more than friendship for me. Once more, there's nothing I can do to make it easier for him. I'll certainly never fake attraction to him in that manner with the "hope" that if I fake it, eventually, my love will spark. We both deserve better than that.

Besides, he will be a catch for some sweet girl one day. The sooner he isn't thinking about me, the sooner he can have the life he deserves.

It's not going to be easy for me to set my best friend free. But it's the right thing to do since I am what is holding him back.

I grab my purse and start for the door. I detour to the bed and give Puppy's side a vigorous rub as I place my forehead on his ear. "You understand platonic relationships, don't you, Puppy?"

He rolls over, exposing his belly for me to rub. I shake my head as I give him a quick belly rub.

All the men in my life are working an angle.

I drive out to Dottie's house faster than I should. I don't know what I think I can accomplish. It's not like I'm going to be able to help put the fire out.

Surely, Jacob called me as a professional courtesy, and the fire is minor. Perhaps it didn't even get to the basement. It may be large because Dottie did go somewhere, leaving nobody at home to report the fire, but the firemen caught it in time to save the documents.

There, that scenario will save my client and the paperwork required to keep her out of prison. I focus my energy on that sequence of events.

I squeeze my eyes tight for a second as I recall that the only family she has left are a couple of nieces that live in Guntersville. That's the sometimes awkward thing about being intimate with people's final will and testament. You have the propensity to know everything about them.

Yet, I don't know everything about Dottie, if the recent visions I pulled from her memory are any indication.

I see an ominous black column of smoke blooming into the powder-blue sky from the hilltop base that Dottie's house sits on top of. It's too large a fire for me to pretend that somebody is burning leaves this morning.

Working my way up the winding road to her house, I know that the Dixie Mafia's evidence has been lost if it existed. If I am to win this case for Dottie, I will have to find another means of proving her assertion.

Jacob was serious. As I pull up, there are more fire engines than last year's Christmas parade.

I find his cruiser and park in front of it. Looking over my right shoulder back at the house, I confirm what the smoke column has already indicated. The windows of the home have exploded outward. Flames lick the underbelly of the aluminum gutters that melt due to the intense heat. A four-foot round hole has appeared at the roof's peak, releasing a tower of flames reaching high into the sky.

The home will be a total loss.

I get out and walk toward the driveway. Jacob meets me halfway up the drive.

"Do I need to write you a ticket, Snow?"

I'm confused. "Why?"

"There's no way you got here that quick driving the speed limit."

I begin to answer him with a joke. I study his expression and am shocked that he is actually angry with me. I think it best to skip over the topic. "Has anybody heard from Dottie?"

"In the last fifteen minutes? No."

I'm afraid to ask the next question. "Inside?"

Jacob frowns. "The firemen rescued some dogs through the side window earlier, but we haven't found any people."

"Well, at least the puppies are safe." I scan the burning building as if I expect Dottie to come bursting out the front door. "I sure do wish we knew where Dottie was."

"That makes two of us," Jacob grumbles. "It's a big house, and because we can't determine if she is home, the fire crew has to treat it as a rescue until they've confirmed no one's alive in there."

"Jacob, even if she is in there, she's not coming out alive."

Jacob crosses his arms and cocks his hip. "Yeah, I was sort of thinking that myself."

We stand in companionable silence, watching the fire crews do their best to douse the flames. The smoke has turned from roiling pitch black to a frothy gray.

"Assuming the old woman isn't home, how's your case coming?"

"I'll know better once we see if the paperwork in the basement is still intact."

Jacob shoots me a sideways glance. "If that's what you're basing your case on, your goose is cooked."

I shake my head, and he grins. "Not even funny."

He gestures with his forefinger and thumb, level with his eyes. "Just a little funny."

"No, it's morbid."

"Eh, a coping mechanism for the job." Jacob's head swivels as he holds his hand up to me. "Hold on a second."

Jacob takes off, jogging toward the street. He certainly commands attention at six foot two and well over two hundred pounds, a baton and Glock bouncing at his side on his belt. He waves down the blue Corolla, slow-rolling in front of the house. Jacob makes a gesture in the air for them to turn around.

The driver quickly turns the car around in a three-point turn and drives back down the hill. Jacob saunters back toward me, his jaw set as he shakes his head.

He points back toward the road. "Now *that's* morbid. They don't have any reason to be up here other than to see what's going on, and I'm sure it would tickle them pink for somebody to be dragging a body bag out of the house right now."

I nod my agreement as we resume watching the crews battle the remnants of the fire. The flames no longer are visible from the exterior of the home. A squad of three firemen have chopped through the front door and are hosing down the house's interior from a few steps in the foyer.

"I never understood why everybody refers to this as a farm," I say.

Jake loops his thumbs onto his belt. "Christmas trees."

"Pardon?"

He looks at me and licks his lips. "I said Christmas trees. Before the Castles bought the place, it used to be a Christmas tree farm."

"Huh. Who knew?"

"I'd say everybody older than us."

"You're in rare form today. Are you gonna hit the road with that act?" I tease.

"I'll be here all week, folks—" He embellishes with a wave of his hand.

This is the Jacob I love to be around. The one that always makes me laugh and keeps it real. The surly, moody Jacob is not enjoyable company.

He looks at me and favors me with a lopsided grin. "I'm not sure if this is an appropriate time to tell you, but honestly, I don't know with our schedules when would be a good time, and I don't want you to hear through the grapevine."

My stomach flutters. I feel both exhilaration for my friend and sadness for me that a local girl has claimed his heart. I know … I planned to let him go from our relationship stunting his growth. Still, I can be melancholy that this season in my life, the season where Jacob is the first friend I share with, is over.

I wait to hear her name.

"I'm leaving town next week."

I'm surprised and admittedly confused. I always assumed he would pick a girl from our county. "Oh?"

He looks away from me. "Yeah, I'm headed up to DC for a job."

I open my mouth and close it. I open it again, and air comes out, but no words. I'm sure I look like a fish struggling for breath right now. I'm simply a woman attempting to comprehend what I'm being told.

"There's not much here for me anymore. Since Mom and Grandma moved down to Florida, there's no family. And if I have any designs on being the police chief, Walt Edison has at least ten years before he retires." He shrugs his massive shoulders. "I figure it's time to broaden my horizons a bit and get some more experience so that I can be a police chief sometime in the future."

"Jacob—I didn't even know you wanted to be a police chief."

He bites his upper lip and stares at me for the longest time. "It's not my *first choice* of what I want to be when I grow up. But now that I understand that what I really want is not an option for me, being a police chief sounds like a great backup plan."

The lump that starts in the back of my throat grows, nearly choking off my breath. I won't make this about me and how this pains me, when I know it is nothing compared to the hurt and disappointment my best friend feels. I do my best to steady my voice. "You'll make the best police chief ever, Jacob."

Having said his piece, he turns his attention back to the fire team at work.

"With you being in DC and me in Baltimore, we'll be able to get lunch together. We need to set a standing date right now. Is the second Tuesday of every month good for you?"

Jacob's eyebrows knit together. "I won't be in DC."

"You said you were going to DC," I say as I gesture with my finger.

"Yes, for orientation. But I won't be stationed there."

"Military?"

"No, it's law enforcement. It's an opportunity Vander hooked me up with."

It's as if a cold hand reaches into my chest and squeezes my heart as the day turns to pitch dark. I don't know what Vander does, but I know it's exceedingly dangerous. And that's okay for Vander, but not Jacob. "Jacob, I don't like the idea of you in the CIA."

He guffaws. "It's not the CIA. Vander's group is domestic. Besides, it's a wonderful opportunity. Vander says, given my past military and law enforcement background, I could be running my own team by the end of the year."

"Own team of what?" I say as I gesture wildly with my hands.

"Investigators, of course."

"Investigating what? What does Vander do? Jacob Hurley, what have you signed up for?"

Jacob looks over his right shoulder and smirks at me. "That's on a need-to-know basis, Snow. And you don't need to know."

The fire chief strides toward us. "Bad news, folks. We found a body."

Chapter 42

I'm so mad at Vander I could just spit. What in the world is he thinking drawing Jacob into his top-secret, cloak-and-dagger universe?

If Vander wants to have a death wish, that's his business. We all knew in high school that Vander was dangerous and not long for this world. But Jacob? My sweet Jacob?

I swear Michael VanDerveer better hope some serial killer takes him out before I see him next. I'll give him a piece of my mind that he won't soon forget.

How is this all becoming so blasted complicated so close to April's victory lap? I should be celebrating escaping this town and at the same time having done so without leaving anybody worse for the wear. But no! Howard has to lose his ever-loving mind and decide to close his law business to be a pizza doughboy, and my best friend decides he wants to join some bad-boy cult reserved for crazy-eyed Southern boys who don't have the sense to get out of the way of a gun.

I swear, the men in my life just chap my butt. It's as if they haven't got the sense God gave a goose.

Turning on one of the switchbacks down from Dottie's place, I take the turn too fast and nearly fly out over the top of the fifty-foot pines. I brake and feel my car slide before the rear tires grip again.

That's it. I'm done. I admit that Granny and Nana are

right. I can't be responsible for anybody but myself. I'm attempting to decide what everybody else should do with their lives. The more I think about it, the more they do something stupid like taking a job someone like Vander offers them.

Bless it. I've got to calm down, or I'm not gonna make it to my twenty-eighth birthday. Knowing my luck, if I were to pass on the same day as Dottie, we would have to share a room in heaven or something.

Don't get me wrong, I hate that she is dead. I genuinely hope that if it was the Dixie Mafia, they didn't make her suffer. But honestly, something was always off with that woman, and even though I wouldn't wish her dead, I'm not particularly upset that I won't have to defend her.

Not knowing what happened to her is going to drive me nuts. And I know, given their lack of investigation on Gil's murder, the local detectives will be more than happy to say Dottie accidentally started a fire and burned herself up.

Nope, I can't focus on that. I need to do something that makes me happy.

When I get home to my apartment, I'm going to turn my phone off so none of the stupid men in my life can interrupt me. I'll put the amulet around my neck, and I'm going to finally master transferring the sphere of light from my right hand to my left. That's what I'm going to do. Before I leave this town, I will master that level of control.

My heartbeat slows and my breathing normalizes as I visualize the beautiful blue-silver orb on my right hand rolling onto my left palm. It makes me happy and centers me.

I pull into my parents' driveway and see a familiar metallic-blue Nova Super Sport. For Pete's sake. I pulled another annoying man into my gravitational pull. Is the man so hard up for cash that he's got to come collect on a Sunday?

I get out of my car and shut the door a little too hard.

I stomp my way to the sliding glass door, assuming Baker Diaz is inside bending my parents' ear about needing a check for the investigation he completed.

Seriously, the man did excellent work. And I'm going to pay him, but a little patience would be appreciated.

I grab hold of the sliding glass door handle, and voices make me turn toward the lake. I cock my head as I take a moment to comprehend what I'm seeing. Daddy is sitting on one of his canvas chairs smoking a cigar, and a man who looks suspiciously like Baker Diaz is next to him drinking a beer. The two men are looking at the edge of the dock where Puppy is having a conniption fit, barking at catfish or something in the water.

Fine. Have a drink and a smoke with my daddy while you wait on me to show and cut you a check.

Have some common sense, Daddy. For all you know, Baker is a serial murderer stalking your daughter.

Whatever Puppy is barking at has his full attention. He's following it to the low-slung plastic platform we use to mount the WaveRunner. Something black and sleek disrupts the water and pulls itself up onto the platform.

Puppy hops onto the floating dock and nips behind the black Lab's ear. The Lab turns and paws at Puppy.

I'm catatonic at the beginning of the dock. "Well, I'll be."

Daddy turns toward me, his half-smoked cigar in his right hand. "There you are."

Regaining my composure, I walk down the dock. "Is that who I think it is?"

Baker turns in his chair and favors me with a smile. "Was somebody looking for a Lab?"

"Where in the heck did you find him?"

Baker laughs. "The one place everybody said not to look."

I stop short of the floating dock and roll my hands out in a questioning manner.

Baker stands and walks toward the two dogs. "Remember when Roman said that Ivy would never take Bailey to her parents?"

"No—"

Baker leans over and pulls the tennis ball from Bailey's mouth. He tosses it a few feet into the water, and Bailey happily dives after it. The dog has obviously exorcised his demons over swimming.

"True story. On a hunch, I went by the parents' place, and when they answered the door, there was a black Lab. I explained the situation to them, and they said that Ivy had dropped him off a couple days earlier, and they couldn't decide what to do."

"What do you mean they couldn't decide what to do? They should have called us."

Baker shrugs. "And we need to discuss that. They said their daughter dropped Bailey off because the longer he was with her, the madder she got at Roman. Even though the whole setup at the river was a hoax to make Roman worry, she was afraid she actually might hurt Bailey. So, to keep that from happening, she dropped him off at her parents' and then headed up toward Washington state. They say she's got girlfriends up there. She plans to lick her wounds with sympathetic ears."

"Well, she better be getting a good lawyer," I say.

Bailey hops back up on the platform. Baker steps down onto it and rubs both dogs. "I need to ask a favor, April."

"What's that?"

"I got Bailey back. I promised her parents that you and Roman wouldn't press charges. That we all could act like everything is right, finalize the divorce since Bailey goes to Roman, and get on with your lives."

"Baker, that's not exactly something you should've promised them without checking with me first."

He glares at me, and there's a cold glint in his eyes that reminds me of Vander when he is in his intense mode.

"With all due respect, I didn't think leaving the dog with them after exposing that I know where the dog is, was a good decision. I'm going to expect that you can convince your client it is in his best interest to drop the charges."

"That is reasonable, April," Daddy says. I didn't see him get up from his chair.

I think it over for a moment. On the one hand, it irks me that Ivy was able to eat up my time and my friends with her little hoax. But truthfully, Roman gets his dog back in good health in the end. Shouldn't that be what's really important?

I sigh. "I'll give it my best shot."

Baker smiles. "I don't want your best shot. I want you to make it happen."

I go inside the house to get an extra sheet to put over my passenger seat for Bailey to ride on. Mama is in the den.

"Mama, do you have an old sheet I can use?"

"Oh, I'm glad you're here. I need to have that conversation with you, April."

I shake my head. "I can't, Mama. I need to get Roman his dog back."

"April, this is important."

"Getting a man on the verge of suicide his dog that he believes dead *is* important."

Mama grits her teeth and narrows her eyes. I'm about to give in because that look really scares me. She turns and plods off toward the linen closet.

She's rummaging through the linen closet, making a mess of her highly organized stacks of linens. The red color has reached her ears, indicating that she is doing my bidding, but I will pay for it dearly later.

Mama swivels and holds out two sheets. "Use these and put them in the wash when you get back."

I move to take them from her, and she pulls them back. "Only if you promise me you'll talk with me when you get back."

"Geez. I promise, Mama," I say.

"I'm going to hold you to it."

I take the sheets from her and quick-walk outside to my car. I make short work of setting both sheets on the seat, tucking them in nicely. Miraculously, when I call Bailey, it's as if he knows I'm taking him home. He stands at the open passenger door until I tell him it's okay to get in. He hops directly onto the passenger seat, turns, and sits down neatly.

Wow, if I could only get Puppy to do that.

I'm at Roman's fifteen minutes later. Bailey whines as we drive up the driveway. When I open the driver's-side door to get out, he jumps over my lap and out the door, leaving me covered with muddy pawprints. So much for his stellar dog riding abilities.

I ring the doorbell twice, and nobody answers. Changing strategy, I call Roman's cell phone.

"April?"

"Where are you, Roman?"

"At home. Why?"

"Come open your door. I've got a surprise for you."

"Okay."

Bailey has started scratching furiously at the front door. "Stop that," I say. It has no effect on the dog.

The door opens. I take a step back when I see Roman. The man has raccoon eyes set two inches deep in his skull, and his skin looks like it hasn't seen the sun in a decade. But when Bailey slams into his legs, knocking him on his butt, the man wraps his arms around the black Lab's neck.

I watch the joy of the reunion. It helps with the stressful things I saw during the supernatural trip this weekend, the death of Dottie, and even the idiotic decision of my best friend to trust Michael VanDerveer.

A man and his dog. A year ago, I never would've understood it. Now I understand perfectly.

"Where on earth did you find him?" Roman hugs Bailey's neck again. "I thought you believed he was dead."

"Listen, we need to talk about something, Roman."

He scratches behind Bailey's ears. Bailey thumps the floor with his hind leg. "Talk about what?"

"Talk about the divorce settlement with Ivy."

"I plan to hang that woman by her toes for the next twelve years."

"That's just it." I gesture toward Bailey. "You have your dog, and we've negotiated everything else on the divorce. All we need to do is have both sides approve it."

"Hardly. She caused considerable emotional damage to Bailey and me."

"Sure, I hear you and understand. But to get Bailey back, I had to promise that you wouldn't press charges against Ivy."

Roman stops rubbing Bailey's ears. "Why would you promise that?"

"Because sometimes getting what you want is more important than vengeance."

Chapter 43

Yes, the feel-good moment of getting Bailey back to Roman was enjoyable. Still, it has knocked me off my schedule for today. Plus, my jeans have muddy dog prints on them. I'm not looking to set a new fashion statement, and especially not when paying my respects.

Coming up my parents' driveway, I'm going so fast I bottom out my IROC. I promised Rhonda I would pick up the flowers before she closes, and although I have plenty of time, the way today has gone, I don't want to push my luck.

I park and run to my apartment. I slam the door behind me, making a beeline for my closet. Where I planned on wearing jeans, I now decide that it will be more appropriate to wear a dress. Nothing fancy, but it seems like the better call.

I nearly jump out of my skin when someone knocks on my door. "Hello?"

The doorknob twists. "April, can I come in?"

"Uh—yes."

"Our talk." Mama raises her eyebrows.

"Mama, can we hit pause? I've got only a few minutes to get down to Rhonda Applewhite's store."

"This will only take a minute."

I turn back toward my closet and roll my eyes so that she can't see. I select a printed cotton dress, hang it on the back of my closet door, and get to peeling my jeans off.

"I owe you an apology."

"For what?" I ask as I try to kick free of the jeans stuck to my ankles.

"On the phone the other day, you asked if I had ever heard of a lock witch."

I pull my T-shirt off and reach for my dress. "Right."

Mama snorts and shakes her head. She looks to be on the verge of tears. I've rarely ever seen Mama cry.

"What's the matter?"

"April, you need to leave."

I screw up my face and laugh. "I know. I told you that when you came in."

"No, baby. I mean, you need to leave Guntersville."

I squat down in my closet, searching for matching shoes. "I'm working on that, too, Mama. I just have a few things to finish up at the office."

"April, you are not listening to me. Loretta told me what happened in Shelbyville. And my mom had told me last week that there might be an issue."

The more I think about it, pumps are not the right choice, and I grab a pair of Keds. "You know what they say, all's well that ends well. Everybody made it home, Mama."

"The lock witch is part of a prophecy. A prophecy that deals specifically with the city of Guntersville."

I pick up my purse. "Mama, all super interesting. And I would love to have this conversation over a bottle of wine, which I believe was the deal. But I've really got to go right now."

"The lock witch, if she joins forces with the key warlock, can open the gates of hell. Or seal them forever."

A nervous laugh escapes me as I freeze in my tracks. "An old wives' tale?"

Mama shakes her head. "Oh, how I wish it were. I've seen it firsthand. Your aunt Dionis was a lock witch, and although by "joining" the prophecy does not mean sexual, she did have a child with a key warlock."

Memories flash of the ghost of my aunt Dionis appearing at my bed during a thunderstorm and handing me the amulet that I've kept frozen in my freezer. I tried to get rid of the amulet twice, and it came back to me.

"Mama—what are you trying to tell me?"

She draws a breath, and it makes her tremble. "I'm sorry. To keep you safe, I may have caused more damage than good."

"No more riddles, Mama."

"Don't you see?"

I think I feel it deep down, but I still want to deny it. The feeling that something is off with me and everyone but me knows what it is.

"April, you are a lock witch."

I stare at her to see if there's more. She doesn't say anything else, and I laugh. "If this is some joke, it's just not that funny."

"It's no joke. As much as I wish it weren't true, you are the lock witch of this generation. If you stay here, your powers will continue to grow, and more supernatural entities will come and attempt to convince you by persuasion or force to join them."

I'm sure I'm staring at Mama as if she's grown a second head. "You're mistaken."

"I'm not. Loretta and Pauline called it when you were born. I was in denial until the day that something tried to grab you in the lake. Then I knew. Your signature was already too large to protect you."

"No. Mama, it's not like that. Look, Nana showed me how to block those voices, and I was fine. I don't know what happened between then and when I came home. Things are certainly different now."

"It's because I put a binding spell on your powers. I had that option with you a minor, and I wasn't overly concerned since you left for college before your eighteenth birthday, which is when it would wear off."

I brace myself against the counter. "A binding spell? What's that?"

She looks down at the floor. "It takes away your supernatural skills until your eighteenth birthday, then they come back into existence."

"But that would mean you have powers—" I stare at her.

Mama arches her eyebrows.

"How do I not know this!"

"You haven't exactly asked."

"It doesn't seem like I should have to. And what gives you the right to bind my gifts?"

"A mother's right to keep her child safe. There was no signature for the entities to follow with your powers bound."

"So, the mental partitions that Nana taught me?"

"They would work now. But before your eighteenth birthday, you had a binding spell that eliminated all of your abilities, which rendered the partitions moot."

I grunt. "You had no right to do that."

Mama's head snaps up, and she looks directly at me. "I'm your mother. I have the right to do whatever it takes to keep you safe."

Anger bubbles up from inside me. I feel the heat rush up my neck, causing my ears to burn. "But you didn't. That didn't make me safer. If anything, it put me in danger because I didn't know what to avoid."

"I know. And you're right. It did not work out the way I meant it to."

"Didn't work out the way you meant it to? Do you realize what sort of danger you put me in?"

"That wasn't the intent."

"So, what? Everybody knew except me?"

"Your grandmothers, of course, and then your father and uncle."

"You're unbelievable. I don't even know what to do with

this right now."

"April, the lock witch loses her powers the longer she's away from the gate. From the time you could talk, you said you were leaving. It hurt my heart to think that you wanted to go, but at the same time, I was relieved because it meant that you would be away and not have to worry about the prophecy.

"But then you just showed up one day from Atlanta, and I thought okay, she's only going to be here for a couple weeks until she gets her feet under her. Now it's been a year, and you're attracting things, if you haven't noticed."

"Of course, I've noticed I'm attracting things!" I scream. "I'm just saying it would've been helpful to know *why* I'm attracting things."

"I was just trying to keep you safe."

I raise my hands. "You know what? I just can't. I'm running late, and I've got something to do. I'll deal with this later."

Chapter 44

I make it to Rhonda's florist shop with five minutes to spare, no thanks to Mama and her secrets. I pay Rhonda for the impressive bouquet, and she all but pushes me out the door.

Driving up to my destination, I can't help but replay in my head what Mama said. One thing I comprehend with absolute clarity: Guntersville never was a safe option for my residence. At least not if I didn't want to have to be fighting off demon suitors my entire life. Yuck.

At least that issue will be easy enough to solve since I will be packing as soon as I finish the last cases at Snow and Associates. Packing—Baltimore—I'm missing something in this puzzle.

Oh, fudge nut! I totally forgot about Lee.

I quickly find his number in my favorites and dial. My call goes directly to voicemail—odd. I try again with the same result. Again, I wish there was some way I could know if he's looking at his phone, seeing my name, and denying the call, or if he has his phone set at one ring before it goes to voicemail.

This is too important to chance. I change directions and speed toward Lee's lake house. I know he is supposed to be down in Birmingham at Marty's mom's place. Still, in case he shows up before I make it there tonight, I want him to be greeted by a note that lets him know how much I love him.

Where I was once just excited to be going to Baltimore with him, now it's become imperative. I can't be sure if all Mama's talk about the prophecy is true or just a bunch of bull malarkey, but I don't want to leave anything to chance.

And bless it. It's got to be better up in Baltimore. Lately, I feel like a juggler with twelve balls in the air. It's impossible for me to take care of everything without dropping a ball or two, like calling your boyfriend and letting him know where you are.

Coming around the bend at Lee's subdivision, I get a tickle in my stomach when I see his truck parked in his driveway. That explains some things. He probably just got back from Birmingham and lay down to nap.

I rush to the front door and trot into the hallway. "Lee! Where are you?"

Walking through the foyer, I look to the left; he's not in the living room. He's not in the kitchen to the right of the home, either. I was correct. He must be taking a nap. I make my way to the master bedroom in a light jog.

"Lee," I say as I enter the bedroom. My eyebrows jump as my jaw drops. I watch him slap three pairs of jeans into a suitcase. "What are you doing?"

He doesn't look at me as he turns back to his dresser. "Going to work."

A nervous laugh escapes me. "You usually pack that much to go throw the ball?"

He shoves a pile of T-shirts on top of the jeans. "I do when I'm traveling out of state."

"I don't understand?"

He looks up and smirks. "Well, that would make two of us."

I move closer to him and raise my hand. "Wait, stop."

"Why? Tell me one reason why, April."

"Why stop, or why not go?"

Lee shrugs. "Either."

"Are you saying you're going to Baltimore?"

"Well, there's certainly nothing holding me here."

I lean my head back as if I've been slapped. "Okay. That's rude."

He finally looks at me. "No. Rude is your significant other never being around because she's traipsing around the countryside with her brothers and ex-lovers."

"Ex-lovers?"

"Don't play coy."

My face wrinkles up as I shake my head. "You don't even know what you're talking about. Listen, I don't know what you're all upset about, but you're not gonna take it out on me."

Lee braces his hands on the bed and leans forward. "You don't know what I'm talking about? About the fact that you're not taking this relationship seriously. I don't feel like you're committed to our relationship lately."

"Well, that's rich. I suppose you're taking it seriously."

"Yes. I'm taking it very seriously."

"Says the guy who hasn't given the girl a ring."

Lee favors me with an incredulous smile. "Is that it? Do you need a ring to be a thoughtful person? Wow, if I'd only known," he mocks.

I sigh. "I didn't mean that. I'm only tired and grouchy."

"Oh, I think you meant it. It's funny, though, because we had this discussion before, and you agreed with me that it wasn't necessary to get married."

"Maybe I've changed my mind. Maybe it's good for both of us to have made a commitment."

"Wow. I must let that one sink in. I kinda thought offering you to come with me was a commitment." Lee snaps his suitcase shut. "You know what? You have your plane ticket, and you can come up anytime you want to. As for me, I'm leaving tonight, and if you follow, great. If you don't, I won't hold it against you."

"Are you breaking up with me?" I ask.

He laughs. "No, April. This is me giving you plenty of room to figure out what you think you want. I know I want you. But I'm also not going to beg for your attention while you spend time with men I don't know, that you dated in the past."

"It wasn't like that. That's not even fair."

Lee picks up his suitcase and brushes by me. "I guess life isn't always fair, April. Lock up on your way out."

Chapter 45

The sting of Lee's rebuke is real as I drive to Whispering Willows cemetery. I can't recall a boyfriend ever being so harsh with me—to my face.

I grit my teeth as I focus on the fact that I had a hand in our temporary speed bump. If I had been thoughtful and kept him in the loop about what I was doing today. Peaches. If I had thought to call him at all...

Until I was concerned about getting out of Guntersville, in case Mama's campfire prophecy story has any validity to it, I hadn't so much as a thought of Lee. It is as if he is some high-priced Uber driver I have scheduled for later in the month.

What is that about? The man I love, and he never crossed my mind?

Wait. It's not like I wasn't fighting witches and a demon, watching my least favorite client burn up in her home from a Mafia hit, and doing the one positive thing to come out of the weekend—reuniting a man with his best friend. Yeah, my cup overfloweth this weekend.

Meanwhile, what was Mr. Jealous up to? Hanging out with his catcher, drinking some beer, and gosh knows what else. Let's be real here. Why didn't he call me?

Oh, well, Lee did call Friday afternoon, but he had forgotten about my trip. That's what started his sulk fest.

I suppose there's plenty of blame to go around if I care

to go down that path. But it's a waste of time. I'll focus on finishing up in Guntersville and getting to Baltimore as quickly as possible to start my new, very sane, predictable life with Lee.

The man I love—and forgot to call.

I drive under the tall stone archway entering into the cemetery. A honeycomb of asphalt single-lane paths divides up the gently rolling hills dotted with willows and oaks. Rhonda, now back in good graces with the cemetery, with my help, gave me Antoine's mother's plot number. As soon as she said G 36, I remember Antoine mentioning it when we first talked in the police station.

Following the crude drawing Rhonda made for me on the back of my invoice, I wind past a giant statue of Jesus in the center of the cemetery. The path carries me over the top of the hill. As I turn right into section G, I notice a lone figure sitting on the ground next to one of the headstones.

Even from a distance, it's easy to identify Antoine from his height.

I slow down and consider if I should give him his time alone and come back tomorrow to pay my respect to his mother. Still, I know Antoine's nature, and he would be welcoming if not appreciative of the company.

Exiting my car with the bouquet in hand, I push my car door without shutting it, so as not to disturb him. Antoine is deep into meditation, and I don't want to startle him.

As I near him, he angles his head toward me and smiles. "She said you might pay a visit."

There's no need to question him. I understand fully. I stand at his side and lower myself into a sitting position, crossing my legs. "I thought I would bring her some flowers to show how much I appreciate what she did for me."

He winks at me. "She said you might be doing that, too."

I hand the flowers to Antoine. He leans forward with his long arm and easily places them in the brass flower vase.

We sit in companionable silence.

Reading the headstone, I see *Melissa "Missy" Lattimore,*

cherished daughter and mother. I do the math and am shocked to realize she died at the young age of 58. It's unfathomable for me to think of my parents, who are of a similar age, not being here for me.

I put my hand on top of Antoine's hand on his thigh. He closes his eyes and sighs.

"I'm sorry she left so soon."

He hangs his head, his dreads shifting and covering his face. "Me too," he says with a strangled voice as I watch a tear land on his crossed legs.

It's unclear to me why Missy sent Antoine on this mission. The mission to warn me about the grays. I'm forever grateful, but I don't understand the connection.

Obviously, I knew Antoine, but we weren't friends, and I never met his mom Missy, although I think I remember seeing her in the stands. Still, how good is the memory of a fourteen-year-old while cheering.

The sun sets, and the air takes on a new chill. "Antoine, I think I'm going to leave now. Where is your car?"

"It's at the hotel."

I squint my eyes. "Is something wrong with it?"

"Nah. It was a nice day, so I wanted to walk to clear my head."

"Can I give you a ride to the hotel?"

"No—I think I'll sit here for a spell longer."

"And walk back alone in the dark?"

He angles his head toward me and flashes that brilliant smile that warms my heart. "I'm never alone, April. Jesus walks with me."

I nod my head and flex my legs to rise. "Promise to reach out to me if you need anything, Antoine," I say as I squeeze his shoulder. He pats my hand with his long fingers.

"Don't worry about me. I'm good."

I touch the smooth granite of Missy's tombstone. "Thank you, Ms. Lattimore."

I'd be lying if I didn't say that I feel uneasy about leaving Antoine by himself. Something is itching at the back of my mind that tells me I shouldn't, but what am I supposed to do? Sit out here and freeze to death?

Reluctantly I start back toward my car. It all seems sort of anti-climactic. This whole time in Guntersville, which according to Mama, never should've taken place, is winding down.

The big mystery left undone at the Imperial theater a few months back has been taken care of. As of today, I have zero cases left pending at Snow and Associates. Howard should be thrilled since he can close the office without leaving anybody in the lurch.

And I'm leaving Guntersville, which is what I always wanted.

To be with a man who doesn't want to marry me and I don't think about if I get too busy.

A gust of wind blows in from the south, lifting grit and the decaying leaves into the air. I shield my face, and still, I feel something's sticking in my right eye. As I stop to extract the grit, I experience a sudden jerking motion, as if someone has tied a nylon rope around my waist and hooked it to the back of a speeding pickup truck.

I panic as all light evaporates. Smell and sound, too. The only sensation I feel is the constant tug on my body and the coldness that is the void. Struggling, I try to get control of my emotions so I can decipher what has taken place.

This is different from past times when I have transferred in between times and places. Those episodes had been from me, allowing my mind to float indiscriminately. Always a dangerous proposition given the numerous holes in my veil barrier.

This is a totally foreign feeling. Something or someone is pulling me toward it, and there is no escape. I have no way to brace my feet and fight the momentum that is picking up speed.

My ears pop as if someone clapped their hands on both ears, rupturing my eardrums. Red, pink, and orange flash before me. I bend over, putting my hands on my knees as I struggle for breath, realizing that the atmosphere is spoiled with acrid smoke.

Cautiously, I tilt my head to better understand where I am and my circumstances. I immediately identify where I am.

I'm on Gunter Avenue, between Snow and Associates and the courthouse. My building is wholly gutted, with smoke smoldering out of it. I only know that it's where Snow and Associates should be because the pile of rubble is in the corner that our building sits on. Rotating toward the courthouse, I see it's in better condition, still standing, but all its windows are gone, and the roof has been burned through.

Fires burn indiscriminately up and down Gunter Avenue from the buildings not yet entirely demolished.

My anxiety level spikes for a second time. This foreign, war-pocked version of my picturesque Southern town is unlike any other travel I have made through the void. Rather than a time or place, this has more of a—dreamlike quality? I am reticent to move since I have no history to draw upon.

I hear a skittering noise to my left and swivel quickly. My muscles clamp tightly as I see a gray tail disappear behind one of the debris fields.

That makes me more cognizant of my surroundings. I look up at the sky, which blooms abnormally with purple and red bruises in constant flux, as if someone is releasing huge dye droplets into the atmosphere from above. As the alternating red-and-purple splotches emanate outward in a rippling motion, another drop hits directly above me.

Instinctively, I pat my hips and back. Of course not. A girl couldn't get lucky enough to be transported with her weapons of choice.

Fine. I'll have to rely on my magical powers to protect myself.

Before I attempt to create a protective shield around me, I already sense that there is an issue. Still, I focus on bringing as much energy as possible into my chest. I concentrate with all my might on creating a shield to protect myself from the witches in this alternate reality.

Nothing happens.

"I told you I learned an awful lot about you, lock witch."

I jerk to my right, looking toward the courtroom. Austin Tate stands at the top of the stairs with his hands in his pocket and legs crossed.

Chapter 46

"Don't call me that," I growl.

Austin ambles down the stairs. "As you wish. I'll call you whatever you want as long as you open the gate like I require."

"I will not do your bidding." I'm talking a tough game, but my knees are shaking. I realize that everything is playing against me as I see multiple witches appearing from the various buildings in my periphery. Not only am I greatly outnumbered, but I also have no means of defending myself.

Austin smirks as he walks toward me. "Oh, I have a multitude of ways of coercing your cooperation."

"I'll die before I help you."

Austin's eyebrows knit as he puckers his lips. "Your bravery has never been in question, lock—April. You would be the last thing I kill." He ticks off his fingers one by one. "Dusty, Chase, that nasty little woman you call Granny, Mama, Daddy, hmm...

"I might find something useful for the witch you call Nana. She's actually sort of hot."

As I think of losing everybody that means something to me, tears come to my eyes, but I refuse to let this demon know how deeply he's threatening me. I ball my fists and convert my fear to anger as effectively as possible.

Austin halts six feet in front of me and crosses his left arm over his chest as he touches the index finger of his right hand to his lip. "Of course, for starters, I think I'll let my girls pull

Puppy apart by his legs." He turns and waves his arms behind him. "Would you like that, ladies?"

Now numbering easily two dozen, the grays jump up and down with anticipation as they wring their spindly hands at the ends of their short arms. "Yes, yes," they cackle.

Austin turns his attention back to me. "So, April. Are we going to do this the easy way, or will you let me kill everyone you love first and then do my bidding?"

The hopelessness settles in on me like a long, moonless winter night. This is an end worse than death. To hopefully spare my family, I will open the gates of hell onto humanity.

I'm a logical girl, and I understand that the devastation and havoc wreaked by the evil entities released could kill the very people I hope to save. I rack my brain for a contingency plan, but nothing comes to mind.

As I think, the witches close in on me, and I am entirely circled.

"Good girl. Submitting at this point is best. I know you want to fight, but it truly is futile."

Austin nods his head at two of the witches. They step forward, and despite my lack of power in this construct of their reality, they look hesitant as they wrap a black chain around my waist. The two ends lead out like a dual leash. They grasp the ends. As they lock the chain in place, I am engulfed by a sadness unlike anything I have felt before.

"I must say I am quite shocked that you bought that little ruse of mine at the theater." He raises his hands and mocks, "Help me, I'm trapped in this finger painting."

"How utterly gullible. Still, I have heard many reports that you could be quite—foolish," Austin says.

The two witches jerk on the chain, and I'm forced forward as we move off Gunter Avenue down Worth Street toward Blount Avenue. Mostly, I look down as they drag me along, but my town's destruction is all but complete when I look up. Every building—every home and storefront—has some damage, and all are on fire.

"Marah, Dinah, and Miriam, open the path for the key," Austin commands.

Three of the grays leap forward in their unnatural manner. They take a position on top of the dike as they begin their incantation in a language I've never heard before. The two witches with my chain pull me past Blount Avenue as the other grays follow in a herd behind us.

"I do hope you don't mind, April. But we will have to summon the key from the last generation to complete the prophecy. Your family has done such an admirable job of keeping you and the current key apart."

I notice the consternation in Austin's expression. It occurs to me he doubts this will work.

"You're an idiot, Austin. Even a hack knows the prophecies must be followed to the letter," I snarl.

"It's a matter of interpretation. It will certainly work."

I'm getting under his skin. It makes me feel good, and a tingle comes to life in my fingers.

I gasp as the lake tears apart. The three witches on the dike chant louder, and a six-foot-wide path, stretching ten feet out into the channel, has already opened and is becoming wider. The amount of energy this must be consuming is mind-boggling.

"You know where the key is?" Austin taunts.

"Which one? The one you need or the one you're going to be disappointed in when it doesn't work?"

"Stop with your silliness. It will work."

"I'm just trying to save you from the disappointment." I gesture by rolling my head and nodding my forehead at the different grays surrounding me. "Your girls will lose confidence in your ability when you fail."

Austin crosses his arms. "You don't know where the key is, do you?"

I roll my eyes and turn my head from him.

"Wow. To think that your father and uncle could keep the truth from you for this long." Austin laughs. "You Snows missed your calling. Y'all could've run a small empire with your ability to keep secrets and be ruthless when you need to be."

I know he's only trying to get in my head, and I try to ignore him. But after my discussion with Mama today, I can't help if it's a sore spot, and I'm liable to believe anything. I watch in horror as the lake continues to part, now thirty feet wide and halfway out into the channel. I can see all the way to the muddy bottom.

My breath catches as I spot the mottled corpse at the bottom of the lake. On either foot, halfway up its shins, are concrete slabs. The entity slides one slab forward, catching mud as it goes. He stops then pulls the opposite foot forward.

"How lovely. The key looks anxious to meet you," Austin says. The key warlock raises his right hand. I'm sure it's my overreactive imagination, but I swear I recognize the hand of the Old Man in the lake, and my blood chills as I begin to pass out.

As my head swims and my vision tunnels close, I feel myself going up with a rush of wind and the sound of something like a vast fan beating against the air. I shake my head clear and look back. The witches have grown wings and are lifting me into the air.

We fly out over the gaping chasm of the lake toward the key. I look up, so I don't have to see the entity that has haunted me since I was a child. The sky continues with its red, pink, and bruised-purple blooms with increased rapidity.

And I know.

This is what my family feared. This is what they sought to protect me from, and despite all their effort, I walked right into it.

As if it were not only prophecy, but fate.

I hear a hiss over the roar of the separated lake water. I turn my head, but there is no need as the two witches rotate us in the air.

"No!" I scream. Unsure if I can be heard over the roar of the water, the witches' wings, and the hissing grays on the dike.

Antoine struts down Worth crossing Blount Avenue. He wears his varsity basketball uniform with the number one and a large "C" on the left side of his chest. He grins from ear to ear.

"Antoine, no!" I scream again, convinced it's futile as he doesn't even look toward me.

A monstrous black creature appears on the dike as Austin transforms into the Hell Kite. He spreads his wings, nearly engulfing all thirty witches remaining on the embankment. His whip-like tail slashes side to side, streaming fluid from the massive stinger at its tip.

Antoine stops fifty feet away from the dike and slaps his hands together, spreading them in a wide arc above his head. It's a familiar motion he used to do as his name was called before a basketball game, a movement he adopted from his favorite NBA player.

The witches fall silent. Austin's tail stops thrashing as his wings retract. All eyes are on the tall, muscular man standing in front of the dike. Waiting. Wondering what he will do.

I try one more time. "Antoine, go home!"

He lifts his chin toward me in acknowledgment.

Antoine starts a full sprint toward the dike.

My face contorts as I'm about to sob.

The witches on the dike broaden their stance as their tiny hands create energy in their palms, and Austin's tail flexes the last three feet with the stinger twitching, waiting to strike.

Antoine reaches the base of the dike, and Austin's tail comes over his shoulder, striking down the front of the embankment as the witches shoot flame, cold, and energy orbs in the same general direction.

My sadness from the imminent demise of my friend turns into a gasp of joy as I watch Antoine fly over the evil masses, gaining altitude while sailing out over the lake. It's as if I'm back in high school cheering below the basketball goal, watching Antoine fly through the air for a slam dunk.

As he's about to crash into us, he turns sideways, separates his hands, and slaps my shoulders roughly. He catches one of the witches with his left elbow as he flies past us and begins his fall into the lake opening.

I watch in horror as he lands feet first in the mud, piledriving himself knee-deep. I suddenly feel different.

More powerful than I've ever felt.

A bright-pink glow melds into the similar colors coming from the sky. Looking at the weight against my chest, I see a familiar object that nearly blinds me with the light it's putting off. Both of my captors turn their faces away from the amulet light.

I bring both arms down against the black chain leading from my waist, and it disintegrates. The two witches turn toward the dike, and as they fly back, I set their wings on fire, causing them to plummet from the sky.

The gasp from the congregation of witches is satisfying, but I have unfinished business. I look down at the bottom of the lake, but I can't bring my powers to bear as the Old Man in the lake disappears into one of the walls of water.

Levitating, I float toward the dike, my body glowing like a beacon led by a pink searchlight. The walls of the lake opening begin to falter, and I notice that the three witches have stopped their incantation.

I turn away from them and find Antoine. Focusing, because of the distance involved and the difficulty of getting it right, I try to save my friend.

A blue bubble encompasses him seconds before the wall of water engulfs Antoine. I wait, wondering if I was successful or if I must dive into the lake and attempt to help him.

I'm grateful when I see the blue ball pop to the surface with Antoine cramped inside. Our eyes meet, and he gives me a thumbs up.

With him safe, it's time for me to throw down with Austin and his entourage. Turning toward them, all the witches have grown wings, and the closest is only a few feet from me. Instinctively I slap my hands and scream, "Be gone all evil!"

A blast of air sucks toward me for a millisecond. There is another millisecond of calm followed by an incredible concussion blast emanating from me, turning the three closest witches into red mist and blowing all of them back toward the dike with a massive fireball.

My ears ring, and I feel as if somebody has hit me in the head with a baseball bat. But you should see the other girls.

Body parts continue to fall out of the sky. A few grays, blown back to Blount Avenue are dragging themselves across the pavement, attempting their escape minus multiple limbs.

It's repulsive.

Austin, the demon version, stands on the dike. His wings are torn off, and his skin smolders. He transforms into his human form, and the right side of his face is burnt off. His nude skin is red and blistered everywhere.

He touches his blistered finger with an exposed tip of a bone to his tongue. "Mmm … delicious. Well done, just the way I like it."

I float toward him, emboldened that now is my moment of opportunity.

Austin points his destroyed finger at me. "The gate will be opened, lock witch, and you will open it for me."

"Yeah, I'm not feeling it, Austin." I grow a sphere in my cupped hands and enjoy its power surge as I float closer. "But hey, if you're foolish enough for another game, come on back. I'll gladly kick your butt again."

"I'll be back. You can count on it like the rain, April. I'll be back for you, and you will be mine."

"You have some serious stalker issues, Austin." I sling the power orb, sidearm, at him.

As it leaves my hand, he makes a swiping gesture with his left hand, and I'm floating in the calm, cool darkness of the void. The current carries me out feet first. I try to fight against it, but I am adrift with no idea which way to go, even if I could control the direction.

I am lost in the void.

Chapter 47

I float for what seems like days—weightless, freezing, and lost. My cheek bumps against another object.

Through the prophetic darkness, I hear a slight noise. It grows in volume and clarity.

"April. Hey, girl. Wake up."

My eyes pop open. Antoine's weathered face is inches from mine.

He smiles and shakes his head. "Darn, girl. You sure know how to make an exit."

I sit up and hug him. "Thank you, Antoine."

His chest shifts under me as he laughs. "I just caught you during a fainting spell. It's not like I kept a shark from eating you."

I pull back and look into his eyes. He doesn't remember.

Antoine was there to save me and knew I needed my amulet. Still, he is unaware of the battle we narrowly escaped as a team. This Antoine kept his friend from bumping her head during a fainting spell.

It confirms my gut feeling I had while in the apocalyptic version of Guntersville on the other side of the veil. I was pulled into an alternate timeline of reality where evil had prevailed.

This is one time I take no joy in being correct.

"Are you okay?"

"Yes. I'm fine now." I scratch my head and take inventory of things. "I point to Missy's grave. Your mama."

He smiles. "She's gone. She says you're out of danger now."

"Well, that's comforting." I laugh.

"And I can go back to Atlanta." He extends his hand to me as he stands

My stomach growls as I accept his hand.

"Darn, girl, you got a demon in there."

"Let's hope not." I tilt my head. "Do you like pizza, Antoine?"

"What's not to like?"

I grin. "Great. My treat."

Putting my curiosity and hurt feelings in a box is not easy. The revelation that Mama is a witch has turned my world cattywampus on its axis.

I have so many questions to ask my grandmothers, too. With Nana, I must debate if traveling to an alternate timeline could help defeat Austin if he keeps to his word and attacks again. I believe Granny can shed more light on the prophecy and help me be better prepared.

What of Austin's claim that Daddy and Howard had a part in the existence of the Old Man in the lake? I suppose demons are the best deceivers. It was Austin attempting to break down my will.

Still, I learned to be in the moment from Grandpa's gift. The moment at hand is to celebrate the unlikely arrival of an old acquaintance who saved my life. It is time to show my appreciation in some small way and savor the victory.

Antoine leans back in his chair and lays his hands across his belly. "Man, I'm as full as a tick. That is the best pizza I have ever eaten. They need to outlaw it. It's dangerous. Folks are liable to just burst from overeating."

I laugh and beam with pride. Howard has turned this dive of a pizza chain into an affordable gourmet pizza parlor.

"You say this is your uncle's place?"

"Yes, this is his next career."

"Wow. I don't see how you stay so skinny."

Antoine obviously is nearsighted since I haven't been called thin since ninth grade.

"How about another Meat Lover's." Howard appears at our table with a hot ten-inch pizza. Steam rolls off the fresh pie.

"No. I can't," Antoine says.

"Can we box it for him to take, Uncle Howard?"

"Sure, we can."

I reach into my purse, pull out a wad of bills, and shove it in Howard's front pocket.

"What are you doing?" he asks.

"Paying for the pizza."

"It was my treat. I'm just glad to see you in here."

"Silly. I can't accept free pizza when I promised Antoine I would buy it. That's like regifting?"

Howard shrugs. "Suit yourself."

"Hey, wait." I catch his arm as he starts for the kitchen. I give him a sideways hug and whisper in his ear, "Thank you for being the best teacher a girl could hope for, and I'm so happy to see you enjoying yourself."

"Follow your heart and do what you love, April. It's the secret recipe to life."

THE END

April's story continues with...

Foolish Haints

A witch out of her element...

An evil specter set on gaining immortality...

A paranormally gifted girl's work is never done.

April accepts the dangerous mission of uncovering the truth behind a series of disappearances on the mysterious coastal island of Turtle Key. Armed with nothing more than her resolve and unreliable supernatural "gifts," April works with her makeshift paranormal team as they face mortal danger and uncover a terrible family secret. Along the way, she grapples with the complicated relationship with her mentor, neighbors, and even her family.

Haint is a Southern variation of the word haunt. It originated in the beliefs of the Gullah Geechee people, one of the many unique cultures that form the tapestry that is Southern folklore and legend.

Have you read the prequels? *My Psychic Ghost-Filled Life* stories are the prequel series to the *My Witchy Psychic Life* novel series of April May Snow.

Click to get your copies today!

My Psychic Ghost-Filled Life Prequel Series

Throw the Amulet

Throw the Bouquet

Throw the Cap

Throw the Dice

Throw the Elbow

Throw the Fastball

Throw the Gauntlet

Throw the Hissy

M. Scott lives outside of Nashville, Tennessee, with his wife and two guard chihuahuas. When he's not writing, he's cooking or taking long walks to smooth out plotlines for the next April May Snow adventure.

Dear Reader,

Thank you for reading April's story. You make her adventures possible. Without you, there would be no point in creating her story.

I'd like to encourage you to post a review on Amazon. A favorable critique from you is a powerful way to support authors you enjoy. It allows our books to be found by additional readers, and frankly, motivates us to continue to produce books. This is especially true for your independents.

Once again, thank you for the support. You are the magic that breathes life into these characters.

M. Scott Swanson

The best way to stay in touch is to join the reader's club!

www.mscottswanson.com

Other ways to stay in touch are:

Like on Amazon

Like on Facebook

Like on Goodreads

You can also reach me at mscottswanson@gmail.com.

I hope your life is filled with

magic and LOVE!